ALAS!
THE ONE THAT
EVIL BRINGS

Fate of Vaeldor
BOOK 1
written by

Ronald G. Bellar

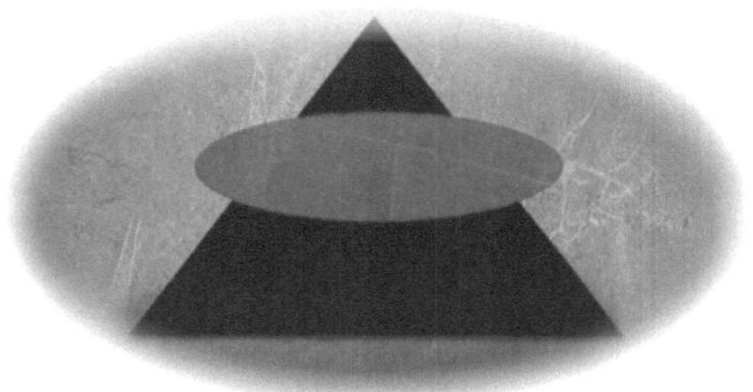

Vaeldor House LLC

Brighton, MI 48114

ALAS! THE ONE THAT EVIL BRINGS

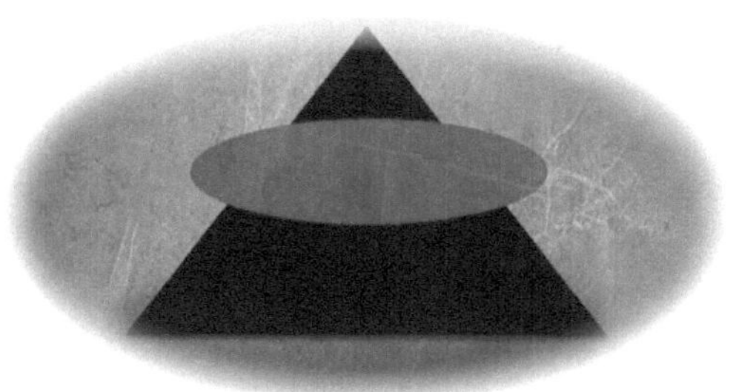

to my wife and son,
Justiina & Ronnie

CONTENTS

North
Pavan
Helmland
Balgorn R.
Lothen F.
Beit
Shield R.
Stone Eagle M.
Vol Maren
Rornibur
Shield R.
Maple Lore F.
Neja
Eastgate
Cafdella
Stony R.
Ellaville
Virch
Sistama
Endless Sea
Urell Coast
Tall Pines F.
Sikilaville
Squire R.
Larkorn
Rivercross
Korban B.
Tikkev City
King Arman L.
Dominelli
Salenti F.
Moclen
Garthglen Bog
Prince Arman R.
Arman F.
Krimburd
Witchdoor
Sarell Desert
Queen Arman L.
Tenvale
High Riser M.
Dakreal F.
Crynora
Philen
Fendora
Holindale
Eraim's Journal Entry 5: Western Vaeldor

Andria
Ekland
Coranthiar M.
Bouldertown
Selt
Harbonan
Vermallon F.
Nira
Batorn Gulf
House of Elgarroth
Orlenfel F.
Tribenor
Benasti F.
Batorn R.
Orlenfel R.
Sendorum
Great East R.
Candermane Tunnel
Varlimor M.
Lake Garaard
Palidur
Morimont
Darmhorng
Kalmaar
Sardina
Starlight L.
Southwood
Serpent's Range
Charndova
Ironside Keep
Barraday
Border Hills
Denvale
Fire Hills
Marcove
Ladall M.
Mentrial F.
Endless Sea
Desert of Fire
Borleag M.
Nomedd
Tarn Arüm Jungle
Eraim's Journal Entry 6: Eastern Vaeldor

Prologue

A Glimpse of the Past

Tell me what you know," Trannum demanded, hovering over a mangled corpse.

The body remained still, revealing nothing.

"So that's how it's going to be." He sighed. "None of you are talking lately."

Trannum gazed at the nearly ten thousand corpses, sorted according to allegiance. To one side were dwarves, elves, and humans, and to the other the minions of Uustaag the Dark, the most terrible warlord ever to have existed. The evil army included goblins, hobgoblins, hairless gorilla-monsters with perfectly black skin, and potato-like creatures possessing a single eye and four tentacles, but no legs or feet. Of the latter two races, Trannum was not sure he *could* question them; he doubted very much they were part of his world. Of course, there were humans among the evil army as well… His own race, so easily corrupted. From the looks of them, the humans had served in every aspect of the enemy force: foot soldiers, archers, knights, and high-ranking officers. Of all the enemy cadavers, *they* should have been the easiest to question, and the officers would perhaps possess knowledge of where their master had found such power…but none of them were talking.

Being the greatest necromancer in all of Vaeldor, it was only natural that Trannum had been asked to investigate the most horrific war ever known. Questioning corpses of the Alliance for Good was easy enough and they were happy to provide all they knew, which was little more than descriptions of battles. Now that Trannum had moved on to the evil forces, however, things were changed. The carcasses refused to reveal any information as to the source of the late warlord's power, and this intrigued Trannum greatly. Never before had he found such stubbornness within those no longer among the living. It was as if they still feared the wrath of their fallen lord.

Of course, the process would have been much easier had Uustaag's body been found after the Battle of Balgorn, but all efforts had proven futile. So naturally a strong fear was festering—a fear the warlord's dark magic had allowed him to survive. This anxiety seemed strongest within the elves, and it was the elves that first approached Trannum for help. Trannum hesitated to accept the task, but then Palidur came calling, hoping to find the source behind the evil power. How could he say no to the Holy City?

With a sigh, Trannum gazed at the swampland to the south. It was a pleasant place as bogs go and home to a few human villages and a small clan of elves. He had chosen the location to conduct his research, for it lay very near to the battleground and most of it was uninhabited. But the only section in which its denizens would allow Trannum to work was a desolate area considered unlivable. Insects were heaviest there, the ground was plagued by quicksand, and rivers overflowed whenever it rained, which occurred more often than not. It was not all bad, though, for Trannum enjoyed the privacy it provided. But not being allowed to transport any corpses into the marsh was ridiculous and inefficient. The inhabitants did not want the bodies "disgracing the hunting grounds and scaring away the game." They allowed the carcasses to fester just outside their northern border, however, and this made no sense. Trannum could, of course, impose his will, but he chose to honor their silly request and made the journey every few days to question the dead. He had hoped the arrangement would work out, but time was becoming an issue. Soon the voices of the dead would begin to fade.

"You leave me no choice." Trannum sighed again, eyeing the carrion birds making happy homes amongst his specimens. The inhabitants of the swamp would not approve, but he had a job to do; a job more important than their petty day-to-day lives.

Trannum raised his hand over the corpse of a hobgoblin and concentrated. The body twitched. Its eyelids snapped open, revealing dry orbs mostly white in color, and even though its chest possessed a gaping hole where it had been skewered by a spear, it rose to its feet and awaited his next command. He did the same with another hobgoblin, a goblin, and a human appearing to be a soldier of significant rank.

"Follow me," Trannum ordered as he entered the swamp, and the zombies obeyed, unable to do otherwise.

CHAPTER 1

A CHILLY SUMMER DAY

Eraim pulled a sword from its sheath. Despicable. The edges were worn; the weight was wrong. Some folks should stick to shoeing horses and mending fences, and leave weaponsmithing to those capable. With a sniff, she returned the blade to the merchant's table.

She spied another small sword with potential—at least the fine leather wrapping about the handle was encouraging—but it was beyond her limited reach. Times like this made Eraim long to be more like a Vermallon elf, or at least more in likeness to her own Salenti clan. Sure, Salenti elves were the smallest of all elves, but Eraim fell short of even her own kin. With a pout, she furrowed her brow.

The merchant followed Eraim's gaze and smiled, extending the weapon for her inspection. She did not even get the blade halfway out when she stopped. More junk.

"Perhaps my fine maiden is at the wrong cart," commented the merchant, a man obviously living well, judging by his fine silk shirt, trimmed hair, and clean hands. His eyes fell to the jewel-encrusted scabbard hanging at Eraim's side.

Eraim instinctively placed a protective hand over the pommel of Mithkahr, reassuring herself the sword was still there. It was a reflex when visiting markets within human cities—thieves were far too common. Mithkahr had been with Eraim for greater than a century. There existed no equal in beauty or balance and its edge was never in need of sharpening. Eraim had no heroic story to tell of how she came by it; no great battle or deadly journey through long-forgotten ruins. She simply stumbled across it, quite by accident, in a market similar to this one. The merchant had not known what he possessed, for the blade was filthy and housed in a mismatched sheath. The moment Eraim held it, she saw it for what it was: an ancient blade forged by elfish smithies with a skill and art long forgotten. She purchased it immediately, with no attempts to haggle, and dressed it up in a scabbard befitting its stature. Even to this day, Eraim continued to upgrade its home, adding only the most exquisite jewels she could acquire.

"I am always in search of fine blades, if you must know," Eraim stated. And she meant it.

"Eraim!" Selanna called. "Come look at this!"

Eraim turned to find her golden-haired companion sifting through an art collection. A nearly toothless smile came to the collector's face, his eyes full of hope at the pending sale, or perhaps he was enchanted by Selanna's beauty. His smile broadened further upon seeing Eraim.

"*Anything* has got to be better than what this man is selling." Eraim slid the blade back into its sheath and dropped it onto the table. "And worry not," she added softly to Mithkahr as she approached Selanna, "I shall never replace you. But would you not like a little sister or brother?"

Mithkahr did not answer. It never did. But Eraim knew it could hear her.

"Is it not just horrid?" Selanna could not contain her giggle as she shared a canvas with Eraim, causing the few teeth the merchant possessed to retreat. "Is it supposed to be a dragon? Or perhaps it is a giant toad with wings."

Though Eraim and Selanna had never actually seen a dragon, due to the reptiles' extinction long before their time, Selanna had collected many paintings of the creatures over the years. And Eraim had to agree this depiction was the absolute worst.

"And this troll ..." Selanna pulled another painting. "It is in a forest.

Everyone knows they live in swamps! Oh, and this one here—"

"Are ya gonna buy somethin'?" The merchant's patience was at an end. "Or are ya jus' gonna insult me art all day?"

"Oh, is there art around here?" Selanna looked from side to side, doing her best impression of one bewildered.

"Jus' move on, missy," the man whined. "Ain't no one gonna buy nothin' with ya pointin' out the flaws of every piece."

"Begging your pardon, sir," Selanna batted her large emerald eyes, "but I was pointing out the *good* features." Selanna flashed her cutest smile, tilting her head slightly to allow her long hair to dangle. She had no need for her spells or charms; the smile normally sufficed to tame the hearts of human men. The merchant, however, was unmoved.

"Ya made yer point," he whined some more. "Now please move on 'bout yer business. A man has to make a livin'." Under his breath, he added, "Blasted elf magicians think they know everything."

One had to be blind or completely naïve not to realize Selanna to be a user of the magical arts. Her green robe was embroidered with strange sigils upon the breast—symbols even Eraim did not understand—and she carried no weapon, save for a small knife. But Selanna was also a full-blooded elf with hearing every bit as keen as others of their race, and Eraim was sure her friend had heard the merchant's mumblings clearly.

"Let us get some tea." Eraim grabbed Selanna by the arm, knowing all too well her friend would not yield until the man was utterly subdued. "There is nothing to earn my interest here anyway."

"Very well." Selanna smirked at the peddler. "A good day to you, sir."

The man waved a hand, as one shooing away a pesky insect.

It was midsummer, not an ideal time for lengthy travel, but as Eraim and Selanna neared the end of their two-week journey home from Vermallon Forest, they decided to see what the merchants of Rivercross had to offer. Crossroads Market was a paved square walled in by two-story buildings of wood and stone, and it was rarely less than three-quarters full. The city was built upon major crossroads connecting the kingdoms of Virch, Moclen, and Neja, and travelers moving west or east around King Arman Lake had few choices but to pass through, lest they dared to journey through Tenvale, the bizarre kingdom of wizards. This fact attracted merchants from near and far, as well as the interesting wares they peddled, and today seemed especially busy. People from all walks of life were always represented, though it looked—and smelled—like there were more farmers and beggars in attendance than any others this day, and two weeks of uncontested sunshine had done nothing to improve the odor.

"I cannot believe the heat today," said Selanna.

Eraim gazed up at her companion, rolling her eyes in full agreement. "But it has done nothing to chase away *this* crowd." She dodged a large woman and found herself face to face with a shrunken head. Its leathery skin was indistinguishable from the strap from which it hung, and BLACKFOOT GOBLIN was written beneath it. Eraim wrinkled her nose and pushed herself from the cart. "Not even the grim shopping could clear this market."

Selanna gave a wry smile. "A plague could not accomplish that."

"This place is positively filthy!" Eraim was unwilling to discover the substance attempting to make her boot a permanent fixture of the marketplace. She wrinkled her nose again. "And it reeks of—"

A man browsing a nearby cart bumped into Eraim, knocking her into a woman that scowled but kept moving.

"My apologies, little girl." The man offered a slight nod and tip of the hat.

Eraim had given up counting the times folks outside Salenti mistook her for a human girl years ago, when it ceased to be amusing. Normally she would turn, tossing her long dark hair to expose her pointed ears, and gaze upon the man with her blue eyes and a smile to leave him weak in the knees. But on this occasion, Eraim issued a glare, her eyes becoming daggers.

"I could truly find it within my heart to forgive you, sir, if you will kindly return me my pouch."

"I...I..." the towering man stammered, unable to deny the accusation.

"You are sorry," Eraim submitted. "And it will not *ever* happen again."

"Yes, miss." He pulled her pouch from the confines of his cloak.

"That is very gracious of you." Eraim smiled and accepted her property. "And I forgive you," she added, shaking his hand. "Off with you now."

Turning, the man slinked away with his head low.

"I hate thieves," Eraim muttered, holding the man's pouch behind her for Selanna to see, and she meant it. A thief stole whatever they could, whenever they could. Eraim used her talents for good, teaching lessons whenever lessons were necessary. She did not need to steal for wealth, not when a simple game of cards or darts could earn her more gold than she could spend. She was no thief.

Selanna smirked. "Perhaps some wine is in order?"

"Indeed." Eraim tested the weight of the pouch, listening to the coins rattle. "And the nice gentleman would like to buy us some lunch as well."

There existed many choices for lunch, as taverns were almost as plentiful as merchants' wagons, so they stopped by the first establishment they came upon: THE HAPPY FISHERMAN. A table was easily managed within the busy room, for several men eagerly parted with their seats before Eraim and her companion, and she and Selanna proceeded to enjoy a pleasant meal at the expense of the would-be-thief. Eraim ordered a bottle of the tavern's finest wine, "all the way from Sardina," or so the barkeep claimed. Eraim found it satisfactory, though typical of Moclen make. The fish, however, was splendid. "Fresh morning catch from the King!" the barkeep bragged. King Arman Lake yielded the tastiest fish Eraim had ever sampled, from sunfish to freshwater sharks, and today's main course was no exception.

After the meal, and keeping the barkeep busy with little reward,

Eraim and Selanna decided to return to the heat of the sun. Eraim looked forward to some fresh air—or at least fresher air—as the tavern had grown quite stale.

"Salenti elves," muttered the barkeep once they reached the door.

It was not a complaint foreign to Eraim's ears. Naturally, most elves in those parts were of Salenti. But with the forest having been long cleared of evil, Eraim knew her kin to enjoy carefree lives, filling their time with merriment and humor—often at the expense of humans. As a result, many business owners considered them pests, and some even refused them service. Selanna delighted in playing the "typical Salenti elf" most days, so when she stopped to make a comment, Eraim urged her friend through the door, tossing the pouch containing the remainder of the thief's coins onto the bar.

"Shall we fetch the horses?" Eraim was eager to return to the road.

"What is the quickest route to the stables?"

"Hmm…" Eraim pursed her lips in thought. "I shall have a look."

She saw the surprise and amusement on Selanna's face. No doubt Selanna was thinking there existed no city where Eraim was at a loss for a hasty route of departure—or escape on a few occasions. Selanna's chuckle did not elude Eraim as she effortlessly scaled the chimney of a nearby building for a better view.

Eraim rose to the rooftop and enjoyed a deep breath above the reek of the city, and for a moment she was caught up in the view. Two seagulls argued over a dead fish to the south upon the shore of King Arman Lake, the water stretching beyond the horizon; the east revealed a covered wagon following the long road to Larkorn along the water's edge; the plains to the north harbored soft fields swaying yellow, white, and green, its peaceful façade marred only by a large graveyard; and to the west, the Korban Bridge spanned the Squire River. Eraim's attention rested upon the bridge, for it never failed to fascinate her. The beautiful construction of white stone arched thirty yards across, and though it was built more than nine centuries prior, the images of dwarfish heroes upon its sides appeared as though they had been carved yesterday. Sure, Stone Eagle dwarves seemed clumsy, lacked manners, and usually showed little in the ways of common sense, but they were capable of great beauty when they were inspired, and of all dwarfish constructions, Eraim felt Korban Bridge to be their finest work.

"Surely you are not having difficulties," called Selanna.

Selanna's knowing smile did not escape Eraim's notice, and with a sigh Eraim returned to the task at hand. She knew how to get to the stables already, but she wished to find a path unhindered by shoppers and wanderers—not every merchant was lucky enough to have landed a spot within the market square, and several were forced to place carts wherever they could along the side streets. Quickly noting an acceptable route, Eraim descended, dropping lightly onto the street.

"It is not far."

"If we ride without stop," Selanna mentioned, "we can make Tikken City before it gets to be too late."

"Splendid!" Eraim smiled.

Of all settlements of humans, Eraim loved Tikken City most. It was one of two free cities, the other being Palidur across the lake, and governed by the Council of Wizards, a group of eleven boasting the great Seac the Seer, prophet of the current century and the next. It was also home to many nobles possessing remarkable jewelry and items of interest, and Eraim enjoyed teaching whatever lessons she saw fit. As well, taverns were open all night, and Eraim seldom needed sleep when gambling or feats of skill could make her additional coins. It was not the bounty that pleased her most, but the looks upon the faces of those she bested.

Selanna, Eraim knew, fancied the city for other reasons. Selanna knew each wizard of the Council by name, and she visited often to offer knowledge, to which the wizards normally scoffed, or to browse through their library, the most extensive collection of books Eraim had ever seen. Selanna enjoyed the many tomes on history, and found them amusing when they differed from Salenti records. But she also claimed to have discovered in them many things Salenti had not the interest to record, or perhaps was uninvolved in, and it was this knowledge in which Selanna reveled.

With a renewed spring in her step, Eraim led the way toward the stables. After only a few paces, however, a breeze, much colder than was normal, stopped them in their tracks. Eraim turned to Selanna, who gazed about the sky. It was clear and not so much as a zephyr had penetrated the city all day. The breeze continued, growing in strength and becoming colder with each moment. Signs rattled and banners waved wildly as the streets were filled with dust, and soon it was as frigid as a midwinter's gale…but then it stopped.

"That was odd." Eraim rubbed her hands, welcoming the warmth of the sun against her skin.

The people about the area shook off the occurrence, laughing and returning to business at hand. "Whoa!" exclaimed one merchant. "The King blows cold today!"

Eraim noticed Selanna's concerned frown. It was an expression Eraim had seen enough to know something was amiss. "What is it?" Her hand moved to Mithkahr.

"The gust came out of the northwest," Selanna said quietly, gazing to the south where the lake lay beyond the mass of buildings. She shook her head. "We should move on."

They continued toward the stables at a quicker pace, passing between many buildings and following the route within Eraim's mind. Upon exiting an alley and stepping onto the main street, the chill had been completely expelled by the hot sun and the dust was settled. It was as if the wind had not blown at all. Eraim was not surprised to hear very little conversation of the strange occurrence from that point. In fact, only one man made mention of it, stating how it would have been wonderful if the wind had remained longer. Sometimes Eraim did not understand humans at all.

After another block, they arrived at the stables. Eraim found their horses, Lilli and Dandi, well cared for and gave the stable hand a generous tip, easily equaling a week's wages.

"Many thanks, my ladies." The man bowed low with great appreciation. He was dressed in what must have been his cleanest shirt tucked into his breeches, though it was obviously well worn, and his hair was combed neatly to one side. Eraim and Selanna shared a giggle, for only a few hours ago, when they released their horses into his care, he had appeared much differently. His shirt looked as though it had been worn for days and his hair was wild and decorated with straw, as if he had slept in the loft. "'Tis robbery though," he added as he stood. "Your fine animals needed no real caring for and made the stalls seem all the fairer while they were here."

"You did not feed her your oats, did you?" Eraim patted Lilli's neck.

"No, no," he assured her. "Just the meal you gave me. That's all. And I fetched fresh water from the King. They wouldn't let me brush them, though. Not that they needed it."

They were, indeed, beautiful animals, being of a special Salenti breed. They grew shorter and leaner than normal horses and were swifter and more intelligent. Eraim took great care of Lilli and the mare returned the favor; faithful companions until the end—quite a bond, considering the horses lived as long as elves themselves.

"You did fine." Eraim tossed another piece of silver.

"You'll always have a stall here, miss!" He bowed again, scanning the straw for the coin he failed to catch.

Lilli and Dandi followed without command as Eraim and Selanna headed toward the city gates, but after a couple of blocks Eraim came to a stop. She thought she had heard a distant scream, and her beliefs were confirmed when she detected another. And another. And another. She turned to Selanna as the screams drew closer and became more numerous.

"What is happening?"

Before Selanna could give a response, several screams came from the Crossroads Market, just down the street—cries of terror and pain. Eraim pulled Mithkahr from its sheath and the blade reflected red in the sunlight. Evil was afoot.

Eraim and Selanna ran back to the market, but the square was hardly how they had left it only an hour ago. Carts were overturned and people ran hysterically in all directions, pursued by walking corpses—undead had invaded the city, still shedding the soil of their graves. Most were skeletal remains dressed loosely in rags, but more gruesome ones were present with rotting flesh that clung to their ghastly bodies. The skeletons rattled upon the pavement and made hissing noises as they clawed at people with bony fingers, and the zombies snarled and feasted upon all that failed to escape.

Three skeletons approached from the left; their bones were yellow where dirt did not cling and fresh blood decorated their fingers. With a quick word, Selanna released three green balls of magic from her open palms, and they struck the undead, dislodging their bones and scattering them about the square.

Eraim heard the scream of a child and took off as fast as her legs could carry her. She found a zombie pinning a small boy to the street, its tattered clothing revealing many gaps of missing flesh, and it growled as it opened its mouth wide. The zombie's yellow teeth moved in on the boy's neck, but it did not enjoy even a taste, for Mithkahr cleaved its head with a single swing. After helping the child through a nearby door, Eraim returned to Selanna's side.

"What is going on?" Eraim asked, bewildered. "Where did these things come from?"

Selanna did not answer. She was focused on two zombies closing in on a merchant seeking shelter beneath a cart. After a hasty chant, a spell of fire streamed from Selanna's fingertips, igniting the walking corpses and dropping them to the street as the flames consumed their bodies almost instantly.

Eraim was then moved to pity. The art merchant Selanna had teased earlier was motionless beneath a zombie, his mouth frozen in a silent scream. She knew Selanna shared the view, for several more spells were unleashed upon the undead. Eraim never liked seeing her friend driven to such ire, but on these rare occasions, Selanna exhibited remarkable power to impress even the most seasoned wizard. With Mithkahr in hand, Eraim assisted in the destruction of the filthy creatures until the market was cleared, but the screams did not cease. They sounded in all directions, near and far. The city was infested.

A score of city guardsmen rushed into the area.

"It's not safe here!" one called out. "Secure yourselves indoors!"

Selanna ignored the order. "Where are they coming from?"

"The graveyard." The guardsman shook his head in disbelief. "Just outside the city. Everyone ever buried there has dug their way out."

Screams sounded nearby to the south, stealing the man's attention.

"Let's move!" he ordered his contingent, and fear was evident in the soldiers' eyes as they hurried from the square.

Eraim's mouth went dry, recalling the size of the graveyard to the north of the city. Hundreds of headstones existed therein. "This place is cursed! We should leave, lest it come down upon us as well."

"We have to help these people," Selanna insisted as more screams sounded not far away. "Come!"

"Stay close," Eraim gave the unnecessary order to Lilli and Dandi.

CHAPTER 2

COUNCIL OF WIZARDS

The Council of Wizards sat upon their thrones within the audience chamber. The semicircle of oaken chairs overlooked the vaulted room from atop a dais, perfectly situated before an enormous half-circle window. Beyond the glass, the late morning sun hovered above the endless ripples of King Arman Lake, but the elderly men faced the room, gazing at their twenty-foot shadows stretching across the polished white floor. Seac the Seer occupied the largest chair in the middle and the others sat to either side, five to the right and five to the left. All remained silent, their wrinkled faces somber and brows furrowed while they pondered the most recent disturbance to their fair city.

Corpses had uprooted from resting places only yesterday and began an assault upon the living. The walls of Tikken City stood strong against the sudden foe and the gates were quickly closed, but the many family crypts within the city were another story—their dead occupants had broken free from their confines and lusted for blood. The city alarm sounded at once, but soldiers were scattered, already fighting undead or rushing to don armor and weapons. Organizing them seemed impossible. Had it not been for Vecnor, in town on a chance visit, things could have been much graver.

Vecnor was unequalled in skill, standing higher than the tall elves of Orlenfel Forest and possessing the strength of ten men. He arrived to the city only a couple days prior on a "holiday," as he put it, and was more than happy to give aid. Vecnor took command of the city defenses, organizing soldiers wherever he found them, and swung a mighty sword with one hand that most men could not wield with two. By all reports, over a hundred undead were felled by Vecnor, and when all was quieted within the city, he led the charge through the gates.

Archers had been raining arrows onto the gathering force of over three thousand walking corpses outside the walls, but most the missiles shattered upon skeletons or stuck into lifeless zombies with little or no effect. With Vecnor at the lead of over a thousand soldiers, however, the undead were defeated before the sun was set.

The Council was not sure what to make of it all and worked through the night, reading from the Prophecy Scrolls to determine if it had been foretold. Since the dawn of time, Seers recorded visions as they understood them. The Sight came from the stars, dreams, and fleeting thoughts, but were seldom clear and often an effort for the entire Council to decipher. Sometimes they prophesized current events, while other times the distant future, and upon occasion the latter never came to be, due to the actions of others to prevent them. It was quite a complicated art, but such were the ways of Vou, the Source of Magic. The only thing the Council knew for sure was that a frigid wind had swept over the city from the northwest, and not long after, the first of the undead were spotted.

The people of Tikken City would understand none of this. They would blame the Council for not forewarning of the sudden rising, and most fingers would point Seac's direction. For nearly eight hundred years, the city had known peace under the Council's rule. With the powerful kingdom of Virch to the north and Palidur across King Arman Lake, Tikken City was a place without fear, comfortably nestled within the bosom of Moclen. Never before had the gates been locked during the light of day. It was most disturbing.

"Pardon me, masters." Mordan broke the silence as he poked his head into the chamber through one of a set of large, oaken doors. Mordan's gray hair was neatly trimmed and his face clean shaven. He was Chief Steward to the Council, and having served them for more than thirty years of his forty-two-year existence, he was a man of order. "Master Vecnor has arrived, per your request."

"Thank you, Mordan." Seac gave a nod. "See him in."

Seac had sent for Vecnor the previous night, wishing to thank him personally for his part in the city's defenses, but the large man proved hard to track down. Most likely he had been patrolling the streets to be sure all corpses were vanquished.

Vecnor entered the chamber, each step resonating about the high ceiling. The warrior was dressed in black plate armor with a helmet tucked beneath his arm, and strapped to his back was his mighty sword, also black — a menacing sight to any he did not call friend. Some referred to Vecnor as Black Death and others Black Rogue, but he often dubbed himself Weapons Master, boasting he could wield a table leg in combat better than most used their own sword. He swore fealty to no king and roamed the lands of Vaeldor, defeating evil wherever he found it in the name of Brondor, the battle god. Vecnor eyed the Council as he came to a halt before them, his blue eyes gleaming with confidence, if not cockiness. With his thumb and index finger, he traced his neatly trimmed mustache and short, pointed beard as he grinned and bowed.

"Greetings, Vecnor," said Seac. "How nice it is to see you again."

"The pleasure, as always, is mine." Vecnor's deep voice reverberated about the chamber.

"We are grateful for your deeds of yesterday, and are indebted to you."

The warrior's laughter filled the room. "Nonsense! You are in need of properly trained soldiers. As for the zombies and skeletons, they were no challenge at all. Sure, they're scary to common folk and part-time guardsmen, but once your Captain Dellen mustered your best, we defeated them with ease. You're lucky it was not worse. Now ghouls... There's a battle worth reckoning!" A glint sparkled in Vecnor's eye.

"Yes." Seac nodded with a sigh. Though he was truly grateful, the Council did not have time for an unrelated battle story. "All the same, if ever you have a request of our fair city, you have but to ask."

Vecnor bowed and strode toward the exit with eager eyes, likely headed to a tavern where many ears waited to hear of his heroics of yesterday and beyond. As he reached the doors, Mordan entered in a rush, bouncing off Vecnor's large frame and nearly crashing to the floor.

"Easy there," said Vecnor, grabbing the steward by the robes and setting him on his feet before departing with a chuckle.

Slightly out of breath, Mordan composed himself, straightening his robes and flattening his hair. He then addressed the Council. "A ship from Palidur has reached our docks, masters."

Seac felt his breathing momentarily cease, afraid of what this might mean. "Escort their messenger here immediately."

Mordan bowed and exited.

Perfect. On the day after the dead had risen, a Palidurian ship arrived to Tikken City's docks. Was it coincidence? Or had the Holy City experienced something similar? Seac supposed he would know the answer to that question soon enough. The very rank of the messenger would reveal much. A common runner or holy soldier would be preferential. Seac would not even mind if it was a priest, though they seldom visited. But if it was a Holy Knight...

The paladins were not easily dealt with. They were Palidur's elite, skilled in both battle and healing. They commanded like generals and fought like champions, always dedicated to their deity and their city, in that order. They demanded respect wherever their roads led, and most kings hearkened to their arrival, lest they fall from the city's better graces.

Seac's thoughts were interrupted when a pair of servants opened the chamber doors. Mordan entered, holding a silver helm within his arms.

"Lady Merssa Goldmace," the steward announced.

The paladin entered with a grim look upon her face. Merssa wore a fine brown cloak, as did all Paladins of Cafior, deity of the land, and her polished silver armor clanged in perfect rhythm with every step as she approached the thrones. Her brown hair was efficiently knotted upon the back of her head and a golden mace swung at her side. Merssa came to a halt before the thrones, and her cold eyes viewed each wizard in turn, finally coming to rest upon Seac. She added a slight nod.

Of all possible messengers, Seac would have preferred anyone else. Merssa was the highest-ranking woman within the Holy City, the only woman to have ever attained the title of Paladin, and in his opinion, she carried a larger chip on her shoulder than other paladins, if that were possible. Though Merssa stood no higher than a Salenti elf, her deeds were great, making her seem six feet tall at times. And even with her youthful—although not particularly attractive— appearance, she carried the wisdom of one much older. This would not be a pleasant visit.

"Greetings, Lady Merssa." Seac returned the nod. "What brings you across the lake?" he added, sure he already knew the answer.

"I have been on a ship since yesterday." Merssa's voice was strong and confident. "The dead have risen."

The other wizards shifted a bit in their seats.

"A winter's wind swept over us," the paladin added, "and we sensed evil within. Not long after, undead infested the land."

"Then it has traveled far," Seac said, mostly to himself.

"You know of what I speak?" Merssa said, more a statement than a question.

"Unfortunately, we do," he replied. "And what of the crypts of Palidur?"

"There was no effect on any of *our* dead." Merssa appeared insulted by the mere hint that such an evil could penetrate the holy walls. "The crypts were inspected immediately upon learning the results of the wind upon the surrounding territories, but they remain at peace. Sardina and Sendorum tell different tales, however. As we speak, the Knights of Palidur hunt the abominations within those realms. I have been sent to see if you, the Council, bear any information as to the origin of this evil, so we can make sure it does not happen a second time."

"Indeed." Seac sighed. "That is the question on our minds at this very moment. For now, all we know is that the wind came out of the northwest."

Merssa raised a brow. "It came upon *us* from due north."

Seac froze. Her words did not make sense…unless the wind had multiple origins. A horrid thought, he attempted to push it aside, but the other wizards began moving their lips, speaking in silent whispers so Merssa could not hear. Some echoed Seac's thoughts while others blamed wind shifts or questioned the accuracy of the paladin's claim.

"Perhaps," Seac said softly, bringing the others to silence. In a stronger tone, he addressed the Holy Knight. "That is a point we shall have to consider as we look into the matter. For now, we must concentrate on what *we* know. And since the wind came from the northwest, we will send a messenger to Neja. Perhaps they have experienced it there as well and we might learn more."

"I shall take that journey." Merssa's voice was filled with contempt. The word "Neja" meant "prison" in the ancient tongue, and was given to the territory by Palidur when lawbreakers fled into the wild country to escape justice many centuries ago. And like all citizens of the Holy City, Merssa made no attempts to conceal her great distaste for the mere mention of the land. "The roads are not safe. And Neja's no place for simple messengers or city guardsmen."

"If…you insist." Seac did not agree with Palidur's view of Neja—many kingdoms did not. With the passage of time, the land had become a prosperous realm and the days of outlaws running it were long over. "But I must insist upon sending one of my subjects. Perhaps Captain Dellen suits you?" The Captain of the City Guard had accompanied Merssa in the past, and she had never complained.

"Dellen will do fine."

The chamber doors swung open, and in strode two elf maidens. A golden-haired elf glided gracefully across the floor, her gaze intent upon Seac, and a smaller, dark-haired elf flanked the first, her eyes moving left and right and taking in her surroundings. Seac had never seen a more beautiful pair, nor a more troubling duo, than Selanna and Eraim in all his years.

"Sorry, masters," Mordan said, rushing behind the elves as quickly as he could while still toting the paladin's silver helmet. "They—"

Seac raised a hand to calm the steward. "It's all right."

The rumblings of the other wizards told a different tale. Seac was the only member of the Council that had spoken to Selanna since her banishment over two decades ago for visiting rooms off limits. He lifted the ban only recently, after the elf mage apologized and promised never to wander again, but the rest of the wizards retained their grudges and kept a careful eye on her. Then there was Eraim. The smaller elf, even to this day, often disappeared into the shadows of a room or hallway, not turning up again until sometime later. Seac heard many arguments from wizards and servants alike in favor of banishing Eraim as well, but he always declined the notion, for there could be found not a shred of proof she had visited any of the places that saw Selanna exiled. But Seac was no fool, and he was sure Eraim had seen many things meant only for the Council's eyes.

"Summon Dellen right away," Seac instructed Mordan.

"Yes, master." Mordan shot the elves a sideways glance before departing.

Merssa was annoyed with the interruption of the elves' arrival. She had known the two for several years now and could not remember a time she had ever seen one without the other. As a matter of fact, Merssa could not recall an occasion when trouble did not follow them, and she was sure this time was no exception, for Selanna's smile was unconvincing. Something was amiss.

"Merssa!" Selanna said in her melodic voice, appearing as if she wished to complete the greeting with an embrace.

"Selanna. Eraim." Merssa acknowledged the two, turning back to the wizards and banishing all thoughts of a hug.

"Do you bring news from Salenti Forest?" Seac addressed the elves, worry evident in the Seer's eyes as to the answer.

"Actually," Selanna replied, "we have just arrived from Rivercross with most dreadful news. But as we rode through your streets, we learned it is no news to you."

Seac sighed. "The undead."

"Correct." Selanna looked to Merssa with concern, then back to the Seer.

"Alas, our experience is not unique," said Seac. "They have also risen in Sendorum, as well as Sardina and probably several other places. And did a cold wind preempt the rising?"

"It did." Selanna gave a nod. "And within I am sure I felt an element of magic."

"It was evil," Merssa stated. Mages often confused the two.

Selanna gasped. "How far has it traveled?"

"We are seeking an answer to that question," Seac replied. "For now, we are uncertain as to its reach, as well as to its origin."

"What about Dominelli?" Eraim asked, the small elf's face given to concern for her home.

"We have had no word from your kin as of yet," said the Seer. "But I doubt the undead would be a match for your folk, had the wind reached that deeply into your forest."

Selanna was suddenly pale. "Could it have come from Helmland?"

Seac's knowing look revealed he had been awaiting that very question, and he responded in a fatherly tone, as one explaining away the shadows of the night. "Helmland is a desolate place, where evil dwelt in days before our city's reckoning. Nothing has stirred there for over a thousand years, since your ancestors and the army of Palidur defeated the Ancient Enemy of the North in the Battle of Balgorn. The many battles fought there are long over, but seem to have bred fear within your bloodline. That is why the elves of Vermallon placed the Guardians within Lothen Forest. But there has been no report of activities in that dead land."

"It is quite vast," Selanna pointed out, "with many dark places to hide from prying eyes."

"That is so," Seac agreed. "However, I doubt our answer lies there. If an evil power has risen, strong enough to summon a wind to raise the dead, I'm sure the Guardians would have seen something. No. I feel our answer lies closer than you think."

Selanna appeared unsatisfied, but fell silent.

Seac returned his attention to Merssa, and it was about time. A twinge of impatience festered while she listened to the exchanges between the Seer and the elves, and she was not sure how much longer she was willing to tolerate it.

"For now, you will be put up in our guest quarters," Seac informed her, "and Dellen shall be briefed and ready to depart tomorrow. Do not hesitate to call upon our servants for anything you require, and thank you for your assistance, Lady Merssa…and you also, Selanna and Eraim. The Council must now meet in private. A good day to all."

The wizards rose and filed silently through a small door to their private chambers. Then, as if feeling a summons, three servants stepped into the room through the larger doors, one bearing Merssa's helmet.

Selanna turned to Merssa with a quizzical look. "Where are you off to?"

"Neja." Merssa uttered the word more calmly than she would have thought possible. All the same, she intended to wash it from her tongue with some wine immediately upon reaching her quarters. "First thing tomorrow. If they're behind this…" Merssa shook her head, her blood suddenly on fire.

"We shall join you, then," said Selanna.

Merssa eyed the two. She had no idea what to expect in the near future, and having the mage around might be beneficial, as well as Eraim. The smaller elf's combative skills would prove better than even Dellen's if the situation called for it, not to mention the other "questionable" talents Eraim possessed. Half the time Merssa did not know if she wanted to thank Eraim or place the elf in irons. "That will be fine."

"What about Salenti?" Eraim asked of her companion. "I would like to know that everything is safe there."

Selanna offered an assuring smile. "Salenti is safe. I am sure."

Eraim hesitated, an objection poised upon her lips. "Very well," she mumbled.

"I will see you both before the dawn." Merssa turned to leave.

"It is only nearing midday," Selanna said. "Though Eraim and I have ridden through the night, we were about to head into the city for something to eat."

Merssa shook her head. "No thank you. I shall remain under the hospitality of the Council. There is much prayer to be said before tomorrow." Beyond that, she did not wish to listen to the elves' constant giggling, as they seemed to find humor in everything.

Merssa gave a slight nod and walked to the doors, where the servant bearing her helmet waited to escort her to her quarters. The other servants' suspicious eyes remained locked upon the elves.

Chapter 3

Korban Bridge

The sky brightened and the stars faded as night retreated with the approach of morning. Merssa's gear was packed, and she had just completed donning her silver armor when a knock fell upon the door.

"Lady Merssa?" Mordan's voice was muffled. "It's time to rise. Breakfast will be ready shortly."

Merssa rolled her eyes and placed her golden mace onto her belt before opening the door. She could see the steward's surprise to find her fully dressed. Folks outside Palidur just did not understand the benefits of an early start.

"This way…my lady." Mordan bowed.

The steward escorted Merssa to the dining hall, an oval chamber large enough to seat fifty. Save for Mordan and a single kitchen servant, Merssa was its only occupant. The servant wore a simple brown dress and clean white apron, and she was obviously unprepared for Merssa's early arrival, stifling a yawn as the door opened. With wide eyes, the woman immediately scrambled in and out of the kitchen through a small door to place breakfast upon the table.

The meal consisted of eggs, ham, bread, and coffee and was probably abundant in flavor, but Merssa barely tasted it. Her mind was imprisoned by the thought of journeying to Neja, a place inhabited by the lowest scum of the lands. Bandits roamed free in the lawless waste, and the reigning monarch was usually the one that could afford the best mercenaries…until another came along with a larger purse and stole their loyalty. It was almost enough to sour the food in Merssa's mouth. For duty, however, she continued to fuel her body with the resources provided to her.

When finished, Mordan led Merssa to the audience chamber, where ten cold thrones sat vacant upon the dais. Vecnor was present, standing near the chairs and speaking with the Captain of the City Guard. Dellen was a large man, but paled in the presence of Vecnor, standing a head shorter. Dellen's rusty-colored, curly hair was well trimmed, as was his full beard and mustache, and he was dressed in guardsman attire, consisting of a chain shirt over which he wore a surcoat of deep blue bearing a circle of eleven stars. By the body language and boisterous laughter, Merssa was sure the two were sharing battle stories. She did not understand how they never tired of such tales, for she often heard the same ones several times over. Their conversation ended abruptly upon her arrival.

"The masters will be along shortly, my lady," Mordan assured her.

Merssa nodded and the steward left them alone.

"Merssa," said Vecnor with a smile. "How nice it is to be in your company again."

"Always a privilege and a pleasure, my lady." Dellen bowed, an ear-to-ear grin splitting the guardsman's face.

Dellen was always happy to see Merssa, and would travel even into dreaded Helmland if she asked. She knew this well, but never returned the sentiment. He was, after all, a guardsman, while she was a Paladin of Cafior!

"Vecnor." She looked up at the towering man. "I did not expect you."

"Dellen and I were enjoying a couple tankards yesterday," Vecnor explained, "when a lackey came bearing news that you were here."

"A *couple* tankards?" Merssa raised a brow, her lips falling just short of a smile. "Do your tales never cease?"

"And when I heard you were traveling to Neja," Vecnor held an impish grin, "I figured you'd be in need of protection."

Merssa gave a wry smile. "That's why I have Dellen." Her words caused the guardsman to blush. Though she was merely returning Vecnor's sarcasm, Dellen always accepted any compliment forthcoming from her lips. It was annoying. If he was not such a loyal and trustworthy soldier, Merssa would never have accepted his assistance. "But you're always welcome," she added to Vecnor, her tone serious again. Outside the Holy Knights, Vecnor was the greatest warrior Merssa had ever met. Deep down she knew there to be no equal to his skill, but pride placed Vecnor second to her paladin companions across the lake. "This is becoming quite a reunion. Selanna and Eraim should be along any moment now."

"Is that so?" Vecnor's smile faded.

Merssa knew the announcement would have an effect. It was not elves in particular that bothered Vecnor—Merssa had seen him in the presence of Vermallon elves upon several occasions—but he was not very fond of Salenti folk, and this fact was always obvious. He did, however, seem comfortable in Eraim's company, the small elf's attitude unlike that of her kin in many situations. Selanna was another story.

The doors swung open and the elves entered.

"And here they are!" Vecnor's sarcastic announcement was accompanied by a grandiose wave.

"Well, what have we here?" Selanna teased. "My favorite mountain."

"Hello, Vecnor," Eraim said in her small voice, standing just above the warrior's waist. Genuine respect shone in the elf's eyes.

"You're both looking lovely as ever," Vecnor commented dully.

"As are you," Dellen added quietly to Merssa.

Merssa gave the guardsman a sideways glance, knowing her appearance to pale greatly in the presence of the elves. She was plain to look at, of this fact she was well aware. But she cared not for the difficulties of romance, instead focusing on her faith to Cafior.

"What's keeping the Council?" she sighed.

Moments later, the door to the private chambers opened and Seac entered. The Seer was alone, appearing as though he had not slept, and he made his way quietly to his throne, seemingly oblivious to the fact that the room bore occupants. Once seated, however, he gazed upon his guests without surprise.

"We have searched long and hard," Seac said, "and though our labors have not been without results, the news, unfortunately, is little and incomplete.

"First of all," the Seer continued, "as for why I did not foresee this most recent evil. It was prophesized many centuries ago, beyond the reckoning of our city. How far beyond I can only guess, for there is no way to know for sure. You see, before the Council's existence, the Seers were solitary prophets, dutifully recording their visions, but the writings were scattered and unorganized. The Council was created to bring their works together, so that all might share in their wisdom to help Vaeldor become a place of peace and prosperity. I cannot say that all writings were found; nothing could be further from the truth. In the days of the Dragon Wars, nearly five hundred years ago by our reckoning, many things were destroyed. But what was recovered was scribed onto what we refer to as the Prophecy Scrolls. We use the Scrolls to piece together the histories of Vaeldor and assist in the foresight of things yet to come. Trying to determine the difference between the two is difficult, for a Seer's vision knows no time, and not all that has happened in the past is known."

"What have you learned?" Merssa asked, her patience waning. She cared not for a deeper insight into the Council, and his little story brought her no closer to resolving the rising of the dead.

"Fortunately," said Seac, "we have discovered a prophecy we feel is related to most recent events. Unfortunately, I believe it to be incomplete." Concern plagued the Seer's face. "I'm sure it is but the first piece of a puzzle, and the others of the Council continue to search for more. I pray they still exist." He shook his head, gazing into nothingness. Returning to those before him, he pulled a scroll from his robes and unrolled it. "It reads:

> *"Power of five, united by one,*
> *Forth on journey, defy the sun.*
> *Summer tastes winter, darkness draws near.*
> *Sleeping do wake, 'neath shadow of fear."*

Seac rolled the parchment and returned it to the confines of his robes. "It is not much, I regret," he spoke directly to Merssa, "but it is all that we have at the moment. Summer has most definitely tasted winter with the blowing of the wind—the Wind of the Dead, as we are calling it—and it is obvious the sleeping refers to the dead."

"But who are the five?" posed Merssa. "And what journey does it refer to?"

"Regretfully," the Seer spread his hands, "there is no way to know that at this time. But as I said, I feel there to be more to this tale, and the Council will not rest until the remaining Scrolls are found." He returned his attention to all of the room's occupants. "I also believe that we should proceed to Neja and speak with Baron Karlsum of Eastgate. You will be provided with my mark so he knows you are messengers of the Council, and since he has called upon us on more than one occasion, he should be willing to share what he knows, if anything. If his information points in a new direction, I warn you this: we do not yet know what is behind this evil. Whatever created the Wind of the Dead must be of great power, for neither I nor any member of the Council could perform such a feat. I recommend you gather as much information as is useful and return immediately." Seac eyed Merssa with the last statement. "Perhaps then we will have learned more here as well."

Merssa stared without emotion. She was no messenger. Her charge was to put an end to this evil, set upon her by the High Order within the Grand Cathedral of Palidur, and she would see it through.

Seac seemed to read Merssa's thoughts and he released a small sigh. He then motioned to the door and Mordan entered, responding to the silent summons.

"Mordan will escort you to the stables," the Seer said. "Good journey to all, and may the Heavens guide you."

Merssa said nothing while the steward led them through the southeast exit of the building and to the Council's personal stables. The early sun was beating down already, making for another hot day, and scattered clouds drifted lazily upon the sky. To the east, a twenty-foot wall prohibited any view of the lake, but the smell of water and squawking of seafowl were heavy upon the air. Two grooms waited with four horses, two of which Merssa knew to belong to the elves, and all saddlebags bulged with supplies. Merssa grabbed the reins of the animal she was sure was meant for her, for the other horse was taller and bore a large hammer she recognized to be Dellen's.

"Begging your pardon, Master Vecnor," said Mordan, "but I only just learned you were accompanying them. I shall have another horse ready in no time."

"That will not be necessary, my good man," Vecnor assured the steward. "I prepared Umbarc this morning." Turning to Merssa, he added, "I'll meet you at the north gate shortly."

Merssa nodded, and Vecnor headed back into the building. "Mount up," she ordered the others.

Life seemed untouched by the rising of the dead as Merssa rode along the stone streets of the city, with the exception of the guards patrolling in larger numbers. Several businesses were opening their doors and sweeping out the previous day's dirt, sleeping drunkards fidgeted within alleyways, searching for more comfortable positions, and several early risers made their way to wherever their day was to take them. Even the Free City Market possessed a few shoppers at the early hour, laughing and inspecting potential purchases while merchants were setting up their wares. How easily commoners forgot the walking corpses that had them locking their doors and left hundreds dead in the streets only two days prior. But that was the way of most people: content to discard such things as bad dreams. It was just another reminder of why folks outside Palidur were vulnerable. Within the Holy City, evil was never forgotten or pushed aside. Merssa shook her head, feeling pity for the citizens of Tikken City.

The north gate was closed tight when Merssa arrived, and many guards kept watch over the surrounding fields from atop the walls. She pulled her company to a halt and they awaited Vecnor.

The Rogue Knight arrived moments later, sitting upon his monstrous steed. Umbarc was of a special breed from the barbarian realm of Andria, where horses of exceptional lifespans grew tall and muscular. The horse was dark in color and its mane and tail long, and within its eyes could be seen a greater intelligence than most animals—Merssa was sure Umbarc could rival that of the elves' much smaller horses. Vecnor once said he received Umbarc as a gift for his help in thwarting an invasion of Andria's lifelong enemies of Ekland, and the animal had been with him for as long as Merssa had known him. Umbarc snorted, announcing their arrival, and the horse's head was held high with pride, very much reflecting its rider.

Dellen signaled the tower, and the cranking of the winch filled their ears as the large gates swung open. Merssa led the way outside and the gates began to close immediately, slamming shut with a resounding boom.

"We'll arrive to Eastgate in four days," Merssa announced.

"Four days?" blurted Dellen. "But even at a good pace it's a five-day journey."

"Then we best not tarry with pointless conversation!" she snapped, causing the guardsman to flinch, and headed north.

Merssa was not the least surprised to find the road completely barren. There existed no villages along the lake between Tikken City and Korban Bridge, so the only traffic one normally expected to encounter were merchants, farmers, hunters, and travelers. But after the undead rising, Merssa doubted anyone would be braving the road today.

Just past noon, Merssa halted to allow for a short break for lunch, and when they returned to the road, she slowed the pace only slightly under the growing heat—there was a schedule to keep. They reached the hottest part of the day and over twenty miles were behind them. All riders and horses were now drenched with perspiration, but Merssa ignored the argumentative stares of the elves and continued. She was brought to an abrupt halt, however, when a familiar wind interrupted an otherwise calm day.

From the northwest stirred a cool breeze, refreshing at first, but rapidly growing in strength and becoming frigid. Merssa's ears, nose, and hands were stung by the cold, and dust and debris temporarily blinded her as it whipped past, shifting downward and upward and spiraling about. After less than a minute, it stopped.

"Not again," murmured Selanna.

"We must go back!" Desperation engulfed Dellen's face.

"That would accomplish nothing!" Merssa scolded. "The Council gave you a task and I suggest you get to it."

Merssa resumed the northward trek, glancing back to see Dellen gazing in the direction of the city. All that existed were the endless fields, the lake, and scattered trees. Merssa had not intended to sound so harsh; everything always seemed to come out that way. Duty was something she understood all too well, but what did the man hope to accomplish by going back now? Tikken City was not without its defenses, and if more undead attacked, this time the guard would be ready. It was foolish, really. Merssa looked back a second time to see the guardsman pushing his horse to catch up.

Another ten miles passed before Merssa slowed again. The scenery changed little, but her attention was drawn to a gathering of bugs near the lake, where tall reeds and cattails marked the water's edge. Insects did not normally alarm Merssa, but the immense number of critters buzzing about caught her eye, and while she studied the area, a feeling of evil—a small tingling upon her scalp and back of her neck—brought her to a complete halt. A rustling came from within the reeds and she caught wind of a putrid odor—that of a rotting carcass. Merssa dismounted and approached the vegetation, pulling her golden mace.

"What is it?" Vecnor was suddenly on Merssa's right with sword ready.

"Evil," she said, gazing at the towering weeds as she crept closer. "I can feel it."

"I can *smell* it!" Eraim sat atop her horse, wrinkling her little nose.

Merssa returned her attention to the lakeside, and Dellen was now on her left bearing the large hammer from his saddle, its handle nearly as long as he was tall. The weeds stood higher than even Vecnor, and Merssa carefully pushed aside the thick stems with her mace to reveal a gruesome sight. Three figures stood knee deep in the water, and their lifeless eyes were not the only features to give them away as undead. Two seemed to be fresh, as zombies go. Their bodies had not begun to decompose and their clothing, typical of farmer's garb, was clean and intact, save for a few rips drenched in blood. The third zombie had obviously been dead much longer. Its yellow, deteriorated skin barely clung to its body, gaps of missing flesh revealed discolored bones, one of its eyes was missing, and grave dirt stained its tattered clothing. The three were feasting upon a corpse dressed similarly to the newer zombies, and they were displeased with the interruption of their meal.

The decayed zombie hissed and lunged for Merssa, moving with surprising speed and nearly catching her off guard. She danced aside and crushed its skull with a single blow.

The other two did not move as swiftly as they emerged from the water with hatred in their eyes, and Vecnor cleaved one in half while Dellen's hammer smashed the head of the other. The torso of Vecnor's victim clawed at the ground and reached for Vecnor's boot, but he turned his blade downward and skewered its skull. It twitched once before ceasing to move.

"Have you ever seen a zombie move like that?" Merssa asked Vecnor, gazing at the one she had felled.

"No," he admitted. "It moved almost like a ghoul, though it lacks a ghoul's stench."

Merssa shook her head. "It was no ghoul." She had encountered ghouls once before, during a raid into an evil temple in Harbnum, and she knew a few things about them. "They would never venture into the daylight. The sun would destroy them."

"I wonder if it is the power of the Wind," Selanna mused. "The older zombie was obviously created a couple days ago with the first blowing, while the other two were surely killed recently and rose earlier today. Perhaps the second coming of the Wind had an increased effect on those already raised."

"If that's so," Dellen released a nervous chuckle, "I'd hate to see one after a third wind."

They all stood in silence. Merssa thought of how quickly the zombie had lunged at her. Had it not been for her extensive training, it might have actually touched her with its filthy, claw-like hands. *It moved almost as swiftly as a ghoul.* Vecnor was right. If Selanna's theory proved true… Merssa hated to think of what would come next. What if the wind could actually create ghouls?

Merssa cleared her throat, snapping the trance that held everyone. "Let's continue." No sense living under the fear of what *might* happen. She would put an end to this evil, and then no one would have to worry about undead anymore.

They moved on, the road bending westward until the setting sun was in their eyes, and as the large orb touched the ground, Korban Bridge came into view. Still a couple hundred yards to the northwest, its white stone reflected orange in the fading light, and upon it dark forms moved about. Merssa squinted, but the bridge was too far away to make anything out. At least for her it was.

"A dwarf!" gasped Eraim. "He battles the undead!"

Merssa led the charge, and the pounding of her companions' hooves followed. Soon the bridge became clearer and she spied the dwarf, ducking and evading the bony claws of skeletal attackers. His large axe destroyed two undead with a single swing and he lowered his shoulder and rammed a third into the water. By the time Merssa reached the melee, only five undead remained.

Merssa swung her mace from atop her horse, knocking the skull from a skeleton. Destroying the head was the quickest way to defeat a zombie, but skeletons were not zombies and the headless warrior continued flailing its arms. Dellen leapt from his saddle, crushing it beneath him and dislodging enough bones to break the curse sustaining its life. Merssa rounded her horse while Vecnor and Eraim joined the fray, destroying a skeleton each, and the dwarf took down the final two.

The battle was over.

Planting the handle of his axe firmly onto the stone and resting his arms across the top of its blade, the stocky dwarf eyed the company. He was tall for his race, standing as high as Eraim, but he was nearly four times the elf's girth. His hair was brown, its dirt content possibly causing it to appear so, and scars decorated his face and hands, marking him a warrior of many years—Merssa would guess him to be no less than two hundred, more than two thirds a dwarf's lifespan. His weapon was of exquisite craftsmanship. The handle, apparently made of bronze, was three feet long with a black leather strap wrapped about most of it, and from the bottom protruded a bronze spike. Its blade looked to be of polished silver, and all about its edge were mysterious runes. A small breeze tugged lightly at the dwarf's beard and the tip danced about his knees, and from beneath his bushy brow, he gave a snort.

"I am Merssa Goldmace of Palidur." Merssa dismounted and placed her mace upon her belt. "Are you all right?"

"I am Poluran of Rornibur." The dwarf's voice was exceptionally deep. "And I am as I was before you showed up: in no need of aid."

"Have you passed through Rivercross?" Merssa paid no mind to the disrespectful attitude. He was a dwarf, after all, and could not be expected to act above his nature.

"Just moments ago," Poluran replied in a more compassionate tone, shaking his head. "These are strange times. The foul wind swept across the land again and rose up all those killed two days ago. Now all that perished today are being mutilated or burned so it won't happen again." The dwarf gazed back at the city to the northeast, where the road disappeared beyond twenty-foot walls. "I think I'll return to Rornibur. These lands are cursed."

"Does the Wind not blow in the Stone Eagles?" Selanna asked. "Is Rornibur free of the walking dead?"

Poluran shrugged. "I know not. I am only on my way back from Morimont, from visiting cousins of mine. I've not been home in almost two years. I only stopped here to pay my respects to Korban the Strong." He eyed the white stones with pride. "Its work is the finest of its kind. Bones as tough as steel!" He stomped a boot to further his claim.

Merssa sighed. "Yes, this we know." She gazed at the city and back to the dwarf. "I thank you for your news and bid you good evening." Grabbing her reins, she addressed her company. "It will do no good to ride into Rivercross, I think. There will be too much fear and confusion, quite possibly hostility. We'll ride farther tonight and camp off the road."

"Would you be headin' north?" Poluran reminded Merssa he was still there.

"We are traveling to Neja, if you must know," she responded impatiently. "You are welcome to accompany us. It would be safer for you. Do you have a horse?"

"Safer indeed!" Poluran grumbled before speaking louder. "I have a mule. She bolted when the skeletons came, but she'll not have gotten far." Turning to the north, he gave a loud whistle. "Melballa! Melballa!" The dwarf ran to the edge of the bridge. "Melballa! *Bistrent*!"

Merssa shook her head. "Why did I offer?" But it was no time to be traveling alone. The undead were relentless, in no need of rest and unable to quench their thirst for blood or the destruction of the living.

At last, a mule emerged from the growing shadows of a few trees north of the bridge, its head bowed in shame.

"I don't know why I keep you!" Poluran climbed onto its pack-laden saddle.

Eraim gasped. "That poor animal. It was not meant to bear such a burden."

Merssa wondered if the elf spoke in reference to the many packages strapped to the saddle, or to the dwarf himself. "Will you be able to keep up?" She eyed the mule with doubt.

"She's a swift one, as her breed goes," Poluran answered. "Lead on!"

Vecnor laughed heartily. "A swift mule! That would be as likely as a swift dwarf!"

Poluran's snort of displeasure was loud enough to encourage additional laughter from the large warrior. Merssa gave a wry smile. She would try to ignore the dwarf's presence for the remainder of the journey.

Merssa led the way, riding around Rivercross and rejoining the road north of the city. They had not ridden far, only another mile or so, when the half-moon fell behind invading clouds and the night grew dark, and Merssa veered into a small grove.

They set up camp and Poluran lit a small fire, seemingly eager to earn his keep. Dinner was eaten quietly, with the exception of the dwarf's rather loud chewing, and all eyes kept watch on the shifting shadows while a light wind rustled through the treetops. The air remained warm and the breeze pleasant, but the night grew darker as clouds consumed the stars. After an hour, Merssa broke the silence.

"Get some rest." She rose to her feet. "We've an early start tomorrow." She stepped from the firelight to take the first watch.

Dellen remained by the fire with Poluran while the elves and Vecnor spread out their blankets. The dwarf pulled a jar of oil and a rag from his pack and began polishing the silver axe blade.

"That's quite a weapon," Dellen commented. He had been admiring it since Poluran joined their little journey. It was a weapon fit for a king.

"It's Clanghorr!" Poluran swelled with pride. "There's no equal."

"What do those runes mean?"

The dwarf shook his head, turning the axe to look at the symbols along the silver edge. "Don't quite know. I've been told it was forged by Meldar himself," he mentioned the dwarfish deity, "and that it is the language of the gods. There's nothing its edge can't cut." After a pause, Poluran ceased in his task and looked at Dellen with a furrowed brow. "So why do you journey to Neja? It's the rising of the dead, is it not?"

Dellen gazed toward the darkness where Merssa had ventured, not so sure she would approve of him speaking of their mission. But he really did not see the harm. "We seek the source of the Wind," he whispered.

Poluran nodded. "In that case, I shall lend you my services." He extended his short, thick arm.

Dellen was a bit reluctant to accept the offer. Perhaps there had been a good reason not to speak of the mission after all. He was suddenly plagued with regret, but it was too late. He clasped arms with the dwarf, not looking forward to the tongue lashing he would surely receive when Merssa found out.

"I best get some sleep," Dellen said, rising to his feet. "I have last watch."

Poluran nodded and resumed polishing.

Dellen awoke to Eraim's hand upon his shoulder. The night remained warm and all seemed quiet. When he rose, he saw Poluran standing alert.

"We dwarves can go days without sleep if need be," Poluran boasted. "I think it best I join you in your duties. Make use of my superior senses."

Eraim rolled her eyes before settling upon her blanket.

Dellen posed no argument, and he and Poluran shared the last watch, sitting against the trunk of a large tree and quietly exchanging stories. Dellen had few to mention, speaking of the couple opportunities he had had to venture from Tikken City on missions with Merssa in the name of the Council. He added that he had spent a holiday within Palidur, and that Merssa had led him to the worship of Cafior. He also explained how he had abandoned the sword for the hammer in combat, for Merssa preferred not to spoil the ground with evil blood, as was the way of most her Order. He felt his cheeks flush when Poluran asked why all of his stories involved the paladin.

"Cafior is held high among my folk," Poluran commented once Dellen finished. "He assists Meldar in the Halls of Stone beneath Vaeldor." The dwarf patted the ground.

Poluran then spoke of his experiences, mentioning battles with giants in the Stone Eagles and goblins within Varlimor. The dwarf also described the splendor of the mines and magnificent halls of Rornibur, pointing out that Rornibur meant "steel bones" in the dwarfish tongue.

"The stone there is much harder to work than any in Vaeldor," Poluran bragged. "And working it has made my clan the strongest dwarves that ever lived! But we don't hold that against the soft-skins." He chuckled quietly at his reference to the dwarves of other mountain chains. "They're still capable of good work. The Palidur Bridge is nice enough."

"Palidur Bridge is a mile long," Dellen pointed out, "and wide enough for four carts abreast. I'd say it's more than nice."

"But it needs occasional maintenance," Poluran said, "while the Korban defies time. Lord Korban gave it as a gift to the king of Moclen more than nine hundred years ago, and it hasn't aged a day!"

"Dwarves of Varlimor built Palidur City as well," Dellen added. "It's considered one of the greatest works of dwarfkind."

"To humans, lad." Poluran was not impressed. "To humans."

Perhaps Poluran had a point. Dellen grew up near the Korban Bridge and saw it often enough, and that probably made the sight of Palidur Bridge seem all the more majestic. But then again, Palidur Bridge was ten times longer than the Korban and supported by great pillars, holding it high above the widest river in all of Vaeldor. Also, in place of the images of dwarves carved upon the sides of the Korban, titanic statues of exquisite detail marked the middle of Palidur Bridge, standing at least five times higher than even the Great Tree at the center of Maple Lore Forest. No. Dellen was sure it was Poluran that was biased. The dwarf only liked the Korban better because it was made by Stone Eagle dwarves. But there was no point arguing the subject further, so Dellen returned to an earlier comment.

"If the stone is so hard to work in Rornibur, why mine it at all?"

"Meldar's Hammer and Anvil!" Poluran blurted. "*Why?*"

Dellen gazed at the campsite with alarm. No one stirred.

Returning to a quieter tone, Poluran explained. "The reward is great, man! Without Rornibur, there's no Korban Bridge, not to mention the buildings we've constructed for many cities. In Rornibur the furnaces burn hotter and we make the strongest steel. The diamonds are the purest and the gemstones more valuable than any others. Why indeed!" He snorted.

There was a moment of silence.

Dellen braved to speak again, changing the subject to recent days, and how he and Vecnor led Tikken City to victory against the undead.

"These are strange times." Poluran shook his head. "My whole journey home has been plagued. First a man tries to lift my pouch in Sardina. Then a group of filthy riders almost runs me over in Sendorum. And that was just the beginning of my misfortunes. After passing through Larkorn, I felt the evil wind. Fought my way west after that...skeletons and zombies coming from all directions, day and night. Some came out of the wild; undead hobgoblins and a few skeletons I couldn't place. But I took down the lot of them. Yeah, the road to Larkorn is much safer thanks to my hand." The dwarf nodded in satisfaction, but a grim expression overtook him. "After reaching Rivercross, things seemed back to normal...until that wind returned." He gazed into the surrounding darkness, as if undead were closing in. "Once Rivercross was quieted, I went to pay my respects to the Mighty Korban, and that's when those blasted skeletons came after me. Then your company arrived." Poluran released a long sigh, gazing at nothing. "I should have stayed in the mountains."

The sky brightened, and all remained quiet within the camp as wisps of smoke rose from the exhausted fire.

"We'd better wake the others," Dellen said. He knew Merssa would not take it well if the sun broke the horizon before he roused her.

Chapter 4

Ellaville

After a small breakfast, they mounted upon reluctant steeds and returned to the road. The clouds became fuller, providing some relief from the sun, but the air grew thick and their clothing clung to them, so Merssa eased the pace, but only slightly.

As they pressed farther northward, the trees grew more scattered and the land began to rise and fall often. Grass still grew in most places, but its green was either faded or completely lost to yellow or brown. The richer growths made finding streams easy enough, and Merssa allowed for short breaks to rest the horses whenever water was accessible. Upon the third such stop, there was quiet conversation. Poluran's voice carried farther than any others while he rambled about things uninteresting to Merssa, but she tuned him out and concentrated upon her own thoughts.

To the distant southeast, beyond all sight, lay Palidur. Merssa's home. The only home she had ever known. She was born within its walls, the daughter and only child of a low-ranking priestess and a holy soldier. It was expected that she would follow in her mother's occupation, for Merssa's link to Cafior was strong, and when she remained small in stature, it was in the direction of the clergy that she was pressed. But Merssa felt a different calling and trained hard in the art of combat. She excelled in her studies, as well as her physical training, and was raised to Paladin by the High Order at the age of twenty, surprising all. Over the next few years Merssa took every mission that came her way, thwarting evil whenever it crossed her path. She quickly rose in rank within the Cafior Sector and her name became well known, and not just because she was the first and only woman to ever attain Holy Knight. But over the past year, Merssa felt less than satisfied with the tasks handed to her; they seemed menial and more appropriate for those of lesser rank. Several times, standing before the Order, she requested a charge more befitting of her skills and rank, and she finally received it.

This was the most important mission the High Order had ever bestowed upon Merssa, and she would not fail. She only wished she had known it would lead her into Neja; it would have been well to have been prepared for that. All the criminals that sought refuge there hundreds of years ago, taunting the soldiers of Palidur and hiding amongst the highlands of the untamed country… It served them right to make it their permanent residence. But now, all of Vaeldor called the prison a kingdom. Anyone could carve a throne and forge a crown; that did not make one a king. Merssa held much respect for the Council of Wizards, but the fact that they backed these criminals infuriated her. It was the Council's endorsement, in her opinion, that gave credibility to the outlaw nation.

"Merssa?"

Vecnor's voice brought her back to the small stream where they were stopped.

"It's been twice as long a break as the others already," he added. "Not that the horses aren't enjoying it, but—"

"Mount up!" she called out.

The remainder of the day moved quietly by as they rode without further stops. They encountered nothing in the desolate terrain, and as dusk approached, they happened upon a small meadow and made camp. A brook ran through the center of the trees, carrying cool water from the distant, dark mountains apparent to the northwest, and the canopy of leaves provided adequate shelter should the darkening clouds decide to wash the land.

"We are two days from Neja," Poluran said, rapping his knuckles upon the ground. "You can feel the land's bones growing strong."

"We've made a good distance," Vecnor commented. "Perhaps we should unload the horses. Give them solid rest tonight."

Merssa nodded, and Dellen and Eraim saw to it. The company settled within the tight quarters and ate a quiet, cold supper.

The night was hot, though a steady breeze made it bearable, and thinning clouds revealed the aging moon and ended the threat of rain. Vecnor leaned against a large oak during the second guard shift, waving his sword in an exercise he often performed when alone. But he never focused on the task; the experience of many years allowed his senses to remain alert, and though the moon sparsely illuminated the meadow, he knew all was well.

It was nearly time to rouse Eraim when Vecnor detected a noise to the west of camp, opposite from where he stood. Something approached, and from the sound he knew there to be more than one, moving upwind like skilled animals on the hunt. He swiftly crossed the campsite and peered through the trees, spying shadows of men several yards away. They were hunched over and moved slowly, and when the breeze shifted, Vecnor caught wind of rotting meat.

"Ghouls!"

Looking back, his companions were still asleep.

"*Mees*! *Mees*!" Vecnor whispered sharply the elfish phrase for alarm.

Almost immediately, Selanna was stirring the others. Eraim joined Vecnor with Mithkahr in hand, and the blade emitted a dim red light.

"Mithkahr senses evil." Eraim wrinkled her nose. "Ghouls?"

"Can you tell how many?" Vecnor asked quietly in the elfish tongue.

Staring into the darkness, Eraim pursed her lips in frustration. "The trees hide most of them. At least a dozen, I would say. The nearest are to the right. Thirty yards."

She had not even glanced to the right.

Vecnor looked back again. Selanna produced a spark from her finger, igniting a collection of sticks, and Poluran and Dellen headed his way with weapons ready. Vecnor halted the two with a hand and pointed to where Eraim detected the nearest ghouls, and they nodded and veered that direction. Merssa's face twisted in disgust as she approached.

"I despise ghouls!"

The paladin made no attempt to conceal her voice, but Vecnor knew it did not matter. The wretched creatures were certainly aware of the company's presence, and they could be heard hissing to each other while they spread out.

"Fall back," Merssa ordered. "Back to the fire."

The three of them retreated to the campsite, and upon arrival Vecnor noticed Selanna was missing.

"Where is Selanna?" Eraim echoed his thought.

Vecnor scanned the woodland, but all he saw was Dellen and Poluran with backs to trees. Dellen held a gauntlet over his nose — the ghouls were near.

Just then, three of the creatures emerged, one next to Dellen and two to Poluran's left, and even in the shadowy light they appeared ghastly. They carried the air of the grave with them, just as zombies, but that's where the similarities ended. The ghouls' odor included a thick aura of spoiling meat to gag anyone with the slightest sense of smell, and their cold, dead skin was grayish blue, never seeming to decompose and covered by wounds oozing a black liquid. Dark tongues eagerly licked sharpened, bloodstained teeth, and they hissed with hatred as their yellowish eyes darted left and right, searching for their next meal.

Poluran struck swiftly, Clanghorr easily slicing a ghoul in two, and Dellen squared off with another. The vile creature remained just out of the guardsman's reach and crouched low to the ground.

"Dellen! He's going to leap!"

Vecnor had only a moment to shout his warning before his attention was drawn to five ghouls charging from nearby trees. He moved to engage and gave a mighty blow to fell one, and with his massive boot he sent another flailing into a tree. To his flanks Merssa and Eraim each fought a ghoul, and he moved in on the fifth one.

The creature circled, just as the one near Dellen had, but Vecnor knew their tactics well. As it crouched low and began walking on hands and feet, a cat ready to pounce, Vecnor feigned an attack. The ghoul took the bait and sprung, but Vecnor dropped to one knee and slashed his sword overhead, slicing the fiend wide open. It was dead before it hit the ground.

Eraim had killed her opponent and presently battled the one Vecnor kicked earlier, and Merssa's foe was unmoving. The paladin's mace shed a golden glow, a familiar sight when she called upon Cafior's wrath to smite her enemy, and as six more ghouls approached, she sped toward them without fear.

By the time Vecnor joined Merssa, she had already struck down two. Vecnor dropped two more and she destroyed another, but the final ghoul sprung onto the paladin's back and put a claw to her throat. Merssa threw the creature to the ground and brought her mace onto its skull at the very moment Vecnor's sword skewered it. Dark blood gushed onto his blade and the body went limp.

No ghouls moved. With the exception of the brook, the meadow was still.

"Damn!" Merssa held her hand tightly against her neck.

"How bad is it?" Vecnor asked.

He knew all too well the wound from a ghoul burned as if on fire. Their sickly, talon-like nails were packed with a filth that killed their victims over time, even if the injury failed to do so. The infected area would rot and spread like a dark rash until the victim succumbed, and days later the corpse would rise again…as a ghoul.

"Blasted hell spawn!" Merssa walked to where her pack rested by the fire.

The paladin pulled free a leather pouch and extracted an herb leaf and small vial. From the vial she sprinkled powder onto the leaf, and then scooped loose dirt from the ground and held it tightly in her fist with a silent prayer upon her lips. When finished, she mixed the dirt into the powder before placing the leaf across her neck, where the skin had already begun to darken around four long scratches. Vecnor stood ready to assist, but as usual Merssa wanted no help.

"Dellen's been hit," Poluran said as he and the guardsman returned.

Dellen's face was twisted in pain and scratches covered his left arm from elbow to wrist.

"The thing leaped like a frog!" the dwarf added.

Merssa wrapped a bandage about her neck to hold the herb in place before inspecting Dellen's wounds. She shook her head, observing the cuts, and Vecnor noticed a bite mark as well.

"Clean his arm as best you can," Merssa instructed Poluran, and she immediately began preparing more herbs.

Vecnor noticed Selanna returning to the campsite and he shot her a questioning glare.

"I heard Dandi calling," the elf explained. "She and Lilli destroyed one of those wretched creatures, but there were two others, and Umbarc could not possibly have gotten them both in time."

"I see you have not lost your touch." Eraim stole Vecnor's attention.

Vecnor half smiled at the small elf as her eyes gleamed in the flickering light. Even within the stench of the fallen ghouls, he was hard pressed to resist such a reaction when speaking with Eraim. She was the perfect combination of beauty and lethality. "And you're as quick as ever," he returned the compliment.

"I have great help." Eraim patted her sheathed blade, which Vecnor did not doubt had already been wiped clean of the foul blood.

"Is it not odd for ghouls to travel about the wild?" Selanna asked. "I thought they inhabited crypts and ruins and such."

"In most places." Vecnor nodded. "But it is strange, I agree."

"Perhaps the Wind has drawn them from their lairs," suggested Eraim.

Poluran snorted, surveying the ghoul bodies. "I'll not stay in this stench!"

The odor the black ichor exuded was growing thicker with every passing moment.

"No." Vecnor sheathed his sword. "We'll have to move on as soon as Merssa's ready. Let's saddle up the horses."

"I have done that already." Selanna smiled. "I did not think we would remain."

While Merssa finished wrapping Dellen's arm, the others gathered their gear. Selanna extinguished the fire with a word once all were ready and they left the trees behind.

They walked the horses while night persisted. The road grew long and dark as the moon struggled to shine through lingering clouds, and though the ghouls fell miles behind, the stench remained. Eraim noticed smatterings of black upon her leather jacket, barely visible in the dark. In fact, she noticed that all but Selanna shared in the horrible decorations. How was it Selanna always seemed to avoid such misfortunes? They could have washed up in the brook before leaving the meadow, but the odor had been so powerful, the company could think of nothing but returning to the road as quickly as possible. That was no excuse for Eraim, however, and she was a bit upset with herself for not having thought of it at the time.

"We would do well to find a stream and wash away this filth," Eraim said, pulling a rag from her saddle and blotting at the spots upon her jacket in vain. It was ruined.

Hours passed and the sky brightened before Merssa called for a halt, and they settled within a field off the road to gain a bit more rest. Eraim would have liked to unload the horses again, for the poor animals appeared every bit as tired as her human companions, but she sensed a bit of a growing temper within the paladin and thought better of asking.

Vecnor sat heavily onto the ground and leaned against a large boulder, falling asleep instantly. Merssa and Dellen were not so lucky, as their burning injuries surely made rest difficult, but weariness eventually overwhelmed them and they passed into slumber. Eraim remained awake with Selanna, and Poluran joined them while they sat upon the ground and watched the sunrise. Only a glimpse of the bright orb did they catch, though, before dark clouds engulfed it.

"I am troubled," Selanna mentioned, just above a whisper. "From what I know, ghouls are not much for travel."

"I hope they were not created by the Wind." Eraim continued to scrub at the filth on her jacket with water from her flask. "Skeletons and zombies are bad enough. If it can create ghouls by the thousands…"

"That smell…" Poluran mumbled to himself.

Eraim heard him clearly. "Not a smell one can easily forget. I recall the last time I encountered —"

"No!" The dwarf was perplexed. "Back in Sendorum, about a week ago, I smelled it when I encountered a very rude group of riders. They were taking up the whole road and I moved aside out of courtesy, but even so they nearly ran into me, as if they hadn't seen me or didn't care. I said a word or two, and I swear one of them growled at me like a dog. Made the hair on the back of my neck stand, it did. I had half a mind to let them sample Clanghorr's edge, but it wasn't worth the trouble." He shook his head.

Selanna stared at Poluran with piercing eyes. "A week ago? Before the first wind? You are positive?"

He nodded. "But it was during the day, albeit a gray one."

"If the day was dark enough…" Selanna pondered, "they might have been protected from the sun. But still, why would —"

"Had I known them to be ghouls," Poluran scowled, "I'd have slain every one of them!"

"Ghouls in cloaks?" Eraim wrinkled her nose. "On horseback? It does not sound believable."

Selanna turned back to Poluran. "What of the horses? I cannot fathom an animal allowing something so foul to sit upon its back, no matter how tame the beast may be."

"Come to think of it," he scratched his chin, "they trotted a steady pace, almost in unison with each step. And their eyes seemed to almost glow blue in the dim light. I thought them to be well trained, but why anyone would let animals go like that I don't rightly understand."

"Let them go?" Selanna furrowed her brow.

"They didn't look to have been brushed in months," the dwarf explained. "And some were missing shoes, by the sound of it. Then there were the scabs—oh, and the flies!"

"Undead horses!" Eraim was filled with horror. The nightmare was getting worse by the moment.

"So it would seem." Selanna gazed into the distance. "But why were ghouls riding horses? And where were they headed? Ghouls do not behave this way." Her last statement was murmured, barely audible even to Eraim.

"I've never encountered ghouls before." Poluran obviously felt a need to defend himself from an accusation voiced in his head. "And I've smelled farmers almost as bad."

He continued to grumble while he pulled a pipe from his belt and filled it with tobacco. He sighed. There was no fire from which to light it. Selanna whispered a strange word and smoke began to issue forth, as the pipe came to life. Poluran nodded in thanks and puffed away, staring onto the unmoving fields. They sat in silence for the next couple hours while Eraim continued with her cleaning task.

Merssa was not happy. She had only wanted to rest an hour, but at least two had passed before Selanna roused her. Selanna claimed they all had needed the sleep, but it was not the elf's place to make such decisions.

"Mount up," Merssa ordered with no attempt to hide her disapproval.

Poluran's brow furrowed. "But what about—"

"There will be no breakfast!" Merssa glared at the dwarf. He could stand to miss a meal or two. Besides, with the ghouls' odor still lingering, she doubted anyone other than Poluran possessed an appetite.

Dark clouds glared menacingly and the air was hot and breezy as they moved on. Trees grew sparser, sometimes lone, depressed figures upon the hard soil, and the road turned west, passing over rolling hills for many miles. The Wind of the Dead returned again a few hours after noon, and as in the past, it was bitterly cold and short lived. Merssa kept a careful watch on the countryside afterward, but saw nothing.

"Perhaps there's no more dead to rise up," Dellen suggested at one point—a morbid thought, but probably correct.

Lunchtime came and went, but Merssa did not stop, not even when she finally began to feel pangs of hunger—either the ghoul stench had faded or she had simply become used to it. She pressed on, trying to make up for the time Selanna had wasted, and the only complaining she detected was the grumblings of Poluran—she was not sure if it came from his mouth or his stomach. With the coming of dusk, Merssa halted off the road upon a field of hard soil and large rocks, and there they settled for the night.

Everyone ate a cold meal from their packs and few words were uttered. Mostly Poluran spoke in his "soft voice" to Dellen, though Merssa was sure anyone within a hundred yards could detect the deep rumblings, and Vecnor made comments about travel time, horse fatigue, and a couple other things. Merssa nodded without listening; she was again lost in thought. Visions of ghouls rising up by the thousands haunted her mind. The Wind had to be stopped.

Morning arrived without interruption and they resumed their pace. They did not travel far, however, before a village brought Merssa to a halt. Several buildings were nestled between two hills and a wide stream cut through its center. Grass did its best to grow along the waterway and created a small field to the southern edge, where a wooden fence surrounded a humble garden—the crops appeared scarcely large enough to fortify the number of houses present, much less the animal pens visible. Why would anyone build a village in such a desolate place?

"That would be Ellaville," said Poluran. "A small farming village."

Eraim frowned while eyeing the surrounding fields. "What could they possibly grow in this wasteland?"

The dwarf shrugged. "Not much. But they do keep sheep and cattle."

"I do not hear any," Eraim said. "And I see no movement either."

Indeed, all was still and quiet.

Merssa led the way down the hill for a closer inspection. Even as they entered the town, she spied no inhabitants or animals, only structures of wood or stone to either side of the bending road. The village appeared abandoned.

"Hello!" Vecnor called out.

There was no answer.

They came upon a couple houses to either side of the road, and Dellen dismounted to check the right side while Vecnor went left.

"Here!" Dellen called.

Merssa dropped from her horse to join the guardsman, and Poluran followed.

"Blood." Dellen held open a broken shutter to reveal a reddish streak upon an interior wall.

Merssa moved to the front door, finding it ajar. She stepped inside with mace ready. "Hello?"

Nothing.

Entering deeper, Merssa discovered overturned furniture and blood splatters marring the floors and walls. But there were no bodies.

She returned to the road, where Vecnor had rejoined Selanna and Eraim. The large warrior reported similar sightings across the street. Merssa ordered more houses to be checked, and the company paired up to execute the command. Vecnor accompanied Merssa as she scouted three more structures, but they were all the same. Upon returning to the road, she was informed the other buildings were no different.

"This is odd," commented Selanna. "Even if the undead killed everyone, there would be remains of some sort."

A light drizzle descended, and over the growing mountains to the west, a rumble of thunder chased a flash of lightning. Though the rain felt refreshing, Merssa was suddenly uneasy, as if undead eyes were watching from vacant buildings.

"Let's go inside and discuss this."

Poluran pointed down the street. "There's the tavern. I've visited it a time or two."

It was a two-story building of wood with four large windows overlooking a long, covered porch. The windows had obviously held glass panes at one time, but broken shards were all that remained. A set of doors between the windows led into the structure, one barely clinging to its lower hinge.

"*Larman's Brew*." Vecnor read the sign aloud.

"Was someone breaking in or breaking out?" posed Poluran, eyeing the windows.

Merssa climbed the steps. The glass was strewn across the porch as well as the tavern floor. "Both," she said. It was the only explanation.

Her attention was stolen when the ailing tavern door collapsed—Vecnor had knocked it loose as he entered the establishment. While the company filed in behind the large warrior, Eraim led the horses onto the porch. The small elf spoke in the elfish tongue and the animal called Lilli whinnied and nodded. Merssa would never understand the relationship Salenti elves shared with their horses, but often she was amazed by it. She followed Eraim inside.

The tavern was in a state of disarray; glass crackled beneath their boots, most tables and chairs were broken, and blood smeared the walls and floor in many areas. Vecnor was dragging a table toward the farthest corner—the cleanest area of the room—and Selanna gathered chairs still possessing four legs. While they did so, Dellen passed through a door behind the bar, reporting there to be an empty kitchen, and Poluran found a few unbroken bottles of wine and a small keg, as well as four mugs that survived whatever it was that had assailed the establishment. With Mithkahr in hand, Eraim ascended the stairs to the second floor, returning shortly to report no persons or undead hiding within the rooms above. Dellen then returned to the horses to fetch food from their packs, and they sat to their first meal of the day.

All things considered, it was the most comfortable accommodations they had had since Tikken City, and they munched and nibbled as the storm arrived. Rain poured heavily, beating upon the roof and exposing a couple leaks, and lightning danced across the sky while thunder pounded fiercely onto the tavern. Through the broken windows came a refreshing mist riding a light breeze, but the company's expressions remained uneasy and no one spoke for several minutes.

"Where are all the people?" Dellen posed the obvious question at last.

"They've been taken," said Merssa, staring blankly at the untouched jerky before her. It was not the memory of the ghoul stench that spoiled her appetite this time, but the fact that she was clueless as to what had happened to this village. The inhabitants had to have been taken elsewhere. It was the only explanation that made sense.

"Where?" Poluran inquired with his mouth full. The sound of the dwarf's chewing had not ceased since they sat down.

"Maybe they escaped," offered Dellen. "They could be hiding in the wilderness. Or run off to another village."

Poluran shook his head. "There are no villages near enough. Only Eastgate. But the farmers would never go *there*."

"With all the blood…" Vecnor sighed. "Like Selanna said, there should be *something* left behind; bones, body parts, some sort of remains. I'd settle for a bloody shirt. If this is the work of the undead…" He sat back in his chair, shaking his head again. "I've never known them to collect bodies. It's not as if they store food for the winter."

Selanna sniffed the air. "There is a faint odor to suggest ghouls."

"It might be *us* you're smelling," Dellen pointed out.

Eraim sat up abruptly, her head cocked to one side. "What was that?"

Everyone fell silent, but all Merssa heard was the pounding of the rain—even the thunder seemed to pause. She raced to the windows and peered outside; the horses were undisturbed and the road nearly flooded. She returned to the table, shaking her head at the questioning look from Vecnor.

"What did you hear?" Vecnor asked quietly to Eraim.

Eraim shook her head slowly. "I thought I heard something. But it is gone now."

"I heard it," said Selanna. "Or rather felt it. Like something sliding across a stone floor."

"A cellar." Vecnor pulled his sword, moving behind the bar upon swift strides.

Dellen was quick to join the large warrior, and Merssa followed as Vecnor opened the kitchen door.

"You three wait here," Merssa instructed Poluran and the elves. "And keep an eye on the road," she added to the dwarf.

She watched Poluran shrug while he poured another mug of ale. He then grabbed his axe and the food Merssa had failed to consume before moving to the broken windows. Merssa shook her head and passed through the doorway.

A small window dully illuminated the kitchen, and it was obvious the fight had not been exclusive to the tavern. Broken pots, plates, and mugs were strewn everywhere, and next to a hearth rested a large cauldron upon its side, its contents decorating the floor. The broth, vegetables, and meat were cold, but a faint, pleasant aroma still clung to the air.

Merssa moved to the window and peeked outside. A flash of lightning highlighted a dog pen behind the building, its twisted gate broken loose and lying several feet away. The pen was empty.

"Here."

Vecnor gained Merssa's attention. He stood above a trapdoor she had not noticed, next to the hearth. He pulled open the door to reveal a dark stairway.

"Dellen," Merssa whispered loudly. "A light."

The guardsman inspected the fireplace, stirring the ashes with a ladle and discovering hot coals within. He blew lightly to resurrect a small glow, and grabbing a candle from the floor, he lit the wick. He headed for the trapdoor, but Merssa snatched the light and led the way down the steps. She was not going to get stuck walking behind the towering men again.

She entered a small cellar. Narrow pathways led around crates, kegs, and sacks, and upon shelves rested jars and bottles. To the side hung a lantern upon a hook, and Merssa lit it before handing the candle back to Dellen, but the new light revealed nothing more.

Thud.

Merssa held her breath. The noise had come from the back wall. Quietly, she made her way around the room to a dark spot on the floor; a clearing of dust in the shape of a crate. She studied the wall beyond and detected the outline of a poorly hidden door. Handing the lantern to Dellen, Merssa pushed the panel, but it did not budge. She tried harder. Nothing. Determined, she stepped back and lowered her shoulder to give it a rush, but Vecnor's large hand halted her and ushered her aside.

A small flame ignited within Merssa's stomach as she watched Vecnor raise a mighty boot to give the door a kick. The big oaf obviously had not realized she was merely testing the door's strength. But she never knew him to pass up an opportunity to show off, and she let it go with a controlled exhale.

The wall gave way to Vecnor's strength, as the secret door broke loose from its hidden hinges, but it opened only slightly. A barricade upon the other side halted its progress, and through the narrow opening issued light and muffled voices. Vecnor lowered his shoulder and rammed through, scattering a pile of furniture and debris upon the other side and inciting screams from beyond.

Huddled within the far corner of a cramped room, Merssa spied a small family. Looks of horror were plastered upon the faces of a short, balding man, a robust woman, and two young boys while they gaped at the black-armored warrior who had crashed into their hiding place. Vecnor stood tall and hit his head on the low ceiling.

"They're alive." He rubbed his head, stepping aside to allow Merssa access.

The bald man's eyes brightened and he released a joyous sigh upon seeing Merssa enter. "Palidur! Thank the gods you've come!"

Chapter 5

Larman's Brew

I am Larman," the balding man said, beaming with pride. "Proprietor. And this is my wife, Fellna, and—"

"Excuse me, Larman," Merssa said, "but we must return upstairs." The small, cramped room was hardly the place to hold any lengthy conversation, and she wished to make sure all was right with the elves and dwarf.

Merssa led the way up the stairs and into the tavern. The rain had tapered off to a light sprinkling, and Poluran still kept watch over the street while Selanna and Eraim spoke quietly at the table. As Merssa made her way toward the elves, Poluran lifted the small keg to join them, eyeing the newcomers. Fellna immediately grabbed a broom and instructed the boys to help tidy up, as if such a feat could be attained, and while the boys gathered broken furniture into a pile, the woman cleaned around the company's table in a vain attempt to be hospitable.

Merssa stood at the head of the table. "We need to know what became of your village, Larman, and we haven't much time." Already they had remained within Ellaville much longer than she had intended.

"Well…" Larman took a seat, scanning the tavern as if searching for the right words to say. "I suppose it all began a few days ago, when the first cold wind blew." The innkeeper shuddered and Poluran poured him a mug of ale. After a deep, shaky drink, Larman continued. "It raised the dead from the graveyard! A nightmare come to life, I tell you." He looked at Merssa. "Had it not been for Olinin, all would have been lost."

"Olinin?" Merssa asked.

"The wizard," Larman said, as if she should have known the name. "From Neja."

Merssa could feel the sneer crossing her lips.

"Truly," Larman insisted. "We haven't the weapons or skills to defend ourselves against such a foe. But as luck would have it, Olinin was in town with his warriors, Belsod and Corlan, and we were able to fight them off. In all, I believe we lost little more than a score. Much better than it would have been had we been forced to rely on our own resources.

"We gathered our dead and gave them burials of highest honor." Larman's eyes were downcast and he shook his head. He seemed about to weep, but he fought back the tears. "We hadn't realized the wind would return and our fallen heroes would rise again." The innkeeper raised his head to meet Merssa's gaze. "But they didn't attack this time. They dug their way out of the fresh graves and walked off to the west."

Poluran refilled Larman's empty mug and the innkeeper drank every last ounce. Fellna then arrived to Larman's aid, placing a comforting hand onto his shoulder.

"What happened to your village?" Merssa prodded. The tale about the zombies was irrelevant. Why couldn't people just get to the point? And this Olinin… He was more likely the culprit. Why else would the zombies head for Neja? Merssa would have to meet this wizard.

"Last night," Larman said with some effort, "all seemed well and normal…as normal as can be *these* days. The missus was preparing meals and the boys were serving drinks. Then she calls me into the kitchen, claiming the stew was going bad. Said the whole kitchen smelled of rotted meat. When I went to see, I noticed the smell was coming from the open window. Thought maybe one of old Kamen's herd had died again, so I told her to close the shutters." He stopped and gazed at the table.

"I did as he told me," Fellna said, "but when I pulled them shut, I heard something hiss at me! I couldn't understand why the dogs weren't barking if something were out back, and I wasn't sure I wanted to find out."

"Ghouls," Merssa murmured to Vecnor.

"Ghouls?" Larman's eyes grew wide and his lip quivered slightly. "Truly?" He looked at Merssa's bandages, as if noticing them for the first time, and then spied the wrappings about Dellen's arm. "I see your journey hasn't been without its *own* dangers."

"We're fine," Merssa assured him. "Please continue."

"Well, after I returned to the tavern, I heard screams outside." Larman seemed to avoid looking at the broken windows. "Some of my patrons ran out to see what was the matter… I never saw them again. Then came the sounds of wood splintering and glass smashing, and a hideous creature peered through one of my windows. I'd never seen anything so vile in all my life. Truly. It is an image I'll not soon forget." He paused to take in a deep breath. "Those that remained inside took it upon themselves to bar the doors and shutter the windows, but that didn't work. The monsters broke in anyway. There was no stopping them. They smiled as they tore people apart." Larman's face grew pale. "I saw no other course of action…I-I had to protect my own. There was nothing I could do for anyone else." He lowered his head in shame. "I gathered my family into the cellar and we stowed away. I had the room built years ago, as a secret storage for my finest products… I never thought it would one day save our lives."

"Soleran answered our prayers," Fellna added, "for the creatures never found us."

"Perhaps." Merssa took slight offense. It was she, a Paladin of Cafior that found them. But she knew many commoners prayed to Soleran the Protector in times of danger. "You were fortunate, for ghouls can smell the living at a hundred yards."

"What about the bodies?" Vecnor inquired. "Where are the dead?"

"Bodies?" Larman gazed about. "There aren't any bodies? Truly? Did the ghouls eat them?"

"You never left the cellar?" Merssa raised a brow.

Larman shook his head. "We barricaded the door and never so much as peeped outside. When everything got quiet, we stayed put to await our saviors." He smiled at Merssa. "And here you are!"

"Well," Merssa sat back, "I don't think you should stay here any longer. You can't survive in that room forever. Pack four bags and leave the rest behind. You'll ride with us to Eastgate."

"Thank you, my lady!" Larman stood and bowed. "Many thanks to all of you!"

"We leave shortly," Merssa mentioned. "You best get packing."

Larman hurried up the stairs, followed by his family, and Merssa turned to the others.

"We'll arrive to Eastgate tomorrow. We can't leave these folks behind to fend for themselves. Who knows if the ghouls will return? Dellen," she addressed the guardsman. "Fix their gear to the horses as best you can." She turned to the elves. "Larman shall ride with you, Eraim. Fellna with you, Selanna. Dellen and I will each take a child."

Eraim's nose wrinkled in disapproval. Merssa could feel the objection rising and she put up a hand and turned away.

"Come, Eraim," Selanna said loudly enough for Merssa to hear. "Let's go break the news to Dandi and Lilli."

Over the next hour, they made ready to ride. Merssa took the time to change Dellen's bandages, as well as her own, and though the wounds were still a bit blackened about the edges, they appeared to be healing nicely. Merssa then made room on her horse for one of the boys, she could not recall his name, while Poluran assisted Dellen with the task of loading the Larman family goods. Upon lifting a very heavy and bulky pack onto Melballa, Poluran frowned.

"Did they pack the cauldron?" the dwarf complained loudly.

Dellen's response spared Merssa the bother.

"They were only allowed four packs." The guardsman pulled a

strap taut. "I imagine they tried to pack all that is dear to them."

Loading Fellna was a chore as well. Selanna's horse was very hesitant, and it took much coaxing from the mage before it allowed the woman to climb aboard. Even then, Vecnor's assistance was necessary to lift Fellna onto the saddle.

All was ready at last and they left the village behind, riding in silence for several miles. The clouds broke up, taking away the rain, and the company was then faced with hordes of insects. Merssa attempted to ignore the critters, allowing her mind to wander to places she would rather be, like her church or her quarters in Palidur, but her passenger stole her attention.

"Did Soleran protect us?" the boy asked. "Or was it Cafior? You *are* a Paladin of Cafior, aren't you?"

"Very good." Merssa was pleased with the question, as well as the opportunity to teach the lad something important. Folks outside Palidur seemed to lack any real knowledge of how the gods worked. "I would say they both did, as well as Arronaus. In Palidur, we believe all three work together to combat evil. Soleran protected you, giving you time to seek shelter. Then you and your family found refuge beneath the ground, which is Cafior's realm, and Arronaus brought the sun and chased away all shadows. Finally, Cafior guided me to your village, so I might escort you to where you will…" She wanted to tell the lad it was a safe place they were headed for, but she could not do so. Neja was the last place Merssa wanted to leave the family. Time, however, presented her with little choice. "To a place that's safer."

"Some say Cafior don't care about this land," the boy said. "That's why the soil is so tough and crops won't grow."

"Cafior cares about all lands!" Merssa snapped. "Even here, though I doubt there are any in these parts that pay homage to him. He is Ruler of the Land and all it provides, be it crops, stones to build castles and walls, or treasures and iron sought in the mines. It would do you well to learn more of His ways before making such comments, but I have not the time to properly teach you."

There was a pause as Merssa felt the boy retreat a bit. But then he spoke again.

"Things don't grow real good out here, but we *do* have lots of stones for building stuff. And I hear there are lots of mines in the Stone Eagles. I just wish it wasn't so hard to grow food."

"There have been many battles fought on these grounds, way before your time." Merssa attempted to speak more gently. "Perhaps the blood of evil that has poured over it for centuries has spoiled it. Or perhaps it is those that dwell in these parts that aren't worthy of richer soil."

She was confident the boy understood, for he asked no more questions for the remainder of the ride.

Dusk approached and they stopped for the night. Vecnor located as nice a site as the terrain allowed, out of view from the road among some large boulders, and they set up camp. Fellna unpacked a large pot from one of her bags, causing Poluran to shake his head at Dellen, and collected portions from the company's rations. Then, with her spices, she put together a tasty stew and the dwarf was quick to forgive as he returned for a second helping. Dellen grew a bit concerned that the odor of the food might attract ghouls, but Vecnor reminded the guardsman that the undead smelled the living, and probably would not heed the pleasant aroma.

Once dinner was finished, there was some light conversation. Merssa chose not to join in, and she and Vecnor sat at the edge of camp, listening while they watched the dark countryside. Larman's family was in complete awe of the lovely elves and asked many questions, and though Vecnor looked uneasy at the thought of them learning about elves from Salenti folk, he remained silent—even when Eraim revealed him to be the Black Rogue, to which Larman gasped and said, "Truly?"

The night was cool, a welcome change, and nothing was seen or heard throughout its duration, allowing for solid rest. With the morning came fairer weather and large, billowy clouds floated lazily overhead. Only a few miles to the northwest, the Stone Eagle

Mountains rose higher than the Varlimor peaks Merssa was accustomed to, and had she been in a better mood she might have taken a moment to admire them.

She applied fresh bandages to the ghoul wounds, pausing only to make sure Fellna remembered they were to leave shortly—the woman was humming loudly while preparing breakfast. For some reason Fellna seemed annoyed with Merssa afterward, commenting that breakfast "didn't have proper time to blend," but in Merssa's opinion it was quite tasty for a campfire meal and more than she had expected. Beyond that, Merssa was starting to feel a little unappreciated. Would the woman rather be locked back in the tavern cellar?

They returned to the road and it veered north a few miles before turning west again, aiming directly for the growing mountains. As the sun rose high overhead, Poluran announced the Stony River to be only a few leagues away and Merssa decided to stop for an early lunch—she pretended not to notice the looks of surprise that ensued. In truth, she was loathing their arrival to Neja, and once the meal was done, she allowed the horses to walk an easy pace.

The Stony River was in sight at last, snaking its way south from the towering peaks, and just before the waterway stood the crumbled ruins of the once proud Warden Tower. The structure's great ramparts pierced the sky in days long past, but all that remained was a ring of stones, thirty yards across and no higher than twenty feet at its tallest point. Markings and symbols decorated it, as Nejans had surely enjoyed a pastime of desecrating its once great memories.

Palidurians had built the tower many centuries before, and though Merssa had never seen it in days when it stood, she could picture the tall sentinel guarding over the only fordable area the Stony River knew. What a thrill it must have been to scale to its highest point and keep watch over the criminals within the wilderness beyond. The low lives thought they had escaped into the wasteland, and they hid amongst the foothills of the Stone Eagles, hoping to lure the Palidurians into ambushes. But Palidur did not give in. Instead, they erected the tower and fortified it with a hundred soldiers, fifty hounds, and two catapults to prevent the thieves and murderers from reentering Vaeldor, for there existed no safer path elsewhere. The north held the impassable mountains; to the south, the eerie Silent Marsh and dangerous Tall Pines Forest claimed all who dared to enter; the west was blocked by the swift and wide Alabar River, boasting many waterfalls along its course; and the Stony River completed the prison walls, for its current was too rapid for swimming and jagged stones hidden throughout its length made the use of boats a dangerous task.

Palidur had guarded the prison for nearly half a century, and added to its population by forcing other lawbreakers across the water. But then a king arose from within and Neja was founded. The Holy City refused to recognize the new king, but after another twenty years, and thwarting many attempts of inmates trying to gain control of the river, Palidur had to abandon its watch for more important matters. Merssa was not completely sure what the other "matters" had been, but they must have been truly important. Otherwise, Palidur could have kept the rogue nation from ever having been counted among the realms of Vaeldor.

Those days were far behind, and presently a simple arched bridge of stone spanned the river. It lacked the splendor of the Korban and Palidur Bridges, having most likely been pieced together by Nejans, and many patches were visible throughout the length of its careless construction. Fifty yards beyond the bridge stood Eastgate, ready to bar entry to the rest of Vaeldor should the Nejans wish to do so, but its gates were wide open.

Merssa took in a deep breath and slowly released it. They had arrived.

Chapter 6

Eastgate

Life seemed undaunted by the cold winds in Eastgate. If not for people boasting of victories over the undead, Merssa would have thought them not to have suffered the same fate. Many even bragged of how they welcomed another attack, if there were any dead left to rise.

The streets were busy, as merchants' tables were placed anywhere space was available, and it left Merssa to wonder if the city possessed a proper marketplace. One merchant claimed his sword and armor to be specially forged to combat the undead, while another called out, "Elixir of anti-undeath! One vial will prevent you or a loved one from returning from the dead to feast upon your family and friends! All the way from Tenvale, the Wizard Kingdom!"

If the merchants weren't bad enough, there were plenty of beggars to add to the experience. The filthy scroungers were laying in alleyways, sitting outside business doors, and wandering through the crowds with their hands out.

Neja was already proving itself a most undesirable realm.

Much to Merssa's surprise, there were many that recognized her as a Palidurian Paladin of Cafior. Some folks scurried from her path and avoided eye contact while others scowled and glared, and there were a few that smiled, as a thief sitting at a table sporting lots of good silver. Merssa ignored them all, holding her head high and secretly wishing one would impede her, so she might make an example of them.

Many jaws dropped at the sight of Vecnor—whether they recognized him from legend or were filled with awe by his size was unclear—but no one dared gaze too long, save for a few suggestively-dressed women. The elves were not only gaped and whistled at, but a few jeers came their way as well. "Come with me little woman!" one called to Eraim. "I'll make a human outta ya!" Of the women onlookers, the comments were more of an envious tone. "This ain't your place!" one yelled. "A bit north for your kind, ain't it?" sneered another.

Poluran snorted. "I've been away so long, I almost forgot why I avoid this place."

Merssa scanned the nearby buildings. "Let's find a tavern." She looked back to Vecnor. "We need to drop off our guests before seeking the *lord* of this pigsty."

"Over there's the Split Skull Haven." Vecnor pointed out a drab-looking structure.

Merssa gave a sniff of disapproval and signaled for a halt. Not only was the name repulsive and the building filthy—not even the street wanderers seemed interested in venturing near it—but Vecnor had pointed it out much too quickly, making it obvious he had been there before. Merssa knew he traveled extensively, but why would he waste time within such a pitiful realm?

They dismounted and unloaded the family's goods before bidding Larman good luck. Fellna and the boys lugged the items into the tavern while Larman thanked the company profusely with many handshakes and hugs. Merssa dreaded her turn for an embrace, but reluctantly allowed the man to show his gratitude.

"I am sorry we brought you to this…place," she said, glaring about the street with disgust.

"Well," Larman rubbed the back of his neck, "it isn't quite what I expected, and I must admit my expectations were low from stories I've heard. All the same," his smile returned, "any place is better than where we were."

Merssa reached for her pouch. "Are you in need of—"

"Oh no!" Larman raised both hands. "Truly. You have done quite enough. Keep your gold. My inn was not without its profits. We'll do well enough."

"I knew I heard coins in those bags," commented Dellen.

Larman smiled and gave a wink. "As soon as opportunity presents itself, I shall buy you all a round." He bade them another farewell and rushed to join his family.

"I could use a drink and a hot meal," Vecnor mentioned after the balding man disappeared.

Merssa looked at the sky and sighed. There was plenty of daylight left and the hot, sticky air was intensifying the city's undesirable smells. Besides that, it was the perfect excuse for putting off her meeting with the baron. "I suppose we have time for a *short* meal." She gazed at the Split Skull. "And this place is probably as good as any, if that's saying much."

"Is it safe to leave our animals?" Dellen eyed three men across the street. They seemed to be taking an interest in the many packs the horses bore.

"Don't worry," Vecnor assured the guardsman and turned to his large steed. "Umbarc. Guard." Vecnor dropped the reins and entered the inn without tethering the animal, and Eraim and Selanna did the same.

"If I don't tie her down," Poluran said, "she'll wander off." The dwarf slapped the reins of Melballa about the hitching post, and Merssa and Dellen secured their mounts as well.

Merssa entered the tavern, and the odor of alcohol and waste hit her like a stone wall—perhaps the streets had not been so foul after all. She noticed Selanna and Eraim sharing similar looks of revulsion, but she dared not wonder what other scents the elves detected.

"I hate this land!" Merssa was uncaring as to who might hear. Grabbing an unoccupied chair from a nearby table where a couple patrons were enjoying a drink, she propped open the door. No one protested.

Besides Merssa's company, only three other tables were

occupied, unless she counted the table with a man passed out upon it. Behind the bar stood a homely barman in dirty clothes, and he glanced at Merssa briefly before looking away.

"You'd be hard pressed to find other taverns of Eastgate more inviting," Vecnor said as Merssa joined him at a table.

"This city is a cesspool!" she spat. "I'll not be eating here."

Vecnor grinned. "At least try the wine. It's the best this side of Stony River."

Merssa sent the large man a sharp glare, but his unwavering smile showed him to remain undaunted.

Larman entered from an interior door, and upon spotting his heroes he grinned and approached.

"So, you're to test my word already? My word is my honor. The first round is on me."

"Again," said Merssa, "I am sorry for bringing you to this *place*."

Glancing about the room, Larman gave an unconvincing smile. "I admit it leaves much to be desired. I shall have a word with the proprietor. This is no way to keep an inn. Truly!" His genuine smile returned. "But back to current matters. At worst the drinks will be a bit watered down." Larman's last comment was uttered quietly with a hand held up so the bartender would not hear. "But after our long journey, I think they're called for. I'll be right back." He scuttled off to the bar.

"Was he on a long journey?" Selanna giggled. "I travel from Salenti to Vermallon at least once a year."

"I've been to Kalmaar to compete in the Tournaments of Brondor," Dellen said, speaking of the annual events held in honor of the battle deity. "I didn't win, though." His face twisted as he rubbed his left shoulder.

"From Rornibur to Morimont, and on occasion to the High Riser Mountains." Poluran nodded in satisfaction.

"I've been to every kingdom in Vaeldor," Vecnor mentioned, almost to himself as he gazed to faraway places upon the table. Returning to the tavern, he looked to the bartender, who was busy filling Larman's order. "Barkeep! Get me some food. And I had better enjoy it!" Vecnor's tone brought alarm to the bartender's face, as well as nervous glances from the other patrons.

Larman made two trips to supply the table with four pitchers of beer, two bottles of wine, and tankards for all. Merssa gazed at her mug doubtfully and pulled a cloth from her pouch to give it a good polishing.

"Alas, I must be off," Larman said. "We need to get settled, and I think the missus has had proper time to tidy the room a bit."

Still plagued with guilt, Merssa chose not to inquire as to the condition of the room, and Larman gave many more thanks before taking his leave.

The bartender placed a wooden platter before Vecnor. A large leg of meat, Merssa unwilling to guess as to what animal it had once belonged, dominated the plate, and surrounding it were potatoes and carrots. The barkeep returned with a side of steaming broth and a chunk of bread, and all smelled surprisingly good.

"I trust this is to your liking," the man said with a near toothless grin. "Pay as you deem worthy." He bowed his head.

"I would not trust vegetables grown in this soil," commented Merssa as she scowled at the plate.

"Oh, they're good all right," the barkeep said. "Grown in a village south of here. Best vegetables you could hope to find anywhere, as far as I can see."

"Then you do not see past the end of your nose!" Merssa caused the man to retreat a step.

"They are actually quite delicious," commented Selanna, having snatched a carrot.

Ignoring the elf, Merssa poured herself a mug of beer and took a sip. It was grossly watered down. She sighed.

Vecnor took a large bite from the leg and nodded in satisfaction. "Two for you." Food rolled about his mouth as he spoke.

"Two silvers is most generous, master!" The barkeep beamed.

"Who said silver?" Vecnor dropped two gold coins onto the table, causing the man to gasp. "I'll expect my second course momentarily."

The barkeep chuckled, but then realized Vecnor to be serious. "You are most noble, my lord!" The man bowed, scooped the coins, and scampered back into the kitchen, no doubt to see what else he could scrape up in a short time.

"Let's not tarry," Merssa said. "We must seek out Baron Karlsum and see what the pig keeper can tell us."

Everyone sipped the less-than-satisfactory drinks while Vecnor ate. After a few minutes, Vecnor stopped to address Dellen.

"Don't just sit there with your mouth watering. Get some food. It's quite tasty!" He took another bite.

Dellen glanced Merssa's way. She shook her head and gazed out the door, wishing they had not stopped.

"Uh, no thanks," the guardsman said. "I'm still full from lunch."

Vecnor snorted a chuckle.

Poluran was practically drooling while he stared at Vecnor's plate. "I could do with a snack." The dwarf turned and bellowed to the barkeep. "An equal share for me, my good man!"

Merssa glared at Poluran, annoyance welling up and about to burst. This "short meal" was going to last a lifetime.

Selanna continued swiping vegetables from Vecnor's plate for Eraim and herself, and the elves giggled whenever Vecnor shook his head or sighed. He poured the broth over the remainder of the food, bringing looks of disgust to the two, and his meal then belonged only to him.

Shortly after Poluran received his platter, the second course was served, consisting of spiced wine, sweetbread, and a piece of cheese. The dwarf proved a quick eater, and even as Vecnor's meal was half consumed, Poluran devoured his entire mystery leg and washed it down with the broth, like it was a fine after-meal wine. Poluran's vegetables remained untouched and he had no help forthcoming from the elves—his mannerisms had sprayed far too many bits of food onto the plate.

The display was more than Merssa cared to witness any longer and she excused herself, deciding to get what little fresh air the city offered. When she neared the doorway, there was a commotion outside—horses' whinnies followed by shouting. Vecnor was suddenly behind Merssa as she exited, his greasy leg still in hand, and they found the men from across the street now outside the tavern. One lay motionless while a second cowered before Umbarc, and Lilli and Dandi neighed threateningly, cornering the third man against the wall. Four additional men approached Umbarc with swords drawn.

"Umbarc! Halt!" Vecnor ordered his mount as it prepared to stomp the groveling man before it.

The large horse obeyed, releasing an angry snort, and the man scrambled behind his comrades before drawing a small sword.

Vecnor turned his attention to the thugs. "What type of men fight horses with swords?" He took a bite of his lunch.

The men hesitated; their faces unsure. The lead figure then smiled.

"You're drunk, my friend." The man's eyes narrowed upon Merssa before returning to Vecnor. "You best finish your meal inside, lest we finish you *and* your fancy friend."

"Enough!" Merssa barked. "*You* best walk away while you still can." She folded her arms across her chest, her mace still hanging at her side.

"Your authority's no good here!" spat another man. "Go back to Palidur!" His sneer faded when Dellen, Poluran, and the elves exited the tavern.

"Your horse killed my friend," the lead figure said to Vecnor, nodding to the limp body in the street. "Now it is only just that the beast be punished."

"Bad Umbarc!" Vecnor scolded. "No apples for you!"

"Very clever." The man held no more humor. "But that will not do. He killed my friend. And now I'm going to kill him!"

The man rushed Umbarc, but never drew near enough as Vecnor's half-eaten leg crashed onto his head and knocked him to the street.

The remaining men charged, and Vecnor swung the drumstick with his long reach, catching the first one full in the face. Vecnor then sidestepped the blade of the second one and brought his fist into the thug's jaw, knocking the man aside. After steering away the third man's sword with his lunch and dodging the blade of the fourth, Vecnor snapped the now almost-bare-bone, knocking one attacker into the other and dropping both to the cobblestones.

A loud stomp and snort sounded to the right, as the leader had apparently recovered and was attempting to sneak up on Vecnor. Now, the man writhed before Umbarc, holding his twisted arm close to his body.

The ruffians slowly regained their feet, but made no further advances. Merssa remained back—she knew Vecnor would not welcome assistance in this matter, and it appeared her companions shared in that knowledge.

"Be gone!" Vecnor threw what was left of the leg bone at their feet. "Before I draw my sword!" He emphasized the final three words with a growl.

The men scattered in separate directions, disappearing into the gathering crowd until all that remained were the dead body and the man cornered by the elves' horses. After a whisper from Eraim, the mounts let the thug go.

"I told you to halt!" Vecnor grabbed Umbarc's chin. "I had it under control."

The horse gave a sharp snort in response, pulling its chin free.

Merssa eyed the mass of onlookers. There were a lot of excited conversations and pointing, and two men dragged the dead body into a nearby alley—most likely to check all pouches and pockets. But there were no city watchmen to be seen. Merssa shook her head. "We're finished here."

While the others mounted, Merssa addressed Poluran.

"We have brought you to Neja. You may go your own path now, wherever it leads, or remain with us." Though she found no joy with the dwarf's company over the past several days, she could not deny he was a competent warrior with a weapon every bit as lethal as Mithkahr. "Either way, I thank you for your skills on the road."

Poluran scratched his chin in thought. "I'm a dwarf of my word. I'll stay. I've no doubt Rornibur will be fine without me a bit longer."

Merssa was not sure what he was talking about, for he had sworn no oaths to her. She heard what sounded like a small gasp from Dellen, but when she glanced at the guardsman he quickly turned away. She returned her attention to the dwarf.

"The road we travel has dangers unknown," Merssa warned. "Already we have seen the likes of ghouls, and we know not what lies ahead."

Poluran shook his head. "Seeing what has become of Ellaville… We're staying until the deed is done." He patted his weapon with these words. "And besides, you folks could use the fighting prowess of a dwarf!"

Merssa stared. Another delusional warrior thinking his weapon was alive in some way. At least he did not speak to his axe the way Eraim spoke to Mithkahr. "So be it." Turning to the others, Merssa mumbled, "Let's get this over with."

While they rode to the far end of Eastgate, Merssa found the city unchanging. Every building was as dirty as the last, and if there existed an area where nobles lived it was not readily apparent. The castle, however, was in good order. Walls surrounded the structure, fifteen feet high with towers throughout its length, and many guards walked the battlements. It appeared as though the place was on high alert.

"If there's danger about," Merssa murmured to Vecnor, "then why are there not more soldiers patrolling the streets?" She had noticed only three guardsmen on the entire two-mile journey across the city.

Merssa approached the large wooden portcullis barring entry into the courtyard, and staring at her from the other side was a middle-aged soldier wearing a chain shirt and leather pants. The man's narrow eyes were untrusting, and remained so even after he was presented with the scroll from Seac. Finally, with a grunt he disappeared.

Beyond the gate, what could be seen of the courtyard lacked the splendor of most castles, as it was devoid of gardens, fountains, and color—save for that of gray and brown. There were small buildings and sculptures of unfamiliar men, and many more guards in mismatched armor moved about, as if newly recruited and dressed in what scraps the armory had to offer. Merssa began to think Baron Karlsum was paranoid, or he knew something she did not. She sighed, trying not to tap her foot while awaiting the gatekeeper's return.

Minutes later the man reappeared, mumbling with every step until reaching the gate. "The lord will see you."

"Splendid," Merssa uttered sarcastically as the gate began to lift.

Soldiers immediately led their horses to the stables; Umbarc, Lilli, and Dandi objected until their masters issued commands, but Melballa seemed eager to get into a stall and practically dragged a guard behind her. Other than the stables, there was a pair of blacksmiths busy at work, a few unmarked outbuildings, and situated to the rear of the courtyard was the keep. The structure was of granite, standing tall and proud and adorned by many spitting gargoyles, and from its towers waved the flag of Neja: a sun rising behind the peaks of two mountains upon a green background.

Two guards stood at attention before large wooden doors bearing Karlsum's coat of arms. It was a fine carving of a double headed axe upon a shield, and sunlight sparkled off the many jewels encrusted along the weapon's haft.

"Glass," snorted Poluran immediately, shaking his head at the fake stones.

The guards opened the doors by large pull rings, and just beyond stood four more soldiers within a vestibule. The company was led by one of these men through another set of doors and down a long corridor, where portraits depicted the four lords of Neja. One was obviously Baron Karlsum, for its frame was much more exquisite than the others. It depicted a tall, muscular man with piercing blue eyes, shoulder-length brown hair falling to either side of his square jaw, and unsmiling, full lips resting beneath a strong nose.

At the end of the hall, another pair of doors were opened to reveal the audience chamber, where Baron Karlsum was seated upon a throne. The baron was dressed in green robes and wore a jeweled crown of silver, and had Merssa been in a good mood she might have laughed in his face. As it was, she was even more disgusted than she thought possible. The portrait's depiction of the lord was almost the opposite of reality, other than he must surely be tall if he were to rise from his seat. His skinny nose was long, a thin mustache stretched down his narrow cheeks, and if he possessed any muscles at all, they were surely lent to the dozen or so guards posted to either side of the room. His eyes were not even blue. They were brown!

"Welcome all!" Karlsum's mustache stretched even thinner upon grinning lips. He scanned the group until focusing upon Merssa. "I see we have a Knight of Palidur."

"Knight of Cafior." Though the titles were interchangeable, Merssa corrected him nonetheless. And while the others bowed, she added, "Let's get right to the point."

Karlsum lifted his chin and arched a single brow. "Indeed." He smiled again, slapping his hands and rubbing them together. "You wish to hear of icy winds, is that not so?" Gazing at Merssa, the baron's smile broadened and he sat back. "My dear, how I know you would like this to be *our* doing." His smile faded and he leaned forward. "But it is not, alas. We have suffered much from its evil. How many can claim to have buried their parents twice, I wonder."

"Who's behind it?" demanded Merssa.

"Now, now." Karlsum waved a finger, sitting back. "Remember where you are. We *do* have laws here, regardless of what you and yours believe. You will not address me in such a tone."

Merssa's lips twisted into a snarl.

"Has the Wind touched your city thrice, as it has south and east of here?" Selanna interjected.

Merssa's cheeks grew suddenly hot. She understood the elf's intent, but this man should not be catered to.

"Indeed, it has!" Karlsum shuddered. "It was most horrible. The family crypt was almost the death of me. The corpses were hideous, with smelly rags and bones. They were reaching for me —"

"What of the undead?" Impatience crept into Selanna's tone.

Lord Karlsum, seeming to realize his sudden descent into hysterics, cleared his throat and took in a deep breath, his eyes calming. "With the second coming, those who perished in the first defense rose up. But it was not the same as the first time. While some attacked, others gathered at the south gate, as if they wished to leave. My guards opened the doors, and sure enough…they left. I pity the poor souls that meet up with them in the wild."

"You allowed them to leave?" Merssa felt every muscle within her body twitch as her anger boiled over. What cowards! And she did not believe for a moment Karlsum felt any pity for small villages such as Ellaville that had little or no protection. He was probably overjoyed to hear the undead had gone. Merssa struggled to calm herself. "Where did they head off *to*?" she asked in a slow, trembling voice.

Just then, a hollow moan echoed throughout the chamber. It rose in pitch, like the wailing of ghosts, and Karlsum paled as he gazed at the vaulted ceiling.

"It howls again!" The baron shuddered, turning to Merssa. "Save us!"

Selanna ran swiftly from the chamber.

Merssa continued staring at Karlsum with disgust. "You sit and rot behind your walls and soldiers! And if there are any gods who will listen, you best pray we find this evil and put an end to it before it's too late!"

She exited the hall, followed by the remainder of her company, and soldiers moved hastily to open all doors before her. Merssa's blood continued to run hot while she considered the waste of time the Council of Wizards had placed before her. She knew traveling to

Neja was a fool's journey, and now she would see at least two weeks pass without a clue as to the Wind's origin.

Outside, Merssa found Selanna gazing at the sky. The late afternoon sun was still high in the west and the large, fluffy clouds seemed unmoving. The Wind had stopped, but guards were scurrying about, manning their stations.

"It comes from Sistama." Selanna used the elfish name for the Silent Marsh.

Merssa's throat was suddenly dry. The swamp was a mysterious place, shrouded in darkness. What history existed of it was scarce, consisting mainly of fireside stories with a wide range of horrors that lurked therein. "You're sure?"

Selanna nodded. "I thought it came from Helmland, but it is not so. The wind came from the south; from Sistama. I have no doubt."

"I hear a great dragon lives there," said Dellen.

"Nonsense." Poluran shook his head. "Those creatures are long gone. It's ghosts that haunt that land."

"*Something* haunts it," said Eraim. "I have lived in Salenti for nearly one-and-a-half centuries, and Sistama has been draped in darkness since before even my days. Something lurks there, that is certain, but I hesitate to guess as to what."

"I have gazed upon it on occasion," Selanna mentioned, "though I never dared to enter. There exists no book in any library to explain how it has come to such darkness. It is an impenetrable black cloud, emitting no sound, and the trees of the Tall Pines that feed upon its waters grow in grossly, twisted shapes. All who have dared to enter have never been seen again."

"I have been there." Vecnor's somber voice came from the doorway of the keep. "It has been ten and two years since my path led me so, but I have seen the desolate marshland from within."

All eyes and ears were upon the large warrior. Merssa was momentarily confused with his timetable, for she believed him to be in his late twenties, and that would have made Vecnor very young for such a venture. His face reflected troubled memories, and after a deep breath he spoke again.

"That is where I first fought the likes of ghouls." Vecnor shook his head. "It is infested with them."

Merssa felt her cheeks flush, and she was no longer concerned with Vecnor's age. "Infested with…? And you said nothing after the ghouls…? After Ellaville?" She found it hard to complete a thought and shook her head to clear it. "That could have saved us a trip to this kingdom of fools!"

"I was hoping it would not come to Sistama," Vecnor explained. "With the dead rising everywhere, it may have been only a coincidence that ghouls came after us in the wild. For all I knew, the Wind created the ones we faced. And had I mentioned it at the time, I'm sure you would have wanted to go there at once." He paused, considering Merssa. "I wanted to be sure before even thinking of crossing its borders. All we know for certain, even now, is that the Wind came from south of here." He addressed all within the company. "Know this: even I, Vecnor, do not wish to go there again, lest there be no other choice."

Merssa stared a moment longer before addressing a nearby guard. "Fetch our horses." She turned to her companions. "Let's restock and make leave of this place. We travel south." She gave Vecnor a sideways glance. "Wherever it takes us."

While they rode back through Eastgate, Merssa witnessed many Nejans rushing about and bearing some form of weapon, be it sword, club, staff, knife, or even a pot or pan. The attitudes of many toward Merssa were changed, as eyes pleaded for help, though there still were some that scowled. She was shocked to see several folks singing, laughing, and toasting the undead. Merssa would never understand these people.

The Split Skull Haven was soon within sight, and Merssa would have chosen to ignore the establishment and forget her whole experience there, but her attention was drawn to a boy rushing toward her from its front door. His arms were flailing and he called her by name.

"Lady Merssa! Lady Merssa!"

It was one of Larman's boys; the one that had ridden with her.

"What is it, boy?" Merssa asked, bringing the company to a halt.

"The inn…" He panted. "My father—"

Merssa bolted her horse forward. As she neared the building, she could not help noticing a slight change in its appearance. White paint was splattered over the sign, still wet, and the word LARMAN'S was placed over SPLIT SKULL. Pulling her mount to a halt, Merssa sighed as she slipped quickly from the saddle.

"What have you done, Larman?"

She rushed into the tavern, followed closely by her companions. Inside, Merssa was shocked to find every table occupied. Patrons stood about, holding drinks and having a good time—she wondered if they were aware that the Wind of the Dead had just blown. Many were gazing at a commotion at the bar, where Larman's feet dangled several inches above the floor as a man twice his size held him up by the collar. Before Merssa could act, Vecnor stepped past her and pushed his way through the crowd. She pursed her lips and followed—once again, he had overstepped himself. She was going to have to have a word with him later.

"What seems to be the trouble, Master Larman?" Vecnor's booming voice carried, bringing the tavern to silence.

"Mind your own—" The thug turned. Slowly, he scanned upward until finding Vecnor's face, a foot above his own.

"No trouble," Larman said with what breath he could muster. The innkeeper's face was red and quickly changing to blue, but it softened to pink when the man lowered him to the floor. "No trouble at all. Truly."

Vecnor glared, his eyes moving to a large bruise upon the bully's cheek; a mark left by the leg bone from earlier that day. "Have we met, little man?"

The thug trembled as he sought escape, but Dellen and Poluran barred the exit with arms across their chests.

"Please, Master Vecnor," Larman said. "I've only just purchased the inn. Don't go breaking it up now."

"V-Vecnor?" The color drained from the man's face. "Black Death?"

Gasps sounded from the onlookers and whispers could be heard. Vecnor's reputation was obviously well known.

"You'll not be coming here again," Vecnor growled. He bent slightly and added, "Ever!"

Vecnor issued a hearty slap onto the man's back, driving him toward the exit, and Dellen and Poluran parted to allow him passage as Dellen opened the door. Poluran stuck out a foot at the last moment, causing the ruffian to tumble head first into the street, and Dellen slammed the door.

Vecnor's eyes passed over the muted onlookers. "Master Larman, my *good* friend! I'll be needing a table and drinks for me and my company." A nearby table was quickly vacated under his gaze, and he smiled and sat down. "How gracious!"

Larman rushed behind the bar. "Drinks coming up!"

Merssa took a seat next to Vecnor, shooting him a sideways glance. "We can only stay a moment."

She would have dealt the street thug a bit more justice, but she understood Vecnor's approach, as well as the grin now etched upon the innkeeper. Larman was a businessman, and he was surely aware that tales of the legendary warrior would spread quickly. Folks would frequent his establishment in hopes of catching a glimpse of Black Death, and ruffians, such as the one that just left, would stay away, fearing retribution if they dared to hassle a friend of Vecnor.

The tavern remained silent and Larman glanced about while pouring the drinks. "Everyone! Back to your business!"

Conversations resumed and the room returned to normal, though most talk turned to tales of Vecnor, the Black Rogue.

"Larman's Haven?" Dellen chuckled. "I wonder just how much gold was in those packs!"

"Enough," Larman said with a wink as he dropped off a round of ale. "But the place came fairly cheap, what, with its lack of business and the rising of the dead and all. The man was more than happy to part with it."

"Business seems very well now," Selanna commented.

"Funny thing." Larman scratched his bald head. "Soon as folks saw me painting over the sign, they started coming in. Truly. The missus has been doing all she can to clean the kitchen and get her special stew ready."

"Why would you want to settle here?" Merssa shook her head in disbelief.

"Not the best place, I know." Larman bobbed his head, glancing about. "But I feel these folks could do with a fine inn, know what I mean? It'll better their spirits, so to speak. Maybe even brighten things up around here."

"I see it's already working." Merssa was unable to contain her sarcasm. "Your recently departed patron seemed to take a great liking to you."

"Begging your pardon, my lady," Larman said hesitantly, "but it was you what brought it on me. You see, he accused me of bringing you here. Called me a Palidur lover. He claimed that if I kept this inn open, others of your city would surely follow."

"Begging *your* pardon," Merssa scoffed, "but Palidurians would not travel so far for a tavern. Especially a Nejan—"

"I quite understand." Larman had the nerve to cut Merssa off, though he winced as he did so. And while her mouth hung open in shock, he continued. "And that's what I told him. He was only trying to stir things up, is all. But thanks to my heroes once again, all is well." Larman beamed. "And now, drink up! I'll fetch a second round for the lot of you—on the house of course. I'm sure you'll fancy the taste a bit more now that the water content has been properly reduced."

Larman returned to the bar, where one of his boys was filling a pitcher with beer.

Poluran was the first to sample the new brew and drained his mug. The dwarf nodded as he wiped the froth from his mustache.

"Much improved!"

"I just hope he survives this place," commented Eraim, watching the barman. "We likely will not be here the next time trouble arises."

"He'll be fine," Vecnor assured the elf, but his attention was elsewhere.

Merssa followed Vecnor's gaze to a corner table, farthest from the door, where two figures were seated. One was thin, seemingly no larger than Selanna, and the other was large to say the least, and obviously a crossbreed of human and hobgoblin. Merssa detested hobgoblins. Unlike the goblins of the mountains, these larger cousins dwelt in forests as bandits, and their raids often included unfortunate victims of rape resulting in offspring known as krukari. Only the strongest krukari usually survived childhood, and being outcasts, they normally led criminal lives as thieves and cutthroats. This particular krukari was gazing Vecnor's way, its small reddish eyes barely visible beneath its bushy, jutting brow, and Merssa knew the look all too well. She saw it every so often when traveling with Vecnor, as there always existed those that would fancy to match skills with the legendary warrior. Rarely did she see Vecnor participate in such worthless ventures, but sometimes he was left with little choice, and over the years Merssa had seen several men humbled or dead.

Larman returned with a couple pitchers. "Soon as I can build my stocks with fine Vircan beer and ale, these folks will learn what they've been missing!"

"They make a fine brew in Virch," commented Poluran, reaching for a pitcher. "But the ale of Rornibur is yet unmatched! You should all be so lucky to taste it one day."

Larman snapped his fingers. "I almost forgot, with all the commotion." Then, in a hushed tone, he said, "I've met some friends of Olinin. You remember? The mage that saved Ellaville from the first attack?"

Merssa held a wry smile, but the innkeeper stared, awaiting some sort of acknowledgement. Reluctantly, she offered a nod and he continued.

"Well, I've met a couple that claim to be companions of his. They say he left. Headed south. And I believe he set out on the very mission you have, from what the skinny fellow said."

"How long ago did he leave?" Merssa asked, wishing Larman would get to the point.

"I'm not sure." The barman furrowed his brow. "But those friends of his are still here. In that corner over there." Larman nodded in the direction of the krukari. "One isn't much for looks, but they may have a bit of news for you. Something useful, I hope."

Merssa glanced again at the table with the krukari. Somehow, she knew there would be no leaving without first confronting the *thing* in the corner. "Thank you, Larman."

"A krukari!" spat Selanna after Larman returned to the bar.

With the exception of the hatred between Palidur and evil, Merssa knew there existed no animosity deeper than that between hobgoblins and elves. The battles between the two races for dominance over the forests outreached the histories of all other wars.

"I knew I smelled something foul." Eraim wrinkled her nose.

"And a marteese is with him," Selanna sneered, pointing out the krukari's companion to be another of mixed race — that of human and elf.

Marteese were not shunned like krukari, and Merssa certainly held no grudges against them. But she knew some elves to feel the impurity of their long-lived race to be in bad taste, a feeling usually strongest among Salenti elves. The fact the marteese held company with a krukari would surely make matters worse in the eyes of Selanna and Eraim.

Merssa stood. "I best have a talk with them."

"I'll go with you," Vecnor said.

She nodded as the warrior rose.

"I shall join you as well." Selanna stood, the elf's glare remaining on the distant table.

Merssa considered the mage. Was there a choice? "All right. But bear in mind that we seek whatever they may know. Try not to insult them. Your dislike for the krukari is only slightly more than my own, if that's possible." Merssa gazed at the krukari again; he seemed more in likeness to a hobgoblin now. His leathery skin bore a brownish hue, his filthy jet-black hair hung down to his shoulders, and beneath his large, flat nose, his lips curled into a grin. She gave a sigh, suddenly more concerned with her own control than that of Selanna's.

At their approach the krukari rose, standing as tall as Dellen but with broader shoulders. The marteese remained seated and smiled, taking an extra moment to admire Selanna.

"To what do we owe the pleasure of such enchanting company?" The marteese tucked his long brown hair behind his pointed ears to show off his elfish heritage. Were it not for the thin mustache, Merssa would have thought him a full elf.

"We would like a moment of your time," Merssa said.

"Anytime." The krukari spoke in a low, scratchy voice. He remained standing and his eyes never strayed from Vecnor, and chairs slid across the floor as a nearby table was quickly vacated.

"We wish to discuss Olinin." Merssa glanced at the krukari. "I have been told you know him."

"Easy, Gruzim," the marteese said to his companion. "Why don't we all have a seat?" He offered the table's two vacant chairs, grinning ear to ear.

Merssa took a seat and Selanna sat to her left. Vecnor grabbed one of the chairs just made available at the neighboring table and placed it on Merssa's right. He hesitated to sit, however, when he noticed the krukari's dead gaze still affixed upon him.

"I am Bayn," the marteese introduced himself. "And this is Gruzim."

Vecnor slowly sat, obviously not wishing to quarrel, and Gruzim gave a pompous grunt and did the same.

"Have you seen Olinin?" Bayn asked in a jovial tone.

"We only know that he has headed south," Merssa replied. "We were hoping you might be able to tell us where exactly he has gotten off to and why."

Bayn's smile dropped, but when he looked at Selanna it returned. "Oh, who can say?" He gave a nonchalant shrug. "He's always here one day and gone the next. Always on the move, Olinin is. Can I buy you a drink?" The question was directed at Selanna.

Selanna's cold expression moved to anger. "You *will* speak to us." The elf's voice was far detached from the light and cheery one Merssa was used to. "And you will tell us what we wish to know, one way or another."

Bayn laughed and put up a hand. "Easy, love. I can see you are a mage, as well as a creature of great beauty. But I must inform you that I, too, am in the study of Vou."

Selanna raised her brow, undaunted, and Bayn shifted uneasily beneath her gaze.

"All right!" He surrendered with a playful chuckle, but then his tone turned serious. "He did head south, with Belsod and Corlan. I believe his trip has something to do with the rising of the dead."

A hush seemed to overcome the tavern with Bayn's last statement, but when Merssa looked around, she saw the patrons still involved in their own affairs.

"How long ago was this?" Selanna's attitude remained cold.

"It has been four days since his departure," Bayn answered. "He arrived here in a rush, the day after the wind first howled across Eastgate. We had only just defeated the uprising when he came bearing news that the ill wind was felt elsewhere. After it happened a second time, he gathered his maps and left. He seemed quite upset."

"Where was he headed?" Merssa asked.

"Who knows?" Bayn resumed his good-humored tone, which faded under Selanna's piercing eyes. "But the maps were of Silent Marsh."

"Why the marsh?" posed Merssa.

"He has studied it most his life," the marteese explained. "At times, he allowed me to see records of his excursions there, but he never shared too much. He warned me to never venture there."

"He has been inside Sistama?" Selanna was shocked.

Bayn nodded. Leaning close, he said softly, "He claims it to be a very cold place. Full of evil." He sat back, and though the krukari seemed unmoved, Bayn appeared quite concerned. "From what I saw, most his attention seemed focused on the western region. I know something there has troubled him for many years."

"Does he believe the Wind to have come from the marsh?" Merssa asked.

Bayn shrugged. "I'm not sure. But it's the swamp he aims for, of that I have no doubt."

Merssa sat in silence, staring at the marteese while she absorbed the information and gathered her thoughts. Everything seemed aimed at the marsh. She pulled a small pouch from her belt and tossed it onto the table. It was the only time Gruzim's attention veered from Vecnor. "Thank you for your time." Merssa rose from her chair.

"No." Bayn pushed back the pouch, drawing a scowl from his partner. "Make sure he returns safely. I owe everything to him. Many people in these parts do. He takes in those who many will not and gives them direction. Regardless of what you may think of me or my companion, Olinin is a great man. He is my—" He looked at Gruzim. "He is our master."

Merssa detected sincerity from the marteese, but the krukari seemed untouched. She scooped up the pouch. "Very well." Turning to Selanna and Vecnor, she nodded for them to follow and headed back to their table.

"What could Olinin have possibly been studying within Sistama?" Selanna posed while they walked.

"I'm not sure," said Vecnor. "I did not venture to the western side. The place was unchanging, each day like the last. I could not see every inch. I could barely see at all."

Merssa heard their words, but her thoughts were elsewhere. "Something still puzzles me." She looked at Selanna as they rejoined their companions. "Olinin believes the Wind to have originated from the Silent Marsh, just as you, or so it would seem. But the Wind that swept across Palidur came out of the north. How is that possible?" Merssa shook her head and looked at Vecnor. "Perhaps the marsh *is* but a coincidence. I do not see how it could be the root of the evil Wind. It's almost as if there are two sources."

Selanna seemed uncomfortable with the suggestion. "Perhaps. But Sistama may yet tell us something we do not know."

Eraim, Dellen, and Poluran watched in silence until the conversation was finished. Dellen then gave an uneasy chuckle.

"Need we ask what was said?" he posed.

"We leave immediately." Merssa looked at the guardsman. "We cannot waste another moment in this place. I'll explain as we ride."

"Ride where?" asked Poluran, his face full of hope the answer would be something other than the obvious.

"South," Merssa replied. "To the Silent Marsh."

CHAPTER 7

CAFDELLA

Larman filled their skins and packed extra food for the road. At Vecnor's request, the innkeeper also supplied several warm blankets and his boys procured fur cloaks from local shops. The innkeeper recommended more than a few times that they spend the night and get a fresh start come morning—he even offered up his best rooms at no charge.

"Thank you," Merssa said as politely as she could, "but we cannot waste another moment." The Wind had returned several times now, and she had no idea what mischief it had wrought upon the lands she loved, nor how many more times it would blow before she ever caught up with this Olinin. But also, Merssa could not bear the thought of spending even a single night within Eastgate—she already felt the need for a weeklong bath to wash the stench from her body.

The company said their goodbyes at last and exited the city, undoing at least one of the many knots plaguing Merssa's stomach. Eastgate faded quickly into the hills and the southern road turned west after only a league, but the company continued south along a trail Vecnor discovered near the Stony River.

The ground fell gradually before them and the river's current sped up as its breadth narrowed to less than fifty yards. They kept as quick a pace as the terrain allowed, but often slowed for Poluran to catch up—the dwarf moved gingerly down some of the slopes, trying not to spill any of the packages or himself onto the trail. It was almost enough for Merssa to demand to know what he kept in all those sacks, but in truth she did not care, nor did she wish to endure the long explanation that would surely ensue.

Dusk was quickly upon them, but Merssa did not stop; Olinin was days ahead. They continued a few more miles after sunset before finally making camp fifty yards from the water's edge, and there Poluran lit a fire and Merssa checked on the ghoul wounds. Her own appeared as three faded scratches and she removed the bandages for good, but Dellen's arm, though much improved, was still a bit darkened and she applied new herbs and redressed it.

Clouds concealed the sky and the starless night was cool and calm. They guarded in shifts, though nothing stirred, and the peaceful sound of rushing water made sleep almost pleasant.

They continued come morning, eating a simple breakfast from atop their horses. Dark clouds rolled overhead on a cool breeze and the smell of rain was heavy within a haze that settled over them; it felt like mid-autumn, though a month of summer was yet ahead. Just after noon, the land leveled and the river slowed a bit, but the water now stretched over a hundred yards to the far bank and jagged boulders decorated its surface. Merssa called for a short break and they rested the horses while eating a cold lunch in silence. It seemed the swampland was on everyone's mind, and not even Poluran found a topic to ramble on about.

The remainder of the day passed swiftly and they encountered nothing, but with the evening came the return of the Wind of the Dead. From due south it passed over the hills and chilled their skin. After less than a minute, it stopped.

"It had blown only yesterday," said Eraim with alarm.

"And it has never blown so late in the day," Dellen added.

Eraim looked to Selanna. "Is the evil growing?"

"There is no way to know." Selanna held a calmness Merssa found strange. "I hesitate to guess until we hear what Sistama has to tell."

The mage was right. Merssa nodded and they moved on.

Eastgate was now better than forty miles to the north, and though the skies continued to threaten, rain never came. Merssa was grateful for this, for the night grew cold. But she remained uneasy with the early arrival of the Wind, not to mention the absence of undead for some time, and cautioned the others to be alert.

Vecnor kept watch on the southern side of camp. It was the darkest part of the night, and every half hour or so he added wood to the fire. Beyond that, there existed no noise outside the river's current. Nearing the end of his shift, he heard the kicking of a stone and turned to see Eraim. Vecnor knew her to have stumbled intentionally, for he would never have detected her approach otherwise.

"All is quiet to the north and west," Eraim reported, looking Vecnor eye to eye while he sat upon the ground.

Even in the darkness, Vecnor found her quite enchanting. He nodded and stared blankly into the night.

"I was wondering," she said hesitantly, "why would anyone venture into Sistama?"

"Who knows?" Vecnor shrugged. "Mages have always been a bit queer to me."

Eraim put her hands on her hips. "I meant you."

"I know. And I meant what I said. Never perform tasks for wizards. You never know where they'll take you."

Eraim furrowed her brow. "For whom did you perform the task?"

Vecnor eyed her. Eraim was the only reason he had not given up on Salenti elves. She was more in likeness to Vermallon elves most the time, and a better warrior than those twice her size. He would have liked nothing better than to share his tale with her, but he could not. He sighed, turning back to the south. "It doesn't matter."

Eraim stood, as if trying to read his face. "You are a real mystery, giant. But one day I will figure you out. You know there is nothing you can hide from me for long." She started back toward her post and paused. "I am glad you are here," she said softly, and disappeared into the darkness.

Eraim's comment warmed him. Vecnor was the greatest warrior in the land, but it had not come without a price. The Black Rogue was all people knew. Outside of Eraim and Merssa, he shared very little of his life with anyone, but even they would never truly know him. And for now, that would have to do. There was a task at hand more important than his life, and he would see it through.

After a few more minutes, they woke Dellen and Poluran for the final shift and settled in for the remainder of the night.

The weather remained unchanged by morning and the cold night gave way to another autumn-like day. Their gear was wet with dew and Merssa felt stiff as they readied to ride, but she ignored the discomfort and they returned to the path. With a sense of urgency, she drove the horses hard, taking advantage of level ground whenever possible. As the late morning sun prevailed, the day quickly grew hot and she eased the pace.

Shortly after noon, Eraim reported there to be an odor of cooking meat, and it was not long before Merssa smelled it as well. Just over the next hill, Merssa spied a village a couple hundred yards to the west, nestled within a lush valley of rich green grass and vibrant trees. A branch of the Stony River passed through its center, and a system of wooden pathways and wheels carried its water to fields where various gardens flourished. Merssa squinted, trying to penetrate the hallucination, but nothing changed; the oasis remained, surrounded by little more than rock and clay as far as the eye could see. She looked to Vecnor questioningly.

Vecnor shook his head. "I've never seen this place."

"The man at Split Skull said he received his vegetables from a village to the south," Eraim reminded Merssa.

The smell of food was mouthwatering, but Merssa harbored doubts. She knew her company greatly desired a closer look, and as curiosity got the better of her, she headed into the valley.

Merssa approached slowly with eyes alert, and she could feel the ground soften as her horse stepped onto the turf. They came upon a wide street of hard-packed dirt that passed through the village, unmarred by horses or wagons, and buildings of stone stood to either side. Wooden fences housed various livestock to the north, and here and there townspeople performed their daily chores. The scene reminded Merssa of Sardina, and she wondered what power allowed such a place to exist within the wasteland of Neja.

Suspicious glances greeted Merssa's company as they entered, and when she attempted to speak with any villagers, they scampered hastily indoors or around buildings. Ahead, a small bridge of stone arched over the stream, and beyond stood a few larger buildings. Merssa made for them, hoping to find an authoritative figure, but before she reached the bridge, a man ran from a small house and barred the way. His shoulders were broad and his face stern, and strapped to his side was an impressive sword.

"Halt!" the man commanded. "Let it be known your name and business."

"Merssa Goldmace and company. We are passing through and were lured by the smell of food. We thought we'd have a bite to eat, lest your village lack hospitality for travelers."

"Nobody travels these parts." The man glanced about their horses, taking a special interest in the many packages upon Melballa. "And those that do seek more than just a bite to eat. From where have you come?"

Merssa was a bit surprised he did not recognize her attire. Even the scum of Eastgate had. "I am a Paladin of Cafior and Palidurian Knight. That alone should assure you we mean no ill toward you or your village."

"Palidur, huh?" The man appeared unimpressed. "I've heard of it. Have you proof?"

Merssa's cheeks grew hot and she felt an explosion building. How dare he ask her for proof! Before she could put him in his place, a second man, this one in brown robes, came hurriedly across the bridge. The newcomer was older and a head taller than the first man, but lanky in build. His dark hair was almost completely receded from his forehead and his large nose made his eyes seem small.

"Pallit!" the man called. "Pallit! It's all right." He reached the first man's side and stood panting for a couple seconds. "These aren't thieves or anything brought about by evil winds." He looked apologetically toward Merssa. "You'll have to forgive Pallit. Between the undead and the people of Eastgate stealing from our fields, you can understand his mistrust of strangers."

Merssa's only response was to shift her glare from Pallit to the newcomer.

"I am Borse, priest and servant to Cafior." The taller man bowed. "I am at your service."

Merssa's jaw dropped. She was not sure what to make of a Cafior priest in Neja. The rich soil might have been proof enough, but she was sure another explanation existed for the unusual growth and she regarded the man with suspicion.

"Come," Borse beckoned. "Let us refresh you and your horses. The villagers will be along for lunch soon, but there's plenty to spare." He walked back over the bridge.

Pallit stepped aside to allow passage, though he still exhibited apprehension. He followed the company across the bridge, and after they dismounted, he led their horses to a trough—with Eraim's help of course.

Merssa stepped to Borse's side to exhibit the manners of Palidur. She introduced herself and the others in turn, but said nothing more, not wanting to reveal too much. She walked with Borse to a two-story building dotted by many round windows, and upon entering found a large hall filled with rows of tables and benches to accommodate at least five hundred. At the moment, the room's only occupant was a woman placing plates and cups upon a table halfway across the chamber's length.

"This is Feast Hall," Borse said as he continued to the far end where a shorter table was set. "Here in Cafdella, we work together and the spoils are shared by all. Please, have a seat and food will be provided shortly." Borse nodded to the woman and she quickly passed through a set of doors. "Don't be shy," he added, seeing the company's hesitation. "Make yourselves comfortable."

Borse sat at the head of the table and Merssa took the seat to his right. Dellen quickly sat next to Merssa and the others found their places.

"Thank you." Merssa continued with the pleasantries.

Borse eyed Merssa with what appeared to be curiosity and amusement combined. "So, what brings you to our humble village, all the way from Palidur?"

"As I said to your warrior," Merssa replied, a bit annoyed at having to repeat herself, "we are passing through."

Borse scratched his nose in thought. "You have come from the north by way of a hunting path, for there exists no road. But you're not dressed as hunters. And the closest settlement other than Eastgate lies many, many leagues to the west." He gave Merssa a sideways glance. "There is nothing south of here except the plague that is the Silent Marsh. Where might you be passing to?"

"Not that it's any of your business," Merssa replied, "but we are following after a mage and his companions."

"You must mean Olinin." Borse seemed oblivious to the beginning of Merssa's statement. "Indeed, he sat at this very table..." Borse trailed off in thought. "I believe it was three or four days ago. A good man, he is." His brow furrowed. "But if it is Olinin you follow, then you must share in his task."

"Task?" Merssa played ignorant.

"Yes," the priest said, his eyes widening. "The wind."

All was silent until the white doors swung open and six women entered, four bearing trays and two carrying pitchers. The trays were covered with beef, pork, lamb, and one overflowed with steaming vegetables, and while the food was placed upon the table, everyone's mug was filled with ale. The women departed, but two returned moments later with four more pitchers, to Poluran's obvious delight—the dwarf had already drained his mug.

"This tastes like home!" Poluran wiped the foam from his mustache and snatched a pitcher before it could be set upon the table.

"And very well it should," said Borse, "for it is Rornibur Brew. The finest ale you could ever hope to sample." Upon a suspicious glance from Poluran, the priest elaborated. "The dwarves bring it in trade for crops. It has been so for over a year now. I fear it has been these exchanges that brought the unwanted attention of Eastgate, however. We would gladly deal with them as well, but they prefer to offer nothing and sneak into our fields at night."

Eraim entered the hall, and her face became aglow at the bounty upon the table. After taking her seat, Borse motioned for silence and bowed his head.

"All Mighty Cafior," the priest prayed, "bless this food you have generously provided, that it may strengthen our bodies and minds in these days of uncertainty."

"Here! Here!" they all concluded, and the eating began.

Poluran was quick to help himself to all three meats, with a few vegetables added to the side. "Must have a bit a fiber," he informed Dellen.

Vecnor and Dellen also filled their plates, and the elves ate lightly from the vegetable tray. Merssa waited until the others were eating before selecting a modest portion—though everything looked and smelled delicious, she did not wish to appear anxious. Borse chose a small meal for himself.

"However did you find this place?" inquired Selanna. "Your village is very beautiful."

"Cafior led me here," Borse replied, "though it was not as you see it now. Much work had to be done. My loyal following tilled the soil, and with faith and prayer, Cafior smiled and brought forth the fertility that was hidden."

"I did not notice a church," said Merssa. "And where are the other priests?"

"Ah, yes." Borse smiled. "I've heard of the temples of Palidur, great in size and unequalled in beauty. Perhaps one day I shall behold them. But here, the village is our temple. We congregate about a large well behind this building. As for other priests, I am the only one."

"You would have me believe that Nejan soil has been made rich about an entire village by a single priest?" Merssa shook her head. "I've heard of such miracles, but it has never been done without the combined efforts of at least five priests of Cafior."

Borse continued to smile. "Alas, I can only say that my labors have been aided by the faithful that journeyed with me. Beyond that, I am ignorant. Cafior's ways cannot always be understood, as I'm sure you'll agree."

"Come, Merssa!" Vecnor chuckled. "Let it be and accept this most generous hospitality. It may be a while before you eat this well again."

Merssa gave Vecnor her sharpest glance, but he smiled and winked in response. The list seemed ever growing of the items she would have to discuss with him later.

"You never answered *my* question." Borse looked at Merssa. "Is it the source of the wind you seek? As Olinin before you?"

"You know for certain that was his quest?" she posed.

He nodded once.

"Yes, that is our quest," stated Selanna, becoming the next to fall under Merssa's glare. "I see no need to hide it from him," the elf reasoned. "Perhaps he can help us. He may know something."

Merssa was going to have to muzzle that mage one day.

"Olinin frequently visits," Borse said. "Usually with Corlan and Belsod, but sometimes alone, when he only wishes for company and relaxation. He and his warriors often venture into the marsh for reasons he has never shared, and upon several occasions have returned with terrible wounds needing my care; evil wounds that blacken the flesh. I believed them to have been caused by ghouls, but Olinin never confirmed this. If ghoul wounds are not tended properly, you see, the skin dies and begins to rot —"

"We are aware of ghoul rot," Merssa stated. Why did everyone feel the need to share useless knowledge before saying anything helpful? "What else can you tell us?" Merssa added a warning glance Selanna's way for silence, but the mage furrowed her brow, as if she did not understand.

"He keeps a boat here," Borse said, "to enter the marsh by way of the river. There is a place not far to the south where the water is safe for travel. It is unknown, most likely due to the fact that it lies very close to the swamp."

"What is it he seeks within Sistama?" Selanna asked. "Do you know?" Now Selanna refused to look Merssa's way at all.

"I've often wondered," Borse admitted, "but I never felt it my place to pry. Occasionally he spoke of an ancient evil, before the swamp fell silent. And not too long ago he mentioned something was growing, but did not say what. When I saw him last, he said, '*The day has come,*' and that he must stop the evil wind. He warned me to move my people, but knew of no safe place to go. I only hope all is not as dire as he fears."

"How long have you known him?" Selanna inquired.

"His name is old in these parts." Borse rubbed the thinning hair upon the back of his head. "I guess I've known of him for as long as I've lived in eastern Neja, that being only slightly more than four years. But from what I've heard, he is over two centuries in age."

"Is he an elf?" Selanna's interest seemed piqued.

"Marteese."

Selanna's shoulders slumped and a wry smile invaded her face.

"And he's made quite a name for himself," Borse added, "helping others not of pure blood. You'll not find anyone in these parts more respected, or in some cases more feared than Olinin. I do hope he's all right."

"Has he taken his boat?" Merssa asked, wishing to return the conversation to more important matters.

"Yes." Borse nodded. "I'm afraid he has."

"Then we must take our leave." Merssa rose and addressed her companions. "He's got four days on us and travels by boat. We'll be lucky if we find him at all."

Many disappointed looks came from the company, as their plates were only half cleared, with the exception of Poluran's—the dwarf was busy with his second helping, and he continued shoveling meat into his mouth as he and the others rose.

Dellen leaned close to Merssa. "Perhaps I should have Borse look at my arm," he whispered.

"Nonsense!" She shot the guardsman a cold glare. His face showed genuine concern, but the lack of confidence in her healing skills did little to please her. "I am not incompetent. You'll be fine soon enough." Turning to Borse, Merssa said, "We'll need our horses immediately."

"At once." Borse motioned to Pallit, who now stood at the hall's entrance. "Though I doubt you'll be able to lead them into the swamp."

"You've been a most gracious host and owe us nothing," Vecnor said with a bow. "But if you would be so kind, I would ask the favor of caring for our horses in the days to come. Once we reach the marsh, I should like to send them back to you."

Borse nodded. "I will care for any that come back to Cafdella, be it horse or other." His tone was almost fatherly. "With a good pace you should be there by nightfall. But from what Olinin has told me, you best camp outside its borders, for it is wise to spend as few nights within as possible."

"Thank you for your concern." Merssa ceased all pretenses of courtesy. "But we are quite capable and I have Cafior to guide me. Good day."

She walked toward the door and heard the others following. Outside, the sun was bright and Pallit arrived with the horses.

"Please forgive our first meeting," Pallit offered. He held the reins of Melballa and Merssa's and Dellen's steeds while Umbarc, Lilli, and Dandi followed on their own. "It has been some time since decent strangers passed this way."

"Do not concern yourself," Selanna said.

The mage had spoken hastily, before Merssa could respond. Merssa knew it was an attempt to keep her from speaking her mind. Though Cafdella was much cleaner than Eastgate, Merssa found it no more hospitable, but she said nothing.

"You do well to protect your lovely home." Eraim smiled, causing the man to blush.

The company mounted and Dellen steered his horse to stand beside Merssa's.

"I'm sorry," the guardsman said quietly.

Merssa stared at him, confused.

"Back there." Dellen nodded toward Feast Hall. "I didn't mean to imply you…couldn't…" He appeared flustered. "I mean, *your* wound—"

"Oh, please!" Merssa sighed. "Don't apologize." She looked him square in the eyes. "You're a good man, Dellen. Believe me, I do not wish for you to incur ghoul rot. If I thought for a second your wound was beyond my skill, I would be the first to take you elsewhere for proper care."

Dellen smiled broadly, apparently hearing only the complimentary portion of the statement. Merssa shook her head and addressed the others.

"Let's ride!"

CHAPTER 8

OLININ

The ground returned to the hard soil Neja was infamous for and grass, where it did grow, took on a straw-like appearance once again. Cafdella faded fast into the distance as the villagers gathered for their afternoon feast, and Merssa noticed the desire in her company's eyes, wishing they had been able to stay longer. But even if she had not been thoroughly disgusted with the realm and its inhabitants, there was no time for personal pleasures.

After another mile, there existed no more signs of life, not even a bird flying overhead, and the sun disappeared, bringing back the feeling of autumn. It was as if a window had existed over Cafdella with shutters wide open to allow summer through. The Stony River remained vast and the opposite bank was now shrouded in mist. Streams branched off to places unknown, but none reached any real depth and crossing was never difficult. The day grew colder, much like the previous night, and dusk arrived sooner than expected.

Reaching the top of the next hill, Merssa came to an abrupt halt. The land below leveled off and was covered by dark soil with scattered trees bent in awkward poses. What few leaves existed upon the pitiful branches hung limp, as the wind diminished to little more than an occasional breath, and from the calm Stony River stretched narrow streams—long twisted fingers, stagnant and covered with algae. Merssa's attention, however, was drawn farther ahead, for less than a hundred yards away a black fog, like the darkest storm cloud descended from the sky, sat idle before them. The view stole her breath and stilled her heart, and she quickly realized the whole company shared in her hesitation. Even the horses were motionless, as if the slightest movement would catch the attention of the Silent Marsh.

Vecnor cleared his throat, breaking the silence. "Perhaps we should camp here and continue tomorrow."

Merssa's eyes narrowed and she put forth her bravest face. "Yes. But no fire." No sense alerting anyone as to their position.

They settled upon the hill and ate from their saddlebags, finding Pallit had filled their packs with salted meats and flatbread, as well as vegetables. Poluran was especially pleased to find his two skins upon Melballa were filled with Rornibur Brew, but the pleasure on the dwarf's face after taking a swig paled in comparison to the joy he had shown only hours ago. Merssa guessed it did not taste so good as before, for even though her rations appeared fresh, they tasted days old. Surely the presence of the bog was praying upon their minds.

Night descended quickly and darkness removed the marsh from sight, but the image haunted Merssa's mind. It felt as though many eyes lurked within the hidden cloud, watching and waiting.

"Let's get some rest," Merssa said at last. "Sitting up all night won't make it any more pleasant tomorrow." Rising, she pulled her mace, feeling a bit more comfortable with its shaft firmly within her grasp. "Same shifts," she added. "Dellen, wake us before first light."

"If the light returns," mumbled Eraim.

It was nearing dawn, and Poluran guarded the direction of the swamp while Dellen watched the west and north. Not a sound was heard, save for the fall of Dellen's boots as the guardsman paced about to stay warm—the man had surrendered his blankets to Merssa and the elves, for the night had grown bitterly cold. Poluran sat upon the ground, wrapped in a couple blankets and finishing off the first skin of ale. Even tainted ale was better than no ale at all.

As the slightest hint of light crept into the night sky to suggest the coming of another day, Dellen could be heard waking the others. Poluran rose to join the guardsman, but then he spotted a figure emerging from the darkness in the direction of the bog.

"Dellen!" he said sharply. "Something's coming!"

Poluran gripped Clanghorr tightly and watched the figure. It stumbled from side to side, but did not move in the manner of a ghoul. Its motions were more of a clumsy nature, as one intoxicated. Poluran was then startled when Eraim spoke quietly into his ear—he had not heard the elf approach.

"It is not a ghoul," Eraim confirmed Poluran's belief, and after another moment she gasped. "It is a man!" Drawing her sword, Eraim ran down the hill. "He is hurt badly!"

"Wait!" Poluran shouted, running after her. "It might be a trap!"

Eraim ignored Poluran's warning, and as she neared the figure, she saw it more clearly. It was a marteese. He stumbled left and right and was covered in black filth, but Eraim noticed no wounds upon his body.

"Are you all right?" She grabbed the marteese's arm as he nearly fell, but he was ice cold and she recoiled, fearing him to be undead.

The marteese collapsed and ceased to move, save for occasional, hard breaths.

"He's out," Eraim said once Poluran arrived, the dwarf holding his weapon ready to strike. Eraim knelt onto the moist ground and cradled the half-human's frozen head onto her lap. "He is alive. He is breathing."

"Help..." The marteese's voice was weak and his eyes opened and locked onto Eraim's. His hair looked to be white and his robes silver beneath black mud, but it was hard to be sure. He writhed, as if in great torment.

"Olinin!" Eraim said as the others approached. "It must be."

"C-c-cold," the marteese stammered as he began to shiver.

"We need a fire," Eraim insisted.

"Poluran," said Merssa.

The dwarf immediately rushed up the hill without a word.

Vecnor scooped up the marteese, and Eraim and the others rushed after his giant strides back to the campsite, where Poluran had begun the task of lighting a fire. After the marteese was set upon the ground, Eraim and Selanna immediately wrapped him in blankets. His face was pale and his quivering lips blue, and he shivered constantly, sometimes erupting into violent shaking. Soon the fire was going, and after Merssa requested a hot cup of water, Dellen filled a pot in the river and began heating it.

"Olinin?" Selanna asked.

The marteese gazed upon Selanna. Shutting his eyes, he nodded.

"Let me take a look at you." Merssa reached for the blankets.

"Don't...trouble yours-s-self," Olinin said. "There is nothing ...y-you can do...P-Palidurian Knight."

Merssa stepped back, appearing shocked at being recognized for what she was. In lighter circumstances Eraim might have found this humorous, as Merssa usually showed disgust when people did not realize her to be a Paladin of Palidur.

"What has happened to you?" Selanna asked, helping to steady Olinin as he started to teeter. But her question fell on deaf ears and the marteese stared longingly into the flames.

"Here." Poluran extended a steaming mug toward Merssa.

The paladin glared at the dwarf in annoyance. Then, with sudden realization, she pulled a small pouch from her belt and withdrew dried herbs. Crumbling the leaves, Merssa added them to the hot water and swirled it to get a good mix.

"Drink this." Merssa handed the mug to Olinin.

The marteese's look was one of hopelessness, but he accepted the mug and drank deeply, seemingly unaffected by the heat of the water. Eraim held her breath as she watched Olinin lower the drink, and moments later his breathing eased a bit, though his coloring remained unchanged. Eraim released her breath. It was an improvement, at least.

"Where are Belsod and Corlan?" Selanna asked.

Olinin continued to stare into the fire and slowly shook his head. "It is more —"

A surge of pain overtook the marteese. After a few seconds, he eased up and continued.

"It is more powerful than I ever believed."

"You found the source behind the Wind?" Merssa used her business-like tone.

"I have f-f-found my end," Olinin mumbled.

"Olinin," Selanna said softly, turning him to face her. He focused on her emerald eyes and his expression calmed. Selanna smiled. "Olinin. What has happened?"

"I was a f-f-fool," he said, just above a whisper. "An arrogant f-fool."

Merssa began shifting her feet, obviously eager to take over the questioning, but Selanna put up a hand and the paladin pursed her lips and remained silent. Some things were better handled with compassion.

Olinin took another drink of the concoction and spoke again. "All these years, I've kept an eye on the s-swamp. W-watching and w-waiting for whatever power existed there to rev-veal itself." He gazed into Selanna's eyes again. "It began more out of curiosity than anything else. I was young and wanted to solve the m-mystery of the Silent Marsh.

"For more than one hundred f-f-fifty years I've watched over it, venturing in whenever I could." Olinin turned back to the fire. "Ghouls and other dangers lurk there, yes, but for a well p-prepared wizard with skilled warriors travel was possible. Some days it seemed the ghouls ignored us, as if they had more important things to do." He turned back to Selanna. "What could be more important than a meal of living flesh? There is no end to their appetite. That is what drives them."

The marteese fell into a fit of coughing for several seconds and Selanna patted him on the back. After the spell passed, he took another drink and continued.

"Instead of being concerned, I felt intrigued and ventured deeper in hopes of discovering an answer to their presence. It was only four years ago when I found it."

Olinin looked around, as if afraid to be overheard. Morning was upon them, revealing the ominous shadows of the marsh once again, and the air seemed cooler, but Eraim realized the chill came from the marteese. He gazed at the dark fog and cringed, turning quickly back to the fire.

"What did you find?" Selanna asked softly.

"In the western reg-gion there exists a stone house—"

A cold wind played with the fire and Olinin's eyes opened wide. But it was not the Wind of the Dead and the breeze subsided.

"A house in the Silent Marsh?" Merssa's disbelief was evident in her voice.

"The first time I saw it, I dared not enter." Olinin gazed at the clouds. "I studied it from the outside, but never for too long, for it seemed the concentration of ghouls was heaviest there. It is old…very old. I am baffled as to how it has withstood the toll of time in that horrid place." He shook his head. "There are no windows and but one door, and not a sound comes from within. But there is a power there; a power unlike any I have ever felt before.

"After two years, I worked up the courage to explore further. It took some convincing to bring Corlan and Belsod to agree, and they're not easily frightened. They were great champions of Neja." Olinin bowed his head.

"Were?" Merssa frowned.

"The place was abandoned." Olinin still seemed not to hear the paladin's words. "We moved from room to room, finding only tattered remains of ancient f-furniture, but I knew s-something was y-yet undiscovered. My companions' fears began to grow and they insisted we depart. So I granted their request, leaving the mystery behind, and we never returned…until recently.

"The first time I felt the wind, I knew it came from the s-swamp, and I knew from where as well. The only source of p-power strong enough to accomplish —"

Another surge of pain nearly overwhelmed Olinin. He drained the remainder of Merssa's brew and calmed, but his breathing became labored and he began to wheeze.

"We returned to the house," he said finally. "B-b-barely any ghouls impeded us, making me a bit n-nervous, but we had to continue. Inside, we found a r-r-room we had not seen before; a hidden library within the b-back b-bedroom. While Corlan and Belsod searched, I scanned the b-b-books, but the titles were unclear, written in some language I have never crossed. One set of runes was common to many books, so I wrote it down."

With a trembling blue hand, Olinin reached into his robes and produced a torn piece of parchment. Selanna accepted it and gazed at the runes scribbled upon it. Eraim took a peek as well, but the symbols made no sense to her.

"It is Ancient Moclen," Selanna said. "From before the existence of Neja or even Virch, when Moclen had a language all its own."

Eraim and the company stared at Selanna in wonder.

"Elgarroth has been teaching it to me," Selanna explained. "Some of his books are written in its script."

Elgarroth. Of course. The ageless wizard. Considered the greatest mage in all Vaeldor by many, he was the reason for Eraim's journey to Vermallon every summer. Selanna insisted on making the trip for training, claiming the wizard to be a mentor, but Eraim was not sure she agreed. Eraim accompanied her friend, enjoying the distraction from everyday life, but what puzzled her was that they never seemed to be expected, and sometimes Elgarroth was not even home. One thing Eraim knew for sure was that Elgarroth was unmistakably of Salenti origin. Why he lived in Vermallon she did not know, and the elders of Salenti refused to speak on all topics referencing the wizard. Eraim did not believe Selanna knew the answer to that question either.

"It is a vast and difficult language," Selanna continued, "but I might be able to…" She studied the parchment, pursing her lips. "If my translation is correct, it says *Tra…Tran…num. Trannum.*"

Though Eraim knew not what it meant, a chill coursed through her body. And from the momentary silence, she was sure the others had felt it as well.

"What, or who, is Trannum?" Selanna asked Olinin.

The marteese shook his head.

"What happened to Corlan and Belsod?" Merssa's patience was apparently at its end.

"They f-f-found a trapdoor bet-t-tween the bookshelves." Olinin addressed Merssa at last. "Beyond was a blue light, pulsing in the darkness below."

He was suddenly out of breath. After a moment, he regained control and continued.

"I decided to go down alone. I wasn't sure what to expect, and if s-something was too great for me, perhaps *they* might at least escape." Olinin's face was filled with guilt and sorrow. "I found a small cellar. It was bare, except for a pedestal upon which rested an orb; the source of the blue light. The power…" His eyes were distant. "I could feel great power within.

"I m-moved closer to get a b-better look, and that's when I heard their screams." Olinin's eyes grew wide. "Corlan was f-first… It echoes in my mind still. Belsod called for me and his voice t-t-trembled. I ran for the stairs… But all went silent. Then the air about the room changed and I turned back, and standing there was a skeleton dressed in tattered black robes.

"Its skull was barely visible beneath its hood, but I c-could see a blue light within its right eye. I c-c-couldn't move. My knees were locked. I tried to speak, but had no voice. It was stroking the orb, like some kind of pet. It says, *'Do you like my little toy? It has taken me centuries to create.'* Still, I could s-say nothing. I could only stand and watch." Fear filled Olinin's eyes while he relived the horror and his voice became hoarse. "It approached m-me, conjuring a ball of deep-blue light in one of its bony hands. It told me it had seen me in its swamp before, and that I had ventured too far, and so my end must come. It lifted me off the f-floor as easily as an empty s-sack, and I could hear whispers of an incantation. The light in its hand grew brighter until it was white, and I could do nothing as it was p-placed upon my head. My insides turned to ice and my head began to swim. And the pain...the pain."

Olinin seemed on the verge of passing out, but Selanna shook him and he blinked rapidly.

"The figure disappeared and I was alone," the marteese said somberly. "I staggered from the house, trying every s-spell I know to counter its touch...but nothing worked. My m-m-mind wandered and I stumbled about while ghouls laughed and hissed and pushed me around. I thought for sure they would devour me, but they weren't interested. They drove me from the marsh."

"How long has it been since you left the house?" Selanna asked.

"I'm not sure." Olinin's teeth began chattering violently. "I'v-v-e lost track. I've not s-s-slept in s-some t-time, unless you count p-p-passing out from the pain." His eyes fell half shut.

"It must have been two days ago," Selanna said to Merssa. "Upon the evening when the Wind came early."

"Where is this house?" Merssa asked abruptly. "How do we get there?"

Olinin's eyes opened wide. "You mustn't go there! My powers were useless. Go! Far away from here."

"The power of Cafior is great," Merssa said with confidence. "Much greater than any wizard's magic. I will find the house with or without your help. Will you tell me how to get there?"

Olinin's wheezing now whistled with every breath. "I have...a map."

He removed a leather tube from his belt and handed it to Selanna with a trembling hand. She pulled from it a rolled parchment and opened it, and Eraim saw it held a sketch of Sistama. Selanna gave a quick, curt nod to Merssa, and Eraim could sense her companion's anger at the way the paladin had spoken. Merssa exhibited a rare look of guilt.

"I thank you, Olinin." Merssa used a softer tone, one Eraim had never heard the paladin employ. "Unfortunately, I know of no cure for what has happened to you. The herbs will only work to ease the pain."

"What about Borse?" Poluran asked. "He has healed him before."

"Those were ghoul wounds!" Merssa snapped.

"No," Olinin said in a weak whisper. "Borse cannot help me." His eyes were almost shut. "Nothing…can…help me…anymore." Olinin leaned heavily onto Selanna and his eyes closed.

There was a moment of silence.

"We should return him to Cafdella at least," suggested Selanna while Vecnor lifted the body, and Eraim could feel the remorse her friend emanated.

"There's no time," Merssa said somberly. "Every day it takes us to find this house… Who knows what will happen?"

"Lilli will carry him," offered Eraim, her heart aching. Though she had not known the wizard, and never really cared much for marteese, Olinin had lost his life trying to rid Vaeldor of a great evil. "We were sending them back to Cafdella anyway."

Merssa nodded. "Prepare the horses."

Selanna and Eraim wrapped a spare blanket about Olinin's body in a vain attempt to relieve the marteese's suffering, but his skin remained ice cold. Merssa said a prayer and Vecnor strapped the wizard to Umbarc, the large horse being more suitable to bear the body.

"If any of you wish to turn back," Merssa said, "this is your last chance."

For a brief moment, Eraim held the words upon her tongue, but they would not come out. She did not wish to set one toe inside that cursed marsh, but she spied the grim faces staring back at the paladin. Even Selanna's gaze was unwavering. They all aimed to continue. Eraim swallowed the words in a hard lump.

"Perhaps you should return to Tikken City," Merssa suggested to Dellen, "and report to the Council."

"I'm not leaving." The guardsman was resolute.

"Very well." Merssa took the map from Selanna. "It's time."

They grabbed their gear from the horses, taking all food, skins, furs, and as many blankets as they could carry. Eraim slung her bow and quiver over her shoulder and whispered to Lilli her instructions, and the horse gave a whinny in response and led the animals north. Before they had gotten far, Dandi gave a harsh snort toward Melballa, who had begun to veer west.

Eraim watched as the horses disappeared over the next hill, and she envied them. Soon the animals would be resting within the valley of Cafdella, while to the south the marsh sat still and foreboding, hungrily awaiting Eraim and her companions.

North L.
Dark R.
North Branch
Snake R.
Slime R.
House
House R.
Flesh Pond
Twisted Wood
West Branch R.
West L.
South Bound R.
South L.

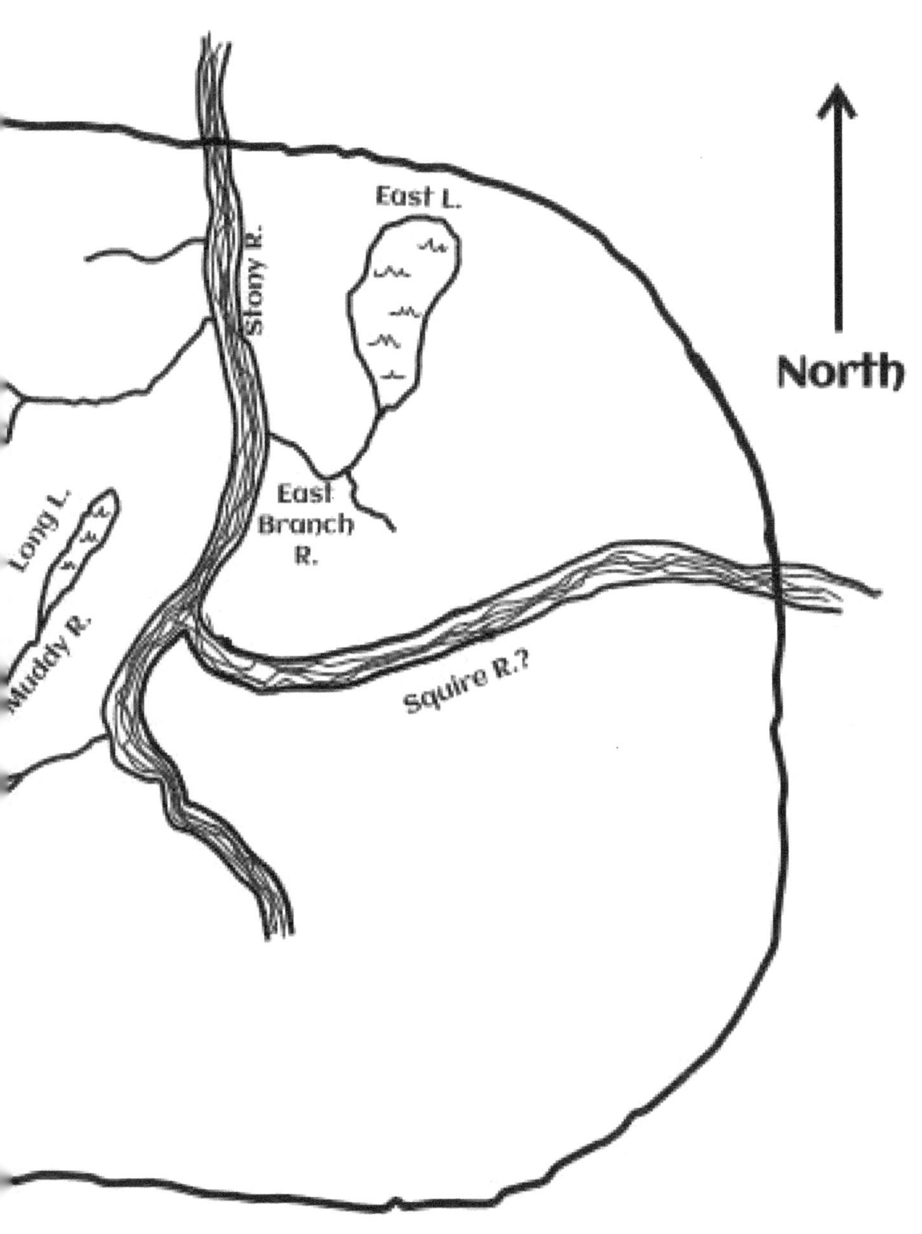

Silent Marsh

Chapter 9

Sistama

Merssa glanced over her shoulder at the members of her company watching the horses disappear over the hill. She sighed and returned her attention to Olinin's map. It was not as if she *wanted* to enter the bog—nobody in possession of their sanity would. But there was no choice in the matter and it was pointless to wish otherwise.

The sketch showed many rivers and lakes, and located upon the western side was a black square labeled HOUSE. Unsure of any of the markings, Merssa handed the parchment to Vecnor.

"Does any of this look familiar?"

Vecnor studied the map and shook his head. "Very little. It's been a while, and Olinin traveled by boat." An idea lit up his face. "That sure would make for a quicker route. Possibly less dangerous."

"What do you suggest?" Merssa posed. "I didn't see one in Cafdella, and we're *not* going back to Eastgate. We must put an end to the Wind as soon as possible; before it grows too powerful. Plan a route by land." She saw the concern etched upon Vecnor's hard face, an expression completely foreign to him, but they could not waste another week.

"Tell the others to find walking sticks," Vecnor said. "The thicker the better. There are many pitfalls in the marsh."

Merssa did as he suggested, and while the company scanned the immediate area, she wandered down the hill to where a fallen tree lay. To her left, the Stony River was hesitant to enter the bog, unmoving to all eyes unwilling to gaze long enough to note otherwise, and the many streams it produced lined the way before her. Little effort was needed to cross the algae-covered rivulets, however, for they proved no deeper than a couple inches and many were narrow enough to step over.

The sounds of Merssa's companions became distant, but then she detected sloshing nearby. Looking back, she was not surprised to find Dellen following her through the mud.

"You shouldn't be down here alone," the guardsman said. His voice was solid and brave, but his eyes betrayed his true feelings for the dark fog growing nearer with every step. Still, he smiled.

With a sigh, Merssa moved on.

The air tasted like early winter and Merssa's breath became thick as she drew almost to within arm's reach of the cloud. She peered into the blackness, but the swamp revealed nothing. There was evil within, however, and it was strong; much stronger than any Merssa had experienced within Sardina or Sendorum, or any other place she had ventured to in the name of Palidur. Her nerves tingled like never before, and she was suddenly aware of her hand grasping the handle of her mace.

"I don't look forward to entering *that*."

Dellen's voice in Merssa's ear caused her to jump.

"Hush!"

Shaking her head, Merssa resumed the task at hand and located a suitable stick, as well as a large branch for Vecnor, who was still staring at the map. After another fruitless glance into the fog, she returned to the hill with Dellen close behind and bearing a staff-like branch of his own.

"We best stay close to the Stony," Vecnor said as Merssa handed him the staff, and all eyes moved to him. "It's our best hope for not getting lost. We'll follow what Olinin named West Branch River to House River. If everything goes well," his voice carried little confidence, "it should take about three days."

Merssa took in a deep breath and released it slowly. "Let's go."

Merssa led the way downhill, focusing on the ground before her as she did her best to gather courage. Though she intentionally avoided looking at the awaiting cloud, she felt its evil chill upon reaching its edge and stopped to allow Vecnor the lead.

The large warrior stood still, gazing at the impenetrable wall of black. Then, with obvious reluctance, he entered the haze. The fog remained undisturbed by Vecnor's movements and swallowed him whole, his form becoming nothing more than a shadow. Merssa hurried to remain a couple paces behind him, and the others followed in single file.

At first there was only darkness, but it was not darkness. It was black air, penetrating Merssa's lungs with every breath, and though it smelled and tasted like nothing, she fought the urge to gag. Then everything changed. Merssa's eyes adjusted, introducing her to a strange world devoid of sunlight, but somehow she could see most things within fifty feet. There existed no color, save for that of different shades of shadow, and it felt like mid-winter. It was a stale cold, though, without wind, and there was no snow or frost and the water showed no signs of icing over. Not a ripple existed on the murky surface of Stony River, if it was indeed still a river—the far end was beyond sight, making it seem immense. Scattered patches of gray reeds and strange vegetation varied from a few inches to a few feet in height along the water's edge, and gnarled trees, bare of leaves and covered in black moss, dotted the landscape like lurching silhouettes within the fog. A sucking sound emitted with every step, as black mud grabbed hold of their boots, but it did not travel far before the bog swallowed it up to maintain its eerie silence. The worst feature, perhaps, was the inescapable stench of ghouls combined with a musty odor, and with every step more of the stink was released. Merssa's scalp tingled constantly to alert her to the surrounding evil, but nothing moved outside her company. She put forth her bravest face, though she doubted any noticed within the cloud, and clutched her mace tightly, her lips moving in a silent prayer as everyone followed Vecnor without a word.

Before long, the bizarre vegetation changed from gray to black, and patches of it extended from the river like gardens. Vecnor steered around them as best he could, but the company was forced through several larger patches, for Vecnor seemed reluctant to allow the river to fall from sight. The walking sticks proved useful then, as pools of soft black muck plagued these areas, anywhere from a foot to ten feet across, but they were easily detected. During a brief stop for Vecnor to consult the map, Poluran tested the depth of one such pool. It was like thick quicksand and appeared eager to accept the entire length of the dwarf's five-foot stick, and when he attempted to retrieve the staff, the muck was reluctant to relinquish its prize. With a jerk, Poluran yanked the stick free, flinging stench-ridden mud onto Selanna's back. Selanna spun with ire.

"We best avoid this stuff," Poluran said nonchalantly, a piece of mud falling from his nose.

Selanna shook her head, no trace of the elf's jovial attitude to be seen, and looked at Merssa with complaining eyes.

Merssa turned to Vecnor, who was rolling the map. "Let's move on."

A short time later, the first branch of Stony River impeded them. The water was dark and impenetrable; perfectly still. Vecnor looked left at the Stony, the body of water unchanged since they entered, then glanced right, as if hoping the smaller river would suddenly end and offer an easy path to the other side. It was not so. With a sigh, he stepped into the water, prodding with his staff until reaching the halfway point of the river's twenty-foot width. The water released a pungent odor, as if it had not been disturbed for years, but rose no higher than Vecnor's waist and he returned to the company. In all places where the water had touched him, a film of dark, acrid slime was left behind.

"It shouldn't be a problem," he said. His gaze went to Poluran and Eraim. "But the shorter ones will want to keep on their toes."

Merssa was surprised he did not look her way as well—she was barely taller than the other two. Poluran released a snort of disapproval.

All packs were handed to Dellen to keep dry, with the exception of Vecnor's, and the company waded forward.

"How are we to ever smell ghouls in this stink?" complained Eraim, holding her little nose while she sat upon Vecnor's shoulder — she had given the large man a pleading look at the water's edge, and he lifted her without effort to place her there.

"Up there you should have a good view!" Selanna said sharply, the water creeping up to the mage's chest.

"This is not going to work!" Poluran's arms were wrapped firmly around Dellen's waist, as the dwarf attempted to keep his mouth above the river.

"Hush!" snapped Merssa. The cold water was up to her neck and the slime had invaded every inch of her body, so she was in no mood to listen to any complaints. She held her mace high, hoping to at least spare it from the filth.

They emerged onto the opposite bank and the swamp seemed twice as cold. Poluran and Selanna immediately retrieved furs from their packs and wrapped them about their shoulders, but Merssa fought the chill, determined to defy the marsh. Merssa also ignored as best she could the shivers assaulting her body as she struggled to keep her teeth from chattering.

They continued another few hundred yards and a second river halted them. It was wider than the last, its far bank barely within view.

"North Branch River," Vecnor said, though Merssa barely heard him. A bit louder, he added, "We'll have to find a better place to ford."

Merssa nodded, and Vecnor led the way west until the river narrowed to fifteen feet. There, he waded forward. The water never rose above his knees and it did not smell so foul as the prior one, but Vecnor's pace seemed hesitant. With determination, he thrust each step forward until he was across, and then nodded back to the company.

Merssa led the others into the water and immediately discovered what had troubled Vecnor, as weeds clutched at her boots. It was like walking through a tangled mess of thread and she fought to keep from stumbling; she could only imagine what it would have been like had Vecnor not made a path already. It was not long before she and the others exited the water, and Merssa was surprised to find none of the mysterious vegetation attached to any of their boots—not a single strand of seaweed, or whatever it was beneath the water, was evident. No matter. It was unimportant. With a nod, Vecnor turned east.

The Stony was beyond sight, and finding it again seemed impossible. Several muck pools rested along the southern bank of the North Branch, much larger than before, and the company was forced north and south, and gained ground east whenever opportunity presented itself. At one point, the North Branch River disappeared for some time and Vecnor's shoulders slumped, but after almost a mile, a large body of water came into view and he breathed a sigh of relief. From the size of it, it could only be the Stony.

They turned south again, and a short distance later a mound came into view, not far from the river's edge. Vecnor headed for it and Merssa made no objection—she could barely dispel the chill clinging tightly to her bones. Even as they ascended onto the drier land, however, Merssa found little comfort, for the stench of decay lingered thicker atop the small hillock. She did find she could see twice as far from the new vantage point, though, as the denser haze was settled below. The Stony River sat motionless to the east, and in all other directions the desolate swamp stretched beyond sight. Above, the haze thinned a bit more, but the sky remained hidden.

The company gathered close and sat next to their packs while Merssa remained standing and kept watch, and she did not object when Vecnor dropped one of the furs onto her shoulders as he passed by. Only Dellen and Poluran showed signs of an appetite, and the two fished through their gear. From the twisted looks on their faces, however, the odor of the swamp must have invaded the salted meats, and from the pile of flatbread and cakes growing at their feet, the moisture had surely destroyed the remainder of their rations.

Dellen sighed as he reluctantly chewed on a hunk of meat. "This has to be the worst meal I have ever had."

"It's not good." Poluran eyed a piece of beef before tossing it into his mouth. "But I've had worse. There was a tavern in Marcove once…" The dwarf paused to drink deeply from his skin and he gagged. "I think I just swallowed a ghoul!"

"Do not speak so loudly!" Merssa glared at Poluran. "Our ears will be our only guard against this swamp."

Merssa returned her attention to the bog, not wholly convinced of her own words. She doubted even the elves could detect a ghoul until it was near enough to strike.

Selanna shook her head, staring at her soiled robes. They were ruined. She had had them specially tailored in Tenvale many years ago, and they had cost her plenty. She had chosen green, her favorite color, and added her name, embroidered with silver thread in the Ancient Moclen text to add mystique. Now, its color was barely discernable and the silver letters illegible, not that any besides Elgarroth and herself could read them. Selanna noticed Merssa's shiny armor completely concealed beneath a layer of filth, but the paladin seemed unconcerned and kept watch on the swamp. This made Selanna think better than to complain.

While gazing at Merssa, a thought occurred to Selanna. Something had been resting in the back of her mind, bothering her for most of the day, and now it had fully formed. Rising to her feet, she approached the paladin.

"I have been thinking about Olinin's story," Selanna said quietly upon reaching Merssa's side. "About the ghouls and how they ignored him. He said it was as if they had something more important to do."

"Yes." Merssa acknowledged Selanna without a glance. "It is odd. Perhaps their hunger is not as strong in this place."

"Poluran spoke of ghouls atop undead horses in Sendorum," Selanna said. "They, too, showed much willpower in not attacking him. He claims they only growled and continued on their way."

Merssa's lips pursed, a sure sign of the fire igniting within her stomach. "Why have I not heard this before?" The paladin's voice shook, and Selanna doubted it was from the cold.

"He told me while you rested outside Ellaville," Selanna defended. "When I woke you, I recall you to have been quite upset with our late start and it found a place to hide in the back of my mind. I only just recalled it now. There is more at work here than mere winds that raise the dead."

They did not have long to ponder this, for the Wind returned out of the west, as if summoned by Selanna's words, and it was much stronger than in the past. Though the swamp seemed cold before, it paled in comparison to the Wind of the Dead and all exposed skin went instantly numb. The fog swirled and thinned, revealing the edge of a lake to the southwest, as well as several dark shapes near and far. The Wind stopped and the haze filled in, swallowing the shapes and hiding them from sight.

"Were those ghouls?" asked Dellen, rising to his feet.

"I believe so." Vecnor scanned the immediate area with sword in hand.

"It is hard to feel their presence," commented Eraim. "Sistama feels so foul… It hides them too well."

"Do you think they saw us?" Poluran turned his head in all directions, as if the ghouls were about to storm the hill.

"If they did not see us," said Merssa, "they have surely smelled us. They know we're here."

"Why haven't they attacked?" Dellen lifted his hammer.

Merssa and Vecnor shared a look, and the tall man shook his head and shrugged.

"Did anyone see how many there were?" Merssa asked.

"Half a dozen to the north," Eraim rotated, pointing as she spoke, "two near the lake, four across the Stony, and at least a score to the distant south along the river's edge. It was hard to tell for sure, but they seemed to be standing very still and facing west, as if listening to something."

"We had better move on," said Merssa. "The ones to the north may be following us." To Vecnor, she added, "We must seek a place from which to defend ourselves before night."

Vecnor nodded, though his expression harbored doubt. "There is still a lot of ground to cover before the day is done, but we should stop if we find another hill such as this. Nights can be very treacherous."

They strapped on their packs and returned to the wetter lands with weapons in hand. The chill seemed to have eased since the Wind had blown, but Selanna knew the swamp to be unchanged and the false sense of warmth was short lived.

After a hundred yards they were forced away from the Stony again, as more patches of muck were placed close together. They moved in a westerly direction for nearly half an hour before clearing the pitfalls, and Vecnor steered back toward the east as much as the terrain allowed, but another hour passed with no sign of the river. A few minutes later, there came a deep splash ahead and to the right, and they followed the sound. They found the Stony at last, but they had been completely turned around. Vecnor put the river to their left again and pressed on, shooting a brief glance at Merssa as he did so.

In that moment, Selanna read the trouble on Vecnor's face. At one time she believed him fearless, but now she was not so sure. Vecnor had been here before and survived, but he seemed reluctant to share any details and Selanna could only imagine the worst. What could possibly have brought a man so strong and skilled to such uneasy silence? And to add to Selanna's anxiety, there was no clue as to what had made the splash that alerted them to the Stony's location, not to mention the fact that not a ripple existed on the water's surface.

Another couple hundred yards fell behind before they were slowed again. More filth plagued the marsh. But unlike the muck pools, these smaller puddles contained black slime with green spots and emitted a stench of festering carcasses with wet feces added for good measure. The fumes watered Selanna's eyes and tested her stomach while Vecnor carefully picked a safe path—a task easily accomplished, for the green spots seemed to glow in the darkness. Only Dellen experienced a close call when he purged what little food he had eaten, and the guardsman would have stumbled into a puddle had Poluran not caught his arm in time. Fortunately, the pools soon ended and faded into the swamp, but the smell would surely persist for some time to come.

They walked a couple more miles and came upon another hill, just as the marsh began to dim further with the encroaching night, and they immediately scaled it. The mound was a bit larger than the previous one and upon it a few trees, taller than any Selanna had seen within the swamp thus far, disappeared into the fog above. The company made a quick search, but no ghouls lurked about and they dropped their gear.

"Where do these poor things find the will to remain standing?" Eraim pondered while inspecting the trees. Their black, slime-coated bark fought desperately to cling to their trunks, and any branches not concealed by the mist showed no signs of ever having sprouted leaves of any kind.

"What's this?" Poluran drew everyone's attention to a blanket, barely visible within the mud near Eraim's feet. The dwarf pulled it free, releasing a fresh cloud of the marsh's stench and driving everyone several steps away. The fabric was tattered, almost entirely eaten up by the marsh. "There is evidence of an attempted fire, too." He looked closely at a collection of sticks. "But it has never seen flame."

"I'll bet Olinin camped here," Vecnor said, "though he didn't mark it on the map." Viewing the surroundings, Vecnor's gaze stopped upon a partial body of water, barely visible to the west. "That must be what he called Long Lake, unless we're lost already."

Merssa's glare showed no humor with the last statement.

"It's no good!" Poluran hovered above the sticks, holding one in each hand. "Everything's too wet. I'll never get a fire going in this place."

Merssa sighed. "We'll have to do without. Pity. It would have done us well with ghouls about."

"We will freeze," Eraim said through chattering teeth as she pulled an extra blanket from her pack.

Selanna stooped next to Poluran. "Let me try." She stared hard at the sticks, concentrating as she whispered her incantation, but she managed only to create a few wisps of smoke. It was no good. Selanna could almost cast the spell in her sleep, but when she pushed upon the sticks to create flame, it was as if they pushed back. She had never felt such a response before and she had no explanation for it. She shook her head. "I am sorry."

Merssa's shoulders slumped as she sighed. "Huddle close."

"We should try to eat something," Vecnor said. "We'll be in need of strength."

Everyone went through their packs. Selanna found that Sistama had wilted her vegetables, even discoloring some, and she discarded the latter, tossing them down the hill. She noticed others doing the same and it seemed a lot of food disappeared into the fog. There looked to be little wrong with a radish other than a bit of droopiness and Selanna decided to give it a taste, but then she noticed Eraim taking in a deep breath before biting into a carrot. There was nothing obviously wrong with the vegetable, but Eraim immediately gagged. Chewing with determination and heaving a few more times before swallowing, Eraim turned a shade paler than was usual. Selanna tossed the radish into the fog.

When all were finished eating, which did not take long, they moved in close and sat back to back, making use of every blanket. Darkness moved in quickly, thicker than when they first entered Sistama, and Selanna doubted even Poluran could see beyond a few feet.

Silence rang in Selanna's ears, interrupted only by the occasional rustling of her companions' movements and the chattering of teeth.

They attempted to guard in shifts and rest from seated positions, but any time Selanna managed sleep, she did not remain so for very long, for ghastly nightmares haunted her dreams—images of endless ghouls.

After what seemed an eternity, the swamp brightened a bit. Morning arrived at last and no ghouls had come. Though Selanna was grateful for this, she wondered how well the day ahead would prove as she forced her stiff joints to move and rose to her feet.

Vecnor rationed out the remainder of the food so they might have a bite for breakfast, but there was very little. Selanna passed on the meal, as did Eraim and Merssa, and stood to one side of the hilltop with Eraim while the paladin took a position on the opposite side. Selanna had borrowed the map from Vecnor and she now studied it, troubled by what she saw and knew: more rivers to cross; ghouls in pursuit while others waited ahead; no food. Pursing her lips, she approached Merssa.

"How long until we reach the house?" Selanna inquired quietly.

"Vecnor says two days." As usual, Merssa spoke without emotion.

"Have you looked at our route?" Selanna glanced at the map. "There is at least one more river to cross, and who knows what else? And with our shortage of supplies…I do not know how long we can survive in this place."

Merssa gave Selanna a sideways glance. "What are you saying?"

"How long would it take if we cut across?"

Merssa bit her lower lip in thought. "Let me see the map."

After looking the parchment over, Merssa approached Vecnor and Selanna followed, remaining a few paces behind. They found the large man spitting out a chunk of meat, a sour look contorting his normally handsome appearance.

"You project two more days, correct?" Merssa asked.

"Maybe three." He wiped his mouth with the back of his hand, gazing into the swamp.

"How long would it be if we cut across?"

Vecnor turned to Merssa with a frown. "That's not an option. You saw how the swamp turned us around when we left the river's side. We'd probably get lost and travel in circles."

"How long would it take?" the paladin repeated.

Vecnor took the map and looked it over. With a sigh, he replied, "If all went well…a bit more than a day. It's hard to say."

"Our supplies are low," Merssa pointed out, "and there's no hope of finding food. Who knows what'll happen if the Wind blows again tomorrow? I'm concerned."

"As am I." Vecnor stared the paladin in the eyes. "But if we get lost, it could take as long as a week to find the house, if we find it at all."

"What if we follow Long Lake?" Merssa pointed to the map. "It is not far to the west. We could round the lake and head for Flesh Pond… I adore these names." Her last comment was uttered to herself, but Selanna heard it clearly. "From there, we round the pond and continue west to House River and then north to the house. If we fall off target, we'll run into either Snake River or West Branch. Either way, we'll be able to regain our course."

Vecnor did not appear convinced.

"I noticed your path has us crossing Muddy River next," Merssa added. "It will take us half the day to get there, and then what if there is no safe place to perform such a feat? We'll end up returning to Long Lake anyway and more time will have been wasted."

"Other than the Stony, the rivers do not seem so deep," Vecnor said slowly. "I crossed many of them when I passed this way before. *That* much I remember."

"How long ago was that?" Merssa posed.

The large warrior eyed the paladin. "It would not be a wise decision."

"I appreciate how you feel," Merssa said, almost apologetically, "but Selanna has brought up a good—"

"*Selanna?*"

The entire group was now listening, and Vecnor showed no

concern for Selanna overhearing him while he stood and towered over Merssa.

"Since when do you value her counsel above mine? Has the swamp clouded your mind? Regardless of how long it's been, I have been here before and she has not."

"Please, Vecnor," Selanna interjected. "Do not be stubborn. If there is a way to get there sooner, we should take it. Nobody wants to be in this place any longer than we have to. Besides, who knows how many ghouls line the path Olinin has set before us? If he has traveled this way often, they surely keep watch on it. Did you not see all of them to the south when the Wind blew yesterday? They may be waiting for us."

"We must go west." Merssa was firm.

Vecnor shook his head. "Very well."

He picked up his staff, his glare resting on Selanna longer than she was comfortable with. Selanna knew he was often unpleased with her company, but she had never felt genuine anger from Vecnor before. She did not like it.

The company gathered their gear and followed Vecnor down the western side of the hill—it was obvious to Selanna he aimed to leave behind anyone not moving fast enough. The swamp moved in, concealing Long Lake, and they headed in the direction of where the water had last been seen, but the way was riddled with more slime pools. There were twice as many of the green-spotted puddles as the previous day and the pace was slow and awkward, and though Vecnor's face darkened with each passing minute, he was not the only one wary of their new route. Poluran was upset as well and bickered to Dellen, easily within Selanna's earshot.

"We've no landmarks now," the dwarf complained. "The river was a perfect guide. I do not wish to get lost in this miserable place!"

Selanna glanced over her shoulder when she heard a deep sucking sound. One of Poluran's legs was nearly down to the thigh in a hidden patch of black slime, one bearing no spots.

"I'll disappear in a pool of ghoul feces!" Poluran bellowed.

Dellen pulled the dwarf up by the arm. "I won't let you sink. I'm right behind you." While the guardsman steadied the stout warrior, he gazed at Merssa marching dutifully behind Vecnor. "I don't think Merssa would make a decision she thought ill of. I'm sure she believes this way to be best."

Selanna returned her attention to the way ahead, so as not to step into a hidden slime pool of her own.

"Or perhaps the elf put a spell on her," Poluran suggested. "You can't trust mages. They—" He realized Selanna and Eraim were staring at him. "Don't stop!" he shrieked. "We'll lose the others!"

Selanna shook her head, and she and Eraim resumed walking, but Poluran went on.

"Meldar's Beard! Can't see but five feet and they want to take a break…"

After a mile, Vecnor surveyed the area with a heavy sigh. "We should have reached the lake by now."

"Let's continue," Merssa said. "It can't be much farther."

With a disapproving glare, Vecnor moved on, and just as Merssa had guessed, a body of water soon stood before them…but it was not Long Lake. A narrow river, no more than twenty feet across, impeded their progress. It was dark and unmoving, like all the swamp's rivers thus far, and the same black reeds that grew along the Stony infested its edges. Upon closer examination, it appeared more like a source for the pools of muck than water.

"Muddy River," Vecnor grumbled.

Sistama had pushed them south of the lake.

Merssa bit her lip, looking up and down the river. "How long will it take to walk around the lake now?"

"Depending on how far south we've drifted," Vecnor said without looking at the paladin, "at least half the day."

Merssa shook her head. "That's no good. We'll have to cross."

Vecnor appeared more than a bit annoyed. He aimed a brief glare Selanna's way before making his way into the reeds.

"Cross *this*?" Poluran gaped at the mud. "It's like bottomless sludge. I nearly lost my staff to a pool of the stuff yesterday!"

"It is a shame you won that struggle!" Selanna spat, remembering the muck he had splashed onto her.

"Unless you two wish to go first," growled Vecnor, standing ankle deep near the bank, "I suggest you rest your tongues."

Merssa watched intently while Vecnor waded into the river. The mud-water revealed nothing beneath its surface, and after only a few feet Vecnor came to an abrupt halt. He jerked one leg forward and then the other, and continued the process as he worked his way across. Merssa wondered if it was another weed infested stream, but she decided not to ask; the large man was in no mood. Selanna was right, though, whether Vecnor wished to see reason or not, and Merssa was sure this was the proper course to take, all things considered. Besides, if there did exist a danger in crossing the water, she was positive Vecnor would mention it. He would not allow his foolish pride to jeopardize the mission.

"Don't stand in one place too long," he cautioned. "Lest you wish to travel the swamp in bare feet."

There. Merssa knew the warning would come.

The mud reached Vecnor's waist near the middle, but receded as he continued, leaving a fresh layer of dark muck where his armor had submerged. He exited onto the opposite bank.

The others proceeded in single file. Selanna went first, followed by Poluran, and then Dellen bearing Eraim—Eraim managed to convince the guardsman to carry her on his back, much to Selanna's obvious disgust and envy. Merssa entered last with mace in hand and quickly learned the reason for Vecnor's warning: the river floor was thick and grabbed hold of her boots with every step. She had to keep moving so it could not claim too firm a grip, and at one point she almost stepped right out of her boot. Ahead, Selanna seemed unhindered, but Poluran, with Clanghorr in one hand and his beard in the other, stopped a couple of times as if stuck. Dellen was close behind and moved the dwarf along, and soon they were all safely across. But the swamp again grew colder and the stench now hung heavier.

Vecnor gazed westward into the dark mist and then south along the river. "We could still make for West Branch." He looked back at Merssa. "Now that we've crossed the *dreaded* river."

Merssa chose to ignore the sarcasm. "We continue west. I do not wish to test any defenses the ghouls have set about Olinin's path." After a brief thought, she added, "Besides, now we don't have to walk around the lake. Missing our target may have actually worked in our favor."

Vecnor shook his head and proceeded west.

Again, Merssa felt a pang of guilt. She knew Vecnor's concern was for the safety of the company. But there was no time to take the long way, not if there was a chance to get there sooner. Duty demanded they try.

A direct trek was impossible, as they encountered uncharted ponds and more patches of slime, but their spirits lightened a bit when the ground rose slightly and lifted them from the more saturated portions of the marsh. After some time, Vecnor spotted a hill, and without a word he veered toward it and ascended. Upon reaching the top, he dropped his pack and the others followed his lead. Merssa decided to allow for the break.

Fatigue was heavy upon all and the food supply was exhausted, but they had plenty of drinkable water, tainted as it was. Vecnor gazed onto the swamp, his face unfriendly and his jaw tight, but the air remained stale and nothing disturbed the fog or made even the slightest noise. Merssa knew he was concerned that they had lost their way again, but she said nothing. Selanna and Eraim wrung out blankets while Dellen and Poluran shared a whispered conversation, but all eyes constantly shifted Vecnor's way every few seconds. Therefore, no one was caught by surprise when he lifted his pack, and everyone fell into rank as he descended the hill.

Another couple miles fell behind, and still there was no sign of

Slime River or Flesh Pond.

"Either we're off our mark again," said Poluran, "or Olinin has erred in his map making."

"Do you wish to take the lead!" snapped Vecnor, lack of sleep, food, and direction obviously wearing upon the man.

"That's enough!" Merssa glared at Poluran. "I'm sure we'll reach the pond before long. Now keep your voice down. There's not been a hint of a ghoul all day and I'd like to keep it that way."

Poluran's jaw dropped and his brow furrowed, as if he had been scolded for no reason. He turned to Dellen for support, but the guardsman's eyes shifted quickly to Merssa and then to the ground, displaying a hint of embarrassment.

"There could be a ghoul twenty paces away and we wouldn't know it," Poluran complained to Dellen, seemingly oblivious to the fact Merssa was still staring at him.

Dellen's cheeks flushed as he glared at the dwarf. Poluran shook his head and sighed, and Merssa fought the urge to do the same. She turned and walked a quickened pace, for Vecnor was now several steps ahead.

After a little more than a mile, the scenery changed. Trees became more frequent, like dark soldiers with arms held high, but unlike the ones the swamp exhibited thus far, they bore leaves—pitiful black growths that drooped heavily. Soon an army of the trees stood before the company and Vecnor stopped.

"The Twisted Wood," Vecnor said evenly. "We're heading south." He glared at Merssa, shaking his head. "Either we bear west to Flesh Pond, or southeast to West Branch."

"It is strange how we keep veering south," Selanna remarked. "It would seem Sistama is trying to keep us on *its* course."

Selanna received a scowl from Vecnor, and Merssa thought she saw the mage flinch. Perhaps it was a trick of the shadows.

"I find it strange as well," Merssa said. "And I don't like it." Unlike Selanna, Merssa did not believe for a second the swamp was alive. Just as Eraim's sword was just a sword, the marsh was just a marsh, albeit one filled with evil. There were surely other powers at work, attempting to force them back toward Olinin's route, and Merssa was not about to submit to another's will; especially not an evil will. She looked left and right. "We head for Flesh Pond."

Vecnor did not seem surprised.

The ground rose steadily and the haze grew thicker as they headed west, trimming visibility to only twenty feet. Merssa was sure Vecnor had been skirting the forest, but after a hundred yards the woodland was suddenly all around them. Trees coated in black and green slime were everywhere, and the smell of the swamp was strong.

Vecnor pushed farther and the twisted forms began leaning menacingly toward them. A loud *crack* sounded and a tree cast down a branch, but Eraim easily jumped aside and Poluran pulled up short to avoid the attack. Vecnor made sure everyone was all right before shooting Merssa a questioning glance. Merssa nodded to proceed.

He pressed on, and Merssa lost all sense of direction as the forest steered them right and left. Soon they were forced to pick their way more carefully, for black roots began clutching at their boots, and at times it seemed a root appeared where there had been none before, causing one of them to stumble or fall. They tightened up their rank so they could assist one another and continued at a slower pace.

After another hundred yards, Merssa noticed the ground to the left held a steady incline — she could have sworn it had been level only moments before. Shortly after, the right side dropped off, falling steeply into a body of water not far below and leaving them upon a narrow ledge. The water was different from what they had encountered thus far; an eerie glow illuminated the diminishing fog above it, as the marsh made no attempts to conceal it, and the opposite bank was barely visible fifty yards away. At first glance the lake appeared to be covered by light-colored mud, but as Merssa gazed longer, she discovered Olinin's motivation for choosing its name: it appeared to be a pool of flesh. Sitting perfectly still, it added another element to the aroma of the swamp: the decomposition of bodily remains. They had reached Flesh Pond.

"Is there no end to the odors of this horrible place?" Eraim held the back of her hand against her nose.

"Well, at least we've found the lake." Merssa eyed the disgusting water. "Now we just have to round it."

With a wary eye upon the water, Vecnor led the way south. But after twenty yards, the ledge narrowed to only a few feet and he stopped, shaking his head.

"I don't trust this. We'll have to put some distance between us and this ledge."

Merssa gazed at the rising land to the left. Somehow it seemed steeper than it had a second ago. "Let's move uphill."

Vecnor ascended, making use of every branch within reach, and Merssa followed his lead. They did not make it far, however, when Vecnor's boot slipped out from under him. He grabbed hold of a large branch and Merssa seized his arm, but the dark limb snapped and he dragged her back toward the ledge. The others of the company had yet to begin the climb and quickly moved aside to avoid being driven into the pond, and Vecnor halted their descent a few feet from the edge, planting his large boot into the trunk of a tree that groaned and creaked and split down the middle. But it held. Rocks and clumps of mud scrambled into the fleshy water and there came a loud hiss followed by a splash farther out. The company froze, but the noises ceased and nothing could be seen within the pond, with the exception of a single ring floating lazily toward the cliff wall.

"What was—"

Eraim's voice was stolen by a high-pitched, inhuman screech. It seemed to come from beyond the pond and lasted several seconds. All was then silent.

"We must find a way to get uphill," Vecnor insisted, his tone urgent.

Merssa agreed with a vigorous nod, her scalp tingling so emphatically that it nearly made her dizzy. Or perhaps it was the fumes of Flesh Pond.

Vecnor tried again to ascend the slope, and this time the company spread out to help seek a traversable path. They used roots and branches and Eraim looped her rope about trees for added support, but branches broke, trees began to bend, and the roots were as slick as the mud. They tried again and again, and each failed attempt found them back on the ledge, which seemed to have grown smaller with every return.

"This is useless!" Vecnor spat. "If we don't head back, we'll have to swim."

Merssa eyed the eerie water. Her skin crawled as its pungent odor continued to sting her eyes and nose. She glanced down the ledge ahead, which appeared to grow narrower until it ceased to exist at all. There was no rounding the lake by that route. "We'll return to where the hill was less treacherous and try to gain ground."

They backtracked to where Vecnor believed they had first discovered the pond, but Merssa was sure he was mistaken; the narrow ledge persisted and the hill to the right was unyielding. Merssa allowed for more attempts to scale the rising land, but the brittle branches and slick mud still denied any advancement. They moved farther along the declining ridge, Flesh Pond growing nearer with every step, and to Merssa's surprise they reached the woodland's end near the northern edge of the lake. There, the moist ground was level with the putrid water and the aroma made Merssa's head spin and her stomach want to heave.

"Sistama will not allow us to pass through this wood!" Selanna's frustrations were readily apparent. Fresh mud covered the front of the mage's robes and her golden hair had lost its glow. "And even if it did, I do not think I wish to know what made the sound on the other side of the pond."

"We'll have to round the forest and make for West Branch," Vecnor said, more than a little perturbed.

"That would take too long." Merssa bit her lip in thought. She had no answer for how they had missed the point of their original encounter with Flesh Pond, where the hill had not existed, and what Selanna was suggesting was impossible. The swamp was not responsible for their misfortunes. There was no way the ground could shift so in just moments; it would take centuries to accomplish what the elf believed to be true. No. They had simply missed the spot they were looking for. With all the fog, mud, and frustration working against them, it was understandable. Still, Merssa was in no hurry to reenter the forest and she had no desire to return to Olinin's path, not while other options remained viable. "We'll find a place to cross the river north of the pond."

"Slime River?" Vecnor raised a brow. "I can guess why Olinin called it that."

"We already stink of the marsh," Merssa pointed out. "What's one more river going to change?" In reality, she did not wish to cross another river. But what choice did they have?

"I don't like the thought of entering that slime," commented Poluran.

"Stay here if you wish!" Merssa had no more patience for bickering. Especially from the dwarf.

Poluran looked to respond, but obviously thought better of it and closed his mouth. A wise decision.

"We should at least stop and rest a bit," Dellen suggested.

Vecnor sighed. "I suppose a break is called for."

"A short one," Merssa said. "But away from the water." She looked nervously across Flesh Pond, the screech still echoing in her mind. Then her attention was drawn to the rising forest ridge. She saw no ledge there anymore and the trees almost seemed to be moving amongst the shadows. Cursed fog! Merssa shook her head and turned away.

They moved several yards from the water before setting down their packs. No words were spoken, with the exception of a few elfish ones between Selanna and Eraim, and no more noises were heard. It seemed like only minutes had passed when Vecnor stood, and they returned to the stench of the pond and headed north.

Vecnor picked up the pace as a gentle rise again lifted them onto firmer land, but when the pond came to an end, the ground stood over twenty feet above the river and did not appear to decline anytime soon. Gazing down, Merssa saw the water did not share the fleshy appearance of the lake; it was covered by the green-freckled slime. At least its odor did not catch her by surprise this time.

"We'll have to continue north," Vecnor said. "There's no way to know the depth of the water…and I'll not jump in to find out."

His last words were drenched in sarcasm, but Merssa let it go without comment. For Vecnor, she could muster some amount of patience yet.

The farther they traveled, the more nauseating the acrid odor of the slime became, and though Merssa was sure all in the company were weary, no one showed any interest in stopping to rest. Just as she, they were probably hoping to cross the water and leave it far behind before nightfall. That time would not come soon enough, however, for the ledge was now thirty feet above the river and the swamp was fast becoming dark.

"It's no use," said Vecnor, coming to a halt. "We have to stop."

Merssa was not pleased, but she nodded. "I know the odor is repulsive, but we should remain here and put our backs to the ledge."

No one argued…at least not with words. The elves' expressions of disappointing surrender and the contorted scowl upon Poluran's face betrayed their true thoughts.

They sat in a semicircle with backs to the ledge and drank from their skins. Merssa's fingers were numb, but she managed not to spill a drop. She was unsure as to whether this was a good thing or not, for the water was the foulest thing she had ever tasted, worse even than yesterday's poor excuse for a meal. She was tempted to pour the remainder onto the ground, but that was not an option.

All were huddled in their blankets, shivering as the chill exceeded that of the previous night. It was not long before Merssa could see no farther than the outline of Vecnor to her left and Dellen to her right, but as time passed, she found no sleep. If not for Poluran's gentle snore, she would have doubted any were able to close their eyes for more than a moment. It must have been a couple hours later when

Eraim's whisper interrupted the night.

"Something is out there. Eyes are upon us."

"I feel them as well," Selanna whispered back. "Wake Poluran."

Merssa heard Eraim carry out the mage's instruction, and from the rustling shadows to the left and right, Dellen and Vecnor were grabbing their weapons and rising to their feet. Merssa readied her mace and stood, allowing the stinging cold to assault her body as her blankets fell to the ground, and Poluran's snoring was replaced by the dwarf's grumbling.

"When I call out," Selanna said for all to hear, "ready your eyes for some light."

Merssa felt the presence of Selanna behind her as the mage stepped into the center of the semicircle, and though the darkness was unmoving, the tingling of Merssa's scalp told her the ghouls must surely be close.

"*Mees*!" Eraim whispered sharply.

"Now!" Selanna shouted.

Merssa squinted, and as she did so she was sure she heard Poluran say "What?"

A brilliant light penetrated the darkness, revealing more than even the daytime allowed. At first Merssa could only detect fuzzy shadows, but she heard the shrieking of ghouls, as well as a curse from Poluran. Then everything came into focus and she saw greater than a score of the undead creatures covering their eyes and tripping over one another in an attempt to retreat.

"Attack!" Merssa called out, and the bright light was suddenly reduced to match that of the marsh's daytime.

Merssa advanced, striking down several of the blinded abominations, and Vecnor wielded his weapon with both hands, equaling her number in kills. Soon more than a dozen lay dead at their feet and Merssa assessed the situation.

Eraim stood before Selanna and had cleaved four ghouls with Mithkahr, but claimed no more as she remained close to the mage, and Dellen had crushed several more with his hammer. Poluran swung his weapon randomly, obviously unable to see, and had not hit a single ghoul. What remained of the undead disappeared into the darkness, a few stumbling, or perhaps jumping into the river.

"Poluran! Cease!" said Selanna, the wind of the dwarf's last swing having surely been felt by the mage.

While Poluran wiped the tears from his eyes, the others returned to reform the semicircle. Selanna brought the light down to a softer glow, illuminating the immediate area only.

"They are gone," Eraim said quietly.

Merssa relaxed the grip on her mace. "Is anyone hurt?"

"My eyes!" Poluran blurted. "The blasted elf blinded me!"

"You are not blind," said Eraim. "She did warn us."

"She did no such thing!" The dwarf continued rubbing his eyes.

"How long can you burn your light?" Merssa asked Selanna, ignoring Poluran.

"Not too long," the mage replied. "This is a strange place. It is draining to maintain it at even this brightness."

"Then I suppose all night would not be possible?" Dellen issued a small chuckle.

Selanna joined Merssa as she glared at the guardsman, causing him to cringe.

"Long enough to get away from these corpses?" asked Merssa, turning back to Selanna.

To this the mage nodded.

They moved a hundred yards north, and once all were settled back within their blankets, Selanna allowed the light to fade, giving way to the darkness of the bog. Not even Poluran's snoring interrupted the remainder of the night, but he was hushed often by Dellen as he grumbled about elves and magic for the next hour or so.

The marsh lightened as the night drew to an end at last, and Vecnor readied to move on without a word, knowing his thoughts would fall on deaf ears. Merssa seemed more stubborn than he knew her to be, if that were possible, and he had been tempted more than once to push his opinions in a more forceful manner. But it was not his place. He headed north without looking back and heard the company follow. Good. That, at least, allowed Vecnor to keep up the appearance he would leave anyone moving too slowly behind.

After a bit more than an hour, the ledge finally began to descend. Vecnor picked up the pace, eager to find a place to cross, and slowed only slightly when the land became level with the river and his boots sank into the soft, damp ground. The odor of the green-freckled river then became almost unbearable — he could not wait to set foot in that!

Vecnor began testing the water right away, wiping the tears the constant sting of the slime brought to his eyes, but either the river floor proved too treacherous, almost like quicksand, or the water too deep. He waded in and out over a stretch of three hundred yards without luck and could no longer contain his frustrations, glaring at any brave enough to make eye contact with him. To make matters worse, Vecnor began to smell as foul as the slime itself, and standing on the shore was no better than standing chest deep within the water. But then he found a spot that provided hope. Near the midpoint of the river's forty-foot span, the water was only just above his waist. The smell, however, was stronger than ever and stung not only his eyes, but his nose, throat, and deep into his lungs as well.

"I think the ghouls bathe here!" Vecnor called back.

Immediately following the comment, a decayed hand emerged from the dark water and grabbed Vecnor's breastplate. Two more clutched at him, one from behind and one to his left, and the heads of three ghouls surfaced, the slimy water gurgling in their throats as they hissed. Vecnor heard Merssa and Dellen call out and rush into the river, but more ghouls sprang up and he knew help would not come.

The creatures must have been underwater for some time, for their bodies were bloated and their flesh sagged. Hands beneath the water clutched at Vecnor's legs and attempted to topple him, but he kicked free from their grasp while bringing his staff around and launching a ghoul into the air. Grabbing the decayed fingers clutching his breastplate, Vecnor bent the wrist back until it snapped and he tossed the creature aside. He continued swinging the large branch, but upon striking the fourth ghoul it broke and he cast it aside, drawing his sword and hacking the remaining undead around him.

Vecnor spied Merssa and Dellen fighting several ghouls—Merssa was almost to her chest in the water, fending off one, while Dellen's hammer crushed another. From the shore, Selanna cast green bolts of magic, bringing ghouls visible pain and chasing them back beneath the river, while Eraim's arrows pierced the skulls of the enemy, sinking one with every shot. But greater than a dozen more ghouls closed in on Merssa, as if drawn to the paladin, and Vecnor knew she would soon be overwhelmed.

Ignoring the burning scratches now plaguing his body, Vecnor hurried toward Merssa, hacking through the undead. As he neared, the enemy's numbers quickly diminished and it seemed the melee was coming to a close, but then two more ghouls emerged, lunging for Merssa from behind.

"No!" shouted Poluran as Dellen jumped between the undead and the paladin. But all the dwarf could do was scramble knee deep into the water while the guardsman was dragged below.

After destroying another ghoul, Merssa turned to where Dellen had disappeared. The guardsman's location was easy to spot, for the bubbles of his breath were escaping, and Merssa plunged into the water.

Vecnor continued to dance about, switching his sword from left hand to right as he dispatched the remaining ghouls with the assistance of the elves. Most the corpses sank, but a few floated about—disgusting remnants of tortured souls, seeping blood only marginally darker than the water itself.

Poluran, now up to his chest in the water, was nearly knocked off his feet when Merssa broke the surface next to him. Slime covered the paladin's body and in her right arm was Dellen, coughing violently. Vecnor stood poised and ready to strike, but no more ghouls revealed themselves.

"Quickly now!" he shouted. "Cross before more arrive!"

Seeing Eraim on the shore, Vecnor moved swiftly and hoisted her onto his shoulder. He then felt the pleading gaze of Selanna.

"On my back." He stooped so the mage could climb aboard.

Merssa was already dragging Dellen onto the far shore while Poluran bobbed up and down near the middle of the river; the dwarf was not moving very quickly and his head began to submerge with each bounce. Vecnor moved up behind Poluran and lifted him with one hand, just as Poluran began to go under again. It was then that Vecnor realized Poluran was dragging Dellen's hammer.

"Unhand me!" Poluran shouted. "You're going to drop me!"

"As you wish." Vecnor lowered the dwarf back into the water.

"No!" Poluran protested. "You've a firm grip already. Don't unbalance yourself on my account!"

Upon reaching the opposite bank, Vecnor set Poluran down and the dwarf ran immediately to Dellen. The guardsman was on hands and knees, coughing and vomiting slimy water while Merssa rummaged through her pack.

Vecnor set the elves onto the ground and pulled Dellen to his feet. "We must move from the shore. Now."

"I'm burning up!" Dellen said through clenched teeth.

"I know it hurts," Vecnor said without sympathy, "but we can't stay. Not even for a moment."

Merssa gave Vecnor a troubled look, but she nodded. "He's right. The ghouls could return in larger numbers. Besides, there's little I can do until my hands stop shaking from the cold."

Vecnor wondered if it was truly the cold that made Merssa's hands tremble. Though the water had been icy, he could see many scratches upon her skin, as well as guilt within her eyes.

Merssa released a long breath, trying to regain her composure. She could not carry out her mission if she worried about whether or not

she had made the right choice. Choices had to be made and it was her duty to make them. If they had not crossed Slime River, it would have been another river. She found some solace in the fact that they should not have to cross any more of the waterways, and now it was time to refocus. A good start would be to carry out Vecnor's suggestion. They needed to get moving.

Merssa stood to one side of Dellen and steadied him while Poluran added support on the opposite side, and they waited for Vecnor, who was procuring a staff from Selanna. It was more like a cane in the warrior's hand, but better than nothing, Merssa supposed, and the only other stick that survived the river belonged to Eraim, so it was even smaller.

Vecnor led the way in a westerly direction, as far as Merssa could tell, and Merssa did her best to shut out the burning of her injuries while they walked. The added weight of Dellen upon Merssa's shoulder did nothing to help in that task, but she pushed on, knowing the guardsman to be in twice as much agony. After a mile the ground began to rise again, lifting them onto firmer land, and Vecnor turned and nodded.

Merssa set Dellen upon the ground and he resumed regurgitating the river water. Poluran immediately started removing the guardsman's armor, and while he did so Merssa took inventory of her supplies. She released a frustrated sigh.

"My herbs are drenched!" Merssa raised a shaky, blackened hand to wipe her left eye, as it had begun to blur, and noticed the blood seeping from her scalp. She ignored it and continued her search for anything useable.

"Let me help," Selanna offered. "Hold out your herbs."

Merssa did as Selanna suggested, and the mage uttered a chant and placed a hand onto the wet leaves. The elf's hand was warm, and for a moment Merssa wished the spell would take hours to complete, but it lasted only a few seconds and the warm hand was taken away. The leaves were dry.

Merssa immediately began blending the herbs with the white

powder. Pulling her small black vial from her pack, she removed the stopper and sprinkled some of its contents onto the mixture.

"That looks like dirt," commented Poluran. He had been watching intently.

"It's soil," Merssa explained, "blessed in the High Temple of Cafior. I dare not use the mud of this place."

"What can I do?" asked Vecnor. The large warrior had walked the perimeter, so his question assured Merssa she had time to do what was necessary.

"Sit," she told him.

"Sit?" His brow furrowed in confusion.

"Sit!" she snapped, and Vecnor complied.

Merssa applied the mixture to Vecnor's cheek, packing it into the scratches, and did the same for the wounds upon his neck and arms.

"Now lay back and give it time to work." If she did not issue the order, she knew Vecnor would continue pacing and slow the healing process.

"What about Dellen?" Poluran asked. "His wounds are many." The dwarf had been shifting from foot to foot while Merssa tended to Vecnor, his face buried in desperation.

"Has he finished purging the river?" Merssa asked.

"I believe so."

Merssa peered over her shoulder. Dellen sat with head bowed, panting.

"Do you have enough herbs?" Poluran appeared doubtful.

"Herbs aren't going to help him," Merssa said softly.

She handed the remaining healing mixture to Poluran and rummaged through her soaked pack. Withdrawing a silver vial inlaid with small pearls, she went to Dellen and placed a hand on his shoulder.

"Do you feel you can drink something?" Merssa asked, her voice returning to its normal, steady tone.

"Perhaps," Dellen said in a hoarse whisper. "I burn all over!"

The guardsman's claim seemed contradictory, for he shivered

constantly. But from the dark gouges, not to mention the sting of the slimy water Merssa felt within her own wounds, she knew him to be in terrible agony.

"It's the venom of the ghouls," she told him. "And the slime doesn't help. I have something that *will* help, though. It is sacred water from the Grand Cathedral in Palidur. It has great healing powers. Now lie back."

Dellen obeyed, and Merssa pulled loose the stopper and poured the contents into his mouth. Before she could pull away, he seized her wrist.

"Thank you, my lady," he said softly. "I thought my eyes had seen you for the last time when those things pulled me under."

Merssa stared hard at him. "Dellen, you must keep your mind about you. If you continue to be distracted while danger lurks under your nose... You're no good if you're dead. Do not try to be my hero. I don't need one. Next time I may not be there for you." She saw his confusion and sighed. "Just lay back and rest now. Take as long as you need. But as soon as you're ready we must move on. I do not know if the ghouls will pursue us."

A twinge of guilt haunted Merssa for speaking to Dellen so while he was hurting, but she did not know what else to do. She had never shown the guardsman any affection that she could recall to make him feel the way he did about her. True, she converted him to the worship of Cafior above all other deities, and perhaps that was when he became infatuated with her. Or perhaps it was before that. Merssa was not sure. Perhaps she *had* brought it on. She did not know. Other than her love for Cafior and her parents, Merssa had not known love in that way or what if felt like — or if she could feel it. Besides, there was not room in her life for that or anything else. Why couldn't Dellen just recognize that and find someone else?

Merssa returned to Poluran, who still held the healing mixture, and with the dwarf's assistance she tended to her own wounds. While she worked, the elves pulled what dry blankets the company possessed and distributed them, each member receiving three. Once

Merssa was finished, they settled in for a short rest.

Merssa was especially cold, as her gear was completely soaked, and she knew Dellen and Poluran to feel the same. Vecnor surrendered his blankets to them, one extra for each, and Merssa did not possess the energy to argue or point out that he needed them as well. She wrapped herself as best she could, but it made little difference. Her wounds burned and the chill made it impossible to stop shaking, and she was sure she felt a fever coming on, so she laid down. She knew she would find no sleep, but closed her eyes nonetheless, allowing Vecnor and the elves keep watch.

Vecnor sat upon the dark ground while Merssa rested, and he pulled the dripping map from his pack. His injuries were already feeling the powers of Merssa's herbs, but he was unconcerned for himself. He almost lost a few members of the company in that river. He had to be more careful, especially in Merssa's case. It was important she survived this ordeal. That was his instruction.

"Where are we headed now?" Eraim inquired, snapping Vecnor from his thoughts as she dropped one of her blankets onto his shoulders.

"West. Snake River shouldn't be more than a few miles. We'll follow it until it breaks north, and if Olinin's map is accurate, we should be able to continue west to the house. We could make it by nightfall, depending on how far north we've traveled."

"I do not think I should like to be there come night," Eraim commented with a nervous chuckle.

Vecnor nodded as he crumpled the map and cast it into the swamp. The ink was smeared and very little was legible. Luckily, he had committed it to memory. Eraim placed a friendly hand upon his shoulder before returning to Selanna.

Nearly half an hour passed while Vecnor kept watch over the dark haze. Nothing stirred, and not even a breeze had brushed against his skin since they stopped, but he felt anxious and looked at

Dellen. The guardsman had ceased coughing a while ago and sat quietly next to Poluran with head bowed. Vecnor rose and approached the two.

"Are you able to move?" he asked Dellen. "There is still a ways to go yet, and I fear staying in one place too long. It would seem our welcome has run out."

"I'm ready," the guardsman said, his voice hoarse but firm, and he stood.

There was a different look in Dellen's eyes and Vecnor was not sure he liked it. He knew how Dellen felt toward Merssa, and the lecture she had given had not escape Vecnor's ears.

"Are you sure? Has your strength—"

"I'm ready!" Dellen picked up his hammer. "The elixir has done its job. Let's move."

Vecnor looked at Poluran, who shrugged. Glancing over his shoulder, Vecnor saw Eraim had roused Merssa and all were ready to go.

Travel remained slow and several hours passed with the land unchanging. Vecnor was no longer sure of which direction they headed, for there were no trees, rivers, or landmarks of any kind, and his concern quickly turned to aggravation.

"Blast!" He stopped for a drink of polluted water from his flask. "We should have made it to the river long ago."

"Let's keep moving." Merssa seemed too calm for Vecnor's liking. "There's been no sign of ghouls since we crossed the river. That at least is good."

"Not if we never find our way again," Vecnor murmured.

They continued without a break. Vecnor's boots were heavy and hunger gripped his stomach, but he pushed the company forward, battling the exhaustion attempting to grab hold as he was eager to see some form of change—anything to prove they had not been traveling in circles.

"There!" Eraim broke the silence, pointing toward a river that had sneaked up on the right.

Vecnor veered toward the water and found it stagnant, just as the others. But he knew they had not encountered it before, for it lacked a slime or mud coating. The ground all around it, however, was soft and wet.

"It must be Snake River," said Poluran with hope. "We're on course then."

Vecnor gazed at the water, and then left and right, shaking his head. He was doubtful. The swamp had not given him any reason to be optimistic. Turning left, he followed the bank, but after a short distance they reached a fork and his heart sank.

"I hate this swamp," Vecnor mumbled and turned to Merssa. "This is the beginning of Snake River. We must have been veering north for hours. There's no chance we'll find the house today. We'll be lucky if we find it tomorrow!"

Merssa gazed at the water and released a long, controlled breath. "Let's not worry about that now. At least we know where we are."

With a shake of his head, Vecnor continued. He was not sure what he had wanted Merssa to say, if anything. And since when did she see the bright side of anything outside of Palidur? He decided to bite his tongue and keep walking.

A few miles farther, the river turned westward—the first bend in the Snake's coils. The company continued until the light failed, trudging along with faces of surrender, and Vecnor searched for a place to stop. But there existed no hills and they were forced to sit in the mud. Taking positions back to back, they settled in for the night.

With the darkness came fear of another ghoul attack, but Merssa urged all to get some sleep while she guarded the first portion of the night. Vecnor agreed, so as to avoid a confrontation, but he remained awake, for Merssa's pale coloring gave him concern. On occasion Vecnor found it hard to focus and drifted to the edge of slumber, but sat up abruptly any time his head began to nod—he could not remember the last time he had felt this tired. Once the swamp brightened a bit, Vecnor pulled himself from the mud and the others did the same. From the faces around him, no one had found sleep.

Before moving on, Merssa checked Vecnor's wounds and informed him they were healing nicely. Her own appeared to be recovering as well, but still showed blackening about the edges. To look at Dellen, one would have never known the ordeal the guardsman had undergone, were it not for the faint scars decorating his body. The elixir Merssa had administered must have been truly potent.

With a heavy heart and reluctant limbs, Vecnor led on. The morning grew late and the scenery changed only slightly, as a few trees dotted the landscape, but his mood lightened when the river began bending southward and a thought occurred to him. He turned to Merssa.

"If we find a point at which to cross, we should take it. The house should only be a short distance south of the next bend. We could be there well before evening. Maybe by noon."

Merssa bit her lip, her eyes wandering but focusing on nothing. There was obvious turmoil within her ashen face, but she nodded. "We best cross, then." She received nervous glances from the rest of the company. "*If* the chance presents itself."

They continued, but the river was unyielding in its width, even as it turned eastward. Vecnor tested its depth in several places, but it rose to his chest after only ten paces or so. Farther along, he was surprised to find the water developing a slight current, and he was further dismayed to discover the ground rising. Though they were again lifted from the mud, the water soon fell beneath them by several feet.

"This is not good," Vecnor said. "The marsh will make us follow the river unto its end."

"What will be will be." Merssa's voice sounded a bit stronger. "There's nothing we can do but press on."

Hope returned to Vecnor after another couple hundred yards, for the channel narrowed to a width of no more than thirty feet and a fallen tree bridged the gap.

"A sign of luck at last!"

He picked up the pace, but none of his companions seemed to share in his enthusiasm. The tree was black, just as the others, but much larger. It seemed broad enough for safe crossing and many scratches were visible, as ghouls had surely used it often.

"Think it'll hold?" Poluran frowned as he eyed the moving water ten feet below. "I recall the trees of Twisted Wood to be brittle."

"I will go first," offered Eraim.

Merssa nodded, and with little effort, Eraim leaped onto the tree and trotted across. It appeared sturdy beneath the elf's light feet, but the river seemed to pick up its pace, as if in anticipation of a meal. Eraim stepped onto the opposite bank, becoming a silhouette in the distance.

"It's a bit slippery," she called back, her voice barely audible. "But I believe it will hold."

"She weighs no more than a bird!" Poluran stared up at Vecnor. "I'm surprised she didn't fly across!"

Selanna went next, appearing as nimble as Eraim, and hopped off the far end. But this did nothing to encourage Poluran. The dwarf shook his head, his eyes wide with fear.

Merssa climbed aboard and moved at a much slower pace. Though similar in height to Selanna, Merssa surely weighed three times as much in her armor, and at times she slid left or right on the black slime that coated the tree. She almost lost her footing a couple times and it seemed the water roared louder with excitement, but she continued cautiously and soon joined the elves.

Dellen went next, immediately falling to hands and knees, and while he crawled the tree creaked and groaned in protest. But in the end, it held and the guardsman stepped onto the opposite bank.

"I'll just wait here." Poluran's lip was quivering.

"You'll be all right," Vecnor insisted.

"Have you looked at the water?"

Vecnor glanced at the river. It was definitely moving much more rapidly, and it lapped against the walls of the channel like a wild animal licking its chops.

"It's alive!" Poluran insisted. "It'll go hungry before it tastes dwarf!"

Vecnor grabbed hold of Poluran and hoisted him up.

"Blast you, human!"

Once upon the tree, however, Poluran followed Dellen's lead and inched forward on hands and knees, stopping often to peer down.

"Don't look at the river!" Vecnor called.

Vecnor detected a few faint mutterings in the dwarfish language, and he knew enough of the speech to almost want to laugh at the choice phrases meant for him. But the swamp had stolen his sense of humor days ago.

Suddenly an arrow sank into the tree very near to Poluran, and the dwarf almost jumped into the water. The arrow was fired from Eraim's bow.

"What're you shooting at, elf?" Poluran roared, hugging the tree as best as his short arms allowed to recapture his balance. The dwarf's eyes then followed a thin rope tied to the arrow and stretching all the way to Dellen's hands. "That's right. The dwarf couldn't possibly cross on his own!"

After a deep breath, Poluran grabbed the rope and fastened it about his waist. He then crawled with a bit more confidence, and though the tree groaned louder, he made it across.

Vecnor saw Poluran untie the rope and toss it at Eraim's feet—he doubted any thanks had been given. And now Vecnor stood alone, the heaviest of them all. The water was raging below, as the river grew angry at the stubborn bridge, and the waves reached high in an attempt to knock it from the ledges.

"Just one more," Vecnor said to the tree, and he hopped onto the trunk.

He walked briskly, showing his balance to almost rival that of the elves, but when he neared the midpoint, there came a loud *crack* and the tree sank a bit—its strength was beginning to wane. Vecnor picked up the pace to a jog, but there was another crack, much louder than the first, and the tree broke free from the northern ledge. He collapsed onto the trunk and slid almost into the water, but the tree remained defiant and held firmly to the southern ridge. The river, however, was strong and the bridge shifted. Vecnor scrambled on hands and feet up the slippery slope, nearly reaching the other side when he felt a great snap beneath him—the tree could withstand the river's will no more. With one last effort, he leaped and caught hold of the ledge as the water swept the bridge away, and Poluran and Dellen grabbed his arms and quickly pulled him up.

"Thank you, my lady," Poluran said quietly, bowing toward the tree as it was thrown about the river and taken away to deeper places of the marsh. "She was no Korban, but her deed will not go forgotten."

"Are you all right?" Merssa asked Vecnor.

"Fine." He attempted to control his panting.

Everyone's attention was drawn back to the river. The water was still and covered by dark algae, as if it had known no current for some time.

"Let's move on," Merssa said, a bit uneasy.

There were no arguments.

Vecnor backtracked along the river until it turned northward, and there he stopped. He prayed Olinin's map had been to scale.

"Straight south from here." Vecnor hoped he had mustered enough confidence to convince the others he believed his words.

They walked with a bit more energy, grateful to leave the mysterious river behind. Black trees were scattered about, but there were no pools of muck or slime-spotted puddles to steer them off course. After a bit more than a mile, Eraim's gasp brought them to a halt.

"There it is." The elf extended a small, filthy, glove-covered finger.

At the edge of the haze rested the shady outline of a small house.

Chapter 10

The Stone Cabin

Just north of a wide river stood a single-story cabin of black stone with a flat roof and but a single door. An overwhelming feeling of woe emanated from it that nearly buckled Merssa's knees, and she found herself hard pressed to move any closer. Faith and duty took hold, however, and she crept forward with weapon ready, not needing to look back to know the others were doing the same.

The ground was firmer than other places of the marsh, feeling almost as hard as Nejan soil, and the thinning fog revealed many twisted shapes standing perfectly still about the area—more pitiful trees forced to exist within the hellish bog. Though the past several hours had left Merssa feeling ill and worn, she felt nothing now but the tingling upon her scalp and back of her neck while she viewed the dark structure ahead.

"Eraim. Selanna. Go around the right." Merssa's voice revealed just how silent the world had become. "Vecnor take the left. See if any other points of entry exist."

"Watch for ghouls," Dellen added.

A needless statement.

The three did as instructed, and the swamp seemed to grow colder and thicker as they disappeared around the sides of the cabin.

"You two follow me," Merssa said to Dellen and Poluran without a glance and approached the door.

The door was normal in size and also made of black stone, only it seemed darker than the rest of the house. A large pull ring was affixed to its right side, but Merssa paid it no heed and took a closer look. Upon the door's surface were two small ovals carved in very fine lines, close together and slightly above her head. The right one was a lighter shade of black and the left one dark blue, barely discernable in the dim light. Merssa's heart leapt when she felt a weight upon her shoulder. It was Dellen's gauntleted hand.

"Shouldn't we wait for the others?" he asked.

Merssa was suddenly aware that her hand was reaching for the pull ring. She shook her head clear, lowering her hand and averting her gaze. "Yes." She cleared her throat. "Do not look too closely at the door. There's something strange about it."

"I don't even wish to gaze upon the house," the guardsman remarked.

"This is odd," said Poluran, standing to the left of the door. The dwarf scrutinized the cabin wall, and before Merssa could stop him, he rapped upon it with his gauntlet, splattering muck—it seemed the house was covered with the same stench-ridden filth that plagued the marsh, though the surrounding area was completely devoid of it. "Hmm." Poluran was oblivious to the fresh mud now decorating his face and beard.

"What are you doing?" Merssa hissed as the dwarf scraped away a patch of sludge with Clanghorr's edge, but then she saw what had caught his interest. The cabin was not black after all, but white beneath the filth.

Poluran gasped, taking a step back. "Rorbak!"

"What?" Merssa was unsure if he was cursing, or making a proclamation of some sort.

"Rorbak," he repeated. "The same stone as Korban Bridge. That is why this place still stands. Rornibur used it to build many great structures in Lord Korban's days." Poluran shook his head. "This cabin must be very old, because the bridge was its final project."

"No other doors," came Vecnor's voice as he and the elves approached.

"No windows either," added Eraim.

"It is just as Olinin said," Selanna reported.

"There is a boat." Eraim raised her brow. "On the shore around the back. Olinin's boat, no doubt."

"And a chimney," said Selanna. "Toward the back right corner."

Merssa addressed the mage. "What do you make of the door? There's something there. Almost like eyes; one black and one blue. I felt drawn. If Dellen hadn't stopped me, I might have already opened it."

Selanna approached cautiously, gazing at the door from top to bottom. "There is a powerful enchantment here." She turned away with a gasp. "It is a spy for its master! And it would lure any who gaze upon it to enter, whether they wish to or not."

"It's only a door!" Poluran approached. "I'll open it."

"No!" Selanna halted him. "It will immediately inform its master." She shook her head, gazing at the black door from several feet away. "Olinin must not have noticed. That is how his presence here was known."

"What do you suggest, then?" complained the dwarf. "Return home? I didn't brave the dangers of the marsh to leave evil to its own affairs. Let Clanghorr's presence be known!" Poluran's last sentence was shouted into the haze above.

"Hush!" Selanna snapped before Merssa could. "Olinin and his men were powerless against the master of this house. I am uncertain as to what chances we stand if the same fate befalls us."

Merssa glared at Poluran, fighting the urge to rip his tongue from his head. Perhaps the swamp was driving the dwarf mad. She took in a deep breath and released it to calm herself before addressing Selanna.

"Is there a way around this magic? Can you get us by it?"

Selanna shook her head. "It has a very powerful aura."

"What about the chimney?" asked Merssa.

"Yes." Selanna brightened. "The smokestack."

"We won't all fit," Vecnor pointed out. "Eraim is probably the only one that can."

"We need not all go by that route," said Selanna. "The enchantment on the door is only triggered if opened from *this* side."

"All right, then." Merssa turned to the smaller elf. "Mind you find the front door immediately. Don't go nosing about."

Eraim looked from Merssa to Vecnor, then back to Merssa, a trace of fear in the elf's eyes and an objection poised upon her lips. Then her shoulders slumped in surrender. "You need not worry of that. I wish to be alone in there for as little time as possible."

"Vecnor and Selanna," Merssa said. "See to it she makes it up safely. Then return at once."

Eraim walked beside Selanna, following Vecnor around the house to where the dark smokestack rose a few feet higher than the roof. It was chipped in several places, but it appeared sturdy. Selanna said nothing, but Eraim detected apprehension within her companion.

"I shall be fine," Eraim said quietly, trying to convince herself as well.

Selanna gave a fleeting smile, eyeing the dark cabin as if it were a sleeping ogre.

The chill from the structure seemed to intensify as they came to a stop next to the chimney. Doing her best to ignore it, Eraim went through her pack and extracted her fine rope—ten yards of a near-weightless weave she had fashioned in Salenti many years ago. She fastened to it a small metal hook and began twirling it while she regarded her target above. Releasing the hook, it sailed up and around the chimney, latching back onto the rope as she gave it a quick twirl and pulled it taut. After a couple tugs, Eraim turned to her companions and gave her best smile under the circumstances.

"All set."

Vecnor gave a half smile and small chuckle, eyeing the rope. He always seemed so impressed with the smallest things Eraim did. But it was not really all that difficult a feat with a little practice.

"Be careful," he told her.

Eraim nodded and began her ascent. The muck-covered exterior made the way slick, but she scaled to the roof without a misstep.

"Disgusting," Eraim declared as she glanced into the dark smokestack.

It was not soot that lined the inside walls, but more of the muck. Eraim stared intently, attempting to pierce the darkness without success, and sniffed the air, but detected nothing other than the stench of the marsh. The only thing she was sure of was that a fire had not burned below in some time, if ever. She gathered her rope and lowered it into the chimney. After one last glance at the concerned faces below, she swung her legs into the square hole and descended into the darkness.

Somehow, the horrid mud had managed to coat every inch of the inside of the smokestack. It was slick, but no more so than soot, so it posed no real challenge and the task was easy enough. Upon reaching the hearth, Eraim discovered absolutely no ashes or wood within the space. It was large, as hearths go, and she did not even have to duck as she slipped into the space beyond.

The room was dark and unrevealing. Eraim detected the presence of a few pieces of furniture nearby, but she was positive nothing living or undead existed therein. Placing her back to the chimney bricks, she pulled Mithkahr.

"Show me," Eraim whispered, and the blade radiated a faint light.

The illumination revealed the room to be a kitchen with walls of white stone. A pair of dark cauldrons rested on their sides among smashed bits of pottery, across the room laid cupboards that had fallen from the wall some time ago, and to Eraim's right was a long counter with tattered sacks that might have once held grain or flour. The only visible exit was a single door to the left.

Eraim felt her skin crawl as she crept quietly to the door, but still nothing moved outside the shadows her light created. Cracking open the door, she saw very little of the room beyond, but she heard and felt nothing moving, so she opened it fully.

A large table, broken in half and missing a leg, dominated a small dining chamber, and upon the other side was a door reinforced with steel bands. There also existed four chairs in various states of ruin and a couple of shelves to the left. Littering the floor below the shelves was a pile of shattered plates.

Eraim entered on full alert, for the table left much of the room in shadow, but the cabin remained silent as she slid around the walls to the right until reaching the door. The door was rotted and split in several places, and it was obvious the rusted bands were all that kept it from collapsing. Fearing what a loud noise might bring, Eraim opened it only slightly and squeezed through.

She stood in the front room. It was filled with what must have once been plush furniture, but their better days were long gone. To Eraim's right was a single wooden door, and in the center of the far wall was the black stone door she was positive led to the outside. She cautiously approached.

The house had given Eraim an eerie feeling even before entering, and now that the door was only a few yards away, her nerves tingled throughout her body, as if a dark presence was right behind her. She moved swiftly and pushed with all her might, and the door swung slowly open to reveal her companions on the other side. Eraim breathed a sigh of relief.

Merssa felt as though she had held her breath the entire time she stood outside the cabin, waiting for the door to open. The marsh remained perfectly silent, as did the house, and she began to wonder if they had seen the last of Eraim. But the door opened at last and the small elf's pale face stared from the darkness beyond, riding a large sigh of relief.

"Selanna," Merssa whispered. "We could use some light."

"Just warn us this time," grumbled Poluran.

"Quiet!" Merssa snapped.

Selanna whispered an incantation and lifted her palm upward, and a small sphere began to glow an inch above her hand, growing brighter as it rose overhead. The mage then led the way inside and the light obediently followed.

The smell of the swamp was alive within the walls of the cabin and the chill seemed intensified. The front room was in tatters, but it did not appear to have been sacked by looters, just ravaged by time — as well as a few claws. Merssa looked from one door to the other upon the opposite wall.

"The door on the right leads to a dining chamber and kitchen," Eraim said in a whisper.

Selanna moved across the room to the left door, curiosity seeming to overcome any fear the mage might have felt, and Merssa followed.

"The bedroom must be through here, then," Selanna deduced, but before the elf could open the door, Vecnor halted her by the shoulder.

"I'll go first."

Vecnor flung the door open, his sword ready, and Selanna's light revealed a quiet hallway with a door to the immediate right and another farther down. Stepping to the first door, Vecnor opened it and they entered a small den. A crumbled desk sat amid a couple toppled bookcases and shredded parchment was strewn about, as well as many tattered books. Broken ink vials had stained the floor in several places, the ancient ink faded, and several quills were broken next to the desk drawer, which lay discarded to the side of the chamber. Merssa gazed upon some of the more intact pieces of parchment and a couple books. Nothing was legible.

"Olinin claimed the library to be in the back bedroom," whispered Selanna.

"Let's move on." Merssa dropped a book back onto the floor.

Vecnor led the way to the far door. Beyond was a bedchamber containing the remains of a four-poster bed, only two posts intact, as well as a toppled chest of drawers where shattered fragments of pottery littered the floor. Feathers covered the area about the bed, having escaped the one-time overstuffed mattress, and the far wall was covered completely by four floor-to-ceiling mirrors, placed close together and almost appearing as one large mirror. Vecnor entered before stepping aside to allow Merssa and Selanna access.

"There's no room for a library here," said Poluran, spying under Dellen's arm from the doorway. "The house isn't big enough."

"It is not as it appears." Selanna stood before the far wall, a sneer crossing the mage's lips as she gazed into one of the mirrors. Her golden hair appeared brown and mud streaked her face, and Merssa could no longer ascertain the color of Selanna's robes, nor see the strange silver writings upon the breast. "It is a simple illusion, really. Not even magical." Selanna touched the glass. "They make the room appear larger than it actually is. One of them is a door, I am sure."

"Search them," Merssa ordered Eraim, doing her best to avoid seeing her own reflection in the mirrors.

"Why don't we just smash them?" Poluran entered with axe raised. "We're wasting time with all this sneaking around. Let's be done with it!"

"Do not be foolish!" Selanna snapped. "That could set off a trap."

"Found it." Eraim stood next to the mirror farthest to the right, which was now ajar. The task had not taken the elf even a minute to accomplish.

Before Merssa could cross the room, Selanna slipped through the opening with Eraim close behind. It was enough to boil Merssa's blood and she moved quickly to join them.

Beyond was surely the library Olinin had described, much bigger than should have been possible—it appeared larger than the entire cabin. Immediately inside the door was a small table and single chair, and to the left four freestanding bookcases formed dark aisles, parallel to the reading area, while floor-to-ceiling shelves covered the walls. Unlike the rest of the house, the furnishings were in working order, though coated by dust, and all seemed muck-free. Thousands of books packed the shelves without an inch to spare.

"Be alert," Merssa said as the others entered.

"It is a powerful magic that allows this room to exist." Selanna gazed about in awe.

"This room seems untouched by the swamp," Eraim said in a hushed voice. "There is no odor. No slime. Nothing."

Selanna moved to the table. "It is just as cold, though."

Upon the tabletop rested four candles within a brass holder. With a single word from Selanna's lips, one of the wicks came to life, and when the mage blew onto the flame it spread to the other wicks. A surprised smile briefly highlighted her face, as if she had not expected the spell to work.

"Pretty handy talent." Poluran offered an energetic nod.

"Shh!" Merssa was more than tired of hearing the dwarf's voice rumbling into the darkness. She turned her attention to the aisles and the tingling upon her scalp began to build, as if something might jump out at any moment. But the library remained still. Merssa took a candle from the holder and handed it to Poluran. "Find the trapdoor."

Poluran looked at the candle, then the paladin, and back to the candle. Was Merssa serious? Find the door? What kind of task was that for Clanghorr? Shaking his head, Poluran took the light and started for the shelves, mumbling to himself.

"I'll help," Dellen offered.

Poluran nodded and handed the candle to the guardsman. "It's best if Clanghorr is ready."

Dellen responded with a wry smile.

They entered the first aisle, moving only a short distance before Poluran spotted a faint light ahead. He immediately grabbed Dellen's arm, as the guardsman seemed absorbed in searching the floor. The reddish light was about waist height at first, then swooped low to the floor and ceased to move. After a couple seconds it rose and moved a bit closer before dropping again. Poluran stepped forward with axe ready… It was Eraim and Mithkahr.

"You should start at the far aisle," Eraim whispered as she stooped to scrutinize the floor in front of her.

"Elves…" Poluran muttered as he shook his head.

The task had not been appointed to Eraim; it was bestowed upon Clanghorr and Poluran. Yet there she was, giving orders as if she were the paladin. Poluran turned to Dellen, who shrugged and headed back the way they had come.

Humans…

Selanna gazed at the shelf nearest the table. Several large, leather-bound tomes existed in various colors with runes of silver or gold, and all of them seemed to be in the Ancient Moclen text. She could not help but wish circumstances had been different, so she might have time to explore their contents.

"Trannum…" Selanna whispered. The runes Olinin had shown her were common to every book.

"But who or what *is* Trannum?" Merssa had been looking at the volumes in vain, for the language was obviously beyond the paladin.

Selanna shook her head, lifting a few books at random for closer inspection and placing them onto the table. Though they were surely very old, they felt as if they had been bound only weeks ago. She then gasped in horror. "The titles…"

"Most deal with the dead or undead," said Vecnor, much to Selanna's shock. "Yes." He answered her questioning stare. "I know a bit of Ancient Moclen."

This was a surprise. Selanna was sure no one outside Elgarroth and herself knew the old tongue. It had taken her almost ten years to learn, and Vecnor could not be much more than thirty years in age. And where did he find someone with the knowledge and time to teach him? Selanna would probably never know. Even if she were to press him, Vecnor would never answer any questions forthcoming from her.

"Indeed, it is necromancy," Selanna said. "But some seem to be research of some sort. Records of something dark."

"But what?" Merssa asked.

Selanna examined the stack of books she had gathered, opening a few at random to peruse the pages as quickly as she could. One referenced Blackfoot goblins, hobgoblins, and the nature of humans; another delved into gates and the summoning of demonic creatures; a third book seemed focused on a source of dark power, but its words were cryptic and she could not grasp them. More than a few books were about the undead, including the likes of zombies, skeletons, and ghouls, but also there were passages about strange creatures Selanna had never heard of and references to *the power of the firstborn spirit* and such. It was all fascinatingly disturbing.

Selanna was about to say something when she felt a cool breeze brush her cheek from the direction of the bookshelves. Merssa must have felt it as well, for the paladin's head snapped toward the aisles. Then Selanna noticed a blue glow deep within the library, and from that direction came Eraim running toward them.

"What have we here?" Poluran tapped the floor with Clanghorr's spike. There was a definite hollow sound from beneath the stone. He knew Dellen had already checked the area, but Dellen was not a dwarf and it was understandable how the human had missed it.

"Is it the door?"

Eraim's voice startled Poluran while he scrutinized the floor on his hands and knees. The elf had evidently finished searching the other three aisles, much too hastily, and decided to check on their progress. But her sword was sheathed, so Poluran had not detected her approach. Well, he could have covered as much ground as she, maybe more, had Dellen not been there to slow him down. Poluran shook his head and leaned closer to the floor, ignoring the elf.

His breath grew thick. "The air's colder here." He slid his finger upon the stone. "A narrow slot… This must be it." Pulling a knife, Poluran worked its edge into the fine crack.

"We should get the others," suggested Eraim.

"I agree," said Dellen.

"I'm not afraid of a skeleton." Poluran continued about his task.

"And Clanghorr is with us." Looking at his companions, he added, "Besides, we must be sure. Can't go back to Merssa with a '*I think we found it.*'" Poluran did his best impression of Eraim, but neither she nor Dellen seemed to find any humor in it.

Humans and elves...

Poluran rocked his knife back and forth until the blade snapped, slicing his hand. "*Brakkeet!*" he cursed in his native tongue, slamming his fist into nearby books.

There was a *click* and the trapdoor popped up slightly, releasing a rush of cold air that extinguished the candle in Dellen's hand. The aisle was not left in darkness, however, for an eerie blue glow filled the cracks of the door. Fear enveloped Poluran. Resenting the emotion, he reached out a trembling hand and lifted the door. The light spilled out to reveal a staircase.

"Wait," said Dellen as Eraim ran swiftly from the aisle. "Let's get Merssa."

Dellen began to move away, but Poluran did not follow. He did not care. There was something about the blue glow Poluran found fascinating and he began to descend. "No," came Dellen's voice, but it was distant—much too distant to be meant for Poluran. All feelings of fear were gone and Poluran found himself in awe as he basked in the light. It called to him, compelling him to have a closer look.

The stairs ended in a small chamber. Its floor was shrouded in a cold mist and the only furnishing was a pedestal in the center, atop of which rested a large orb that emitted the strange blue light. Poluran stepped forward, gazing into the sphere, and spied a swirling blue vapor trapped within. An extreme cold surrounded the orb, but little did he feel it; his attention was held by the endless depths of the spiraling fog...

Eraim shouted something in elfish Merssa could not understand, but she recognized the alarm on the faces of Selanna and Vecnor as the two rushed to follow the small elf toward the blue glow. Merssa did not have the speed to keep up with Vecnor's long strides nor the swiftness of the elves, and her mud-saturated armor did nothing to improve the matter, so she lagged behind.

"He went down!" Dellen's voice called out from the last aisle.

By the time Merssa rounded the final bookshelf, Selanna and Vecnor were already descending narrow steps into the floor, followed by Eraim and Dellen. Merssa brought up the rear, her frustrations running high.

"Do not touch it!" yelled Selanna from the bottom step.

Merssa saw the mage enter the blue glow, and all but Dellen followed. The guardsman was as a statue at the termination of the stairwell, allowing Merssa no access, and she peeked beneath his arm into a small chamber.

Vecnor and the elves stood before a pedestal, and upon it a large orb shed the blue light and issued a steady mist that fell to the floor. Beyond, Poluran backed away toward the far end of the room, clutching his right forearm as if it were in terrible pain, and Merssa was sure there was frost upon the dwarf's gauntlet.

Merssa's attention was drawn to the orb. A mist swirled within, and while she stared it reversed direction and picked up speed. It rose from the orb, taking the shape of a large blue skull, and the right eye shone brightly.

"Who dares to disturb my house?" the skull demanded in a hoarse whisper. "All trespassers have forfeit their lives!"

The skull dissolved into a billowing mass of blood-red smoke. Poluran scrambled to a dark corner and Vecnor and the elves retreated as it snaked toward the stairs, increasing in mass and forming a pillar, and from it came a low growl, like the purr of a hungry lion. The mist retreated back into the orb, again filling the room with the eerie blue light, but the chamber seemed suddenly smaller, for it left behind a horrific beast.

The creature was covered in scales that glistened red, defying the blue glow. Its elongated snout ended in flaring nostrils emitting wisps of black smoke, and a dark, forked tongue licked its scaly lips.

Massive arms stretched to its knees, ending in three fingered claws, and it hunched over on trunk-like legs to fit within the boundaries of the room, disguising its true height. A short, massive tail swayed back and forth while its beady black eyes gazed at the intruders, and it released a hideous roar, bathing the room in searing steam and revealing multiple rows of teeth.

"Hezeb!" Selanna's eyes were wide. "From the pits of Hell!"

Vecnor stood before the beast, and behind him Mithkahr's red hue intensified. Eraim muttered something in the elfish tongue and the light faded as she slipped into the shadows of the nearest corner.

Merssa's heart pounded and the tingling on the back of her neck was stronger than she could ever recall—never before had she been faced with such pure evil. She attempted to enter, but Dellen was frozen in place and she could not move him. The thought of kicking him into the chamber crossed her mind, but she feared something awful might happen if she knocked the paralyzed guardsman to the floor. Merssa shouted his name and shook him as hard as she could while keeping watch on her companions.

A giant among most, Vecnor appeared small in the face of the demon, but the monster maneuvered feebly about the chamber as Vecnor's blade flashed about and scored many wounds. He cut deep into its hide with a force to fell any beast, but Merssa gaped in disbelief as very little of the creature's black blood escaped and the wounds closed before her eyes.

"Mortal weapons cannot defeat it!" shouted Selanna.

The mage placed her hands overhead, uttering a magical word, and a green ball of light launched from her open palms, striking the demon square on the chest. The attack served only to push the monster back a step and it remained unharmed.

Vecnor drove the demon a couple more paces with his shoulder, but Hezeb thrust a large claw into his side, ripping through armor and flesh. Vecnor winced as the creature's massive jaws opened wide enough to swallow his head whole, but the bite did not come. Instead, the demon emitted a roar toward the ceiling.

Mithkahr had bitten deep into Hezeb's back and smoking blood issued—a wound not so easily overcome. Eraim leaped over the lashing tail and dealt another gash onto its flank as she landed, causing the demon to roar again.

Hezeb cast Vecnor aside with little effort and spun to face its new attacker. It hesitated upon spotting the small elf, but recovered quickly and lunged with both claws. Eraim evaded the strike, but it seemed the attack was not meant for her and the demon slapped Mithkahr from her hand. The monster then bore down with gnashing teeth, but Selanna released another green ball, striking Hezeb where its wounds still bled. The attack produced a more profound effect this time and the creature hissed in anger, and Eraim danced out of reach while it turned on Selanna.

Merssa was granted access when Vecnor crashed into Dellen and knocked the guardsman into the wall. She moved to the front of the mage, her mace emitting its golden glow, and the advancing demon balked as it snarled with hatred. Merssa sensed uneasiness, if not a touch of fear, as it was faced with the power of her deity.

"By the Might of Cafior," Merssa said in a commanding tone, "I will smite thee! Back to Hell with you!"

She advanced, swinging her mace in circles to either side, and while she did so the golden glow encompassed her entire body. The light touched the demon and the creature recoiled, as if burned. Merssa pressed, crashing the weapon into its jaw and then chest and driving the monster to the far wall. Hezeb towered above her and gave a mighty roar before bearing down with savage attacks, but she remained vigilant, even when the demon's claw gouged her shoulder. Merssa continued the assault, each strike producing a spark of golden light and wracking the beast with more pain, and flashes of magic assisted from behind her—more green spheres of light.

Hezeb seemed little concerned with Selanna's attacks and remained focused on Merssa. It belched fire from the depths of Hell and she was burned and blinded as she retreated and rolled to one knee. From out of the flames came the monster's gnashing teeth in pursuit, but before they could strike, Dellen knocked Merssa aside and intercepted the full fury of the attack. Five rows of teeth sank deep into the guardsman's chest and lifted him from the floor. With a jerk of the demon's head, Dellen was tossed aside and Hezeb's eyes returned to Merssa.

Merssa's mind went numb and her golden glow faded. Hezeb attacked again, but Vecnor shouldered the beast and drove it into the pedestal. The stand must have been made of the same stone as the house, for it remained unharmed, but the orb was knocked free and rolled away.

"Taste Clanghorr!"

Poluran advanced with malice in his eyes. The axe struck the creature upon the thigh, scoring a wound deeper than even Mithkahr could manage and inciting a deafening roar.

Hezeb knocked Vecnor to the floor and slapped Poluran to the corner where the orb had settled. Its beady eyes returned to Merssa and it advanced, a distinct limp hampering its movements.

Merssa regained her feet and met the foul beast.

"Cafior!"

She brought her mace across with enough force to match even Vecnor's strength, knocking the demon's head to the side. Her weapon struck again and again, until Hezeb seemed no longer able to move, and with one final blow there came a crackling sound and the red smoke returned. The fog billowed from the floor, engulfing the beast and causing Merssa to jump back. There was a flash and the demon and mist were gone. The only light remaining was the sickening blue glow of the orb.

Merssa knelt next to Dellen and took his hand. She felt Selanna's presence suddenly next to her and she glanced quickly about to find the others. Vecnor staggered to a wall and dropped to one knee, and Eraim was quickly by the warrior's side. Poluran remained in the corner where he had landed, staring in disbelief at Dellen while the orb next to him highlighted his expression in a hideous manner.

Dellen was conscious, and he gazed into Merssa's eyes as blood escaped his lips.

"You're beyond my care," Merssa said softly. "Even if I could heal the wound, the demon's venom is in your blood." She shook her head.

"As long as you're safe." Dellen's voice was barely above a whisper. His eyes then stared blankly forward as his last breath escaped.

Merssa closed his eyes. "Cafior guide you from here and ever after."

"Merssa?" Eraim spoke softly, now standing nearby. "I am sorry," the small elf glanced over her shoulder, "but Vecnor is not well."

Merssa looked to Vecnor. The large man sat against the wall with eyes shut.

The blue glow then grew brighter and the air began to stir. Merssa turned to where the orb rested and saw it begin to pulsate with a white light. The room grew colder and was suddenly filled with a torrent of rushing air—the Wind of the Dead.

"No!" Poluran's eyes grew wide as he scrambled to his feet, and he brought down Clanghorr, heedless of the protest shouted by Selanna.

There was an explosion and the room went dark.

CHAPTER 11

No Way Out

It felt as though thousands of shards of glass had washed over Merssa's body, but she could not tell if they had scored any serious wounds in the wake of the burning pain of the demon's attack. In the darkness that engulfed the room, Merssa did not even know if she was bleeding. Then came Selanna's light, rising slowly to the ceiling.

Poluran lay upside down within an adjacent corner from where he had struck the orb, and nothing remained to show the sphere had ever existed, not even a single piece of glass. The dwarf's entire body was covered in frost and he rolled over, shivering. The rest of the company possessed several small scratches in addition to any wounds the demon had inflicted.

"We best be on our way," Selanna said, the small cuts decorating the left side of the elf's face. "I felt a great surge of power when the orb shattered, and it will not go unnoticed by its creator. We must depart before it is too late."

Merssa gazed at Dellen's lifeless face. Why had he done that? She was prepared to die fighting for Cafior, but she could not fathom sacrificing one life for another. There was no point to it. And now the thing she had done or not done to make Dellen act so foolishly had led to his death, and there was nothing she could do to change it. Why? It almost made Merssa want to weep, but she could not give in to weakness.

Merssa winced as she rose to her feet, reminded of the wounds she had sustained. Her shoulder was moist where the demon's claw penetrated her armor and the left side of her body burned from the fire—she hated to think of what would have happened had she caught the full blast. Turning to Vecnor, she saw the warrior still seated against the wall and his eyes were half shut.

Upon reaching Vecnor's side, Merssa found all exposed skin scratched up, as he had obviously made no attempts to shield himself from the shower of glass. But it was the wound in Vecnor's side that concerned Merssa; it was deep and much blood had been lost. Fishing through her pack, she produced a silver vial identical to the one she had used to cure Dellen of the ghoul wounds after the river attack.

"Drink this," Merssa instructed Vecnor, and while he did so she shook her head. "I'm sorry," she whispered. "I was not prepared for this. I…" Her gaze fell to the floor.

"His death is not on you," Vecnor said with some effort. "No one here was ready for such a fight."

Merssa glanced at the large man, not wholly agreeing with his words. It was her duty to be prepared. And she was not speaking only of Dellen's death, but of everything: Neja, the swamp, Hezeb. Merssa gazed at Dellen; the captain that would never return home. What a waste.

"The elixir would work better if you could rest a bit," she told Vecnor, "but Selanna informs me that is not possible."

The pain in Merssa's shoulder made her want to scream as she helped the large man to his feet, but she held it within. Already color was returning to Vecnor's face and his wound was beginning to close. His small scratches had disappeared entirely.

"I'll recover," Vecnor said with a bit of strain. "But what about you?"

Merssa followed his gaze to where her armor was blackened and her exposed skin blistered, and from the way his eyes widened upon seeing her face… She dared not think of what the fire had done there. Then Vecnor's attention fell to where blood seeped from the armor of her slumped shoulder.

"I'll be fine." Merssa attempted to sound strong, but she could detect the tremble in her own voice. She possessed no more healing waters and her supply of herbs and dry bandages was exhausted. She had no choice but to bear it.

To the rear of the chamber, Eraim was placing a blanket over Poluran's shoulders. The dwarf stared hard at the floor.

"Are you able to move?" Eraim asked.

"It's all my fault," Poluran mumbled without raising his head. "Why did I touch that blasted thing? I don't even remember doing it. I only —"

"Now is not the time." Eraim was blunt, impressing Merssa. But then the elf moved to pity. "Look, we came to bring an end to the Wind. Somehow, I believe one of us would have touched it. There was no avoiding the battle with Hezeb. Besides that, Dellen chose his fate."

"Perhaps." Poluran's expression held little consolation.

Dellen chose his fate. The words echoed in Merssa's head. She was not accustomed to Eraim speaking with such wisdom, and they were words Merssa would have to remember. It was not her fault. Blame would have to lay with the foolish guardsman.

"We must go!" Selanna stood near the stairs, her voice urgent.

Merssa joined the mage and detected a faint howl. It was not the call of wolves or the like, but an inhuman wail, as one in pain. Many answering howls followed.

"The ghouls are coming," Selanna warned.

"And from the sounds of them," added Eraim, now standing next to them, "there are hundreds."

"Go," Merssa told the elves. "We're right behind you."

Selanna took one last look at the room before addressing her small, glowing sphere. "Stay."

The elves hurried up the steps, and the light remained behind.

Merssa turned to see Vecnor stepping next to Poluran. The dwarf stood near Dellen's body with tear-filled eyes.

"I hate to leave him in such a place." Poluran sniffed.

Vecnor lifted Dellen with some effort. "Get his hammer."

While Poluran lifted the weapon, Merssa headed up the stairs, her body fighting her with every step. The more she moved, however, the easier it became and she picked up the pace slightly.

Upon entering the dark library, Merssa followed the distant light of the candles to the other side of the room, and there caught up with the elves. Eraim stood with sword ready while Selanna was stuffing a few books into a sack. Merssa did not have the strength to demand to know what the mage was doing, so she grabbed a candle and stepped through the mirror-door, unwilling to look at her reflection while she crossed the bedroom.

Merssa limped down the hallway and the howling grew louder, but as soon as she entered the front room it stopped. The black door remained closed and the room was empty. Merssa heard the others moving down the hallway to join her, so she went to the front door and opened it. Her jaw dropped and her breathing halted while she gazed upon the sea of ghouls standing perfectly still within the marsh. Eraim said there were hundreds, but if not for the fog, Merssa was sure she would have seen thousands. Dark eyes glared with hatred, and with a shrill cry from the middle of the pack, the creatures advanced.

Merssa slammed the door and turned back to the room. From the faces of the company, she knew them to have viewed the horrid sight.

"Barricade the door!" she ordered, for the moment forgetting about her injuries and rushing to one end of the tattered couch.

"I will take care of this," said Selanna. The mage chanted a few words and the door took on a brief green glow. "That will hold them for a little while."

Seconds later the door rattled, as if something had struck it. It rattled again, and then came scratching and pounding, as the ghouls attempted to gain access.

"We must find a way out!" Eraim seemed on the border of hysteria.

"What's it matter?" Poluran scowled. "Even if we found another way, how would we ever survive? Did you not see the army awaiting us?"

"The boat!" Eraim looked at the dwarf. "If we can make it to the boat, we have a chance."

Selanna started for the door Eraim claimed led to a dining chamber, another sphere of light appearing above the mage's head. "Follow me."

As soon as Selanna opened the iron-bound door, it fell from its hinges and crashed to the floor, inciting a curse from the mage's lips. With a sigh of frustration, she stepped over it and around a broken table before passing through another door.

Merssa worked hard to ignore the pain while she pursued the elves, and Poluran and Vecnor walked behind her. She was not sure what the mage was up to, but she was out of ideas and followed in silence. A brief curiosity crossed Merssa's mind while she walked through the dining room: why would a dining room exist? When she entered the kitchen, she found its existence equally puzzling. No one could possibly have ever lived here.

"Everyone stay back." Selanna gazed at the rear wall; the only bare wall within the room. "This place could use a back door."

Poluran looked to object as Selanna began to chant, but Merssa held out a hand to silence him. Selanna finished the incantation and threw her hands forward with fingers wide, and a green orb struck the wall with a resounding clap of thunder. Selanna was thrown from her feet, and Vecnor, still holding Dellen over one shoulder, caught the mage with his free arm and stumbled with a grunt. The spell did not leave even the slightest mark on the wall, and now Merssa's ears were ringing.

"This house is made of rorbak!" Poluran shouted.

Selanna stared at the dwarf, panting as Vecnor set her on her feet.

"Your spells can't harm it," Poluran said. "We're trapped!"

All was silent, with the exception of the distant scratching and pounding from the front room.

"At least we destroyed the orb," Merssa said with as much conviction as she could muster. She did not wish to die here, but what could they do? They could not defeat an army of ghouls, and she was in no condition to try.

Vecnor set Dellen on the floor. As he began to rise, he stopped, his gaze locked on the fireplace. "What about the hearth?"

"The hearth?" Merssa was confused. "Only Eraim can fit through it."

Poluran stared at Vecnor, eyes widening with hope. The dwarf raced into the large fireplace, unnecessarily ducking his head, and after a couple raps upon the back wall with his axe, he shouted, "It's brick! There's no rorbak here! Clanghorr can carve a path!"

Merssa's spirits lifted as she and the elves moved closer to see, and at that moment there came a crash from the front room.

"Clear the way." Selanna stepped before the hearth.

The elf repeated her previous spell while Poluran scrambled out of the fireplace. The green orb struck the back of the hearth and there was another explosion, this time of bricks shattering. The smokestack collapsed in a cloud of dust and muck, pouring into the kitchen and coating the company in yet another layer of filth. But now a hole existed to the outside, just atop the debris within the back of the fireplace.

"Go!" shouted Vecnor with a cough as he lifted Dellen.

Merssa pulled her mace and crawled over the bricks. The explosion had destroyed dozens of ghouls, but a few mangled corpses slowly rose and screamed blood-curdling alarms before she could silence them. Selanna and Eraim exited and ran immediately toward the river and Poluran followed, dragging Dellen's hammer. Vecnor crawled out last and pulled the guardsman's body through after.

Merssa turned to face the front of the cabin, where ghouls were rounding the corner, and she heard Vecnor draw his sword. "Get Dellen to the boat!" she ordered. "I'm right behind you."

Vecnor considered grabbing Merssa and running for the boat; she was in no condition to hold off an army of ghouls. Even he could not perform such a task, and his strength was nearly fully returned, thanks to the elixir Merssa had given him. But he hoisted Dellen over his shoulder to carry out the order, hesitating only when a pair of ghouls poked their heads through the hole in the cabin. Vecnor swiftly decapitated both with a single swing of his blade and glanced once more at Merssa. The paladin stood bravely before greater than a score of ghouls. The creatures were halted, seemingly held in check by the golden glow surrounding her mace. Vecnor bolted for the river.

Eraim and Selanna were already sliding the boat halfway onto the water when Vecnor arrived. It was a good-sized craft and he placed Dellen in the middle, but as the others moved to board, four ghouls emerged from the murky river and grabbed hold of the vessel.

"Has all the swamp's minions come to us?" shouted Eraim.

"We have no time for this!" Selanna's frustrations had reached a level unseen by Vecnor.

Vecnor looked back to see a legion of ghouls pursuing Merssa through the fog. The paladin was not moving very fast, but she was able to remain ahead of the awkward gait of the undead. Selanna spoke in a thunderous voice and Vecnor returned his attention to the river in time to see the ghouls there burst into flames. The undead shrieked and submerged, but every time a limb resurfaced it remained alight. He wondered if the fire continued to burn beneath the water.

Merssa arrived, about twenty yards ahead of the charging ghouls. "Everyone in!" she commanded.

Vecnor steadied the boat while the company climbed aboard. Poluran and Eraim sat in the middle near Dellen and Selanna stood at the head. Merssa sat toward the rear, where Vecnor boarded as he pushed off.

"There are no oars!" Merssa looked frantically about the craft. "Where are the blasted oars?"

"Leave all to me." Selanna was suddenly calm.

Vecnor watched the charging undead reach the riverbank while the mage recited her spell. Selanna then blew softly and the boat began to move, as if the sails had caught a sudden wind, but the air remained stale and there existed no sails upon the craft. Ghouls screamed in outrage and some jumped into the water to give pursuit, but the boat picked up speed and the cries were swallowed by the marsh.

The boat drifted southward, and the mage's unblinking eyes shone yellow while she stared into the fog ahead. Vecnor knew not what Selanna could see that he could not, and he was not sure he wanted to. Though his hearing fell short of that of the elves', even he detected the passing hisses of angry ghouls as the creatures failed to impede their progress. They followed House River for many miles until reaching West Branch, and there Selanna fell hard onto her seat and her eyes dimmed. The boat came to a halt.

"Which way now?" Poluran turned to Merssa.

"We could head back to Stony," Merssa said to Vecnor. "And from there make our way up Squire River to King Arman."

Vecnor shook his head. "That would lead us back into the heart of the marsh. Besides that, Olinin's map showed nothing of the eastern side. We have no idea what twists exist there."

"Alas, I do not think I could take us that far," Selanna said as she began to sway.

Eraim moved quickly to steady the mage. There had been no food or rest in some time, and Vecnor was sure the power Selanna expended in the battle against Hezeb, destroying the chimney, and guiding the boat had exhausted her beyond all others of the company.

"Are you all right?" Merssa asked the mage.

"A bit dizzy," Selanna admitted. "I will be fine."

A thought occurred to Vecnor. "Tall Pines is only a few miles away. That would be the quickest way out of this place."

"It is a dangerous woodland," warned Poluran. "But I suppose I'd rather face the forest than this bog, given the choice. That is, as long as the ghouls don't follow us."

"If they pursue," said Eraim, "at least the battleground will be fairer. Besides, my feet long for dry ground. Any dry ground!"

"As do mine." Poluran nodded. "And for that I'd definitely risk the forest."

Merssa turned to Selanna. "Have you enough strength for that?"

Selanna nodded and stood again. With a deep breath, the mage's eyes lit up and the boat headed west.

Vecnor kept his ears alert to the surroundings, but his focus was upon Merssa. The paladin sat, intently watching the swamp with mace ready while the boat raced along, but he was sure her strength would not hold. Even within the fog he could see Merssa's face was drained of all color. Vecnor hoped at least the bleeding of her wounds had stopped, but the small gathering of blood beneath her proved that hope to be futile. Merssa would not last much longer if they did not rest soon.

Nothing opposed them while they glided across the water. Soon the fog thinned and scattered silhouettes of trees were everywhere, much larger than those of the swamp. The river expanded, flooding the woodland floor, and the tall forms moved in on the company, resembling evergreens without any needles. Many disappeared into the mist upon trunks greater than five feet in diameter while others were bent over, gazing wickedly upon the boat or twisted in frozen cries of anguish.

Eraim eyed the trees with pity. "The poor things are forced to feed off Sistama's waters."

The air became fairer, and Vecnor was suddenly aware of how used to the swamp's chill he had become. The others must have felt the same, for all shivering eased, with the exception of Poluran's—the dwarf still exhibited frost over portions of his body. The fog continued to grow lighter, becoming a normal mist, and the welcome sound of insects greeted them. Vecnor did not even mind when the critters buzzed close by, for it made the world seem normal again, but the pests wanted no part of them, save for a few adventurous flies.

The river narrowed again and Selanna slowed to maneuver about the many rocks that now lined the way. A menacing tree moaned and lunged into their path, and Selanna would have been cast into the water when she halted the boat had Eraim not pulled the mage down. The tree sent a wave over the company and the water was cool, though it seemed warm after the venture through the swamp. Vecnor also realized the river to be free of slime.

"Sistama is angry with us," Eraim said. "It must have some control yet over the trees."

The comment almost seemed to bring color back to Merssa's face, even if only to roll her eyes.

Selanna rose and steered them to the southern bank. There, Vecnor stepped into the water and pulled the boat ashore. He lifted Dellen while Poluran grabbed the large hammer, and Eraim gave Selanna a shoulder to lean on as the elves exited the craft followed by Merssa. The ground was moist but firm, and a warm welcome to the muck of the marsh.

"There's no time to rest," Vecnor said as the others started falling to a knee or searching for a dry place to sit. "Not yet. We must get away from the river."

Though he desperately wished to stop, they needed to put a little distance behind them in case the ghouls pursued. Merssa reluctantly nodded and the company followed him in single file as he headed south.

Soon the ground was completely dry, and after half a mile the mangled trees gave way to healthy firs. Some trunks reached almost ten feet in diameter and rose to greater than sixty feet in height—still dwarves compared to the pines within the middle of the woodland that gave the forest its name. A bit farther and the air cleared as the sun shone through wide gaps between the trees. Until that moment, Vecnor would have thought it to be nearer to dusk, but it was only a few hours past noon.

Vecnor located a bright grassy spot and halted, breathing deeply and thawing his limbs beneath the summer sun. Even Poluran seemed to find comfort, though the dwarf still shivered a bit and frost somehow clung to his facial hair. The songs of birds warmed Vecnor's heart and brought a small smile to Eraim, and at last the swamp felt far behind. No ghouls would come here, not beneath the sunlight. Vecnor turned to Merssa and nodded.

"We'll take a short break," Merssa said, her face extremely pale.

"Perhaps we should tend to your wounds," Vecnor suggested.

"I have no more herbs." Her voice was lacking in strength.

"We'll just have to clean you up as best we can, then." Vecnor offered the best smile he could muster.

While Poluran assisted Merssa with removing her breast plate, Vecnor went through his pack and pulled the driest shirts he could find before tearing them into strips. He gave his waterskin a shake... It was almost empty. Though he preferred to find fresh water, there was no time and he carefully cleaned her wounds as best he could, emptying his waterskin, as well as Eraim's. The area where the demon's claw had struck the paladin was gruesome, but as luck would have it the creature's fire had cauterized the wound almost completely. Merssa winced while Vecnor tended to it, but said nothing, and he used the cloth strips to dress it. For Merssa's burns, there was nothing to be done. It seemed half her body was blackened or red and blisters were plentiful. Vecnor shook his head.

"You did well." Merssa failed to produce a convincing smile. "As well as could be expected. I will not slow us down."

Vecnor gave a wry smile. He was not worried in the least of Merssa slowing them down. He would carry her all the way to Palidur if need be.

"We should get moving," Merssa said, wincing as she rose to her feet. Her brain was obviously functioning normally.

Vecnor nodded and turned to Eraim and Selanna. They had evidently heard the paladin's words, for Eraim was already assisting Selanna to stand. He lifted Dellen's body and they continued south.

The forest opened up, sporting lush vegetation and rocks of various sizes. Animals were heard, consisting mostly of birds, but nothing was seen, and with the arrival of dusk, they stopped within a small clearing. While Eraim and Poluran gathered wood, Selanna slumped next to a tree, her head bowed, and Merssa lowered herself gingerly onto the ground. Vecnor set Dellen nearby and kept watch on the paladin and mage.

"We're having ourselves a fire tonight!" Poluran boasted, returning with three times as much wood as Eraim carried.

While the dwarf worked on lighting the fire, the others went through their packs. They discarded all items ruined by the marsh, which was everything for most of them, including the packs themselves. As darkness moved in, the blazing campfire provided relief from a cool breeze that reminded them of their wet clothing. Vecnor added more wood to the fire and all but Selanna crept closer—the mage had not moved since they stopped.

Poluran stared into the dancing flames, gazing occasionally toward Dellen's body. "Do you think the ghouls will pursue now that the sun has gone?"

"They're relentless trackers," said Merssa, the blistered side of her face turned away from the fire. "If they do, they'll march all night. I only hope the boat ride has afforded us time enough to rest."

"At least we will be able to smell them coming." Eraim gave a wry smile.

"Don't be so sure." Vecnor poked at the fire with a long stick. "Our own odor is just as bad."

"What about the creatures of the forest?" posed Poluran. "Even if the ghouls fail to catch us, we still have them to deal with."

Vecnor released the smallest of chuckles. It was a concern he had heard expressed many times throughout his life. "You live under the fears of ancient times, when the likes of ogres and wolves roamed the forest. But it was a dragon that kept people out in days of old, and now its spirit does so as well. I've been through this woodland many times. Most the ogres moved on to live in Benasti Forest, and the ones that remain won't venture near the swamp. The wolves, however, are as much a threat now as ever. They'll take food wherever they find it, but I doubt they'd be interested in us in our condition."

"Let's be thankful for that, at least." Poluran's eyes shifted about the bushes, as if searching for hidden canines.

Under Merssa's orders, Vecnor took the first watch for the night, but that was as far as he carried out her instructions. He woke no one when the time came for the second or third shifts, choosing to guard the entire night. He could tell by the way they twitched and tossed that their dreams were haunted, but any rest was better than none.

Come morning, Vecnor and Poluran gathered rocks into a large pile. They then positioned Dellen with hammer from feet to chest and built a cairn upon him. With heads bowed, Merssa said a prayer to Cafior and the company said their goodbyes.

They headed south in silence. Merssa walked beside Vecnor, keeping up well considering the pain she surely endured, and Vecnor slowed his pace to make certain she would last the day — only slightly, so Merssa would not notice. Selanna still had not spoken a word, but the elf's color was returning.

"How long do you figure we'll be in this forest?" inquired Merssa as the sun began its descent.

"If my guess as to our location is correct," Vecnor replied, "we'll clear the trees by sundown. But we should keep walking through the night if you're able."

"I'm able."

Merssa's tone left no room for argument. By the way she moved, Vecnor guessed her body had gone numb some time ago. After a minute she spoke again

"Have you ever faced anything…?"

"Never." Vecnor sighed. "I've fought many battles. I've faced great evils. I have even taken on creatures of the Underworld on occasion. But Hezeb… That was a first. I'll bet Selanna only knew of its name from her studies."

Merssa nodded and said nothing more.

The highlight of the day was an encounter with a small brook running from right to left. It was no more than a few feet wide and only inches deep, but they drank from it and washed themselves as best they could before filling their skins. Only Merssa showed no joy, but she cleaned her wounds and redressed them with more of Vecnor's torn shirts.

The shadows of the trees lengthened, and Poluran seemed dismayed to learn they were not stopping to camp. Soon after, the trees gave way to rolling fields of lavender wild flowers, appearing almost black in the fading light. A warm breeze swept across their faces and Vecnor paused to enjoy a deep rush of fragrant air. Selanna closed her eyes and tilted her head back as the wind attempted to move her dirty hair without success, but then her eyes snapped open.

"Food!" Selanna gazed to the southeast. It was the first word she had spoken since the boat.

"I smell it too!" Eraim was filled with glee.

Vecnor found it pleasant to see Eraim smile. He knew not how the elf maintained her beauty, even with the sludge streaks still decorating parts of her face.

"It must be Sikilaville!" Eraim's excitement grew. "It is ten leagues north of Salenti!"

Poluran inhaled deeply. "Ah! My left arm for a hearty feast and ale!"

Vecnor doubted the dwarf smelled anything but imagination.

"Dry clothes and a warm bed," added Eraim.

"Perhaps we can attain some horses." Merssa spoke in her businesslike tone. "We must return to Tikken City at once."

Eraim and Selanna took the lead, following the scent like wolves on the hunt. The fields were overgrown with tall grass and weeds nearly three feet in height, but the dry blades were preferable to the touch of the horrid plant growths of the marsh. After almost a mile, they reached the top of a hill and halted.

The moon was nearly full in the clear night sky and a few stars peeked here and there. Behind the company, the towers of Tall Pines were distant, dark shadows, while to the south the land rolled as far as the eye could see. Nestled at the bottom of the hill was a large village.

Vecnor detected the aroma of food, and music and merriment carried to his ears. Most the commotion seemed concentrated to the western end of town, where lights were abundant, and Eraim and Selanna immediately started toward them. They happened upon a hunting path sharing the direction they sought and followed it to a tavern at the edge of the village. Several patrons stood outside the establishment, enjoying tankards and singing and dancing, and a shingle above the door read TRAPPER'S INN.

Merssa was relieved to have finally made it back to civilization—any civilization. She might have even welcomed the sight of Eastgate... Maybe. Her breaths were growing shallow and her lungs began to burn. She needed food and rest, but more importantly she needed a horse with which to return to Palidur. If her wounds were to overcome her, she needed to complete her mission first.

"Do we have anything to purchase food with?" Poluran asked, checking his belt where his pouch once existed. It must have come off somewhere in the swamp.

Merssa sighed. She had not thought about finances. Checking her pouch, she shook her head. "I have some. But not enough for horses."

"Do not worry yourselves." Eraim smiled. "I will take care of it."

Merssa shot the elf a sharp, accusatory glance.

"I did not say I was going to steal anything!" Eraim held mock offense, pulling a pouch from a concealed location beneath her filthy clothing. The elf poured the contents into her hand, revealing many small sapphires and emeralds that sparkled in the moonlight. "I always keep a little something, just in case." Eraim returned the gems to the pouch and tucked it away.

"Bless you, elf!" roared Poluran. "I could kiss you!"

It was, perhaps, the first time Merssa had seen Eraim exhibit an expression without a hint of beauty. But it did not last long.

"We could buy a whole wagon of kegs!" The dwarf was starry eyed.

"Let's just get some food and beds for the night," Vecnor suggested. "Before we collapse."

They proceeded toward the tavern, and the merriment on the street halted as all attention fell upon the company, still covered with the filth of the swamp — as well as the stench. The locals parted before the grim face of Vecnor, holding their collective breaths while he led the way into the tavern without a word.

The room was packed, but jaws dropped, the music stopped, and the tavern fell deathly silent. A tall, thin man in a brown apron pushed through the crowd, waving a hand before his face as he neared the company.

"Whew!" The man turned and yelled over his shoulder. "Prack! Get the water heating!" He extended a hand, braving the odor, and Vecnor accepted it with a firm shake. "Name's Wirth. We have baths and whatever else you find need for. But come! Let's get you from this room. No sense ruining the celebration."

They followed Wirth from the tavern to the adjoining inn, and at the end of a long corridor filled with many doors, Wirth pulled a ring of keys and unlocked the final door. Beyond was a private lounge filled with comfortable chairs and a large fireplace, and all about the walls hung the heads of many successful hunting trips. Before the hearth was the pelt of a large bear, golden in color, and two smaller doors were on the back wall.

"Do not sit! I beg you!" Wirth spoke to Poluran, who had been approaching one of the over-stuffed chairs. "That is, at least not until you've had a good cleaning and change of clothes. Prack is heating the water as we speak. Are there any immediate needs?"

"Clean bandages would be appreciated," Merssa replied.

"Food and ale," Poluran added.

"Very good." Wirth viewed Merssa, his eyes filled with concern.

"Prack shall fetch suitable bandages, and food will be ready once you've washed up."

"What are you celebrating?" asked Selanna. "If you do not mind me asking."

"Why, the end of the evil wind, of course." Wirth's smile faded slightly. "Haven't you heard? Every couple days or so, that awful wind plagued our land. But yesterday was different. About the time it normally arrived, all we felt was a cold breeze, lasting a second at most. And today there has been no sign of it. Everyone is quite excited." Though Wirth's tone was one of joy, a hint of doubt showed in his eyes.

"You do not feel as the others?" Selanna posed.

Wirth's smile dropped altogether. "Let me just say," he rubbed his chin as he gazed at the trophies with pride, "I once led a more exciting life. I have trod where most men would never dare. I have seen…" he glanced at Merssa, "and smelled things no one should ever have to. It is no mystery the direction from where the wind had come, nor is it a mystery to me where you have been. And from the looks on your faces, I would guess the end of the wind is not the end, but the beginning of something we do not yet understand." Wirth cleared his throat and smiled broadly again. "But enough. Let's not ruin this joyous evening for the simple folk of Sikilaville…not to mention the extra business it brings my way." His last comment was made in a hushed voice. "Prack should be along any moment now." Wirth opened the door. "If you think of anything else you require, let him know when he arrives. You'll be undisturbed, I'll see to that. Mind the furniture." He directed the last comment toward Poluran before exiting.

The room remained silent; all heads downcast in thought. Then a knock fell upon the door and it swung open. Standing there was a short round man. He was not so large as Larman and a simple look was in his eyes.

"Masters." The man spoke with a mouth full of saliva and bowed. "I am Prack, your humble servant. If you will please follow me."

Prack led them back up the corridor and opened the last door on the left. Beyond were two more doors within a short hall, one to either side.

"Gentlemens to the left, womens to the right." A bit of spittle escaped while Prack spoke. "You'll find towels and garments in the bathing chambers. I hopes they fit. I have an eye for such things."

Selanna and Eraim thanked Prack, and they all reported to their proper rooms.

Two of the baths were full of steaming water and the elves immediately disrobed and entered them. Merssa was relieved to find the third tub contained lukewarm water, and further impressed that healing herbs had been provided, though they were nowhere near the quality she was used to.

Merssa cared for her wounds as best she could. The burns covered her left side, nearly from head to toe, and several areas exhibited infection and were warm to the touch—the muck and journey through the forest had done nothing to improve her condition, and she would need to tend to her injuries further when better supplies were available. Merssa's thoughts were interrupted by a sudden silence and she looked at the elves, who quickly turned away and began speaking quietly to each other again. Yes. She must surely appear horrible.

They took extra time to wash away the filth of the marsh, Merssa dabbing herself as delicately as possible, and once they had finished, or rather the water had become too filthy, they dried off and dressed in the clothing provided.

Merssa shook her head at the drab garb meant for her, a commoner's brown tunic and leggings, but she thought better of complaining. Her own garments would not do, and all others she had packed for the journey were destroyed.

Selanna and Eraim found their apparel amusing. Selanna's was not much more than a white tunic with a rope belt, and Eraim's was obviously an outfit for a young boy. It lightened Merssa's heart to see the elves' sense of humor return, as the two could not stop giggling while they dressed. Her mood darkened again when she painfully donned the tunic and leggings.

Upon seeing Vecnor and Poluran, the elves burst into laughter — evidently Sikilaville was not accustomed to fitting warriors of their unique sizes. Vecnor could only fasten a couple buttons near his waistline, revealing his muscular chest, and he looked to split the seams of his trousers at any moment. To accommodate Poluran's girth, the dwarf was provided pants and a shirt for a robust human — Prack's own garments, Merssa thought — and he had to do a lot of rolling of the sleeves and leggings to get them to fit. But at least the bath seemed to have finally expelled his shivers.

Prack, who had been waiting outside the doors like a loyal sentry, smiled upon seeing them exit, but then he scratched his head, not realizing the target of the elves' laughter. So he laughed along.

The servant led them back to the private chamber, and it was obvious the festivities within the tavern were still going strong. Merssa could not help but think it foolish to allow them to believe the evil was defeated, but she had not the time or strength to educate them.

"They'll be going all night," Prack informed them. "I hopes it don't disturb you."

Merssa almost laughed at the comment. She planned on collapsing the moment she finished eating.

Inside the private room, the hearth was blazing and there was a spread to feed ten men set upon a table that had not been there earlier. Merssa saw venison, beef, chicken, corn, beans, cheese, butter, and more; and to drink there were a few choices of wine, four pitchers of dark ale and beer, and a small flask containing brandy, according to Prack.

"If you runs out of food," Prack said, "I can brings more."

"This is more than enough," Merssa assured him.

"Let's not be too hasty, woman!" Poluran rubbed his hands with delight.

Merssa chose to ignore the manner in which the dwarf had

addressed her. It would take too much energy to teach him proper etiquette, and even if she made the attempt, he probably would not understand.

"Do you requires anything else?" the servant asked.

"Some rags and oil," said Poluran. "Don't need anything rusting on us," he explained to the others.

"If at all possible," Merssa added, "we need five horses. Prepped and ready to depart come morning."

"I'll sees what I can do." Prack handed Merssa two keys. "These are for the outer door and bedroom doors." He pointed to the two smaller doors. "Good evening to all." He left.

"Before we begin," Merssa gained the company's attention, just as Poluran opened his mouth wide to accept a piece of meat, "I would like to raise a cup to Dellen."

Eraim poured everyone a glass of wine and Merssa continued.

"May he forever sit at the feet of Cafior in the halls of His Blessed Realm."

"Here! Here!"

They drank deeply from their goblets.

Merssa almost felt embarrassed to be awakened by a knock on her door. She could tell the hour must be nearing ten. The last time she recalled sleeping that late was as a child, when her mother had to rouse her for breakfast in preparation for the lessons of the day ahead. Selanna and Eraim had been asleep as well, but were now fully alert. Merssa rose, feeling stiffer than the previous night, and exited the room, trying her best to show none of the pain she felt.

Within the lounge was Prack and a few barmaids, the latter bearing trays of breakfast. The other bedroom door opened and Vecnor stepped through, followed shortly by Poluran. The dwarf's face was not yet fully awake.

They were treated to eggs, bacon, sausage, oatmeal, and fresh bread along with breakfast wine, coffee, and milk. Merssa thought it the best food she had ever tasted, but perhaps the past few days made it seem so.

After eating, they donned their armor and weapons. Though the task was extremely painful, Merssa was relieved to cover up the peasant clothing, and her armor shone silver and her mace gold—Poluran had been thorough in his polishing, and not a trace of the marsh was evident. Selanna's robe was beyond cleaning and Eraim chose not to keep her spotty leather armor, so the elves continued to proudly display the clothing provided by Prack. Eraim even requested a boy's hat the previous night, and the elf had her hair tucked up into it to complete the look. Prack beamed with pride while he led them to the tavern.

The room was full, but with the exception of Selanna and Eraim, the company received only glances, as most likely no one recognized them as the filthy arrivals from the previous night. Outside, Merssa noticed Wirth arguing with a man covered in dirt and she headed for the door.

"And see how I treat *you* in the future!" the innkeeper yelled as Merssa and her companions exited the building.

The dirty man walked away, brushing Wirth off with a wave.

"Ready to go, I see," Wirth said, his tone lightening as he smiled at the company's approach. He then addressed the elves. "And looking quite lovely without that garbage all over you."

"All loaded," another man said to the innkeeper, holding the reins of three horses laden with packs.

"I've supplied you with plenty of food." Wirth's expression moved to disappointment. "I'm afraid three horses were all I could gather, alas. I do apologize."

"Nonsense!" Selanna smiled at the innkeeper. "You have been more than hospitable. We greatly appreciate all you have done."

"Yes," Merssa said. "I never knew how generous folks of these parts could be." She nodded to Eraim, and the elf extended the pouch of jewels.

"That's quite unnecessary." Wirth pushed it away. "I wish you safe journey and luck on whatever road lies ahead."

"Please," Merssa said. "You've given us much with nothing in return."

"Believe me," Wirth lowered his voice, "I do well enough. I consider myself privileged to have served you."

"Thank you." Eraim gave him as big a hug as her short arms allowed.

Wirth blushed. "A hug from a maiden so fair is reward beyond gold!"

They bade Wirth and Prack farewell, with many more thanks, and mounted up. Vecnor rode alone and the elves shared a horse, leaving Merssa to double up with Poluran. She was less than enthusiastic about the arrangement, but Vecnor was much too large to share a horse with anyone. At least she would not have to walk to Tikken City, she supposed.

"How much did you give him?" Selanna inquired of Eraim after the horses had walked a short distance.

The small elf smiled. "Much more than these horses could ever be worth."

"We've a seven-day ride ahead," Vecnor informed Merssa.

"We'll make it in six."

Vecnor smiled and the elves giggled.

Merssa shook her head. She would never understand how they found things so funny all the time. Launching her horse down the street, she nearly threw Poluran from the saddle. The others followed and Sikilaville quickly faded into the hills.

The road was clear and the weather pleasant. They traveled throughout the days, breaking only when the horses needed it, and continued well into the nights before stopping to rest. Selanna knew it was a hard pace, but she posed no objection. The horses were fresh, so they would be all right, and Merssa's coloring did not appear to be worsening, which surprised Selanna after witnessing the paladin's wounds in the bath. Besides that, Selanna desired to return to Tikken City just as much as Merssa, and from the lack of complaining, the others probably felt the same. When they did stop for camp, the rests were short and they picked up with the first hint of light. Selanna did not sleep much, using these times to read from the tomes she procured from the library within the cabin. They were fascinating, disturbing, and confusing all at once, and she had to read slowly to try and understand all she could.

They skirted Salenti Forest on the second day, and though Sistama lay more than forty miles to the north, beyond all sight, Selanna could feel its chill. Eraim, Selanna noticed, kept gazing longingly at the forest, no doubt yearning to slip into the trees and return home.

The next few days came and went, and still they did not see a ghoul, zombie, skeleton, or even a traveler. While the sun dipped low on the fifth day, Korban Bridge stood to the left, proud as ever in the waning light, but even Poluran did not view it the same. The great white stones were now reminiscent of the ageless house of the marsh; the tomb that almost was their own. Selanna felt pity for the dwarf, wondering if he would ever gaze upon it with prideful eyes again.

That evening the horses began to falter and Eraim expressed concern for their wellbeing. So Merssa called for camp earlier than usual, stopping a few miles west of King Arman and less than a day from Tikken City. Dinner was quiet, though pleasant, and they settled in for some sleep.

Selanna paced about during her shift to guard, becoming alarmed when the night grew unusually dark. Her attention lifted skyward as rolling storm clouds engulfed the stars and moon, and the fire flickered within a cool breeze until it failed altogether and everything went black. Then something caught her eye: a blue light twinkling in the distant north. Staring hard, Selanna spotted a bowed figure upon Korban Bridge. It was fully cloaked in shadow, but somehow she saw it perfectly. The hood rose slowly and she stood paralyzed, for beneath it was a skull, and in its right eye shone the blue light that had grabbed her attention. The skull opened its mouth and released a howling wind that blew ice cold upon her skin…

Selanna awoke with a start. She was lying upon one of the tomes she had been studying. The fire still burned, the moon and stars were very much visible, and only a few clouds decorated the sky. Gazing to the northwest, Korban Bridge was well beyond sight.

"Do you hear something?" Merssa sat upon a flat boulder, just outside the firelight.

"No." Selanna rose and joined the paladin, almost feeling foolish. "I hear nothing."

Merssa loosened the grip on her mace. "What stirs a mage from rest, then?"

"Time will tell." Selanna sighed, gazing at the stars. "It was a dream. While I was guarding, I saw a skeletal figure upon Korban Bridge."

Merssa gave a small chuckle. "*You* were on *guard* duty? It must have been a nightmare!"

"Why Merssa Goldmace," Selanna teased, "did you make fun?"

Merssa's smile faded and the *paladin* returned, gazing into the quiet night. "Relax. It was only a dream."

Selanna drew in a deep breath. "Perhaps, Goldmace. But in any case, I really should return to my *guard* detail." She smiled and walked back to lie on her blanket.

The next day their pace quickened without protest—Selanna was sure everyone could feel the city drawing nearer. As noon came and went, people were seen working in fields, and lunch was an event unknown to the company as they pressed on. The air grew hot through the early afternoon hours, but cooled off when the sun rolled toward the west, reflecting off the buildings of Tikken City less than a mile away.

They neared the city and the gates opened and horns sounded, no doubt to alert the Council as to the company's arrival. Citizens glanced their way and some gathered to see what the commotion was about. Many cheered Vecnor and there were some that waved to Merssa, obviously recognizing her to be a Palidurian Knight, but no one knew where they had been or what they had seen, and it was probably for the best. After the company passed through the open gates of the Council Building, servants rushed to take their horses and usher them inside.

Chapter 12

Council of Trannum

The servants saw the company to private rooms to allow them to clean from the road and don fresh clothing. At Merssa's request she was brought healing herbs from the Council's personal gardens—some of her injuries had begun to ooze and she had taken on a slight fever—and she tended to the wounds immediately. The burns and scabs were dreadful, but she was confident they would heal now that they had been properly treated. She washed up before dressing in appropriate attire she had left behind… When was it? A couple weeks ago? She could not quite recall. Anyway, it did not matter. Her attention went to her armor. Normally Merssa would not think of reporting to the wizards without it, but the thought of putting it on made her head swim, especially after days of the metal constantly scraping against her skin while she rode. With a sigh, she left it behind.

A servant awaited in the hallway to escort Merssa to the audience chamber, and Selanna and Eraim were with him. Eraim was dressed in a long green tunic with brown hose and a brown belt and Selanna wore a Council robe—it was good to see them properly attired again. But earlier Merssa heard the elves give implicit instructions for their Prack-clothes to be cleaned and returned at once… She would never understand those two.

They arrived to the chamber, and the members of the Council were seated before the enormous half-circle window displaying King Arman Lake. The long shadows of the city stretched onto the water, highlighted red by the setting sun, but the attention of the Council was focused on Poluran, sitting in one of five chairs placed before the wizards and eating noisily from a bowl. Merssa took the seat farthest from the dwarf and Selanna and Eraim sat next to her, leaving one chair vacant. Eraim glanced about, a bit concerned.

"Have you seen Vecnor?" Eraim posed to Merssa.

Merssa shook her head, now curious herself. But nothing more was said of the matter, for Seac raised a hand to begin the meeting and Mordan led the servants from the room. Concern was deeply etched upon the Seer's face.

"I have heard that Dellen did not return," Seac said.

"Please," Merssa attempted to hide her discomfort while rising to her feet. "Allow me to tell our tale in full. Then you shall hear of Dellen's fate and all else we've uncovered."

"Of course." Seac leaned back in his large chair. "Proceed, Merssa Goldmace."

Merssa began by speaking of the undead along the shore of King Arman Lake, and the possible increased effect of additional winds upon the zombies. She then spoke about the skeletons on Korban Bridge, as well as their meeting with Poluran—the dwarf placed his bowl upon the floor, stood, and bowed, his eyes shifting nervously from wizard to wizard. Merssa said very little of Eastgate, other than pointing out that Karlsum was a useless prop to hold up a crown and keep a throne warm, and mentioned nothing of Cafdella. She spoke of Olinin, followed by their trek through the marsh, and felt anger when describing the battle with Hezeb, followed by sorrow with the telling of Dellen's demise. She concluded with the name Trannum and the destruction of the orb. To her left, she detected Selanna's fidgeting, no doubt wanting to add to the story, but Merssa left no openings for the elf, and upon finishing her tale she sat.

The Council had listened with no signs of emotion, their unblinking eyes focused upon Merssa, and only Seac seemed the least bit upset with the death of the Captain of the Guard. The room was then silent until Seac spoke.

"Thus far it has been very much the way the Scrolls tell it. We have indeed found what we believe to be the remainder of the prophecy." The Seer pulled four rolled pieces of parchment from within his robes and read them aloud.

> *"Power of five, united by one,*
> *Forth on journey, defy the sun.*
> *Summer tastes winter, darkness draws near,*
> *Sleeping do wake 'neath shadow of fear.*
>
> *"From edge of old, bond does break,*
> *At last revealed, One all did forsake.*
> *Evil long subdued, the One long sought.*
> *Centuries pass, power hard bought.*
>
> *"Alas! the One that Evil brings,*
> *Takes the lands, takes the kings.*
> *Forces gather, dark secrets unknown.*
> *Death march begins from One's throne.*
> *Under sunless sky, o'er blanket of cold,*
> *Fall of strength by treacheries unfold.*
> *Dark power grows, living join through death.*
> *By might of Lords, Hallowed Land is wrest.*
>
> *"Many a hero, born to die.*
> *Trial of time, the battles cry.*
> *Companies four, to take the test,*
> *Set forth on perilous quest.*
> *Seek to end at dark throne,*
> *Might and strength of Evil Bone.*
> *Power shatters, dust does fall.*
> *Eyes open in shadowy hall."*

Seac read with perfect continuity, unrolling each scroll in turn and handing them to the wizard on his left. Once finished, he addressed the company.

"The first Scroll, which you've heard before, speaks of the Wind of the Dead."

"And Trannum must be the One," Selanna said, much to the chagrin of several Council members by the looks on their faces. "He is the writer of the many books we saw, and I believe him to be undead, himself; the Evil Bone, as the prophecy says. It was he that cursed Olinin and summoned Hezeb; a feat he accomplished without even being there."

"And he must be the creator of the orb," Eraim added, "for he referred to it as his '*toy*' when speaking to Olinin."

"He'll have to do without his toy now." Poluran patted Clanghorr.

"I believe I saw him as well," Selanna said. "Though I do not claim to be a seer, I had a vision in my dreams last night, of a skeletal figure upon Korban Bridge. It was robed in —"

"Black," Seac finished for the elf, "with a blue light shining from the right eye."

"Yes." Selanna's brow furrowed.

"About the time you claim Poluran to have destroyed the orb," the Seer explained, "I had a vision of my own. I saw the figure you speak of, doubled over as if in dire pain. I was not sure what it meant, or why it came to me when it did. Perhaps I know now."

"But who *is* Trannum?" Merssa asked. "You are the Council of Wizards. Surely someone here must know something of that name."

After a moment of silent stares from the wizards, one of the entry doors swung open and Mordan stepped inside.

"Please forgive me, masters." The steward bowed. "He insisted I grant him immediate audience."

"Who?" Seac demanded with obvious impatience.

As the other door swung open on its own, Mordan answered. "Master Elgarroth Sandanari of Vermallon."

Standing in the doorway was an elf dressed in white robes. His hood was down, revealing long white hair tucked behind pointed ears, and large green eyes shone bright upon his chiseled face. He was only slightly taller than Eraim and appeared no older, and his physical presence seemed no more threatening than that of a child's. But Merssa knew better. Though she had never actually met Elgarroth, stories from reputable sources warned her so. And now that she had seen him, she understood why many in Palidur considered it odd for Elgarroth to be counted among Vermallon elves, for his physical features were obviously that of the Salenti clan. Elgarroth was constantly shrouded in mystery and considered hard to approach, and for this reason Palidur bore no trust for him, feeling the elf must surely be hiding something.

Selanna and Eraim stood and bowed as the wizard neared. The Council bowed heads from their seats, but irritation was evident on most their faces. Poluran remained seated, apparently unsure of how to act. Merssa stood tall.

"What brings you, Elgarroth of Vermallon?" Seac posed.

"All of you." The elf waved his hand in a wide arc. "I thought, perhaps, I might be of some assistance."

"Indeed, you may." Though Seac's face showed annoyance, his eyes held relief, perhaps due to the rumor that the elf wizard possessed more knowledge about Vaeldor lore than any other living being. "Tell us what you know of the name Trannum."

Elgarroth stepped into the center of the semicircle of thrones, a perplexed look upon the elf's face. "Why do you ask?"

Merssa sighed. She had heard that getting a direct answer from the elf wizard tended to prove difficult. After only just meeting Elgarroth, she had no doubt the rumor was true.

"We found tomes within a cabin deep inside Sistama," Selanna said. "They were written by Trannum in Ancient Moclen."

"Trannum?" Elgarroth mused, looking at Selanna. "He was…a necromancer and a researcher." Elgarroth directed his gaze back to the Council. "He headed the research into the might and power of the Ancient Enemy of the North… Uustaag the Dark."

At the mention of the name, many faces within the room went

pale. There was still an extraordinary number of folks outside Palidur that feared saying it aloud, though there no longer existed any that lived in the days when the evil warlord reigned. Uustaag was a krukari, skilled in the arts of combat and dark magic, and it was said he sold his soul to the vilest of all evil deities, Thard'Dun. Uustaag was responsible for the largest gathering of evil beings and conquered much of Vaeldor, until his undoing in the legendary Battle of Balgorn, when the forces of Palidur cast him into Balgorn River. The water took on a reddish appearance that day, said to be the Blood of Uustaag, and was thereafter called Blood River. The body was never found and there existed many, especially among the elves, that believed his spirit still lurked about the desolate lands north of the Stone Eagle Mountains.

"Please." Seac held up his hand. "We do not speak that name here."

"My apologies." Elgarroth bowed. "Trannum, as I said, was a necromancer. He studied the dead, both those that fell at the hands of…" Elgarroth paused, choosing his next words, "the Enemy…and those in league with him, in hopes of determining where the warlord found his power. This was necessary to make sure such an evil was never again brought to be. But that was a very long time ago. Over four centuries before that of your city's reckoning, if I have my dates correct."

"And what became of this research?" posed the Seer.

Elgarroth stared at Seac. "The research was never completed. Trannum disappeared and was never heard from again, as history tells it."

"Nevertheless," Selanna said, "he has survived all these years, in one form or another."

Selanna went on to speak of the cabin and all they encountered within, the elf's version varying only slightly from Merssa's. Elgarroth listened intently, but nothing seemed surprising or shocking to him.

"So, you believe Trannum to have become a creature of his own studies?" Elgarroth raised a brow. "A walking corpse?"

"And this we have determined without your help." The wizard to Seac's right did nothing to conceal his contempt, catching Merssa by surprise, as the other members rarely spoke. "And now is the time to act."

"Act upon what?" Merssa was instantly annoyed. Other than the name Trannum and the reading of the Scrolls, there was no information to act *on*.

"You see," the Seer explained, flashing a disapproving glance toward his colleague, "when a magical item is crafted, it is filled with energy from its creator. Energy that cannot be reclaimed if that item is destroyed."

"What are you saying?" Merssa demanded.

Selanna perked up with sudden understanding. "He is weakened! That is why you saw him in pain."

Seac nodded.

"Perhaps." Elgarroth appeared a bit troubled. "But how long this condition will last is not certain. It depends on how much of his power was contained within the orb."

"It was very powerful," said Eraim. "Perhaps he did not survive its destruction."

"That would be most unlikely." Elgarroth offered a fatherly smile.

"How much power could he possibly still possess?" Poluran posed. "If I understand you wizards and elves rightly, he must have surely been destroyed. That was the most powerful trinket I have ever come across, save for Clanghorr." The dwarf patted his axe.

"Though I do not expect all here to understand," Elgarroth said, though Merssa was sure he meant her, "it is not likely he placed all his power within a single item, and thus, he will not be fully drained by its destruction."

"But he and the item would have been linked," Seac added, "and the shock of the loss will no doubt hinder him for weeks, perhaps months. That is why it is vitally important he be sought immediately and without delay."

"But where shall we find him?" Merssa was growing impatient with the contest of magical knowledge between wizards.

"That, unfortunately, is where the problem lies," said the Seer.

Elgarroth stared at Merssa, as if considering, and then he sighed. "From all you have said, you may already know the answer. Weariness, perhaps, clouds your mind."

The statement was almost enough to move Merssa to anger. She assumed the mysterious wizard would provide some useful information, but she had been mistaken. She had every intention of voicing her frustrations when a thought occurred to her. "The house!" All eyes turned Merssa's way. "Poluran. What did you call that white stone?"

"Rorbak." The dwarf was happy to contribute. "The toughest bones in all of Vaeldor. Why, the Mighty Korban—"

"Yes, yes." Merssa was unwilling to listen to yet another pointless story. "You said it's not used anymore."

"No." Poluran shook his head sadly. "The area where it was harvested became cursed long before my days and we had to forsake it. Not even my great-great-great-grandfather had ever laid eyes upon the raw stock. It's—"

"But yet, the house is made of this rorbak." Merssa halted the dwarf's story yet again, turning to the Council. "The stone must have come from the place Poluran speaks of."

"Perhaps it is Trannum that cursed the area," suggested Selanna. "To keep the dwarves away. Perhaps *that* is where he resides."

Merssa sighed. It was a weak assumption, but what else did they have? She turned to Poluran. "Where is this rorbak? Do you know?"

Poluran shrugged. "Only in legend. But I do know where the Forbidden Area lies."

"Will you take me there?"

The dwarf nodded. "I will see this unto its end. Besides, I have always desired to see rorbak in its true form."

"How far is it from here?" Merssa asked.

Poluran scratched his nose in thought. "I would have to say at least two weeks, as humans travel." He was oblivious to any insult issued.

Merssa turned to the Council. "We must depart immediately. We'll need fresh horses and gear."

"Perhaps you should depart in the morning," suggested Seac. "The day is already spent, and I do not think your wounds have had ample time to heal."

Behind the Seer, the window revealed the moon's reflection upon the water. Merssa considered her company. Though their faces were determined, they could not hide their weariness, and suddenly she felt the sting of her own wounds again. Her shoulders slumped in surrender and she addressed the Council.

"Very well. We shall rest tonight. But mind you, I wish to leave before the sun touches the King." Merssa turned to her companions. "Any of the current company willing to join me at that time are welcome."

To this Selanna, Eraim, and Poluran nodded. Selanna then addressed the Seer.

"What of the remainder of the prophecy? Do you know what it all means?"

"We are working on that," said Seac. "At the moment, we are most curious as to the *power of five*."

Eraim gasped. "What if Trannum is only one of five?"

"Let us first deal with what we know," the Seer suggested, "and not get caught up in all the possible interpretations. For now, I think it best you get some rest. It appears you have a long journey ahead."

Seac nodded to the doors, and they opened as Mordan entered.

"Please escort our guests to their quarters," the Seer said. "Be sure they have all they require."

The steward bowed, and Merssa and her company followed him from the chamber.

Upon reaching her room, Merssa was pleasantly surprised to find a vial resting upon her nightstand. It was from Palidur, identical to the ones she had administered in the Silent Marsh to Dellen and Vecnor. She could not help but smile and breathe a sigh of relief.

Seac noticed Elgarroth had remained within the chamber after Merssa's company departed. The elf wizard smiled, as if awaiting a question. Sure, Seac had plenty of questions for the *timeless* wizard, and many more were uttered silently between Council members, enough to cloud Seac's mind. He commanded for silence in his head to end the chatter and he addressed the elf.

"If Trannum was a researcher, as you claim, then why have none of us heard of him? Surely there would exist *some* report on the dark subject he pursued. But I've not heard of any such matters in all the libraries I have visited."

"The answer to that question, I cannot say." Elgarroth spread his hands, as if he had nothing to hide. "I have shared with you all I can of the name Trannum."

"All that you can?" Seac raised a brow. "Or all that you will?" The elf was surely withholding something.

Elgarroth smiled. "It is enough to know what he was and what he did with his life. That is a good place to start." The elf approached the doors, pausing as he reached them. "And perhaps it would be wise to never underestimate the unknown. But I shall look into this matter further." He left.

Seac gazed at the door as it closed. He knew the game, providing just enough information to keep others motivated. The Council had to play it all too often when dealing with lords and kings. Seac did not appreciate being one of the players, but at the moment, what choice did he have?

"There will not be any rest until we make some sense of the Scrolls," Seac said to the other wizards.

Selanna awaited Elgarroth within the corridor. She was surprised with his arrival, for she had never seen him outside his Vermallon home, and she was sure there to be something he had yet to tell her. He was, after all, her mentor.

She recalled when Elgarroth had taken her on as a pupil, a bit more than fifty years ago. Selanna had made the journey to Vermallon to seek him out, even though Elgarroth knew not who she was, and it only took her a month of pestering him until he agreed to the arrangement. Elgarroth imparted much knowledge, sharing secrets of the land and ways of ancient times, and taught to her spells long forgotten. Selanna loved him as a father, feeling at complete ease in his presence, and for this reason much of her Salenti kin considered her queer. But it was all worth it.

"Master," Selanna said in the elfish tongue with a smile as Elgarroth exited the audience chamber. "It gives me great hope that you are here."

Elgarroth returned the smile. "Walk with me."

He led her through the front doors of the building, and while in the presence of the great wizard, Selanna noticed the servants normally charged with keeping an eye on her maintained a greater distance, giving her and Elgarroth almost complete privacy. Stars dotted the sky about the aging moon and a cool breeze drifted across the lake, and they strolled along the vast flower gardens covering the northern half of the courtyard.

"You are certain it is Trannum you seek?" Elgarroth asked at last.

"I found many books," Selanna replied. "A few of them I took, but I have not had sufficient time to read them, since they are in Ancient Moclen. I have looked into them a little, and what I have learned is most disturbing. And then there is the house. It is certainly the place where he conducted his research, otherwise the books would not be there. And the ghouls…" Selanna was mortified by the memories. "He was a necromancer, so you say, and there is much undead about the area. But surely he could not have created all those ghouls by himself. And what of the Wind? I cannot fathom the power *that* must have required. Surely it must have taken several wizards to perform such a feat. The prophecy does speak of the *power of five*."

"Indeed." Elgarroth gazed upon the flowers. Most had closed for the evening, but their aroma prevailed into the night. "He possessed the power to create undead, though he rarely used it. He preferred to speak with corpses, and animated them only when they would not obey him otherwise, for zombies were more susceptible to his will. That is one reason why he was chosen to take on the burden of the research, the other being that his power was unmatched. To delve so closely to such a strong and evil energy would spoil those of lesser ability, and they would surely succumb to it."

"Perhaps *he* was not strong enough," Selanna suggested.

"If he was not," Elgarroth raised his brow, "then I know of no one that was." After a moment, he added, "Still, strange things occurred after he began his work." Elgarroth gazed off to the northwest. "Sistama was once called *Gothnelli*."

"Gothnelli?" Selanna was confused by his use of the elfish word for hunting ground.

"It was not always as you see it today," Elgarroth explained. "Once, decent folk lived within its borders. It provided all anyone could need for survival. But that was another time."

"Did you know it before its transformation?" Selanna attempted to gain a clue as to his true age.

Elgarroth left her question unanswered. "Trannum conducted his studies there. He felt it was a safe distance from the Enemy's fortress and it provided seclusion. But the swamp grew dark a few years later and he was never seen nor heard from again. If the evil indeed overcame him, perhaps it was he that corrupted the marsh, causing all that lived there to succumb to his will…as ghouls!"

"Was he that powerful?" Selanna was astonished. "Could he change an entire swamp to become…what it has become? Was he capable of transforming all those poor souls into ghouls?"

Elgarroth offered a small smile and shook his head. "I do not believe so. At least, not when his research began. But who knows what he uncovered? I always suspected he met an untimely end, and it often worried me that he and his work were never discovered. On occasion I looked into Sistama, in hopes of uncovering some clue as to what befell him and Gothnelli. But alas, the swamp is dark and treacherous, and nothing could be found. I only wish I had known Olinin."

"*You* ventured into Sistama, master?"

"I did not say that."

"Oh." Selanna knew he would offer no more information in that direction, so she returned to the topic at hand. "Why was there no investigation when the marsh darkened? Why was not an army sent? Did they not worry of what became of the necromancer or the swamp's inhabitants?"

"You have many questions." Elgarroth gave a wry smile. "But what you must remember is that Trannum's studies followed the greatest war of Vaeldor; greater even than the Dragon Wars. There were no armies left to march or soldiers willing to risk their lives. The war was over and peace was accepted. Inhabitants of the area knew the marsh befell some unknown evil and assumed it took Trannum with it. And since the darkness seemed to haunt only those venturing too near, the swamp was left alone. Of course, now is a different matter."

"You do not believe Trannum is weakened at all, do you?" Selanna asked.

"You best get some rest." He placed a fatherly hand upon her shoulder, as if her question had not been spoken. "You shall be in need of strength, and I sense you are not quite yourself."

Selanna sighed. "My powers are not yet fully regained. Sistama took almost all I possess. Using magic there was like running in water." Looking to her mentor, she asked, "Will I see you tomorrow?"

"I do not know." Elgarroth gazed at the night sky. "I need to look into some things."

Selanna smiled, knowing she would get no better answer. As she turned to leave, she stopped. "You know, one day I shall be as powerful as you," she said, as she always did when they were about to part.

Elgarroth smiled. "Take care of yourself."

Selanna walked the corridors leading back to her chamber, and all the while she thought about their conversation. Some of it made sense and some of it did not — a typical meeting with the great wizard. But one thing she knew: eventually it would all make sense. She had known Elgarroth long enough to realize that.

She arrived to her room and found Eraim awake. Upon the nightstand rested an open journal, a jar of ink, and a quill, still wet. Selanna glanced at the most recent entry and saw that Eraim had written down the prophecy read by Seac, word for word. Selanna often wondered why her friend insisted on documenting even the smallest excursions from Salenti Forest, especially when Eraim seemed to remember everything she had ever seen, heard, or read.

"There is no returning to Dominelli before we depart, is there?" Eraim's face showed she already knew the answer. "I do miss the trees."

"As do I." Selanna offered a halfhearted smile before blowing out the single candle illuminating the room.

"At least we might retrieve Lilli and Dandi from Cafdella," Eraim said with a bit more energy. "I miss them terribly as well."

"That would be nice." Selanna was still distracted by Elgarroth's words. "Let us get some rest."

Chapter 13

Back Again

The following morning, Merssa sat within the dining hall, her half-eaten breakfast before her. Though the elixir from Palidur had sealed her wounds and reduced her burns to mere pink blotches that carried no pain, her appetite was lacking. Selanna and Eraim sat across from Merssa, equally disinterested in the meal, but Poluran had cleaned his plate at least twice already. With the exception of the dwarf's mannerisms, the hall was quiet.

Merssa gazed through a large round window revealing fading stars with the brightening sky. She expected to have received word from the Council, something new to report about their research on the matter of Trannum, but there had been nothing. Even the conversation with Mordan had borne no fruit.

"The masters are quite busy with their arduous task, and wish you well on your journey," the steward had informed Merssa after she inquired.

"What about Master Elgarroth?" Selanna asked Mordan.

"And Vecnor?" added Eraim.

"I have not seen them since yesterday," Mordan replied. "And neither was provided a room for the night."

The elves seemed disappointed, but not surprised, and the expressions had yet to leave their faces.

"Let's go." Merssa could waste no more time awaiting further assistance from the wizards.

A servant escorted them to the stables, where three horses and a mule awaited. The saddlebags bulged with supplies and there were two canteens per animal, as well as plenty of ropes, spikes, warm cloaks, blankets, and other gear for mountain travel.

"I cannot wait to see Lilli!" A glimmer of joy lightened Eraim's face. She wore a brand-new leather jacket, perfectly fitted—how could the elf have procured one so quickly?

"I doubt we'll have time." Merssa checked on the horse she was to ride. "Poluran informs me we need to venture to the far side of Neja. Routing through Cafdella would add a couple days to the journey, and that is not time we have to spare."

Eraim's shoulders slumped and she emitted a small sigh.

Poluran's eyes moved to pity. "Take heart, little one. We shall see our beasts again."

"Lilli is not a beast!" Eraim frowned. "And why would you wish to reunite with Melballa? You do nothing but complain about her. It is a wonder she has not run away."

"She understands me," Poluran explained, at which point Eraim's face changed to one of humor.

A large shadow appeared within the stables, and Merssa knew right away it could only belong to Vecnor.

"Where have you been?" She was both annoyed with the warrior's absence and relieved with his sudden reappearance.

"Tending to affairs." Vecnor stepped forward, revealing his presence to the others. Behind him was another horse, ready to ride.

"Well, you were almost left behind." Merssa mounted. More likely he had been visiting taverns.

"I am glad you are still with us," said Eraim, her face showing obvious relief.

"I couldn't leave Umbarc to the care of others for too long." Vecnor gave the small elf a wink.

"For longer than you think," muttered Eraim, her bottom lip sticking out.

"We depart now." Merssa began toward the gate. The last thing she needed was an argument with Vecnor over retrieving a horse.

They rode while most the city slept, and when the gates of Tikken City shut behind them no one looked back. The morning was cool, but soon the sun climbed over King Arman and brought back the heat of summer, now half over. As the day wore on, they saw more and more travelers upon the road, perhaps on their way to Tikken City for the day's market. Some smiled and nodded in greeting while others went quietly about their business.

Dusk neared as they reached Korban Bridge, and a brief flashback of Poluran combating skeletons crossed Merssa's mind. As the horses' hooves echoed off the stone, she gazed at Squire River. The water floated lazily from the direction of the Silent Marsh, the swamp lying miles away and beyond even the elves' sight, but it appeared as clean as a fresh mountain stream. Poluran paused to pay respects to the white bridge and bowed his head, but his eyes lacked the gleam they once exhibited, when Merssa had first met him.

They stopped in Rivercross for the night, and Eraim secured rooms at an inn she and Selanna recommended. Merssa and the elves turned in, but Vecnor expressed a desire to visit the common room for a drink and Poluran eagerly joined him.

Poluran followed his large companion into a crowded tavern. His tongue was primed for good ale, but he knew he would have to settle for whatever brew the likes of humans could muster. It was not too bad, and while Vecnor consumed a couple tankards of beer, Poluran downed three mugs and lit his long pipe. Neither of them spoke; they were content to watch the guests unwind from the day's toils. The patrons were enjoying life. It seemed they would rather forget the whole ordeal of the undead than live in fear of it. Poluran did not blame them. He wished he could forget as well.

"Vecnor!" a man sneered as he pushed his way through the room. "Is that you, you *dog*?"

Approaching was a homely man with many scars upon his face. He stood over six feet with short black hair that looked as though he had cut it himself with a dull knife, and his long nose was crooked, probably having been broken several times. A snarl was upon his thin lips while he glared and his hand rested upon the pommel of an impressive sword.

"I got a score to settle with you!" the stranger announced as a hush captured the crowd. The man slammed his tankard onto the table, spilling half its contents and splattering some onto Poluran's face. "Nobody buys me a drink and leaves before I can return the gesture!" The man extended his arm with a grin and the room breathed a collective sigh of relief.

"Vikur." Vecnor stood and grasped the man's arm. "It's been a while."

"Been years," Vikur corrected. "Too long, by me. And look at you, not a day older. How is that fair?"

"What brings you this way?" Vecnor asked.

"If I were to wager on it," Vikur scratched his stubbly chin, "I'd say the same thing that has you sitting here at this very moment." He grabbed a nearby chair from a patron who had just stood to reach for an item across the table, and paid no heed to the complaints that ensued when the man sat onto the floor.

"Poluran," Vecnor said, "this is Vikur, Lord of Ironside Keep and the richest man I know."

"Ironside Keep?" Poluran wiped the droplets of beer from his face, trying to appear unimpressed. In truth he was a bit shocked, for Ironside Keep and its line of lords were well respected among Varlimor dwarves, who led in its construction several centuries before. Poluran, himself, had enjoyed a few excursions into the keep's tavern more than fifty years ago with his Morimont cousins. But the loud-mouthed man before him did not seem worthy of respect. "The ale is a good brew there," was the only pleasantry he could think of to say.

"I buy it from Morimont!" Vikur laughed, slapping Poluran hard upon the back, and though he appeared thin, he exhibited much strength. "By the size of you, I'd say you're from Bornibur."

"*Rornibur*," Poluran corrected, but Vikur did not seem to notice.

"Have you traveled with Vecnor long?" Vikur asked, but he did not wait for an answer before speaking again. "He and I go way back. Nearly fifteen years to my recollection." Vikur gleamed with excitement. "When we were back to back, nothing could stop us!"

Vecnor gave a wry smile.

"Why, there was one time we took on two score of goblins by ourselves!" the man continued. "That was a battle to behold!"

Visions of ghouls and Hezeb passed through Poluran's mind. He was not impressed.

"Oh!" Vikur looked back across the tavern room. "I almost forgot my little brother." He bellowed in a voice to carry a hundred yards, "Arkor! Over here!"

A man began working his way toward them, standing a head shorter than Vikur and bearing no resemblance to suggest a relationship existed. The man's dark hair was neatly trimmed to his shoulders and he possessed piercing blue eyes—actually quite comely, as humans went, except for the frown upon his face. In his right hand he held a tankard, and in place of his left hand was a black hook.

"Arkor!" Vikur said. "You know Vecnor. And this is Polermin."

"Polu-*ran*!" Poluran snorted.

"Yes." Vikur chuckled. "Find a chair and join us."

Arkor saw no open chairs. But unlike Vikur, he placed his tankard on the table and went to the other side of the tavern to procure one. Poluran already preferred Arkor to the older brother.

"How are things back home?" Vecnor asked.

"Not well." Vikur's face became stone. "The cold winds blew right through the pass. Next thing I know, there's noises coming from the crypt. I called Arkor, figuring it to be thieves, but boy was I surprised to find the entire bloodline returning to claim the throne! We had to destroy every last one of them, including my father." Vikur looked away and turned back with a maniacal grin as Arkor returned. "I finally got even with the bastard for leaving me the keep and ruining my life! How I miss the battle!"

"Such a position should be considered an honor," Poluran informed Vikur. "Perhaps you should give lordship to your brother if you're not worthy."

"No thanks," said Arkor in a deep voice. "That is one thing my brother and I have in common. Neither of us wishes to be tied to that place. Besides, tradition claims the eldest." Arkor gave a sideways glance toward his brother.

"And you don't mess with tradition!" Vikur said mockingly. "Don't get me wrong, it's quite a living. I've more gold than I could spend in ten lifetimes. But I do miss the rush of a good fight!"

"After clearing out the crypt," Arkor added to the report while his brother seemed to revel in thought, "we dispatched several undead wandering the pass. Then I headed into Sardina to see what I could find out, but by the time I reached Charndova the wind returned."

"And so," Vikur spoke over his brother, "I decided to look into it personally. My brother and me, that is. It's been a confusing trail, though." He shook his head. "The wind came out of the southwest, but villages around Palidur claim it came from due north. And here in Rivercross it blew from the northwest. It has been impossible to track down its source."

Vecnor seemed intrigued. Poluran found it a bit confusing. The Wind hit Ironside Keep from the southwest?

"The gatekeeper of Palidur told me Merssa sailed to Tikken City and had been gone a week," Vikur continued, "so I says to my brother, 'I'll bet she's searching for the source, and I bet Vecnor's with her.' Now, knowing you couldn't possibly survive without my blade, I decided to head to Tikken City. And here you are! Saving me a day's travel."

"I've seen Vecnor fight." Poluran raised a brow. "And I doubt your sword is as good as your tongue."

Vikur laughed heartily and slapped Poluran on the back again. "I like you, Ponerman!"

"Poluran," Poluran grumbled.

"We leave early tomorrow," Vecnor said with half a smirk. "If you wish to join us, I suggest you get some sleep. That's what I'm going to do." He rose and gave a slight bow. "Until tomorrow."

Vecnor walked from the table, leaving his mug almost full. Poluran snatched it and downed its contents, not wanting to leave a free drink for the braggart. He glared at Vikur a moment longer before following his companion.

Come morning, the company was treated to a large, hot breakfast. It did not escape Poluran that Eraim had handed a generous sized pouch to the sleepy innkeeper—he wondered just how many pouches were hidden upon the elf's tiny body—and now he and the others reaped the benefits. Knowing there was nothing between Rivercross and Eastgate with Ellaville devastated as it was, Poluran was very appreciative and left not one crumb of his fair share behind. Merssa then dropped her napkin onto her plate, signifying the meal was ended. Too bad. At least there had been no sign of Vikur.

"Guess your friend had a change of mind," Poluran said to Vecnor. "Probably scared."

"What friend?" Merssa was suddenly alert.

"They'll be along." Vecnor seemed confident. "Arkor is probably pushing his brother out the door at this very moment."

"Vikur…" Merssa sighed, shaking her head. "Well, I suppose his sword may come in handy, as well as his brother's. But he rides to the rear."

"Please!" Poluran raised a hand. "I've no need for his company there."

"Get used to it," Merssa said. "I can't concentrate with his constant babbling." She glared at Vecnor. "Keep him away from me."

Poluran did not understand why Merssa acted as though the rear of the travel order was considered a punishment. He had been there since the beginning of this adventure and it was an important job.

"I have often wondered how Arkor is doing," mentioned Selanna to Eraim.

"Yes." Eraim smirked. "I wonder how he has been getting along since…his arm."

"I wonder if he still blames me." Selanna grinned. "How was I to know that thing was still alive?"

"What happened to his arm?" Poluran inquired.

"Oh…nothing." Eraim shared a humorous look with the mage.

The brothers entered the tavern. Sleep was heavy on Vikur's face and his hair was uncombed, and he was dressed in a chain shirt and dusty brown cape. Arkor wore a dark suit of chain and black cape, and it was now evident that his left arm was missing from just below the elbow. Several straps held in place a wooden shaft with a groove running down the middle, and attached at the end was the black hook. A sword and knife were sheathed at his side and he carried a small quiver of arrows meant for a crossbow, but oddly enough there was not a crossbow to be seen. Contrary to his brother, Arkor was wide awake and ready for travel. His face, however, grimaced upon seeing the elves.

"Ah!" Vikur licked his lips. "Just what I need. A good breakfast."

"Breakfast is over." Merssa stood. "We're leaving."

Vikur smiled. "Of course! We must move out before that sun shows its ugly face. Let the journey begin!"

"It began over a week ago," Poluran grumbled.

They retrieved their horses from the stables, the Ironside brothers possessing regal mounts, and headed north along the barren road. Vecnor and Merssa led the way with Arkor close behind, and the elves rode a few paces back while Poluran and Vikur brought up the rear. The Lord of the Keep passed the time talking about his various scars and seemingly tracing the origin of each, but Poluran only half listened, still annoyed with the man's placement in rank. That evening, when Merssa announced Vikur was to share the final leg of the night watch with Poluran as well, Poluran felt he might explode.

To Poluran's surprise, the human quickly grew on him. About halfway through their guard shift, Vikur inquired as to Poluran's adventures and experiences, much to Poluran's delight, and he found the Ironside lord could listen as well as talk — that is, when you could get the man to stop talking.

On the following evening, Vikur spoke more of Ironside Keep, and Poluran could tell the man cared a great deal for the stronghold, regardless of previous words. Vikur had trained throughout his youth in preparation to rule over the mountain pass, and when that day seemed far off, he honed his skills battling bandits, goblins, and hobgoblins, as well as other evil beings that plagued the surrounding lands. But those fighting days came to an end when his father passed on, and like any seasoned warrior yet in his prime, Vikur longed for the battlefield. Vikur was fascinated with Clanghorr and shared his own blade, explaining it to be the ruling sword of Ironside, forged by dwarves of Varlimor when the stronghold was young. The weapon was exquisite, with excellent balance, and its edges showed much use. When Poluran offered to give it a good cleaning and sharpening, Vikur readily agreed.

Early on the third day since leaving Rivercross, the company came upon Ellaville. Dark windows gazed at them and signs of looting were apparent, as many additional doors and windows had been smashed since their last visit.

"This is where you found the innkeeper and his family?" Vikur asked Poluran.

Poluran nodded, pointing toward the tavern. "Right over there."

"I feel eyes upon us," Eraim alerted them in a hushed voice.

The company fell silent, and nothing made a sound other than the horses as they proceeded cautiously down the road. Poluran looked from side to side and was suddenly aware that Eraim was missing — Selanna held the reins of the elf's unencumbered beast. Strangely, no one else seemed to notice, or perhaps they did not care.

Poluran was also intrigued when Arkor extracted a small metal piece from a pouch and slid it into the end of the wooden arm. The one-armed man skillfully attached a cord to each end and pulled it taut onto a small hook before placing one of the arrows into the groove, converting the arm into a crossbow in less than a dozen seconds. It seemed to Poluran that he was the only one amazed with the efficiency in which Arkor operated, and he realized he was truly an outsider, as the others clearly had much experience working together. Poluran returned his attention to the quiet buildings to either side of the street.

As they reached the front of Larman's Brew, the voice of a man called out, halting their progress.

"Hello! My, don't you all look wealthy!"

It was definitely coming from the tavern, but there was nobody to be seen. Merssa started toward the building.

"I wouldn't go there if I were you," the voice warned, bringing her to a stop. "Take a look around."

A dozen archers showed themselves from atop the surrounding buildings.

"What do you want?" demanded Merssa.

"This is *our* village," the voice replied. "You have trespassed, and now you must pay. I'd say twenty gold each sounds fair."

"We could pay it," Vecnor said, earning himself a glare from Merssa.

Didn't the paladin realize there were more important matters at hand? Should they really waste time in a confrontation with mere thugs?

"I do not pay the ransom of bandits!" Merssa hissed. "Ever!"

"I think you'll feel differently," the voice said, obviously overhearing Merssa's words, and an arrow struck the ground very near to her horse.

"Get ready," Vikur whispered to Poluran. "And stay close."

Merssa nodded to Selanna and the mage raised her hands. Vecnor and the paladin then charged the tavern, leaping from their horses when they neared the porch, and Poluran followed Vikur, riding up beside Selanna as many arrows were released from above.

The missiles shattered upon an invisible barrier, and after the volley ended, Selanna lowered her hands. Arkor depressed a small rod now protruding beneath his wooden arm and his crossbow fired, dropping a bandit from a rooftop. Selanna launched two small green spheres, and a couple more bandits screamed as they were cast from sight.

From the tavern issued half a dozen warriors to meet Vecnor and Merssa. The large man and paladin handled them easily, Vecnor taking out four while Merssa dispatched the rest, and Poluran charged to give aid as eight more jumped through the large, broken windows and surrounded the two. But a loud whistle sounded and the bandits halted.

"Cease!" the voice from the tavern commanded. It no longer sounded smug, but a bit shaky. "Please accept…our deepest apologies. We have detained you good folk by mistake."

The bandits looked at one another in confusion.

"Stand down!" The voice was more forceful, and the thugs backed away.

Merssa, Vecnor, and Poluran slowly stepped from the porch, their eyes trained on the bandits before them.

"Let us depart," said Selanna. "Before our good fortune changes."

They mounted and rode quickly from the village. Eraim's saddle remained empty, and once they were a couple hundred yards away Selanna called for a halt. Moments later, Eraim came running down the road with Mithkahr in hand.

"What took so long?" Selanna asked while Eraim mounted. "A second more and they would have released another volley."

Eraim shrugged with a smile and sheathed her weapon. "He was on the second floor. I had to find which room he was hiding in. Next time we could trade places if you wish."

Selanna shook her head. "I will handle the magic. You do…what you do."

"I don't like leaving that scum behind to threaten other travelers." Merssa's face was filled with frustration.

"We have more pressing matters," Vecnor said. "Besides, the only travelers passing through here are either Nejan or on their way to Neja. I wouldn't think you'd mind."

Merssa sighed and urged her horse on, but Poluran was sure the paladin's face softened a bit; perhaps even showed the hint of a smirk.

The sun raced across the sky while Merssa pushed the horses much harder than the last time they traveled this stretch, and as night moved in, the Stony River came into view. Beyond the water the lights of Eastgate burned.

"Let's make straight for Larman's," Merssa said. "We'll get some food and rest and be on our way before the city awakens."

CHAPTER 14

LARMAN'S HAVEN

Larman's Haven proved even more popular since Merssa's last visit. Music was playing, patrons singing and dancing, and there was constant laughter. Larman served drinks with the broadest of smiles while Fellna tended bar and passed tankards to her sons, who scurried off to assist their father. The tavern reminded Merssa of Cafdella—a bright spot in a sea of darkness. It was not long before Larman spotted her company, and glee overcame the innkeeper as he rushed over.

"What joy!" Larman surprised Merssa with a giant embrace. "What great fate has befallen me this evening!" He released his grip and beamed at the faces before him. "My favorite paladin and company! But there are two I've not had the pleasure of meeting." Larman held up his hand as Vikur's mouth opened. "All in good time. We're full up, but I'm sure I can clear a table."

"No!" Merssa caught Larman's arm before he could disappear. "Perhaps a private room? If one is available? We need a meal and an early rise."

"I see." The innkeeper showed a bit of disappointment. "To be sure. Follow me."

Larman led them from the tavern and down a short corridor while he fiddled with a large ring of keys. He unlocked a door to the left side of the hall, revealing a private dining chamber. It appeared to have been prepped for nobles, as a decent-sized table was covered by a fine white linen and set with polished silver and crystal goblets.

"I take it there's a bit of that nasty business yet to attend to," Larman said after all had entered. He shook his head. "That's a shame. I told my loyal customers that it was you guys what put an end to the Wind, regardless of what Baron Karlsum claims."

"That swine!" grumbled Merssa under her breath. She could only imagine what stories the cad was telling.

"I shall have rooms ready once you've finished your meal," Larman said. "Kitchen's been closed for a short while, but I'm sure there's still hot food. I'll fetch it at once." He promptly exited.

"Is he a *close* friend of yours?" Vikur gave Merssa a wink.

Merssa ignored him while she removed her breastplate and made herself more comfortable. She then sat at the head of the table.

Larman's sons entered, toting four pitchers of ale and seven mugs. In a flash, the lads set them on the table and were gone. Moments later, before even Poluran could down his first mug, Larman returned with a couple large platters. They were covered with meat, vegetables, partial loaves of bread, and pieces of cheese—likely leftovers from the dinner crowd.

"Lots here for all!" The barman maintained his smile. "I'm afraid it's warm at best. But I did not wish to keep you waiting."

"Thank you, Larman," said Merssa. "This will be sufficient."

"Master Dellen did not return?" The innkeeper looked about the room. "Strange, but I didn't realize he was missing. I stacked some extra food with him in mind. He did love Fellna's cooking!"

"He's...not with us anymore." Merssa could think of no better way to phrase it. "He met an ill fate in the Silent Marsh."

"No!" Larman gasped in shock. "I am sorry. I didn't know."

"Do not worry yourself." Merssa hoped the innkeeper would leave it at that. She did not wish to relive the story one more time.

"So!" Larman clapped his hands together in an apparent attempt to lighten the mood. "Who have you brought into my fine establishment tonight?"

"This is Vikur and Arkor." Merssa waved a hand at the two. "Lords of Ironside Keep in the Varlimor Mountains."

"*I'm* the Lord of the Keep," Vikur voiced his correction, extending his arm. "Arkor is my little brother."

Arkor shook his head at the introduction.

"I am Larman." The innkeeper clasped arms with Vikur. "Is Ironside Keep near Tikken City?" he asked as he massaged his arm, Vikur having evidently given it a good squeeze.

Vikur gaped, his lips moving for several seconds without making a sound. "Good heavens, man!" he finally blurted. "It's more than two hundred fifty leagues from here! Amongst the mountains that separate Kalmaar and Marcove from all of Vaeldor!"

"My apologies," Larman said. "Those sound like splendid places. Truly. And it's always grand to see new faces." The innkeeper snapped his fingers and turned to Merssa. "That reminds me. Two days ago, a fellow was here asking about you folks. I told him I was a personal friend."

"Did he have a name?" Merssa raised a brow.

"Yes indeed," Larman replied, searching the ceiling for the answer. "A nice chap, he seemed. He has a room here at the inn. Paid a whole month in adv—"

"His name?" Merssa had very little patience to offer after spending days with Vikur.

"Pallit!" Larman raised a triumphant finger. "Pallit's the name. And he had your horses with him. I'd recognize that Umbarc and the lovely maidens' horses anywhere. Once you've ridden on one of those wonderful creatures, a regular horse could never seem so pleasant."

"This is splendid news!" Eraim bounced with excitement and gave Larman a hasty hug. "You must fetch him right away!"

"I'll notify him you've arrived." The innkeeper bowed and exited.

Merssa released a sigh. The exchange between the elf and barman had happened so quickly that there was no chance to question Larman further before he had gone.

Suddenly the only sound was that of Poluran's slurping and chewing—the dwarf had been eating all the while. The rest of the company filled their plates, lest they be deprived of supper altogether.

Only moments past before a knock fell on the door. Eraim opened it without delay, but the elf's excitement dwindled when she was faced with Bayn and Gruzim. The two bore somber looks and invited themselves into the room. Gruzim gazed briefly in Vecnor's direction, a slight sneer crossing the krukari's face.

"I thought I saw you enter," Bayn said with a large smile. "And I doubt you've returned for Eastgate's fine hospitality."

Merssa glared at them. She had not planned on ever seeing them again and she was in no mood. "What do you want?"

"A warrior from a village south of here brought us Olinin's body," Bayn replied, and there was a hint of pain in the marteese's voice as he shut the door. "We buried him."

"I'm sorry," Merssa said with as much feeling as she could muster. "But—"

"And from the way you rushed through the tavern," Bayn added, "I sensed there to be unfinished business. I must—" The marteese looked over his shoulder at Gruzim. "*We* must be allowed to assist you. I'm sure you don't welcome the likes of us, but Master Olinin was all the family I had. You must allow me to help bring justice to the ones responsible."

"And how do you expect to succeed where your master failed?" Merssa's question came out colder than she had intended, but since the marteese saw fit to interrupt her, she did not really care.

"I don't," Bayn admitted. "But I do expect to be of some use to you in your efforts. Gruzim is mighty and I am skilled with both the blade and magical arts."

Merssa hesitated while she thought on the matter. She caught Vecnor's disapproving glance, and normally she would have readily agreed with him. But the danger before them was unknown, and if the swamp was any indication of what to expect, she felt they could use a couple more hands. Besides, from Bayn's attitude, Merssa knew the marteese to be sincere, though she did not believe the krukari felt the same.

"We're in need of brave soldiers," she said at last. "But I warn you, we have seen dreadful things on the path of this evil, and have lost one companion already. I fear our way will darken further as we continue."

"We are ready." Bayn stood up straight. "We pledge ourselves to your service." He bowed.

Gruzim offered a snort.

Another knock came, and Eraim opened the door a crack to take a peek. The elf then became giddy and threw it open to reveal Larman and Pallit.

"We need a larger room." The innkeeper gazed at the new occupants.

"We'll be fine," Merssa said.

"Very good!" Larman smiled. "I must return to the tavern then. The missus must be going frantic! I shall send one of my boys with more drink. Will there be anything else?"

Vecnor waved Larman off while chewing on some meat and the innkeeper departed.

"Pallit!" Eraim gave the man a hug. "You brought my companion back to me!"

Pallit tried but failed to conceal his smile before the lovely elf. "Actually, it was Borse that sent me. He thought you might return this way."

Merssa wondered how the priest could possibly have known that.

"How is Borse?" Vecnor asked.

"He's troubled." Pallit frowned. "Once he received Olinin's body, he knew he must learn what he could, and he prayed over the wizard for almost an entire night, speaking to the corpse as if it were alive. He entered what looked like a trance and I left him to his work. When I returned later, he snapped free and uttered two words." Pallit stopped speaking and glanced about the room.

"And what were they?" demanded Merssa after what seemed an eternity of silence.

"Is it…all right to speak?" Pallit regarded the unfamiliar faces with distrust.

"It will have to be." Merssa had allowed the newcomers to join, so there was no point in excluding them.

Pallit nodded. "White stone."

"White stone," Poluran repeated, gazing blankly at the table. "Rorbak."

"Yes." Pallit nodded. "I thought of rorbak as well."

Poluran's shock was replaced by suspicion. "How do *you* know of rorbak?"

"I spent much time in the western parts of the Stone Eagles," Pallit explained. "I was one of the King's Rangers nearly four years ago. As some of you may know, the Stone Eagles are not a safe place. Many creatures lurk within, as well as outlaws. My squad patrolled the mountains north of Vol Maren, keeping the area safe from unfriendly beings. Many times I encountered dwarves, and they often assisted in vanquishing enemies of the people. But after a few years, they confided in me their true reason for venturing so far west of Rornibur. They quested for rorbak."

Though everyone listened intently, Poluran was absolutely enmeshed by every word.

"They explained that a curse surrounded the white stone," Pallit continued, "bringing death to any entering the Forbidden Area, and that they aimed to reclaim it from the evil spirits in the name of Rornibur. So I kept an eye out, and some days I left my patrol to join them, for I wished to return the help they had given over the years. Then, one day we found it... The white stone. So wondrous it was that even I marveled at it." Pallit shook his head, pained with the memory.

"They immediately began to mine the rock," Pallit glanced at Poluran, "but it was hard to work and night came swiftly, so we set up camp." He took in a deep breath and released it slowly. "Then the curse came upon us in the dark. Foul creatures emerged from the shadows. They appeared undead, but seemed intelligent and bore weapons. Their skin was a sickly yellow color and wrapped tightly about their bones, and their haunting eyes burned blue. The stench of death was about them, but they didn't smell at all like ghouls. We slew many, but their numbers were unyielding. Most the dwarves had fallen and I felt to collapse…" Pallit looked at Merssa. "That's when I first met Borse.

"Though I had heard of the hermit priest," Pallit returned his attention to all within the room, "I had never actually met him until that night. His voice came out of the darkness, and the longer he spoke the more powerful it became. Strength returned to me and the campfire grew brighter, revealing the enemy as well as Borse. He stood without fear and the creatures retreated beyond the rocks, dragging with them their dead to leave no evidence as to their existence. In the end," Pallit shook his head, "only two dwarves of the score I accompanied remained, and I've not seen them since." He turned to Merssa. "I left the king's service that day, after the power of Cafior touched me — no, enveloped me. I felt a new purpose in life, and I now serve Him by protecting and serving Borse."

Merssa viewed Pallit with doubt. "Borse couldn't destroy the creatures?" More proof the lanky man could not be a true priest of Cafior.

"He said the root of evil there was too strong," Pallit explained. "He healed our wounds and led us from that accursed place. Whether you choose to believe it or not, he is a great man."

Merssa gave a wry smile.

"Would you be able to find this place again?" Selanna asked Pallit. "The home of the rorbak?"

Merssa gave Selanna a sharp glance. "We have Poluran."

"Yes." Poluran nodded. "But Pallit has *been* there. Though I know of the general area, it is a good fifteen to twenty-mile span of climbing and searching. It could take months to find. Maybe longer."

Merssa stared at the dwarf, many comments racing through her mind. This was the sole reason she had brought him. Why hadn't he mentioned his incompetence before they left Tikken City?

"It is not a place I would ever care to see again," admitted Pallit, "but Borse requested that I assist you in any way you require. I am at your service." He bowed. "I'll be in the tavern come morning, if my company is acceptable." He exited the room.

"We must take our leave as well," said Bayn. "We will also await you in the tavern in the morning."

Bayn and Gruzim departed.

"I shall make sure Lilli and Dandi are well." Eraim headed for the door and Selanna joined her.

"Now there are ten of us," Merssa murmured.

"Perhaps it is for the best," Vecnor said quietly. "Though I feel much better about Pallit than I do the krukari."

"I have no more trust for him than you do." Merssa gazed at the door, as if Gruzim were still standing there.

Vecnor nodded. "I shall keep an eye on him."

"Let's see if Larman has our rooms ready." Merssa sighed. "I need some rest."

CHAPTER 15

HAUNTED STONE

The next morning, Larman awoke the company with plenty of time to eat, even by Merssa's standards, which impressed her. Vikur was visibly unpleased with the early hour, but once he inhaled deeply the smell of eggs and pastries, a smile came to his lips and all was well.

While the company ate, the innkeeper's boys fetched the horses and restocked all supplies, and as the sky brightened, Merssa pushed everyone to saddle up. Now that they had been reunited with their horses, the spares from Tikken City were given to Pallit, Bayn, and Gruzim, and one was made to carry most of the gear. The final mule was given to Larman as a gift, inciting many humble "not necessary" comments, but the innkeeper's eyes revealed extreme delight.

Before long, they departed for Vol Maren, capital city of Neja. The last thing Merssa wanted was to tour the realm of outlaws, but she had grown used to the fact that there was no choice. With any luck, it would not be necessary to hold audience with the king once they arrived. Merssa was not sure she could take one more criminal posing as royalty.

Merssa rode at the lead with Vecnor, and behind her were Selanna and Eraim and then Arkor. Next was Bayn, the marteese dressed in leather and possessing a simple sword, and beside him was Gruzim. The krukari wore a dirty chain shirt beneath a tattered blood-red cloak, and at his side was a large sword. More impressive than the blade, though, was the spear fastened to Gruzim's horse. The shaft was no less than eight feet in length and the long spearhead appeared to be sharpened along both edges, allowing it to be used as a slashing weapon as well as a piercing one. Though Bayn often whistled a merry tune while the company rode, Gruzim's brow was perpetually furrowed and the krukari stared blankly forward.

Poluran had requested Pallit's company in rank, and Merssa posed no objection—she had had every intention of placing the ranger with the dwarf and Vikur. While they rode, she often heard Poluran and Pallit conversing in the dwarfish language, which did not surprise her, but Merssa was impressed to hear Vikur speaking it fluently as well—she could not picture the Lord of the Keep learning how to spell his own name.

The day was dry and long and Merssa chose not to speak much, instead keeping an eye on the surroundings. The high mountains to the north seemed a pleasant visage, if you could forget where you were, but with the passing of the day, they lost their appeal and became nothing more than a wall to the right. The land grew harder as early evening approached, rising and falling often with sloping roads that pushed them farther south, and trees were almost non-existent while straw-like grass gave way to dry fields dotted with boulders of various sizes. It was a true wasteland.

"How can anyone live here?" Eraim said aloud, sharing Merssa's opinion.

"Hunting is very prosperous around these parts," Pallit answered matter-of-factly. "There are also many rivers and ponds for fishing. Then there's the granite. Nejan stone is in great demand by surrounding realms, and they pay handsomely for it. And there's always the mining. The mountains north of Vol Maren contain iron and crystal deposits of many sorts."

"Oh." Eraim's expression lacked conviction, eyeing the collection of large birds circling overhead.

Merssa thought the better question was: how could a wasteland exist so far north? The deserts she was aware of existed in the south of Vaeldor. She could think of only one other northern region sharing

Neja's quality, and that was Helmland, realm of Uustaag the Dark of old. More signs of how Neja's citizens had spoiled the land.

The road continued for two days before they encountered a village. Its citizens seemed unconcerned with the company's presence, and after a decent meal and a night of sleeping in beds, they returned to the road early the next morning. They happened upon a small hamlet a couple days later and the people were friendly and hospitable, even to Merssa. Either no one minded the presence of a paladin, or they did not know or recognize what Merssa was—she could only assume it was the latter.

On the fifth day since leaving Eastgate, the mountains became breathtaking. Where the clouds allowed, Merssa gazed upon peaks reaching heights to almost make her dizzy imagining the view they provided. As the day waned, the sun dipped low and reflected orange off the rooftops of Vol Maren to the west.

The city was vast and surrounded by a great wall of stone with towers every hundred yards throughout its length. To the north, a magnificent castle was set upon a hill with the tallest towers Merssa had ever seen, and a walled road of stone connected the castle's drawbridge to the city below. The craftsmanship was surprisingly exquisite; probably constructed by hired help from neighboring kingdoms or dwarves of Rornibur.

"We should pick up a few more supplies before tomorrow," Pallit said after riding to the front. "We don't have enough gear for everyone here." He regarded their packs. "You should probably let me handle it. They'll charge you thrice what they ought to."

Merssa nodded and they passed through the open gates.

Before them, chains of stone buildings were strung together along paved streets of brick. The smell of cooking was heavy in the air—a pleasant difference from the odors of Eastgate—and though a touch dusty, the buildings were relatively clean. Vol Maren was bustling as its nightlife prepared to begin, and runners lit lanterns upon tall poles while miners and hunters were returning from the day's labors. Merssa spied archers lining the catwalks, eyes intent upon the surrounding territory, and large ballistae were mounted atop every tower.

"It is as if we entered a dungeon," commented Eraim, echoing Merssa's thoughts.

"The mountains hold many beasts." Pallit gazed at the peaks to the north. "Twice in my days, ogres attacked the city, smashing portions of the walls before we fended them off. I've seen two-headed giants, and some hunters claim to have seen a dragon." He smiled as Eraim and Selanna looked at him with disbelief. "But I never saw one."

"Let's find an inn close to the gates," Merssa said to Pallit. She could already feel the stares—evidently in Vol Maren they knew a Palidurian when they saw one.

"Yes." Bayn scanned the locals walking about. "Folks here won't be as friendly as those in Eastgate when they see you."

"I do not fear the scum of this city!" Merssa glared at the marteese. "I wish to have an easy departure before morning."

"That won't be possible," Pallit said. "Soon the gates will be locked until dawn. They will not open them early for anyone, save the king himself."

"Terrific," Merssa muttered.

"I know of a good place to stay, though," Pallit added. "And I'll see to it the horses are cared for." The ranger directed his last comment to the elves. "Unless they're skilled at climbing, they'll have to be comfortable here until we return."

Eraim's mouth opened slightly in protest.

"Don't worry." Pallit held up a hand. "I trust these stables."

Eraim's wry smile held little consolation, but she conceded with a sigh.

Pallit led the way, maneuvering along the streets. They passed many lively taverns, as well as dark figures darting in and out of alleys, and although Merssa felt eyes follow her, no one impeded their progress as they arrived to what could only be the northeast corner of the walled city. There, Pallit stopped before a two-story building labeled OGRE'S BREATH TAVERN.

"It's no equal to the food at Larman's," Pallit admitted, "but it'll do."

They stepped inside, and it was immediately apparent many knew Pallit's name. He was greeted by smiles, slaps on the back, and clasping of arms as patrons welcomed him from his "long absence." It did not take long for stares to fall Merssa's way, but Pallit made an announcement that she was a friend and to be treated as family. Merssa was not comfortable with the comment, but thought better of saying anything to the contrary. The patrons put forth smiles with some effort, and even pulled out a chair for her at a large table where room was made for the company. Pallit excused himself to tend to the horses and gain the supplies he desired, and he shared a quiet word with the barman before departing.

The company enjoyed drinks and a hot supper, and from conversations it was obvious off-duty King's Rangers frequented the establishment, perhaps filling its entire muster. Music began to play and laughter filled the room while drinks flowed heavily, and patrons did their best to ignore Merssa's presence. She could not help but notice a man stationed at the door, apparently informing new arrivals of her attendance to avoid confrontations. A couple fights broke out away from the company's table, but were short lived with barely a bottle or mug broken. Vecnor seemed fidgety, obviously hoping one of the brawls might creep close enough for him to join in the fun, but his wish went unfulfilled.

Supper was long over when Pallit returned.

"Where have you been?" Merssa was more than annoyed with the ranger's lengthy absence. Were the stables back in Eastgate?

"I ran across some old friends," Pallit explained, no more loudly than was necessary. "It would seem the Wind came upon Vol Maren from the north."

Merssa noticed concern in Selanna's expression.

"As near as I can figure," Pallit added, "it seems to have come from the direction of the rorbak."

At the mention of the white stone, Poluran set his mug down and listened intently.

"There's been other strange activities in the mountains as well," Pallit continued. "The rangers found signs of travel over the last few weeks. Groups of twenty or more. But there's been no evidence of fires or any other remnants of campsites. Only small fragments of cloth and boot imprints."

"Perhaps they are undead," suggested Selanna. "They would have no need to camp."

"I only pray it isn't the creatures I encountered near the rorbak." Pallit shook his head. "I never wish to face the likes of them again."

"It's time we turn in," Merssa said. "We best get a good night's rest." With her last words she glared at Vikur, who had just bellowed for another round.

Breakfast awaited the company well before dawn, much to Merssa's liking. But unlike the meal at Larman's, the Ogre's Breath served tepid porridge with a side of mystery meat and a pot of watery tea, and the grumpy proprietor looked to have fallen asleep a few times on his feet.

"Is anyone besides Poluran and myself skilled in mountain travel?" Pallit asked while they choked down the gruel.

"My little brother and I," Vikur boasted. "Why, it's been a tradition in our family to travel to Morimont every—"

"I am." Vecnor ended the babbling warrior's story.

"Very good." Pallit nodded. "Poluran and I will take the lead with Vecnor in the middle, and the brothers of Ironside will take the rear and make sure no one falls behind. It'll seem well in the beginning, but that's only because the paths have been well maintained. The Stone Eagles can be quite treacherous, so be on your guard."

Merssa stared at Pallit. Perhaps he did not realize *she* made the decisions. But with her lack of knowledge of the terrain, she could not raise a valid argument. Even in Palidur, the perils of the Stone

Eagles were well documented.

"If we meet up with a patrol," Pallit continued, "leave your weapons sheathed. I'll deal with them."

Pallit saw to it each of them carried a coil of rope, a pouch of spikes, torches, two skins of water, food, and firewood—the latter, he explained, was not easy to come by in the mountains. He also supplied boots, slightly ill fitted for some, but there was no time to have proper pairs made. Poluran declined the footwear, for his boots were more than appropriate for the journey, not to mention he would have been hard pressed to fit his extremely wide feet into a human pair. Eraim complained hers were too large and hideous, but Pallit insisted, and not even the small elf's charming smile seemed able to sway him. The elves were also displeased with the amount of weight they were made to bear, but Pallit assured them it was all necessary for survival. Against Pallit's wishes, Gruzim insisted on bringing the long spear, and under the intimidating glare of the krukari, the ranger did not appear willing to argue.

As the sun touched the walls of Vol Maren, the company stood before the stone gates. The rattling of a great chain echoed into the mountains as an unseen winch began to turn, and the massive doors slowly opened.

"Good hunting, Pallit!" a guard called down, and Pallit waved without a glance as they exited.

The company turned north, following a well-worn path along the city wall, and it was not long before they entered the foothills. The trails were not hard to spot, as they were wide enough for two horses abreast, and travel was surprisingly tame. As the day wore on, however, the pathways narrowed and the company made several stops, for constant upward slopes brought swift fatigue. Only Poluran seemed unaffected, and he showed obvious signs of disapproval with the many breaks.

As dusk closed in, they settled within a small area surrounded almost entirely by large boulders. It was a ranger campsite, Pallit informed them, and was set against a cliff wall to allow only a narrow point of access. In the middle, a fire pit showed signs of frequent use, and Pallit uncovered a cache of firewood the rangers kept among the rocks, explaining that he did not wish to use their own supply until it was necessary. The night grew cool and the winds picked up, but the boulders were excellent shields and the howling sounded worse than it felt. Still, they pulled up their blankets and crept closer to the fire.

Pallit organized the night watch, taking the first duty himself. Poluran would follow, then Vecnor, and finally Vikur and Arkor would share the final shift. Merssa's frustrations grew, for she normally guarded a good portion of the night, but she was not used to this type of travel and her shoulders felt heavy, so again she conceded to the ranger and did her best to sleep.

The night passed quietly and morning dawned. While Merssa and the others gathered their gear and ate a cold breakfast, Poluran extinguished the fire and Pallit climbed atop a boulder to have a look around.

"You best ration your water," Pallit suggested as he jumped down, watching Merssa drink deeply from her skin. "There'll be no clean streams for a few days at least."

Merssa wiped her mouth, eyeing the ranger with disdain. She was not some young adventurer, out for the first time.

"I could never live in the mountains," said Eraim with a sigh as she massaged her feet.

"We've not reached the old birds yet," Poluran informed the elf. "But don't worry, we should be out of the foothills by tonight."

"*Foothills*?" Eraim gasped to Selanna.

They moved on, the day much like the last, and still encountered nothing, save for a few eagles soaring about the sky. At dusk they again stopped within a ranger campsite, this one bare of firewood and forcing them to dip into their own stock. Eraim and Selanna were relieved, for they used all the elves carried to get through the night.

Though a bit later than Poluran's prediction, the following day brought more treacherous paths and steeper slopes, and a constant breeze tugged at their cloaks as they entered the mountains. Sheer cliffs rose high above, many of their peaks beyond sight, and narrow ledges put most nerves on edge while they scooted along with great caution. Poluran gazed about with a smile and took in a deep breath, as one relieved to finally be home.

Breaks came more often, but were briefer than Pallit recommended—they needed to reach Trannum before the necromancer regained too much power, so Merssa kept things moving. Pallit remained alert and stopped often to listen, but there was nothing to be heard, save for the wind in their ears.

Near midday they had their first encounter. Eight of the King's Rangers approached from the northwest and split up, obviously having spotted the company. A few remained on the trail with bows ready while the others disappeared, but then the lead figure smiled.

"Pallit!" The man's shoulders eased and he stepped forward. "How the blazes are you?"

At these words, the hidden rangers returned to the path and greeted their long-departed comrade.

"Good to see you, Bril." Pallit locked arms with the leader.

"How's the easy life treating you?" Bril asked with a chuckle.

"I'm well." Pallit smiled. "But I see *your* wits are lacking." He gazed over his shoulder at Merssa and the others. "You were well within view before you spotted us."

Bril scanned the company, regarding Gruzim and Merssa a moment longer than the others. "And what are you doing in these parts?"

"How are the paths ahead?" Pallit asked, avoiding the question.

"All is calm enough," Bril replied. "We've not seen much for days as a matter of fact. Not since the winds that raised the dead. Did you hear about that?"

"Then all is quiet?" Pallit posed.

"Too quiet if you ask me." Bril frowned. "It's as if the mountains are empty. But what company is it you keep now? Looks like a strange grouping, if you ask me."

Pallit glanced over his shoulder again, his eyes dropping to spy

Merssa's shifting feet—she desperately wished to take over the questioning. He turned back to Bril. "How long since you've been to Barren Trails?"

"They're still patrolled once a month." The man scratched his chin. "Why? Is that where you're aiming for?"

"Are you on your way back to the city?" Pallit inquired nonchalantly.

Bril broke into a grin. "Yeah. It's been good seeing you again. You really should return to us."

"Perhaps." Pallit smiled and they locked arms again.

The rangers bade Pallit farewell and both groups went their separate ways, eyeing each other as they passed. Merssa was surprised Bril had not pressed further into their business within the mountains, but she was more annoyed with Pallit for neglecting to ask of the mysterious mountain travelers he spoke of in Vol Maren.

Many forks were laid before them as they continued up the sloping paths, but Pallit never hesitated, following a route as if the other trails did not exist.

"You're positive we're headed the right way?" Merssa piped in at one point, feeling the itch to say something.

"As much as I've tried to forget," Pallit replied, "the way is burned in my mind."

Night came and they stopped at another campsite. They were greeted with loaded bows, as four rangers had already settled there, but the weapons were lowered upon seeing Pallit. The rangers viewed the company with suspicion, but just as the previous patrol, they never pressed Pallit too hard for any explanations. There again was no news of any creatures lurking about, and the men showed the same concern that all seemed too quiet. At Pallit's request, the rangers guarded until morning, allowing the company solid rest.

With the rising of the sun, Merssa awoke to find Pallit standing at the edge of the campsite. The rangers were gone.

"Wake the others and gather all the wood from the ranger's stock," Pallit instructed Poluran. "We won't be following the paths much longer."

They ate a quick meal and returned to the trail. After a quarter-mile, Pallit came to a halt.

"It'll be rough from here on," he said, pulling a knotted rope from his pack. "It's best if we move single file. Footing will be difficult, so use the rope for balance."

Pallit passed the length of rope back, and they formed a chain before entering what could only be the Barren Trails, for most the time Merssa was not sure a path actually existed. The rope proved useful, as loose rocks caused several of them to stumble on inclines, but it became even more important when they left the paths altogether. They were forced to climb more frequently, and though most cliffs were small, some rose more than twenty yards. The air grew thinner and only Pallit and Poluran spoke, giving directions and pointing out safe holds for hands or feet, but with every passing hour the way became more arduous and they stopped often to catch their breaths. They made good use of the equipment Pallit had procured, and Merssa was grateful he insisted on acquiring it.

As dusk drew near, Pallit located level ground next to a small brook and they made ready for camp. He scouted the area while Poluran made a fire, and the rest of the company sat heavily upon the ground. Even Vikur and Arkor appeared unable to walk another step.

"It was a good day," Pallit said to Merssa as he took a seat, a satisfied look on the ranger's face.

"Good by human standards," Poluran remarked. The dwarf looked up, noticing the glares cast toward him by Merssa and Arkor. "I said it was *good*!" He shook his head, mumbling about humans and their inability to accept compliments.

"We best be on guard tonight," Pallit mentioned. "The Eagles have been far too quiet."

Merssa fought the urge to rest, but before she knew it, she was seated against a cliff wall and observing the others. Arkor was seated, his eyes closed; Bayn and Gruzim shared a quiet conversation;

Vecnor stood, gazing onto the darkening mountains; and Pallit and Poluran were deep into a conversation about rorbak and the curse. Merssa's focus then fell upon Vikur and the elves.

Vikur knelt and scooped a handful of cool water from the brook, closing his eyes and washing away his thirst. He enjoyed a couple more handfuls before opening his eyes, and then noticed Selanna and Eraim had removed their boots to wash their little feet, just upstream from where he was. Vikur gave a sarcastic smile while they giggled, and he sat back against a boulder. A reflection of the sun's dying light flashed across Vikur's face, and he moved swiftly past the elves to fish an object from the water. Merssa rose to investigate.

"What's this?" Vikur handed the item to Pallit.

Merssa saw it was a silver clasp, and engraved upon it was the head of an eagle over twin hammers upon an anvil.

"This is of Rornibur." Pallit placed it into Poluran's eagerly awaiting hand. "We're close. Tomorrow, perhaps."

Poluran stared at the clasp and his shoulders slumped. Most likely it had been dropped by his fallen kin. He slid it into his pouch.

With fatigue heavy upon all, Pallit scheduled everyone a short shift throughout the night to keep watch, instructing them to maintain the fire, for the night would become extremely cold. Merssa closed her eyes and listened to the campfire dancing with the breeze, and sleep found her quickly.

Merssa woke at the touch of Vecnor's hand; he had awakened her for the final watch of the night. Normally Merssa guarded the first shift, but she had informed Pallit she would be taking the final leg. That way she could be sure they got an early start.

It was cold, and Merssa's breath clouded her vision whenever the wind was not blowing, but all remained quiet and she heard and saw nothing. With the slightest hint of morning, she stirred the company, ignoring the complaints of the elves and Vikur. By the time the sun's light touched them, they had packed their gear and refilled their skins and left the brook behind.

The day crawled by as the way became rough, and often they doubled back in search of alternate routes. Sometimes no easier path existed, however, and they returned to their original course. It was almost enough to drive Merssa to take the lead, and when Pallit called for yet another break to quietly consult with Poluran, her confidence waned further.

"Do you know the way or not?" Merssa demanded.

"It's a bit tricky," Pallit explained. "I know of which direction we need to go, but finding a route safe for all…" He shook his head.

"We'll go whichever way we must," she said. "There'll be no more delays."

After these words, Pallit led them along more difficult treks and the climbs became more tedious. Frustrations began to rise for most with the scrapes and bruises that resulted, but they labored throughout the day. As Merssa suspected, they were all perfectly capable of keeping up without any major mishaps, and she grew annoyed with herself for not having spoken sooner.

The day was spent and the sky turned orange when Pallit came to a halt.

"We've arrived," he said gravely.

Poluran scrambled atop a boulder to have a better look, the dwarf's expression desperate. He gasped. "Rorbak!"

Merssa maneuvered about until she could see what Poluran spied, and there it was, not a hundred yards ahead. White stone. It lay scattered in strange formations, rising like pillars to twenty feet in height or resting as boulders with flat tops and bottoms. Portions of some mountainsides appeared to be made entirely of the substance.

Poluran scrambled from his perch and made for the rorbak, seemingly forgetful of the legendary curse. He had not made it far when he came to an abrupt halt, gazing at a piece of armor fifty feet away. He moved swiftly toward it and the others ran to keep up.

It was a breastplate of dwarfish make and size, and several more pieces of armor were strewn about. Some contained skeletal remains of former owners, but most were empty shells and the straps showed evidence of having been ripped apart. Poluran removed his helmet and bowed his head.

"Let's move on," said Pallit softly, placing a gentle hand upon the dwarf's shoulder.

With weapons drawn, they proceeded until the white rock was all around. The air was cool, almost as cold as the previous night, and carried the stale smell of aged bandages. Some of the stones were stained with old blood—more evidence of the battle Pallit had mentioned.

"What do we do now?" questioned Bayn as the sun's light began to fail.

Selanna scrutinized a wall of rorbak. "There must be an opening in one of these cliff walls."

"Then we best get searching while the light lasts," Merssa said.

Pallit shook his head, scanning the sky with nervous eyes. "There's not enough. Let us not forget about the curse that came upon me and the dwarves. We need to be clear of this area before nightfall, and I saw a spot from which we can protect ourselves."

Merssa was silent. Pallit was right, and she reluctantly nodded.

Pallit led them at a quick pace back the way they had come, a couple hundred yards to a small area surrounded on two sides by high walls of stone. They set down their gear and Poluran took stock of the wood supply, announcing enough remained for a couple more nights. The dwarf made a large fire, as the night had grown bitterly cold, and the company shifted uncomfortably every time the wind blew. But it was not the weather that disturbed Merssa's sleep—visions of yellow-skinned ghouls with glowing blue eyes prevented any prolonged rest.

With morning came many looks of relief—obviously others had shared in Merssa's restless night. They returned to the rorbak with a sense of urgency and spread out to inspect as much ground as possible. They often wandered in circles and searched over the same places two or three times, but as lunchtime came and went without a break, there was no luck. Just after midday, Selanna shouted.

"Here!"

The mage's voice did not echo far before the wind swept it away. She stood before a flat mountain wall of white stone, and her keen vision must have spied something well hidden. Merssa had seen Vikur check the exact area and she remembered searching it herself. Somehow, they had both missed something.

Poluran scrutinized the rock and his eyes grew wide. "A door!"

"Let me have a look," said Eraim, removing her leather gloves.

The small elf ran her slender hands about the stone, her face buried in concentration. After a few minutes she depressed an area of rock into the mountain wall. There was a hollow *click* followed by the rattling of a chain, and a large door swung slowly inward.

Eraim jumped back and unsheathed Mithkahr while the others held their weapons ready, as if an army of undead awaited on the other side. The door swung fully open, revealing a large chamber, and the high sun traveled only slightly into its depth, leaving most of it in shadow. All was quiet.

"Light some torches," Merssa said. "Quickly!"

Bayn used his magic to create sparks, and in short order three torches were ready. Vikur grabbed one, as did Vecnor, and Bayn held on to the third. Vecnor moved to Merssa's side.

Merssa held her golden mace tightly as immense evil clutched at the medallion of Cafior beneath her armor. After a quiet prayer, the feeling faded.

"Let's go." She stepped forward.

Chapter 16

Halls of the Dead

Each footfall echoed into the darkness above, rising to heights unknown as Merssa led the way inside. The edges of the chamber remained in shadow, and the air was like an early winter morning and carried the reek of decay. Other than the company's movements, nothing made a sound.

Selanna sent forth her magical light, and its brightness increased as it floated to the middle of the vast room, revealing the hall in its entirety. It was octagonal in shape, but it was not made of rorbak; the white stone began and ended with the door while the floor and walls were gray. Each section of wall contained a single wooden door, and upon the floor in the middle of the chamber was painted a large black triangle with a blue oval in its center, the edges of the oval extending beyond two of the triangle's borders.

"I wonder if these doors bear the same magic as the one in the marsh." Poluran's voice carried across the chamber. "Opening one could alert the skeleton wizard."

"Our presence is certainly known." Merssa had no doubt. With the power the undead wizard had exhibited thus far, there was no way one could intrude upon the creature's home without its knowledge. And Merssa knew it was surely here, for the tingling sensation on the back of her neck was unmistakable.

Merssa moved to the first door on the right. It opened with little effort and revealed an ominous laboratory. Stone slabs filled the chamber like crude tables, and upon them were many glass jars, most of them empty but a few containing dark liquids. Across the room a few of the slabs held various decaying body parts and bones, and from them a rancid odor blurred Merssa's vision.

"How vile!" Merssa closed the door before removing her gauntlet to wipe away her tears. "Vikur," she addressed the warrior. "Take Arkor, Pallit, Bayn, and Gruzim and start with the doors the other way. Call if you find *anything*. The rest of you follow me."

She tried the next door. It was stuck. Applying a bit more force, it flew open and Merssa stumbled into a room much like the last. With a sigh, she backed out and pulled it shut.

The next door led into a large room containing dozens of weapon racks, but only a few unremarkable swords and spears were present. Merssa led the way in for a closer look, until Vecnor's torch illuminated the far corners, but there was nothing more.

"Battle!" Eraim ran from the chamber.

They all hurried after the elf, and as Merssa neared the door, her ears picked up the sound of combat. Ghouls were pouring from a door across the chamber, and Vecnor led the charge to give aid.

Vikur was at the front, hacking with his blade as the undead advanced, and Arkor was beside him. The one-armed warrior cut down a ghoul, and when another bit into his wooden arm, it fell victim to the merciless ripping of his hook across its throat.

Gruzim was squared off with ghouls spilling to the right side of the door. With a slash of his spear, the krukari decapitated one, and he brought the butt into another and knocked it into one of its own. Before the creatures recovered, Gruzim spun the weapon and thrust it clear through both, and in one fluent motion, he yanked them toward him as he unsheathed his sword. Black ichor splattered him as he proceeded to hack the heads from their bodies in a most brutal manner—he did not seem to mind, and his lip curled into what must have been a grin.

Bayn was to the left side, issuing sparks to blind a ghoul before cutting it down. The marteese failed to notice two others sneaking up from the side, but Pallit was there and destroyed them with his broadsword. A fourth ghoul looked to spring upon the ranger, but as it crouched low, Pallit flipped a small axe from his belt and split its skull.

A dozen ghouls lay dead upon the floor by the time Vecnor and Eraim arrived, and the fiends continued to issue through the door, easily tripling that number. Vecnor joined the Ironside brothers while Eraim ran to Bayn—the marteese was hard pressed by three ghouls after four others stole Pallit's attention. Bayn defended himself, giving ground and unwilling to chance an attack, but once Mithkahr slew two, the marteese finished off the third.

Merssa arrived ahead of Poluran and turned her attention to a ghoul looking to spring upon Arkor's back. She crushed the creature's skull with one mighty swing before moving to Arkor's side, and there she faced two more. The ghouls seemed frantic in their attacks, failing to employ many of the tactics shown in past battles, and Merssa and Arkor dispatched all before them with little difficulty.

The room returned to silence. Over fifty corpses littered the floor, their dark blood seeping into large puddles and their stench permeating the chamber.

"Now that is foul!" Vikur put his arm over his mouth.

Poluran shrugged, surrounded by several detached limbs—obvious victims of Clanghorr's edge. The dwarf seemed unaffected, and Merssa understood. Having survived the Silent Marsh, she was not sure the stench would ever affect her the same again.

"Is anyone hurt?" Merssa asked.

"My arm," replied Bayn. The marteese held his hand over his bicep, blood evident through his fingers, and three scratches were upon his cheek.

"My leg!" Pallit said through clenched teeth.

Lying at the ranger's feet was a legless ghoul corpse with fresh blood upon its teeth. From the looks of it, the creature must have lost its lower body to Clanghorr and crawled up behind Pallit to make good one last attack. Poluran avoided eye contact with Merssa and the ranger, leading Merssa to believe that must surely be the case.

Merssa tended first to Bayn and then Pallit. Upon seeing the ranger's wound more closely, she was surprised he could still walk.

"You best stay off your feet when opportunity presents itself," she said. "Or the holes will not close. Perhaps when we return to Vol Maren—"

"*If* we return." Pallit rose to his feet.

"That's the last of them." Vikur exited the ghoul room with Arkor and Vecnor close behind.

"The room's a dead end," added Vecnor.

"All right, then," Merssa said. "Back to the other doors. There's something here and we must find it."

They returned to their groups and checked the remaining doors, finding only empty rooms and a couple more laboratories. It seemed the ghouls were the only inhabitants.

"Whatever was here is gone now," commented Bayn while they wandered toward the middle of the chamber, where Selanna's light still obediently hovered. "Obviously the former occupants are the mysterious travelers the rangers spoke of."

"No." Merssa did not believe that for a second. "I feel something much stronger than ghouls."

"Perhaps it is the remnants of evil," suggested Bayn.

"Merssa!" called Poluran. "Here!" The dwarf squatted within the triangle in the center of the room.

"What is it?" Merssa joined the dwarf, ready to reprimand him if he was wasting her time.

Poluran traced his finger in a three-foot circle around the center of the oval. "There's a seam in the stone."

"I see it!" Eraim moved closer to get a better look. "It is like the pupil of the eye, or something."

Merssa saw nothing.

"And listen." Poluran tapped the stone with Clanghorr's bronze spike. "It's hollow."

"Right there." Eraim pointed at the oval, pulling a knife. "The crack widens enough to fit a tool."

All Merssa saw was what appeared to be a chip in the stone; a flaw, perhaps, upon an otherwise smooth surface.

Eraim worked her knife into the chip, sinking the blade four inches into the floor. She pried at the stone, but the weapon snapped.

"Stand aside," said Gruzim in his gravelly voice as he stepped forward with his spear, specks of ghoul ichor still adorning the krukari's armor and parts of his face. He turned the weapon down and thrust it into the crack—Poluran only just cleared the spot in time—and the spearhead sparked as it sliced through the broken knife. The krukari pulled back on the shaft and the thick wood held strong, barely bending beneath the weight of the stone. A frigid gust escaped as the circle lifted a few inches.

Vecnor passed his torch to Eraim and placed both hands beneath the stone. He moved it aside to reveal a dark hole, and Eraim returned the torch so they could peer down. Iron rungs were set into the wall of a shaft falling a short distance to a landing. From there, steps descended deeper into the cold ground.

Merssa placed her mace onto her belt and pushed past Vecnor. She lowered herself, grabbing hold of the cold rungs, and descended safely to the landing. A chill penetrated her boots and she pulled her weapon and glanced about, but her breath was blinding and she could not see far into the darkness. Vecnor joined Merssa with his torch, illuminating the stairs, and she immediately started downward.

The clambering of the others filing down the rungs echoed before Merssa, and after a short distance she felt a great emptiness to her left as the wall gave way to a sheer drop. She could neither see nor feel a floor or ceiling in that direction and all sound was swallowed by the darkness therein.

The stairs continued and Merssa hugged the right side, not wanting to chance a hasty descent into the depths unknown. After a couple hundred feet she came to another landing. The chasm now stood before her as well as to the left, and to the right were leering demonic skulls, carved into the stone about an archway. Beyond, a corridor traveled a short distance to an identical arch, foreboding and causing Merssa's scalp to tingle even more. But at least there were walls on both sides.

Merssa and Vecnor stepped cautiously beneath the skulls and along the hallway, stopping at the second arch to peer into a large chamber. The torchlight failed to reach its borders in any direction, but Merssa noticed several smaller alcoves veiled in cobwebs and bearing the same eerie skulls, every five feet to either side of the entrance as far as the light revealed. A thick layer of dust covered the floor, save for a worn path from where she stood and straight into the darkness.

"Hold up your torch," Selanna's voice instructed from behind, and Vecnor complied.

Merssa heard the mage recite a short spell and the fire flared, revealing the room in its entirety. Merssa had to squint at first, but she saw greater than a hundred of the smaller arches, as they continued around the rectangular chamber and to the far side, where the path terminated twenty yards away at another larger arch and corridor beyond.

"I do not like this room," said Eraim, now squeezed next to Merssa at the entryway, and Merssa noticed Mithkahr radiated a red tint.

"Nobody likes it," said Merssa. "Keep your wits about you."

Merssa led the way down the path with Vecnor at her side. Glancing back, she saw everyone walking two by two, taking care to avoid stepping outside the path's parameters. Good. They were showing some sense. Nearly three-quarters across the chamber, Vecnor nudged Merssa and pointed the torch toward the smaller archways. The webs were swaying, though the air remained completely still.

"Ready yourselves," Vecnor said for all to hear.

Suddenly a skeletal warrior stepped from each of the smaller alcoves, dressed in rusted armor and bearing a shield. They raised battered swords, as if paying homage to an unseen king, and charged.

Vecnor stepped to the left of the path and Merssa turned to the right. Merssa swung her mace, shattering the ribcage and spine of a skeleton, and after fending off the attack of another, she rammed into its shield, stepping from the path and driving it back into the alcove from where it came. A blade struck her arm, but the dull edge left a small wound at best and she turned on its wielder, reducing it to a pile of bones. Merssa then returned to the path before the undead could separate her from her companions.

Behind Merssa, Vecnor had crushed five undead soldiers, and down the path Eraim and Selanna stood back to back—the smaller elf brought swift destruction with Mithkahr while the mage had shattered nearly a dozen skeletons with magical green spheres. Farther along, Poluran and Pallit fought to the left side while Gruzim and Bayn fought to the right, and Arkor and Vikur stood to the rear, holding the undead there at bay.

Merssa returned her focus to the skeletons, and though they proved less effective than the ghouls, reinforcements issued from the alcoves faster than the abominations fell.

"There are too many!" came Bayn's voice.

Merssa crumbled four more of the enemy before chancing another glance. Bayn had lost his weapon and was employing magic to fend off the warriors of bone; blood dripped from the marteese's scalp and his left arm hung low. Next to Bayn, Gruzim twirled the long spear and smashed skeletons with the haft, but offered no aid, and all others of the company seemed to have all they could handle.

Merssa destroyed another three undead in an attempt to make her way toward the back, but then Vecnor dropped the torch and lifted the shield of a fallen skeleton. He rammed a path to Bayn, smashing all enemies between them, and arrived just as the half-elf looked to yield. Hope returned to Bayn and he mustered the courage to continue the fight.

The dropped torches began to fail, but Selanna's floating light appeared, rising to the center of the chamber. Merssa smashed three more skeletons before she noticed Eraim was now limping and

Pallit's bandages were completely red. Most the company seemed to have taken injuries, and still the undead charged from the alcoves, endless in number. The battle would never end.

Selanna's voice rose above the din, shaking the room like thunder. The mage stomped her foot and the floor shook violently to the right side of the path, staggering all skeletons there and halting their advance.

"Go!" Selanna shouted. "Leave this room!"

"This way!" called Merssa as the company concentrated their efforts to the other side of the room. She stepped to the left of the arch, destroying all skeletons impeding her and opening a path for the others.

Dropping the shield and lifting Bayn onto his shoulder, Vecnor fought his way past Merssa and beyond the arch. Poluran followed, giving assistance to Pallit, and Gruzim was close behind. Merssa continued to keep the archway clear, glancing back to see what had delayed the others.

"I cannot hold them forever!" Selanna shouted to Vikur and Arkor, the elf's arms beginning to shake while the skeletons continued to dance.

The brothers made a dash toward the exit, but Vikur halted upon reaching Eraim.

"Go!" Vikur yelled to the small elf, stepping in to take her place in defense of Selanna's flank.

Eraim hesitated, seemingly unwilling to leave Selanna.

Vecnor returned and stepped next to the Lord of the Keep. "Eraim! Get out!"

Eraim conceded at last, making for the exit as quickly as her wounded leg allowed.

Selanna stomped her foot again, uttering a word that echoed about the chamber. The floor before the mage cracked and launched the skeletons into the air, and their bones shattered upon the floor seconds later, depleting the right side of all enemies.

"Go!" Selanna said, racing toward Merssa.

"Move!" Vecnor yelled at Vikur as replacements already began emerging from the alcoves.

Merssa continued to keep the archway clear as Selanna ran past, and Poluran was with her, destroying two and three skeletons at a time. Vikur passed through the arch and the dwarf followed, and Vecnor came last, slowing to lift Merssa as he exited the chamber.

"How dare you!" was all Merssa managed before they were clear of the room.

As Vecnor sat Merssa down within the hallway, Selanna spoke an incomprehensible command and the archway took on a brief green glow. All skeletons attempting to pursue bounced off a magical barrier then, the glow returning with each strike.

"That will hold them for a while," Selanna said and turned to Merssa. "Perhaps you should tend to their wounds, while my powers endure."

Merssa watched the skeletons beat upon the barrier, and then gazed down the corridor stretching twenty yards before turning right. The rage she felt for Vecnor was quickly replaced by duty.

"Vecnor and Vikur," she addressed the warriors. "Watch the way ahead."

Vecnor nodded and the two moved down the hallway with swords ready.

"Bayn's cut up," Eraim mentioned to Merssa.

A gash ran deep along the marteese's arm, and Merssa had to stitch it with a needle from her pack. Once finished, she prepared herbs and wrapped the wound, as well as his leg, and for a few smaller injuries she performed a quick cleaning. While Merssa worked, Pallit pulled herbs from his pack and prepared them in much the same way before tending to his own leg and a couple cuts upon Arkor's arm. Merssa said nothing, but kept an eye on his handiwork while she went to Eraim.

The small elf had suffered a gash similar to Bayn's, though not quite as deep, and Merssa cared for it in the same manner. Poluran possessed minor cuts, but refused to waste time and insisted they move on. Merssa did not argue, nor did she check her own wounds, knowing them to be mere scratches. If Gruzim had sustained any injuries, they were not apparent, so Merssa quickly inspected the ranger's work.

"This will have to do," she commented after checking Pallit's leg. The ranger had actually done a fine job, but Merssa did not feel like issuing any compliments.

She went to where Vecnor and Vikur kept watch to look them over. Vikur showed a few small cuts, but he waved Merssa off, and Vecnor appeared unharmed.

Turning back, Merssa noticed some of the company getting a little too comfortable upon the floor. "Let's press on," she said, and they climbed to their feet.

Poluran quickly lit a couple new torches and Selanna allowed her light to fade. Merssa took one of the torches and handed it to Vecnor before leading the way down the corridor and around the bend.

The hallway stretched with many doors to the left and right, and Merssa and Vecnor opened each in turn. The doors revealed rooms practically bare but showing evidence of recent use, and after another bend the corridor terminated with a set of oversized doors bearing large brass pull rings. Merssa grabbed hold of the left ring and pulled open the door.

The room beyond was round with another set of doors on the far side. A circle containing a five-pointed star dominated the chamber floor, apparently drawn in blood, and within the middle of the star rested a large skull adorned by strange runes, also apparently written in blood. The skull was possibly that of a ram, but it was twice as large and a long horn protruded from its forehead. The circle left only a narrow path around its circumference to the opposite doors.

The tingling on Merssa's scalp was stronger than it had been since the days within the marsh. "Evil is strong here. Be on your guard...and do not enter the circle." Better safe than sorry.

Merssa moved left and Vecnor stood to the right, ushering the others to follow the paladin in single file while he kept a watchful eye on the skull.

"It's a pentagram," said Bayn when he entered.

"But what purpose does it serve?" asked Eraim.

"Either to keep something in or something out," Selanna replied. "Hopefully we will not learn that answer."

Merssa made her way to the opposite doors, where pull rings made of bone protruded from large, fanged skulls. With a scowl of disgust, she grabbed hold of one ring, but the gasps of her companions caused her to pause. Turning, Merssa saw wisps of red smoke rising from the skull within the pentagram.

Poluran shook his head. "Not again."

"*Mees!*" shouted Selanna. "Open the doors. We must get out of here!"

Merssa tried, but the doors would not budge. "They're locked!"

The smoke snaked toward the ceiling, increasing in mass.

"Destroy the skull!" shouted Vikur as he ran into the pentagram.

"No!" cried Selanna.

Fire erupted from beneath the ram-like skull, reaching the ceiling and spreading throughout the circle—Vikur dove from the pentagram just before it engulfed him. Within the flames a large shape took form, and seconds later the fire sank into the floor. The skull was gone, and in its place stood a fell beast almost as tall as the room. From the middle of its ram-like head jutted a long horn, and its reddish-brown skin was like old leather with bony spikes decorating much of its body. Its hands seemed twice as large as they should have been, each with six clawed fingers, and red, catlike eyes surveyed the room as its toothy maw opened into an evil grin. It emitted a low gurgling, and with a snort of black smoke from its large nostrils came the scent of sulfur.

"Ragab!" Selanna gasped. "The door!"

Eraim immediately made her way toward Merssa. The demon's attention followed the small elf as a thick black tongue tasted its lipless mouth, but Vikur caught its eye when he stepped to the edge of the circle and emitted a battle cry. The creature appeared amused with the display, smiling as a growl rolled in the back of its throat. With a sneer, Vikur charged.

"No!" Selanna shouted from halfway around the room. "It cannot leave the pentagram!"

The Lord of the Keep paid Selanna no heed as he advanced upon Ragab. He slashed his sword, but the demon caught the blade in one of its large hands and there was the ringing of steel on steel. The monster ripped the weapon free and cast it aside as it thrust the horn atop its head, but Vikur tumbled skillfully from the circle, evading the deadly strike. He rolled to his feet, wearing a satisfied grin as he glanced at the open doors — Eraim had picked the lock.

Ragab's attention went to the doors, where Eraim, Pallit, and Gruzim were already through. Merssa stood boldly at the edge of the pentagram with mace in hand while Bayn and Poluran made for the exit, and with a prayer upon her lips, the warmth and protection of Cafior surrounded Merssa with its golden aura. The demon roared, releasing an invisible force from its gaping maw, and Merssa was launched from her feet. Everything around her began to spin and her body went numb.

Vecnor saw Merssa fly into the wall, and Bayn barely retreated in time to avoid being struck by her body. The paladin slumped, unmoving as her glow faded, and Poluran moved to shield her from any further attack while the marteese stepped toward the circle.

Bayn uttered hasty words, and from the marteese's outstretched hand was launched a stream of sparks that struck Ragab full in the face, but the spell bore no visible effect and the demon answered with another roar, this time spitting flames that engulfed the marteese. Bayn screamed as he collapsed, and the monster turned toward Merssa and Poluran.

Vecnor advanced, swinging his sword and cutting into Ragab's hide. Dark-green blood sprayed his armor and the demon growled and turned to face him, but then it received another wound, as Vikur returned with Arkor's sword and struck it on the left flank. Unlike Hezeb, the wounds remained and Vecnor's spirit rose.

Ragab answered with a vicious backhand, its bony spurs striking Vikur in the face and casting the warrior from the pentagram, and it brought up its other hand in time to knock aside Vecnor's blade as Vecnor delivered another attack. The beast countered with a headbutt, but Vecnor retreated from the circle, evading the two-foot spike. Selanna then jumped between Vecnor and the demon as Ragab issued another stream of fire from its mouth, and with hands held forward, the mage pushed the flames aside.

Merssa was back on her feet and surrounded by the golden glow; Arkor, Bayne, and Poluran were gone. The paladin stepped into the pentagram, ready to strike, but the demon must have sensed her approach. It lowered to all fours and spun about, sticking out its long leg and catching Merssa off guard. Her feet were kicked out from under her and the golden glow faded as her mace slipped from her grasp. Ragab rose, placing a large foot upon Merssa's chest and pinning her to the floor.

Vecnor advanced, but he was forced to jump back again, narrowly escaping the creature's lashing claw, and Vikur moved to Vecnor's side. Blood ran from the Lord of the Keep's scalp and a few gashes on his cheek.

"This is a quick one, friend," Vikur scowled through clenched teeth.

"Left and right," Vecnor said.

The Lord of the Keep nodded, and while Vikur darted right, Vecnor moved left.

Ragab's gaze followed Vecnor, and the demon roared as it had earlier at Merssa. Vecnor felt as if a wall had suddenly slammed into his body, but he braced himself against the force and it served only to stagger him. Ragab then spun to meet Vikur and thrust its long horn clear through the warrior's chest. Vikur stared with wide eyes as his body went limp and he was cast aside.

Vecnor moved quickly, shouldering the creature's leg and

knocking the foot from atop the paladin. Merssa scrambled free from the circle while arrows issued from beyond the open door, obviously dealt from Eraim's bow, but the missiles shattered harmlessly upon the demon's hide.

Selanna gained the monster's full attention when her voice rang out, and from the elf's fingertips came forks of lightning that surrounded the demon's body. Selanna continued to chant while the beast writhed, and its shrill shriek pained Vecnor's ears. The lightning grew brighter as Selanna stepped into the pentagram and Ragab lunged for her, but Vecnor brought his blade down hard onto its back. The demon disappeared in a rush of red smoke with an eerie hiss, but its gurgling remained a few seconds longer, almost as mocking laughter. The mist dissipated, leaving behind the ram-like skull that now exhibited a long crack across its top.

Merssa winced as she picked up her mace and entered the circle. After a deep breath, the paladin brought her weapon down and shattered the skull. Nothing came as a result and Vecnor relaxed the grip on his weapon.

Arkor stepped into the chamber, looking from Selanna to Merssa. "Bayn's dead. He was gone before I took him from the room." The one-armed warrior's eyes widened when he noticed his brother lying upon the floor. "Vikur?"

"I could use a little help." Vikur's voice was strained as he pushed himself up to sit against the wall. The warrior's right hand was held tightly over his left shoulder, covered in blood—the horn had just missed its mark.

Arkor rushed to his brother's side. "Are you all right?"

It was a rare show of concern from the one-armed warrior.

"Let me see." Merssa rushed over. She pulled her healing pouch from her waist and inspected the wound on both sides. "You'll be all right…eventually."

Arkor nodded and his grim expression returned. He glanced about, spying his sword lying to one side of the room and Vikur's to the other. "You really should learn to hold on to your weapons, brother." Arkor moved to retrieve the blades.

Merssa treated Vikur's shoulder and made a sling to hold his arm.

"I can't move it," Vikur mumbled through clenched teeth.

Merssa gazed at the shoulder and shook her head. "You won't be of much use now."

The paladin always knew just what to say!

"Still better than most." Vikur grinned, but a surge of pain overtook him.

Merssa helped the wounded warrior to his feet and Arkor returned the blades to their sheaths.

Satisfied Vikur was in good hands, Vecnor turned to exit the room. But then he noticed Selanna leaning against the wall, shoulders slumped and face pale—the mage had obviously used much of her strength within the last two rooms. He took her by the arm and led her through the door.

Within the hallway, Eraim was laying a cloak over Bayn's burnt body while Gruzim relaxed against the wall, chewing on some dried meat. Poluran and Pallit stood guard over a couple closed doors, one halfway down the corridor's length and the other at its termination.

Vecnor released his hold on Selanna and she placed a hand on the wall with a nod of thanks. He went to Poluran and Pallit to see if there was anything to report, noticing that some of the flames that had killed Bayn had also scorched the dwarf.

"I would have liked to have helped," Poluran said quietly. "But I couldn't leave the wounded. Something might have come." He nodded toward the doors.

"I understand." Vecnor saw shame on Poluran's face. Even if it were fear that stayed the dwarf, Vecnor would have understood.

"The krukari," Arkor whispered to Vecnor after stepping into the hallway. "He showed no remorse for the fallen marteese."

"I wouldn't think he would." Vecnor gave Gruzim a sideways glance. "But this is not the place for such discussions."

Merssa and Vikur entered the corridor at last, the Lord of Ironside moving gingerly, and Merssa closed the door.

"How are you, mage?" Merssa asked Selanna. "You don't look well."

"I was just resting a moment." Selanna rose to her full height, putting forth her best—although unconvincing—look. "I am ready."

Vecnor watched as Merssa regarded each of the company in turn. Pallit and Eraim were practically working on one leg each, Vikur was unable to fight, and Poluran had been burned. Other than Vecnor, only the dwarf and Gruzim appeared able to continue. Merssa's shoulders slumped.

The paladin glanced back at the door, as if the thought crossed her mind to turn back, but shook her head. Leaving was definitely not an option. This was one of those moments when Vecnor knew Merssa's thoughts, as if she spoke only to him. If the necromancer was here and had regained his power, most of the company would certainly perish; perhaps all of them. But what fate would claim them if they returned to the room of skeletons? Selanna would not be able to assist them and they were in no shape to run across before being overwhelmed. Even if they did defeat Trannum, they may never escape this horrid tomb.

"Let's go." Merssa's face was grim, and she headed past Vecnor toward the next two doors without checking to see if anyone followed.

Merssa bit her lip. She was desperate. The weight of Palidur was upon her. Duty called, and she could not fail her beloved city. She could not fail Cafior. She could not fail the people of Vaeldor. But more than that, at the moment, she could not fail her friends. It was not a feeling Merssa was accustomed to, and she was not sure what to make of it. Continuing on was certain death for many of them, but perhaps she and Vecnor possessed enough strength…

She opened the first door down the hall, and from above her head, Vecnor's torch illuminated an awesome sight. The room was filled with a dragon's horde. Coins covered the floor and chests overflowed with gold and jewels. Dust covered all, however, showing the owner's lack of interest. Merssa shook her head and closed the door. Better the others did not know what lay beyond.

Advancing farther down the hallway, the air grew colder still. An intense evil coursed through Merssa's body and she found it hard to keep her hands from shaking. She opened the final door to reveal a laboratory illuminated by many candles, and though an icy breeze issued from the room and danced wildly with the company's torches, the small flames upon the wicks remained perfectly still. Many books lined the wall to the right, and to the left tables were covered with bottles of fluids and strange components. Upon the wall opposite the door was an ominous arch, drawn in black and covered with runes. The interior of the arch was filled with a darkness that seemed to move, and before it a black podium of stone held an open tome. But what held Merssa's attention was the hooded skeletal figure in black robes that turned one of the tome's pages, and from its right eye shone a pale blue light.

"Welcome," the figure said in a scratchy voice without moving its mouth or looking up. "I've been awaiting your visit."

"Trannum!" Merssa stepped forward with her mace ready. But when the figure's head lifted to gaze at her, fear froze her legs.

"That is a name I've not heard in quite some time." Its voice became deep and hollow, though its jaw was still unmoving. It made a noise that could only be a chuckle. "Someone has done much research to discern that…or…" it paused, drumming bony fingers upon the podium, "there is one whose memory is long."

"Your evil is at an end!" Merssa found the strength to take a couple more steps. She heard the others filing in behind her, adding to her strength, and she took another step.

"No!" Trannum hissed, halting Merssa again. "It has only just begun!"

Trannum waved a skeletal hand, as if beckoning a servant, and from the dark arch issued six creatures. They looked to have once been human, but their skin was a dirty yellowish color and wrapped tightly about their bones, and small points of blue light shone from within their hollow eye sockets—they were more horrifying than Pallit had described. Holding swords against their chests, they stepped to either side of their master.

"You see," Trannum said, "I could kill you…now, if I wanted to. Yes, even you, Merssa Goldmace of Palidur."

Merssa was caught off guard and her mouth fell open. How did the creature know her name?

"And I do not need my dunarchins to do so." Trannum waved an introductory hand toward the undead warriors.

"Dunarchins!" Selanna whispered harshly into Merssa's ear. "It translates to firstborn in Ancient Moclen. Several pages from one of the tomes of the marsh spoke of them."

"Yes," said Trannum, ending the word with a hiss. "You are correct, Selanna."

Selanna became rigid, seemingly surprised the creature knew her name.

"The spiritual energy only firstborns possess make them more cunning than ghouls," Trannum explained. "They are more like the living, and possess many other powers as well, not the least the ability to walk beneath the sun."

"His strength is great. Much greater than I had hoped," Selanna whispered to Merssa, as if the skeleton mage could not hear the words. "We cannot win this battle. Not now."

A fire was lit within Merssa. The elf might count on spells for power, but she had Cafior! "Your soldiers are no match for us!" Merssa spat. "And as for you—"

"Vecnor?" Selanna pleaded, and at that moment the large man placed his metal hand upon Merssa's shoulder.

"He has not attacked," Vecnor said loud enough for all to hear. "He must wish to speak."

Merssa turned to see Vecnor staring down at her.

"And there's no harm in listening," he added.

Merssa was shocked. How dare he? But she spied the others

behind him and was reminded of the condition of her company. Turning back, Merssa glared with hatred.

Trannum released another dry chuckle. "Very perceptive, Vecnor."

"What do you mean, you've been awaiting our visit?" Merssa demanded.

"Ever since you entered the area of the white stone, I have felt your presence," Trannum explained. "I allowed you to enter, for it was my choosing to speak with you."

"Allowed us?" Poluran's voice reached a level Merssa did not know possible. "You've had your dogs on us every step!"

"Mere guards." The skeleton waved a dismissive, bony hand. "I couldn't have you arrive all brave and healthy. Why, then I'd be forced to kill you. But I have other plans."

"If it's a deal you wish—" Merssa said.

"I do not deal with mortals!" the necromancer hissed, the glow from his eye growing brighter. The light dimmed and he spoke in a calmer tone. "Your presence is with purpose."

"I have but one purpose!" Merssa's ire returned.

Trannum pointed a finger and the door slammed shut behind them. With a wave of his hand, Merssa's injuries began to pulse and she cringed, using what strength remained to stay on her feet. From the noises behind her, she knew the others were wracked with pain as well.

"Look at yourselves…" Trannum said mockingly. "You've barely enough strength to challenge my soldiers, let alone *my* power!" The necromancer lowered his hand and the pain subsided. "But your deaths are not my wish…yet. That will come with time."

Merssa glared as the weight of duty returned. She could attack; Cafior was with her. Perhaps that would be enough. But if it was not, her friends would surely perish. In Palidur faith and duty were always held high above all things, and they demanded Merssa destroy this abomination, a feat she would willingly forfeit her own life to achieve. But never before had she been tested so. Tears welled in her eyes and she put her mace to her side. Hopefully Cafior would understand her failure.

"Good." The dry voice sounded pleased. "I allowed you to enter so that you may take a message to your *Council* of *Wizards*." The final words were uttered with disgust.

An image entered Merssa's mind, and she saw legions of undead marching across fields—hordes of skeletons, zombies, and ghouls led by the yellow-skinned warriors. In their wake lay cities in ruin while dark figures rode large beasts in the sky. Merssa's heart sank and fear gripped her soul, and she heard Trannum's voice, as if in a dream.

"Soon the time will come to wage war upon the living. That is why I send you back with this warning: to resist me is to join my ranks. I shall grant mercy to those that lay down their arms and surrender. I will allow *them* to live out their menial lives in my new world."

The scene shifted to show the living working as slaves while undead guards looked on. Merssa saw her company among the slaves, hauling large stones to build dark fortresses.

The vision ended and Merssa stood outside the mountain, amongst the rorbak and surrounded by her companions. The slamming of the stone door behind her echoed down the mountainside, but still Merssa heard the necromancer's voice.

"Go now, back to your lands and tell your folk. I cannot be stopped. I cannot be defeated. Oppose me and suffer my wrath!"

All was silent and the chill that encompassed the mountains faded, giving in to the sun's warmth. Merssa realized there was no more pain and every wound she had received was gone. Her companions' injuries had vanished as well, but their faces were as haunted as she felt. A deep sense of hopelessness consumed Merssa, and all at once she and the others began to trek down the mountainside.

CHAPTER 17

TROUBLED MINDS

Weapons sheathed and heads bowed, the company made their way toward Vol Maren. No one spoke and neither Pallit nor Poluran seemed interested in leading the way, so Vecnor took on the duty of securing ropes and finding safe routes. His companions were reluctant to obey some of his commands and he was often forced to voice harsh words or get physical to keep them moving. Selanna needed the most assistance, as she possessed little strength, and Vecnor carried her much of the time—the elf simply leaned against him and set her head upon his shoulder like an infant. Nothing impeded their progress throughout the day, and just as the journey to the tomb, none of the Stone Eagle's usual denizens were to be seen.

They arrived to the first ranger campsite outside the Barren Trails just after dark. There was no wood for a fire, but no one seemed to care, and though none possessed an appetite, Vecnor made sure they received ample water.

The remainder of the journey passed in much the same way. They slept little, but Vecnor stopped every evening and remained awake, guarding through the nights and making sure no one wandered off into the darkness. Only once did they encounter rangers. The patrol looked puzzled as to Pallit's melancholic mood, but did nothing to hamper the company's progress—probably due to the hardened glare Vecnor shared with them.

After a few days they were back in Vol Maren, arriving just

before the massive gates were locked for the night. Vecnor set them up in rooms at the Ogre's Breath and put each one to bed.

"A good night's rest will set you right," he told them each in turn.

Merssa awoke the next morning. Or was it closer to noon? It did not matter. The past few days were like a dream, as if she had floated within a dark cloud down the mountainside. And now she awoke on a bed, still dressed in her armor. She vaguely remembered Vecnor putting her there. Did he say something before he left? Merssa could not quite recall. Rising to her feet, she left the room and headed to the tavern, as if by reflex.

Upon arrival, Merssa saw the rest of her company sitting at a table. Breakfast was set before them, but they all sat in silence and the food was untouched. Merssa took a seat.

"I wonder where Vecnor has gotten off to," said Eraim after a moment. The elf's voice seemed tired.

Merssa gazed around the room. Vecnor was not present. "It doesn't matter." She did not have time to worry about such things. "I must return to Palidur."

Merssa grabbed some fruit bread and exited the tavern.

Upon arriving to the stables, Merssa noticed the others of the company had followed. She hoped they did not slow her down—she needed to get to Palidur to inform them of the impending doom.

"How long has the large horse been gone?" Eraim inquired of the stable boy, alerting Merssa to the fact that Umbarc was missing.

"Don't know, miss," the boy said. "I only got here this morning. But Presnin, he worked yesterday, he tells me a large man paid well to make sure your horses were prepped this morning. The giant horse you speak of was here yesterday morning, that much I do know, but it was gone before I arrived *this* morning."

So Vecnor left early. Probably wanted to get as far away from the tomb as possible. Merssa did not blame him.

They mounted and exited the city onto the road for Eastgate. The day was dry and already hot, and a few clouds hovered above the mountain peaks to the north.

"I'll ride as far as Stony River," said Poluran to Merssa. "It's closer to home for me."

Merssa nodded, not really paying attention to the words. Her mind was far off, trying to explain to the High Order that all was lost.

Days passed, one blending into the next, and though Merssa could not recall the journey, Eastgate was suddenly upon them. There was a distance yet to cover and she held no desire to stop, but she headed for Larman's Haven and the others followed. They entered the tavern and found Vecnor standing at the head of a large table. Borse was with him. The priest rose and greeted them with a smile.

"Welcome all," Borse said. "Please, come and sit."

Merssa was reluctant to accept the offer. Besides the High Order, she needed to let the Council of Wizards know all was lost, so there was much to do. But she did as instructed and the others joined her.

"Vecnor has told me of your journey." Borse's voice seemed distant, yet near, and it continued. "It all seems most disturbing, to be sure."

Merssa shrugged. "It's hopeless," she said, barely above a whisper as tears welled up.

"We shall see." Borse placed his hand upon hers; it was the first inner warmth Merssa could recall in some time. "Let's all have a drink and we'll discuss your encounter with this most evil being."

Everyone reached for the tankard before them and took a sip.

"You see," Borse said, "your journey through Silent Marsh, Sistama to some, was most unpleasant. But you did what you had to do." Though his voice still sounded far off, it seemed to draw nearer and grow stronger as it circled the table. "The death of Dellen is a loss to us all, for he was a fine man. But to encounter Hezeb and Ragab, two demons of Hell in one lifetime… That, my friends, is what legends are made of: brave warriors conquering great evils in the name of all that is holy and good. I am *very* impressed." Borse's voice continued to slowly circle. "And finally, face to face with the necromancer himself… I cannot find the words to describe your bravery! There are certainly no others in Vaeldor that could live through all you have seen."

Merssa felt compelled to lift her head, and she viewed the others as they did the same. Their faces were ashen, but color returned in a rush.

"Pallit, my dear friend," Borse said, placing his hand upon the ranger's shoulder. "You swore never to enter the area of rorbak again, but did exactly that.

"Vikur and Arkor." The priest moved to stand between the brothers. "All the way from the Varlimor Mountains with more confidence and skill than a platoon of soldiers in any army.

"Poluran. A mighty warrior bearing a mighty weapon. There has been nothing you two could not overcome.

"Gruzim. Your life cannot have been an easy one. But you endure, rising above all that would otherwise belittle your existence, and have achieved the strength to rival that of a giant."

Borse continued around the table, placing a fatherly hand upon each as he spoke, and with every visit a light was rekindled.

"Eraim and Selanna. Never before has a pair shown such a perfect combination of power, resourcefulness, and cunning.

"And finally, Merssa, the shining jewel of Palidur. Very wise priests there are in the Holy City to send one so faithful on this most important task. I am sure Cafior looks upon you and smiles."

Borse took his seat, and all eyes were trained upon him. "So what do we do next?"

Merssa's courage and strength returned in a rush as the shadows cast by Trannum were vanquished. The tavern was empty—not even Larman was in the room—and Merssa could not recall if there had been any patrons present when they arrived. She saw Borse as if for the first time, and he appeared wise and powerful. He was surrounded by a warm aura that touched Merssa's heart and restored hope. She was seeing him for whom he was, and not just a mere citizen of Neja. Borse was indeed a very holy man and a righteous and powerful servant to Cafior. A tear rolled down Merssa's cheek, as she was overwhelmed with remorse at the way she had treated him. Borse did not come from Palidur, the holiest of cities, but he lived in a wasteland among thieves and bandits, caring for those that would defy such a life and devote themselves to Cafior, the same deity Merssa dedicated her life to. She suddenly felt very small.

Borse's aura faded and he was a simple man again, aged in appearance with a seemingly permanent smile. "What do we do next?" he repeated.

Merssa blinked rapidly, as if waking from a trance. "Well...uh," she stammered, wiping her eyes.

"We go back and destroy that vile thing!" Vikur pounded his fist on the table, and Poluran, Pallit, and Arkor echoed the warrior's action.

"I do not believe the necromancer is there anymore," Borse said, regaining their attention. "From what Vecnor has told me, it sounds as though he departed after your encounter."

"The coward has flown!" Poluran growled. "He knew we would return!"

"We'll track the dog!" said Vikur. "Eraim is the finest tracker in all the land!"

"No." Merssa brought the burst of courage to an end, turning all eyes on her. "We'll do as he instructed."

The company stared in disbelief and their jaws dropped.

"We'll return to our lands and warn our kings and lords, as he demands," Merssa added. "But not to surrender. We'll prepare for his coming with steel. We'll fight this abomination and his minions with all we have!"

A pounding of fists ensued with a roar of approval.

"Then let's go!" Poluran stood and lifted Clanghorr. "While the fire burns hot!"

"Ease yourself, Master Poluran." Borse chuckled. "Perhaps a

good rest is in order. You have long journeys ahead, and you've come far with little nourishment. So relax now. Heal your bodies."

With his last words, Merssa's passion lightened and hunger and fatigue set in. Borse walked to the kitchen door and rapped three times before turning back to the table.

"Master Larman has prepared a meal, your horses have been stabled, and warm beds await."

Larman and Fellna entered bearing trays of food, and the innkeeper could not conceal his smile.

"All right then." Larman placed two trays on the table and rubbed his hands. "Are there any here in need of a refill?"

"That's a good man!" Poluran quickly drained his mug and slammed it onto the table.

Vikur's mug hit at the same time.

"Let's do it, Polerbin!" The Lord of the Keep grinned.

"Keep 'em coming!" The dwarf accepted the challenge.

The food was plentiful and spirits high as the company enjoyed the private party. Pallit revealed the desire to consume as much ale as Poluran and Vikur, and the three laughed heartily into the late hours. Arkor smiled now and again while listening to his brother's stories, often shaking his head or rolling his eyes, but he refused to confirm or deny any claims Vikur boasted. Selanna and Eraim kept to themselves, speaking to each other in their native tongue and enjoying a few laughs. But not all seemed to take part in the festivities, and Gruzim ate quietly, retiring to his room shortly after the food was gone.

Merssa sat next to Borse, eating slowly and sneaking glances at the priest while he continued to smile and sip from his mug.

"I have misjudged you," she said apologetically after clearing her throat. "You are indeed a priest worthy of respect."

"I have never taken offense." Borse placed a warm hand on Merssa's arm. "Respect is earned, not handed out freely, and especially not in places such as *Neja*."

Merssa gave a small smile, a bit embarrassed, and a thought

struck her. "You should come to Palidur! You could do good there. You could teach—"

"I have the utmost respect for the Holy City and the faith it spreads." Borse chuckled. "But I have always been among the people. That is where I belong."

"Perhaps you would be surprised," Merssa said softly, gazing at her tankard with a touch of disappointment. "Have you ever been there?"

"I've never been far beyond the borders of Neja," Borse admitted. "There is much work to be done here, I think you'll agree." He stared into her eyes, and it felt to her he saw beyond their drab brown color, piercing deep and into her heart. He smiled. "Perhaps I *would* be surprised. It has been a while since I made a pilgrimage."

"Have you a horse?" Merssa could barely contain her excitement. She was not entirely sure what was coming over her, and at the moment she did not care.

"I have things to attend to in Cafdella," Borse said, causing her smile to retreat. "But I'll meet you there. In a couple weeks, I think."

"I'm glad." Merssa hoped he was not only humoring her. "Ask for me at the north gate. They'll know where to find me."

"Why don't you get some rest now," Borse suggested. "Yours has been the longest journey of them all."

Merssa was not sure what he meant, but she nodded and rose to her feet. When she reached the door leading to the inn rooms, she looked back. Vikur, Poluran, and Pallit continued with their fun, toasting anything that came to mind and laughing up a storm, and Merssa saw they were the tavern's only occupants—even Borse was gone. She had not noticed the priest's departure, nor that of the elves', but that did not matter. She felt like she would sleep well. Borse would visit Palidur. He was a man of his word, of that Merssa was sure. She smiled and walked with a bit of a hop to her step.

The spell of the necromancer was lifted and the company's spirits returned. Their melancholy faces had been more than Vecnor could bear, and he traveled long and hard to get to Borse, so the priest could set things right. And now, even as their feast began, Vecnor felt a great wariness overtake him and he slipped quietly from the corner of the room where he had observed. It was time to gain some much-needed rest.

Standing in the hallway were Eraim and Selanna. Vecnor had not noticed their departure from the tavern.

"We really must thank you, Vecnor." Selanna used a tone foreign to her. She appeared quite humbled.

"It was Borse's doing," Vecnor said.

"But you saw things for what they were." The mage furrowed her brow. "It puzzles me that you were not affected the same as the rest of us, though. It takes great power to tamper with the mind of an elf, and even greater power with that of an elf mage. But you..."

Vecnor shrugged. "Just strong willed, I guess."

"I will not pry." Selanna held up her hands, returning to her usual, jovial self. "I am still much too weak to match wits with *you*."

"We are forever grateful, regardless," Eraim added, looking into his eyes and moving to pity. "How long has it been since last you slept?"

"I have chosen not to count the days." Vecnor sighed. "But sleep will be mine at last. Good night."

Eraim and Selanna embraced him and pulled him down to place kisses on his cheeks before allowing him to retire to his room.

Chapter 18

Power of Five

Night gave way to twilight, and soon the breakfast crowd would arrive. There was little time to return the room to its proper state, Larman thought as he gazed upon Poluran, Vikur, and Pallit, the three snoring louder than even Fellna could muster.

Poluran was lying upon a table, a tankard firmly grasped within each hand, and the other two were seated to either side of the dwarf, Vikur's head bowed while Pallit appeared to be sitting with his eyes closed. The rest of the tables and chairs were arranged around the room for reasons Larman could only guess—most likely to reenact some heroic battle of the past. Perhaps he should not have given them free reign to refill their mugs last night.

To Larman's relief, Merssa and Eraim arrived, and the two maidens roused the men and assisted them to rooms to sleep off the remainder of their intoxication. Larman's boys then reported for duty and all was made ready before the first patron passed through the door.

Merssa was not surprised to find the sleeping warriors within the tavern room come morning; she heard them laughing long into the night before sleep claimed her. Normally it would have bothered her to no end—there was an enemy to prepare for and long distances to cover—but other things were on Merssa's mind. She was not completely sure why, or if it was a good thing, but she could not wait to see Borse.

After putting the men to bed, Merssa returned to the tavern to find Larman had pushed together a couple tables to accommodate her party, and she and Eraim took a seat. It was not long before Borse, Selanna, and Arkor joined them for breakfast. There was conversation then, but it was kept light and no one spoke of the necromancer. A part of Merssa was glad for this, for it was an ugly topic, but another part told her she was growing weak while her enemy grew stronger. It was a turmoil she decided to ignore, however. At least for the time being.

After breakfast, Merssa joined Eraim to make sure the horses were ready for travel. Eraim shot Merssa a quizzical, almost amused expression that brought Merssa instant irritation—it was not the first time she had performed such a task! Then Eraim smirked for some reason, almost bursting into laughter when Merssa informed the stable hand that she and her company did not expect to leave until after lunch. What? There was nothing wrong with passing a couple more hours within the tavern and having a bite before hitting the road. Merssa would never understand Salenti elves.

When lunch began, the company was all present and took their seats. Pallit and Vikur did not look to be in the best of health and passed on all food, but Poluran readily accepted a large meal to fulfill both lunch and the breakfast he had missed. To Merssa's surprise Gruzim joined them, sitting without a word and eating in silence. She had expected the krukari to part ways at first opportunity.

"Has anyone seen Vecnor?" Eraim asked.

"Beggin' your pardon," Larman said while delivering more food to Poluran, "but Master Vecnor left in the middle of the night."

Merssa had forgotten Vecnor was even in Eastgate. She hated when he disappeared; she would have liked to have spoken to him about the past week. "Did he say where he was headed?" She made no attempt to mask her annoyance.

"I'm sorry." Larman frowned. "I didn't feel it my place to pry.

Figured you folks know your business."

Merssa released a heavy sigh. What was Vecnor hiding?

Shortly after noon, Borse and Pallit bade everyone farewell. Before they could depart, Merssa reconfirmed Borse's plans to visit Palidur, and she watched as the two rode off to the south until they were gone. Though she had desired to give the tall man an embrace, she was able to resist the urge and spare herself any more snickering from Selanna and Eraim. Merssa turned to address her company, pausing when she spotted the grins upon the Salenti elves… She should have just given the goodbye hug.

"I am off to Tikken City. Any of you are welcome to join me if you wish, for all or part of the journey as suits you."

"We shall join you," Vikur said. "I wish to hear for myself what the Council has to say about all of this."

"I am sure Rornibur would be most interested to learn of the Forbidden Area," Poluran scratched his chin, "but they shall have to wait a bit longer. This task is too important. And as I said before, I intend to see this until its end."

Gruzim stood, dressed for travel. Again, Merssa had expected the krukari to disappear to whatever life awaited him, but there he was, staring at her and not speaking until she raised a brow.

"I'm done with this place," was all he said in his deep, gravelly voice.

Merssa stared, wanting to turn the krukari away. Then she thought of Borse and what he would do, and after a deep breath she nodded. But always, she knew, she would keep a watchful eye on him.

The road seemed short, as nothing impeded them. Even Ellaville was deserted—either the bandits had moved on or thought better of revealing themselves a second time. Merssa was tempted to search for the thugs, but returning to Palidur grew more urgent with every passing hour and they continued.

After four days they passed through the gates of Tikken City. The streets were alive with merchants and shoppers and all seemed well, and though a few distrusting stares were directed Gruzim's way, the krukari passed unnoticed for the most part — the majority of the city's inhabitants were accustomed to all walks of life. Within the Council Building, servants scurried about in great haste, and after whispering to one of his staff and sending the man on some errand, Mordan smiled at the company.

"Welcome back, Lady Merssa." The steward bowed. "Please follow me."

Mordan escorted them into the audience chamber, and every step echoed into the vaulted ceiling while ten empty thrones gazed upon the company.

"I apologize for leaving you alone." Mordan shot a sideways glance at Eraim and Selanna. "I trust you will remain here and await the Council. They know of your arrival and should be along shortly."

"You have my word," Merssa assured him.

After another glance at the elves and one toward Gruzim, the steward bowed and exited.

"I shall be boarding my ship for Palidur without delay," Merssa informed the others. "I wish to thank you all for your skills and bravery, and I invite you to remain in my company for any additional orders I might receive."

"Yes." Eraim seemed to be suppressing in a giggle. "You must get back before Bor—"

"I must inform the High Order of all I have learned." Merssa had no interest in the remainder of the elf's sentence. "Let us not forget of the horrors we have witnessed."

Eraim's smile did not falter and Selanna joined her. Merssa turned to the small door, awaiting the wizards.

Several minutes passed before the door opened and a single robed figure entered. Merssa was surprised to see it was not Seac.

"I am Craldek." The wizard spoke in a surprisingly high voice as he stood before the second throne to the left of Seac's. "I do apologize for the delay." Though his words were contrite, his tone was one of arrogance.

"Where is Seac?" Merssa was suddenly concerned for the aging Seer.

"We are quite busy at the moment," Craldek explained. "But we are most interested in hearing your tale, and I'll have Mordan see to it you're taken care of until we are ready to—"

"What?" Merssa could not contain her outrage. "There's no time to delay. I must return—"

"I assure you all is well at the moment." The wizard spoke a bit more authoritatively, showing less patience than Seac usually extended. "We have learned much of the name Trannum since you departed, and of the prophecy. Though I'm sure you believe time to be short, *we* feel the necromancer is not a hasty creature. We have already sent word to Palidur of your experiences within Silent Marsh, though we know the High Order will resist hearing explanations from anyone other than their *own* messenger. But trust me when I say that a few more days will bring no harm."

Merssa's face grew hot at the reference to her as a *messenger* and she fought to control herself. After a deep breath, she said, "So be it."

Several days passed. Merssa's patience was at its end, but it seemed there was no one to receive her ire, with the exception of Mordan. The poor steward was weary from his daily duties, however, as well as with making himself available for Merssa and her company whenever necessary, and she had not the heart to add to his distress.

Poluran and the brothers of Ironside spent most their time within the many taverns of the city, Merssa gathered from conversations she overheard, and it seemed Vikur made no attempts to conceal his wealth as he bought rounds for the entire room at least once a day. Gruzim also disappeared into the city often to places unknown, but always returned at dusk for supper.

Selanna and Eraim remained on the Council grounds, usually within the vast library or walking the flower gardens, but sometimes Selanna retired to her room to study from the tomes of the marsh.

During these periods, Eraim passed the time wandering the halls, and no less than two servants accompanied the small elf to keep an eye on her, or at least to attempt to keep up and make sure no unauthorized rooms were disturbed. Merssa often heard moans of frustration from the staff, for it seemed Eraim had turned it into a game, disappearing and leaping from dark places when they least expected it.

Merssa remained in her room for the most part, burdened by her duty to report to Palidur and the thought that Borse might arrive to the Holy City before her. At times the priest was all Merssa thought about, and this troubled her further; she needed to remain focused to serve Cafior and Palidur.

On the third day, Seac held a private council with Merssa. Merssa spoke of her meeting with the necromancer and the warning the creature bestowed, as well as how Borse had cleansed her company's minds of the dark poison Trannum had set there. Seac did not seemed surprised by anything Merssa said; it was as if he had heard the news already. Well, Merssa thought, he was the Seer, after all.

"Intriguing," Seac commented upon the completion of Merssa's report. "But rest assured, pieces are falling into place. Be patient but a little longer."

On the sixth night, Mordan escorted Merssa again to the audience chamber. The room's only occupants were Selanna and Eraim, but the steward assured Merssa the Council would be along at any moment. Gruzim entered shortly after, apparently straight from the dining chamber—the krukari held a drumstick in his greasy hand.

"I had to send a messenger into the city to summon the others," Mordan told Merssa. "I imagine the Council will begin without them."

Merssa nodded.

Moments later, the small door opened and the members of the Council entered. Selanna nearly jumped in delight when Elgarroth followed at the end of the line of wizards, and she gave him a slight bow of the head while the Council took their seats.

"I have much to tell you, master," Selanna said in a hushed voice as Elgarroth stood beside her and Merssa.

"In good time." Elgarroth patted Selanna's arm.

"After many hours of research and deliberation, we have news." Seac gained everyone's attention. "From Merssa's report, information provided by Elgarroth, and the Scrolls, there is no doubt that the enemy we face is Trannum, necromancer of old and researcher into the Ancient Enemy of the North, some four-and-a-half centuries before our reckoning." The next moment was filled with a sigh issued by Selanna, prompting the Seer to add, "Though there are some that already felt this to be true, we had to be certain. After all, this makes him more than a thousand years in age; twice the lifespan than that of an elf."

"But he does not *live*." Merssa did not understand why everyone spoke as if the creature were a living thing. It made no sense. "He's undead. Just as the rest of his creations."

"Yes." Seac raised a hand. "He *is* undead, but he is *unlike* his other creations. He has maintained his power throughout the years, and added to it a new strength; the strength of an enemy long defeated.

"Trannum was chief researcher into the Ancient Enemy, and dealt with its dark power after its fall," Seac continued. "We believe him to have uncovered something too seductive to resist and he fell into shadow, succumbing to the darkness and disappearing for many centuries. Now, it seems, he has renewed the quest the Ancient Enemy failed to achieve: the destruction of Vaeldor as we know it."

Merssa could not believe she waited days to hear this. "Then we must act immediately! While we stand here, he is surely preparing his next move. Palidur has conquered this type of evil before, let us not forget."

"That is true." The Seer nodded. "But we no longer know where Trannum is, and therein lies the problem."

Merssa's shoulders dropped. She had almost forgotten. Vecnor reported to Borse that the presence of evil within the mountains seemed to fade after the meeting with the necromancer, and she knew this to be true. Poisoned though her thoughts had been at the time, Merssa recalled the way the air had lightened with the slamming of the stone door.

"Besides that," Seac added, "Trannum has had several centuries to make his plans, and hasty actions will surely play into them. Also, there is the matter of the prophecy and the *power of five.*"

"*United by one…*" murmured Eraim.

Selanna's eyes widened and her gaze snapped to the Seer. "It does not refer to Trannum!"

Seac shook his head. "No, it does not. We believe in this verse, the 'one' does not refer to Trannum, as it does in others. We believe it refers to the orb that was destroyed."

"There are more orbs!" Selanna said. "That would explain why the Wind came from so many directions. In Palidur it came from the north, while Vikur tells us it came to Ironside Keep out of the west."

"And Witchdoor of Tenvale reported a westerly wind," Seac added, "while Darmhorng of Kalmaar felt it from the northwest."

"Do we know if it still blows in any of these places?" asked Merssa.

"It does not," the Seer replied. "With the destruction of the orb in the Silent Marsh, the Wind has ceased everywhere."

The doors flew open and Vikur strode in, followed by Arkor and Poluran. From the grins on their faces and their glassy eyes, it was obvious they had enjoyed several tankards.

"You started without me?" Vikur's voice boomed.

"Please, Lord Vikur." Seac held up a hand for silence.

"No!" Vikur bellowed. "Dispense with the formalities. Here, I am just Vikur."

"Vikur, then." Seac lowered his hand, visibly upset with the interruption. "We have been discussing Trannum and the orbs."

"Orbs?" Poluran frowned. "There's more than one?"

Merssa glared at Vikur and Poluran until their mouths closed.

Seac turned back to Merssa. "So now it is the orbs that must be dealt with. Trannum will no doubt wish their safe return, for each possesses a great amount of his power."

"What makes you believe he has not already recovered them?" Merssa's question came out harshly, and she did not care. The skeleton wizard had been allowed days to do whatever he wished while she sat in a guestroom doing nothing.

"Not a week ago I had a vision," the Seer said. "It was of the necromancer standing upon Korban Bridge. He raised a bony hand, and undead creatures stepped from the shadows, forming into four groups. They marched forth, one group to the south and all others bearing east. It is our belief they have set out to find the orbs."

"But surely they already know where the orbs are," Merssa stated. "And since we have wasted days with idleness, we haven't a chance to overcome them."

"The undead have disadvantages." Seac raised a finger. "Most can only travel by night. Also, the Wind of the Dead has led to the creation of the Death Seekers, as they are called; riders that hunt the walking corpses day and night across many lands. And as for knowing where the orbs are located, already our scouts have found the original locations of each, but it seems they have been moved. We believe those that guarded them lost contact with their master when the orb in the marsh was destroyed, and with the Death Seekers about, these *guardians* must have sought places to hide them until help can arrive. Either that, or others have stumbled upon the orbs, unaware of their true nature."

"And what if Trannum should start his war while we're hunting orbs?" posed Merssa.

"That is not a likely event," Elgarroth replied. "Trannum will surely concentrate his energy upon regaining them. He will not want any more destroyed."

"He seemed quite powerful without them," Merssa pointed out.

"That is because they still exist," Elgarroth explained. "And while they do he can draw from them, even if he does not possess them."

Merssa bit her lip. She was tired of all this magic talk. She shook her head and turned to Seac. "I don't understand this as well as I should like. But the Council has always proven wise and I shall trust in it. If it is your counsel that the orbs be sought, then that is what I will explain to the High Order. And seeing that Trannum is already days ahead of us, I must take leave immediately."

"But which orb do we seek first?" inquired Poluran.

"They must all be found without delay," replied Seac. "Therefore, we have sent word to many that may be of assistance in the matter. We were also hoping that you, Lady Merssa, might be able to gather others you trust. The search for all four orbs must commence immediately and simultaneously."

"I see." Merssa realized the Council meant to break up her company. She glanced at what remained of her companions: the elves, a dwarf, the Ironside brothers, and a krukari. Perhaps it was for the best. "I will muster what I can."

"And, as I have mentioned," the Seer added, "we have scouts that already seek information as to the orbs' whereabouts, so no time will be lost while you prepare. They have already provided starting points for each orb: Sendorum, southern Sardina, northern Kalmaar, and southern Moclen."

"I will seek the one in Sendorum," said Merssa. "That is the one that plagued Palidur and the surrounding villages."

"We'll form a company to seek the orb in Sardina." Arkor spoke for himself and his brother. "It is surely the one responsible for waking our ancestors, a day I'll not easily forget."

Vikur cleared his throat. "Actually, you must handle that one without me, little brother. I have strong ties with King Karrak, and my sword belongs to him before any other. I will lead the expedition into Kalmaar."

"This is a beginning." Seac appeared satisfied. "In another room are two that answered our call already. Brem is a priest of Frayorna, and Melac a mage out of Moclen that we have known for some time."

"I know Brem." Poluran nodded in approval. "He is a marteese from Neja. A good man."

"Where shall the lovely elf maidens venture to?" Vikur smiled at Selanna and Eraim.

"Sardina." Selanna did not hesitate, but she appeared confused, as if the voice was not her own. She glanced at Elgarroth, who paid her no mind—his attention never strayed from the Council. Selanna's gaze returned to the Seer. "It lies close to the borders of Tenvale," she added with some thought. "If the orb is within the Wizard Kingdom, there will be need for one with my skills."

"That's three of the four." Merssa sighed. "Who's to go into southern Moclen?"

"That shall be me," said Poluran. "One of us should stay here, and it would appear all of you intend to head east."

"It is settled then." Seac sat back in his chair.

The next few hours were spent pouring over maps and learning what information the Council's scouts had uncovered during the previous week. Names of cities and villages were shared, as well as the contacts to be found within each. Merssa paid the utmost attention when briefed on the Sendorum orb, but her mind wandered as talk shifted to that of the others. She needed to return to Palidur soon.

Afterwards, the hall was emptied and everyone readied their gear for travel. They then said their goodbyes to Poluran before heading to the docks.

"Mind you all find success," Poluran said. "I can't go hunting them *all* down. I am but one dwarf!"

CHAPTER 19

PALIDUR

Merssa's ship sailed through the night, docking the next morning among a score of ships bearing the flag of Palidur: a dark-blue gauntleted fist rising between two mountains beneath the blazing sun upon a sky-blue background—a fine representation of the unity of the three deities: Soleran, Cafior, and Arronaus. The wooden docks extended hundreds of feet from a shore of silver stone, and three white towers kept watch over the King Arman. Connecting the towers was a wall, thirty feet high and fifteen feet thick, also painted white. The wall encompassed the Holy City's mass of tall white buildings, and every hundred yards throughout its length stood another tower, fifty feet high and topped by either a catapult or ballistae. Several guards walked the battlements while they eyed Merssa's ship and held ready their crossbows. She was home!

From the desk in her cabin, Merssa retrieved her freshly polished medallion of gold depicting two mountains. She had been up most the night cleaning the remnants of the Silent Marsh from the holy symbol in preparation of her homecoming, and after displaying it proudly about her neck, she strapped on her fine brown cloak. Stepping from the ship, Merssa heard the Grand Cathedral bell chime ten times to announce the hour and she took in a deep breath. It felt as if she had been gone a year.

Behind Merssa walked Selanna and Eraim, and Lilli and Dandi followed. Arkor and Vikur staggered onto the dock a moment later—

the ride had not agreed with their stomachs and they needed time to clean themselves.

"Why people travel by boat when there are plenty of fine horses, I'll never understand," said Vikur.

After one of the ship's crew handed Vikur and Arkor the reins to their horses, Merssa proceeded.

She led the way from the docks and onto the silver stones, where several guards in dark-blue cloaks bowed upon recognizing Merssa and cleared the way. Forty yards up the street, a gate interrupted the massive wall and the portcullis lifted to allow her access.

The streets of stone continued beyond the gate, but the color was blue as the night sky to represent the deity Soleran. Most inhabitants donned cloaks or robes of the same hue and greeted Merssa as they passed, but their smiles dropped quickly while they viewed her companions with suspicion. This was to be expected, for Palidur was not a place of hospitality, it was a bastion for Good and Law, and its citizens were right to be wary of non-Palidurians, or outlanders, spending even the briefest moment within their hallowed walls. It was not arrogance, but an attitude proven to ward off evil. Of the three religions, the Soleran Sector was the most tolerant of outlanders, and in times of danger was even known to house peasants and commoners until the threat could be vanquished, for Soleran was Defender of the Defenseless. But Merssa's companions were hardly defenseless, so they were watched with critical eyes, even within the Soleran Sector, regardless of Merssa's presence.

Merssa continued at a pace to cause Vikur to comment on the churning of his tender stomach, and they soon reached a divider—smaller walls separating the city into its three sectors of worship. In times of war, divider gates could be closed if any part of the city was breached, but the gate stood wide open and Merssa passed through. The street and typical garb of the inhabitants then became brown to represent Cafior.

Merssa grew anxious and dropped the horses off at the nearest stables, issuing explicit instructions to give the animals the best possible care—the elves appeared uneasy with leaving their mares behind, even so. They continued east, and Merssa picked up the pace until coming to a halt outside a four-story structure. It was a typical building of residence, made up of small apartments to board the city's inhabitants. One such building could house sixty to a hundred citizens, and there existed at least two hundred of them within the Cafior Sector alone. The city held plenty of room for the compact housing, for it did not waste much space on taverns or inns and there existed no markets. There were many churches, however, as well as stables, smithies, armories, food stores, and a few larger homes for the higher-ranking paladins and priests, the latter missing within the Soleran Sector, for the religion forbade exploits of wealth or luxury. Merssa ushered her companions into her cozy, two-room dwelling on the second floor, instructing them to wait there while she ran a quick errand.

She made her way to the north gate. Unlike the gate at the docks, it stood between two larger towers and its opening was two carts wide and twenty yards deep. From the outside, two massive doors of oak barred entry, each twenty feet high and three feet thick. Any wishing to enter would first announce their business to the tower guards, and if allowed beyond the doors, they were met by an iron portcullis consisting of bars three inches thick and strengthened by crossbeams every few feet. They were then questioned and looked over by the gate captain while the doors shut behind them, and if satisfied, the captain signaled for the raising of the portcullis and allowed entry. Such were the ways of the city, and if Borse had passed through, the captain would have record of it.

Merssa called for the gate captain. The man obviously recognized her, for he smiled and greeted her by name, but Merssa failed to recall his. She conversed briefly with him, inquiring if Borse had arrived, and was pleased to learn that no one under any such name had reported to the gate. Merssa left firm instructions that she was to be notified the moment Borse arrived, and that he was to be treated with the utmost respect—outlander priests were not always held in as high regard as priests of Palidur, for they lacked the benefits of Palidurian teachings. Even *she* had not met well with Borse in Cafdella.

Merssa returned to her quarters, where Vikur and Selanna occupied the only two chairs. Arkor sat uncomfortably on the floor with a pouty expression.

"Is he here yet?" Selanna grinned.

"Who?" Merssa tried to appear aloof, but she felt her cheeks flush.

"Borse!" Eraim poked her head out from the bedroom.

"There are important matters to attend to." Merssa shifted to irritation, a look coming much easier. "I'm off to the Grand Cathedral."

Selanna stood. "I wish to go."

Merssa sighed. She knew the High Order would not meet well with such a request, but some of the Council of Wizard's points still escaped her comprehension. She might need Selanna to explain properly. "All right." Merssa gave in with a nod.

"I don't want to stay in this—" Arkor cut himself short under Merssa's glare. "I need air."

"All right, we'll all go." Merssa felt as a mother speaking to her bored children. "But the rest of you will have to wait outside." Under her breath, she added, "I don't know that they'll even allow Selanna admittance."

Merssa led the way to the center of the city, where the dividers connected to yet another wall, this one encircling the inner sanctum. Enclosed was the Grand Cathedral, four times larger than the Council Building of Tikken City. Within were the great halls of worship to the three deities, as well as the High Temple. The domed rooftop rose high above the walls with the bell tower resting atop its center, and the sun shone onto its white stone, reflecting off runes of silver. Around the dome were angelic statues bearing weapons, as if to protect the city's most holy structure, and when the company passed through the open gates, they encountered more of the statues adorning a street of silver stones.

The street continued around the front of the structure, but Merssa headed for the near entrance, where brown steps led to a set of doors. Before the doors stood two sentries in brown cloaks.

"Good to see you've returned, Lady Merssa," the sentry to the right greeted her in a fashion befitting a Knight of Palidur. "The Order has been informed of your arrival and awaits your presence."

The other sentry sneered, gazing past Merssa. "I see you have company."

Merssa glanced at her companions. Eraim concentrated on the cathedral dome, probably contemplating climbing the structure; Arkor was irritated; Vikur searched his fingernails for something; and Selanna stared intently at the cathedral soldiers. Merssa turned back to the guards.

"They have journeyed far with me and faced great evils in the name of Palidur. I request admittance for one of them, Selanna, for she may be better able to present certain views to assist the Order."

The second sentry scowled. "That is not possible. The law doesn't allow —"

Merssa's glare halted his tongue. Though she stood only as high as his chest, he shrank before her. "Do not take such a tone before me! Go and place my request!"

"Yes, L-Lady Merssa." The guard disappeared through the doors.

"My apologies," the first sentry offered, though his expression showed his true feelings. "He forgot his place."

Merssa stared a few seconds longer, unsatisfied, and then walked down the steps to Selanna.

"I do not think they'll grant you audience. I'm sorry, but no outlander has ever set foot within the Grand Cathedral."

Selanna nodded with a sigh.

The second sentry returned with a sour, dutiful expression. "Your request has been respectfully denied by the High Order," he said, as if reciting an order. "But your presence is requested immediately."

"You may return to my quarters," Merssa suggested to the others after a moment, and Vikur rolled his eyes. "Or…there is a tavern called Pleasant Vale, back the way we came. The Pleasant Vale." Merssa repeated the name slowly the second time, so there would be no misunderstandings.

"There's a name to make one tremble!" Vikur kidded.

"Stay out of trouble." Merssa pointed at Vikur. "I mean it. Your usual mannerisms will not be tolerated."

Merssa climbed the steps and entered the cathedral, the first sentry opening one of the doors and giving a cold, sideways glare toward the second sentry as she passed.

She walked along a wide corridor with an arched ceiling, and beneath her a long brown carpet stretched the length of the hall atop a marbled floor of white and brown. To either side stood statues of the many founders of the Cafior Sector, tall and proud, and a few doors were set here and there. Merssa continued to the end, where two more sentries stood before a second set of doors. The soldiers stepped aside and opened the doors without a word, allowing her access into the High Temple.

The marbled floor continued, adding two shades of blue to its design, and the walls of the chamber were colored silver. The ceiling vaulted more than thirty feet overhead with exquisite statues around the arch, and sunlight streamed through stained glass windows, displaying beautiful patterns upon the pews. Candles burned in various places about three altars near the center, and at the northern end, upon a dais behind the Grand Altar, were six colored thrones. Upon two brown thrones sat Jerove and Arduer, High Priest and High Paladin of Merssa's order, the dark-blue seats in the middle were occupied by Nilborg and Soren of the Soleran Sector, and seated upon the light-blue thrones representing Arronaus were Garren and Trakinir. The High Order of Palidur gazed upon Merssa in silence, each wearing an exquisite robe matching the color of their throne, save for Nilborg and Soren, who bore robes of modest quality.

"We were about to send an escort for you." Jerove's impatience was obvious.

"Please forgive my delay, Your Excellencies." Merssa stepped forward and bowed low. "The news I bring is grave."

"Indeed," said Garren, the Arronaus priest doing nothing to conceal his disapproval. "Tikken City sent word over a week ago, telling us of one called Trannum. We had to hear from a Council lackey of the possible force behind the Wind, with no further explanation as to who Trannum is."

"Trannum was a great and terrible necromancer," Merssa explained. "And he is indeed behind the evil."

"You say he *is* behind it?" Arduer, the High Paladin of her order, raised a brow. "Then you did not bring an end to it?"

"No," Merssa said somberly. "Though the Wind of the Dead has ceased, I fear the evil has only begun. With permission of the Order, I would tell all I have seen and heard, from the beginning."

"You may speak," said Jerove.

Merssa told her tale of the expedition into the Silent Marsh and all she encountered therein. She spoke of the journey into the Stone Eagle Mountains and the chilling tomb beneath the rorbak, the message Trannum bestowed upon her and her companions, and concluded with the discussion of the *power of five*.

"The wizards of the Council feel we must track down the remaining orbs," she added, "lest the prophecy take full shape."

"Or, perhaps we should strike at the very root." Trakinir had been drumming his fingers upon the light-blue stone affixed to the pommel of his holy sword. "You say Trannum draws power from the orbs. Then without him, would the orbs not prove worthless?"

"I do not believe that to be the case," Merssa said. "Besides that, he was much too powerful—"

"For the band of outlanders that accompanied you," Jerove finished.

"The wizards all agree." Merssa addressed the High Priest of her order. "And Elgarroth himself—"

"They also agreed to send you hastily into Trannum's clutches," Garren pointed out. Merssa had always felt a bit of disdain from the Arronaus priest; Garren never seemed to support her ascension to Paladin. "Had you returned here first, as duty commanded, we would have sent you into Neja with a proper force, and the necromancer would have been vanquished."

"We have much respect for the Council across the lake, as do you," Arduer added with a slightly softer tone, as if he sensed Merssa's growing frustration. "But even *they* cannot see all. If that were so, we would hardly have need of our High Order." The High Paladin waved a hand toward his colleagues, who snickered under their breaths—with the exception of the Soleran representatives, who maintained faces of stone.

"In this matter, however," Merssa stated firmly, "I believe them to be correct. I was there, and the likes of those that accompanied me, though outlanders they may be, were both brave and competent. Trannum has now disappeared and his minions seek the orbs, and for us to waste time searching for him…" She shook her head. "Have you not heard the prophecy?"

"We have," confirmed Nilborg, the priest breaking the silence of the Soleran representatives. "And I, for one, agree with Merssa and the Council of Wizards. The verse, *Hallowed Land is wrest,* is most disturbing. Could our arrogance prove our downfall?"

The Cafior and Arronaus members gazed at Nilborg, their fleeting looks of outrage not escaping Merssa's notice, but the Soleran priest was undaunted. Next to Nilborg, Soren bore a troubled look and shifted uneasily, evidently undecided in the matter.

"We will speak on this subject," Arduer said at last, and then he addressed Merssa. "Await us in the Cafior Temple."

Merssa bowed and exited.

She returned down the hall and entered the Cafior Temple. There, she stared blankly at several candles burning before a small altar. The altar was a finely crafted piece of black onyx, topped by a golden anvil with a pair of hammers set upon it—a symbol of Cafior's

Might. Merssa took in a deep breath and released it slowly.

Most of her surprise lay with the members of her own order, Arduer and Jerove. In the past they had always heeded her council. She had brokered peace between rival lords in Sardina, ended a hobgoblin assault upon Sendorum, and routed goblin raiders attempting to pillage settlements to the east near the Varlimor Mountains. She always investigated, assessed, and reported, and Arduer and Jerove always agreed with her plan of action. Then the job would get done. Of course, those particular situations had not been quite so dark as this one. *Was* her counsel wise? Was she wrong?

Merssa lit a candle and prayed.

CHAPTER 20

DECISION OF THE HIGH ORDER

Eraim considered the many statues jutting from the rooftop of the Grand Cathedral around the dome, and she could not help but wonder how quickly she could scale from the street to the top of the building, ring the bell, and return.

"Let's find that tavern!" Vikur stole her attention, rubbing his hands together.

"Have you ever been to a Palidur tavern?" inquired Selanna. "It is probably not what you expect."

"As long as there's beer!" Vikur laughed.

They made their way back toward Merssa's quarters, but had no luck finding the Pleasant Vale. Eraim considered asking for directions, but the streets became packed with leering eyes and she thought better of it. After wandering aimlessly for some time, three men in brown cloaks approached them.

"Are you lost?" asked one without greetings or pleasantries.

"No, my fine man." Vikur smiled. "We're looking for a place to get a drink, and perhaps a bite."

"There's a very nice tavern in Courtin," the man suggested, speaking of a village Eraim knew to be a few miles outside Palidur.

Vikur broke into laughter. "Very good, sir! But my hunger would not survive the walk."

"They sell horses in Dellabville," offered the second man, mentioning a village not quite as distant. "You could be there before dusk if you leave now."

Vikur's chuckle became a bit labored and his face grew red.

"We are awaiting Lady Merssa," Selanna said. "And I do not believe she would appreciate having to track us down to any of those places when she is finished speaking with the High Order."

The three men stared at Selanna, obviously knowing of Merssa. Of course, one would probably be hard pressed to find anyone within the Cafior Sector that did not.

"Perhaps you should await her in her quarters, then," suggested the third man, maintaining the pompous tone the others carried.

"Thank you." Selanna bowed before walking down the street. Eraim and the brothers followed.

"They sure make you feel welcome," commented Arkor.

Eraim understood the one-armed warrior's sarcasm, and for the most part she agreed. But even so, Arkor had been wearing his pout since they arrived.

"We are *not* welcome here," Selanna reminded them. "No outsiders are. But even so, as long as the banners of Palidur fly high and proud, all people of surrounding lands sleep well in their beds at night. We best be on good behavior."

Eraim was a bit surprised to hear her friend speak so. She had never known Selanna to defend the Holy City. In fact, Eraim often heard Selanna tease Merssa with threats of bringing all of Dominelli to show Palidur a proper night life, which was never met with any humor.

"You sure put those men in their place, brother," Arkor murmured to Vikur. "Perhaps it would be best if we just return—"

"A tavern!" Vikur pointed to a building not far away.

"*The Holy Sentinel*?" Eraim observed the sign. "Merssa said to go to the Pleasant Vale."

"Nonsense!" said Vikur. "Drinks are on me!"

Before Eraim could voice her protest, the Lord of the Keep was away on swift strides.

He led the way into the establishment. Unlike normal taverns, there existed no roaring laughter, no music, and no singing. Not even a game of cards or darts was underway. There were a few small groups of well-dressed patrons eating and sharing quiet conversation, but activities ceased and all eyes fell upon the door.

"Beer and meals for four!" Vikur walked to an open table.

"You know," the barkeep said, "Courtin has—"

"A very nice tavern!" Vikur finished. "But it does not even begin to compare to the Holy Sentiment!"

A couple patrons chuckled arrogantly.

Vikur seated himself before noticing Eraim and the others still stood in the doorway. He motioned for them to join him and they reluctantly obeyed. The barman stared a moment longer in disbelief before turning to the other patrons. One of the men nodded and the barkeep delivered the tankards.

"There's no charge." The nervous barman spoke in a low voice. "So long as you quietly drain your mugs and be on your way."

"Nonsense!" Vikur slammed five gold coins onto the table. "This ought to buy at least three tales to share with my friends!"

The barman seemed unpleased, and he hesitantly scooped up the coins before returning to the bar.

"Drink up!" Vikur raised his mug and emptied it in one long drink.

Shortly after, the barkeep returned with four bowls of lukewarm broth and half a loaf of day-old bread.

"Thank you, my good man." Vikur broke off a piece of the loaf. "Another beer, if you don't mind." Turning to the others, he added, "Eat your fill," and he dunked the bread into a bowl.

"No thanks." Selanna slid her bowl aside.

Eraim did the same while regarding the other patrons. They wore the same fine brown cloaks as Merssa, and proudly displayed about their necks were well-crafted medallions of Cafior. Eraim was confident they were not ordinary citizens of Palidur.

Vikur proceeded to tell a few stories. Eraim had heard them many times before, but a few of the facts were changed as he "remembered" things omitted in the past. After the first tale Eraim was sure they would be thrown out, but the locals seemed amused, as an audience to a puppet show. An hour later, Vikur thanked the proprietor for his "fine hospitality" and slapped another five coins onto the bar, and they left at last.

Eraim felt as if she had held her breath the entire time she sat at the table. Stepping beneath the sun, she released a long exhale.

"And now I'm ready to return to Merssa's cave." Vikur scratched his neck and gazed about, thoroughly confused.

Eraim did not understand why no one ever seemed to pay attention when walking in strange places. Sure, the buildings all appeared similar, but she remembered every turn they took while seeking the Pleasant Vale. With a sigh, she guided them back to Merssa's quarters.

As they neared their destination, three men approached on a direct path. Two were dressed in shiny silver armor with light-blue cloaks, and the third man walked a couple paces behind, dressed in priestly robes of the same color. Eraim knew them to be of the Arronaus Sector, deity of the sky.

"Clear the way!" commanded one of the warriors.

Selanna and Eraim immediately moved to the side and Vikur joined them. Arkor feigned a sideways step and bumped shoulders with the one who gave the order. The warrior came to an immediate halt and glared at Arkor, the two standing eye to eye and their faces inches apart. Eraim felt helpless and Selanna stood with mouth agape, seemingly at a loss for words and offering no assistance in the matter.

"Step aside," said the warrior through clenched teeth, "lest I personally escort you outside the city walls."

"This isn't your sector," Arkor growled. "The road is wide enough for everyone."

"Stand down, little brother," Vikur warned in a low voice.

Eraim had seen Arkor like this in the past. The one-armed warrior never liked taking orders from those he did not know and respect. Eraim also knew the situation would most likely worsen.

"This isn't your city!" retorted the man. "And while you are a guest here, I suggest you heed the counsel of your *wiser* brother and stand aside."

Yes. That would definitely do it. Eraim was powerless to stop what would surely come next and Selanna still seemed to be held in shock. Even Vikur's shoulders slumped.

Arkor turned to continue up the street, giving the Arronaus warrior a shove and nearly knocking him from his feet. The man swung his cloak aside and reached for the hilt of his fancy sword, his eyes filled with fury.

"What is the meaning of this?" demanded Merssa, suddenly appearing from the south.

"These...people—" the warrior spat.

"Are with me, Rholmar," Merssa finished.

"You?" Rholmar looked at her in disbelief. "Why do you bring this..." he looked Arkor up and down, "this *filth* into our city?"

"It is my business," Merssa said sharply. "Now I suggest you return to yours."

Merssa strode past Rholmar without another word, and Selanna and Vikur followed. Eraim moved last, waiting for Arkor and Rholmar to finish eyeing each other before moving on.

They proceeded toward Merssa's quarters, and Eraim saw Vikur nudge Arkor and nod toward the paladin. Eraim knew Vikur meant for his brother to apologize or offer a word of thanks, but she also knew Arkor felt no appreciation for the intervention. It had something to do with the pride of human males.

"Our apologies," Vikur offered. "Thank you for not letting the situation get out of hand."

Merssa spun where she stood, turning angry eyes upon the brothers. "Rholmar is a respected Paladin of Arronaus. Do not ever put me in such a position again." She entered the building, adding, "Perhaps next time I'll let *him* handle it."

Vikur gave a warning glare toward his brother, as if expecting a comment to follow. Arkor bit his tongue.

After climbing the steps to Merssa's apartment, Merssa's mood immediately lightened. Borse stood outside her door with Pallit, as well as a soldier wearing a brown cloak.

"Ah, Merssa, my dear." Borse held a gentle smile.

It did not escape Eraim's notice that Merssa appeared ready to run to the priest, perhaps even give him an embrace. But the paladin's pace only reached a brisk walk and she clasped arms with the gangly man. Merssa's self-restraint caused Eraim to grin.

"Welcome, Borse," Merssa said, her lips breaking into a smile. "Welcome, Pallit." She clasped arms with the ranger.

"This fine man was kind enough to lead us to your quarters." Borse looked to the soldier, who stood with mouth agape, evidently unaccustomed to seeing Merssa behave so.

Merssa's smile dropped as she addressed the guard. "That will be all. You may return to the gate."

"Thank you, Lady Merssa!" The man bowed and descended the stairs.

Sizing up the company, Merssa sighed. "Perhaps we should go to Pleasant Vale. I don't believe we would be comfortable in my quarters."

Merssa led the way back outside and down the street to the tavern Eraim and the others could not find, only a block away. The white building appeared as the others around it, standing two stories tall with a simple door and a couple shuttered windows. There was no sign marking it as the Pleasant Vale or anything else. Vikur shook his head.

Merssa stepped into the Pleasant Vale, feeling a bit lighter on her feet than she had only moments ago, after her meeting with the High Order. The barroom held only eight patrons, leaving several tables open, and she pulled a few of them together while Vikur and Pallit gathered chairs. Merssa then spoke to the barkeep, who immediately took on the task of making sure everyone was served drinks and a proper meal.

Vikur brightened as he viewed the bounty placed before them: steaming meat, vegetables, hot broth, flatbread, and a large piece of cheese. "Now that's a meal! That Holy Sentryol—"

"Holy Sentinel?" Merssa snapped her head Vikur's direction. There was no way they visited that establishment. Probably one of Vikur's dumb jokes.

"Well..." Vikur shrugged. "There's not even a sign on this building! We couldn't find it, so we went to the other place."

"That tavern is for paladins," Merssa scolded. "I'm surprised they didn't throw you from the city." Actually, she was shocked they were not in jail.

"And what a city it is." Borse gained Merssa's attention. "I wish we could've arrived sooner, but the roads stretched longer than we anticipated."

"Any sooner and you would have been waiting for *us*," Selanna said with a smile. "We had been, for several days, guests of the Council of Wizards. We only just arrived today ourselves."

"True." Merssa was still annoyed with the wizards. "For a group of wise men, the Council is not always very quick with their information."

Borse and Pallit proceeded to share their journey from Neja while the others began to eat. It was an uneventful tale, spotted with humorous remarks here and there. At the story's conclusion, Borse again complimented the splendor of the Holy City and Pallit nodded in agreement, but Merssa detected uneasiness within the ranger. She then shared with Borse the words of the Council of Wizards.

"So you are to seek the orbs, then?" Borse raised a brow.

Merssa's mood darkened as she relived her meeting with the High Order. The past hour had been pleasant in more ways than one; she got to see Borse, and she had been able to forget about the words spoken to her by the city's leaders, even if only for a moment. There was no pleasant way to say it, so Merssa's tone became business-like.

"The orbs are no longer my concern. Palidur has decided to crush this evil at its core. We will seek out Trannum." A dark cloud descended upon Merssa with her words. She had led the company since the beginning, making the tough decisions and keeping them focused. And now she was forbidden from seeing it through. Looks of shock surrounded the table, with the exception of Borse.

"What about the orbs?" Vikur asked.

"We are not even sure where Trannum is anymore," Eraim pointed out.

"We found him once," Merssa waved a hand, "he will be found again." She looked at the company and hastily added, "But this does not mean you shouldn't go after the orbs. It only means I will not be there to help."

"But earlier you said—" began Vikur.

"I spoke hastily!" Merssa did not wish to be reminded. "Now I've had time to put thought to it."

"You? Or the Order?" murmured Arkor, and the lack of respect did not escape Merssa.

"Watch your tongue!"

"Now, now." Borse raised a calming hand. "I'm sure Merssa has her reasons. It is not for us to choose her path."

"But how can we achieve success without Merssa?" questioned Eraim, her eyes wide with genuine concern.

"Pallit and I shall offer our services," Borse said with a slight nod.

Merssa was taken by surprise, and the turmoil in her stomach grew. "Is that wise? You have many who follow you, and I'm sure they anxiously await your return."

"I shan't be returning." Borse patted her hand. "I've always been somewhat of a pilgrim, and my people knew Cafior would lead me away one day."

Merssa's mind raced. She had not anticipated this. She knew what she *wanted* to do, but she had her orders. "I shall see to it everyone has a place to stay tonight," she said. It was the only thing she could think of to change the subject.

Vikur sat back with a sigh. "Good. I thought we were going to squeeze into your place."

Merssa glared at the Lord of the Keep before returning her gaze to the others. "We have quarters usually reserved for religious and royal guests. I'll secure a suite there. But you *will* mind yourselves." Her warning was directed toward the Ironside brothers.

Once the meal was ended, they gathered their gear from Merssa's quarters and she led them to a smaller building down the street, where she spoke to the building manager. He was reluctant to provide a suite for her guests, even after Merssa pointed out that Vikur was Lord of Ironside Keep, so she resorted to a more direct approach.

"You *will* give me a key!" Merssa placed all the frustrations of the day into her glare.

She received the key.

The private suite was similar to Merssa's apartment, except that it was immense in comparison with two luxurious bedrooms and a plush living area. The room was stocked with grapes, flatbread, and a decanter of wine, and Merssa saw to it they were supplied with additional food and a small keg of beer so they would have no cause to wander the streets. Hopefully, that would keep them out of trouble.

With the sky darkening, Borse left Pallit with the others and joined Merssa for a walk and breath of fresh air. Merssa led him along the streets, showing off various areas of the Cafior Sector and the church she frequented most often. She also explained the city's three factions and how they worked together to thwart evil. At the center of the city, Merssa showed Borse the Grand Cathedral and he gazed upon it in awe, inquiring of its interior splendor, but her shoulders dropped and she explained he could not enter. This did not seem to diminish Borse's experience, however, and he settled for her descriptions with a smile. Merssa spoke of the High Order and how they were responsible for all major decisions affecting the city, and she stopped by each statue adorning the silver street and introduced the saints by name. There was so much to share, Merssa hoped she had not missed anything.

They headed back through the Cafior Sector as the stars found their places in the sky. Oil lamps upon tall poles illuminated the streets and windows became aglow. Finally, Merssa found the courage to speak of the situation at hand.

"It's my duty to seek Trannum," she explained. "It's not necessarily my own opinion."

"I know." Borse glanced her way. "Duty is a powerful thing."

"It is." Merssa nodded. "Palidur was created through duty and honor, and has stood thus long because of those traditions."

"And a strong city it is." Borse gazed at the white buildings surrounding them.

"Am I wrong?" she asked, just above a whisper.

"That is not for me to say."

Merssa's shoulders slumped again. Borse was wise, and she had hoped for something more.

"You have a duty to your city." Borse looked her in the eyes. "It is the way you know things to be, and I am not one to change that."

"That's one of the things I admire about you." Merssa gave him a soft smile. "Your acceptance of everything around you. You emanate warmth and wisdom. That is why I must know your thoughts on this matter."

"For me," Borse said, "duty is in my service to Cafior above all other things. That is why I have never settled in one place for too long. It is He who guides me."

"Then you believe it is Cafior's will to seek the orbs?" Merssa asked.

"Of course not." He smiled as he shook his head. "I do not pretend to truly know His will. But the orbs are a creation of evil, as you have explained, and must be destroyed. Cafior stands for all that is good, and I do not *believe* He would like to see those objects returned to their master. That is the information upon which I have based my decision."

"I tried to convince them," Merssa said after another moment of silence. "But they wouldn't listen. I almost feel they are eager to march into Neja, and this gives them the opportunity." Her own words caught her by surprise. It was not that long ago that she would have looked forward to joining a militant expedition into the realm of outlaws.

"Do your laws bind you to march with them?" inquired Borse.

"They do," she said regretfully. "I would lose my rank if I went against the High Order. I could then lose my quarters and place here in Palidur." Tears welled in her eyes. "This is my home. I was born here. And no matter where life takes me, I can't wait to pass through the gates and return to my beautiful city."

Borse placed a gentle hand upon her back. It was warm and reassuring, but did little to comfort Merssa at the moment.

"It seems to me you fear banishment more than loss of rank or anything else," he commented. "Was the High Order unanimous in its decision?"

Merssa accidentally allowed a sniffle to escape before her reply. "Actually...no. Nilborg, the High Priest of Soleran, sided with me. But he was outnumbered." She came to a sudden halt, thoughts racing through her mind. "That's it!" She could not conceal her smile as an idea began to form. "Thank you, Borse!" Merssa pulled him down and placed a kiss on his cheek.

"What did I do to deserve that?" he asked with a chuckle.

"It's getting late." Merssa pointed to a building two doors up the street. "The guest quarters are right there. I cannot explain right now, but I'll see you at breakfast."

Merssa hurried back the way they had come, glancing one last time to see Borse wave before she rounded a corner. She entered the Soleran Sector, and did not slow until reaching the church where Nilborg resided. Upon entering, Merssa requested immediate audience with the High Priest, and the servant that met her disappeared to see if His Excellency was up for a late visit.

Merssa gazed at the shadowy worship room to the right, where a few candles scarcely revealed the altar and empty pews. The statue of Soleran, a kind-faced warrior holding aloft his Sword of Justice, was well illuminated as always, but Merssa hardly noticed this time. Her heart raced as her mind tried to wrap itself around the words she needed to convince Nilborg to see things her way; to persuade him to enact his rights as one of the High Order and —

Her thoughts were interrupted when the servant returned, motioning for her to follow.

Merssa was delivered to a study filled with many books and scrolls. Half the tomes were open and Nilborg was busy writing in one, but he broke from his work and smiled.

"Lady Merssa Goldmace," the priest said. He was the oldest of all the High Priests within the city and almost thirty years Merssa's elder, but Nilborg always appeared much younger, keeping a clean-shaven face and well-trimmed dark hair. Only the wrinkles about his eyes gave him away. "What brings you here at this hour?"

"Your Excellence." Merssa bowed. "I must know, is it still your belief that the orbs should be sought?"

"It is," Nilborg said after a brief pause, raising a brow. "But the Order has voted."

"But you see, you could still pursue that route." Merssa paused for a deep breath in an attempt to contain her excitement. "Any member of the High Order can call for an expedition —"

"I know of the laws." Nilborg put up a hand to silence her, breaking into a small smile. "It is actually something I am considering at this very moment."

"You must include me!" Merssa's eyes grew wide. "You are allowed to choose those from other sectors that are willing —"

Nilborg raised his hand again. "Yes, yes, Merssa." He shook his head and chuckled, then stared at her and sighed while drumming his fingers on the desk. "You make the decision an easy one. I will plan such an expedition. And you will be its commander."

Merssa's face broke into a grin and she desperately wished to give the priest a hug. "It will be an honor to assist you in this matter!"

"The honor is all mine," Nilborg said. "But now you must tell me all that you know. I'll have my steward take a message to the Grand Cathedral in the morning and inform them of my intentions."

Merssa spent most the night within the Soleran Church, giving a complete account of her expedition and omitting no details. They discussed the orbs' last known resting places, as told by the Council of Wizards, and made a list of others they might include in their mission—the law allowed ten willing citizens of rank from the Holy City.

"That is all we can do for now." Nilborg yawned. The hour had grown late. "Perhaps we should get some rest before the sun rises in a couple hours. We'll continue after lunch."

"Thank you!" Merssa bowed.

"Thank *you*, Lady Merssa Goldmace."

Merssa's summons to the High Temple of Cafior came the next morning, before she had had a chance to join her companions for breakfast. She was then confronted by Jerove and Arduer, who impressed upon her the disapproval Nilborg's expedition met with the majority of the High Order. The two were visibly upset, and it appeared to Merssa that Nilborg had convinced them she had had no hand in it, for Jerove expressed outrage in the High Priest of Soleran choosing her to lead the expedition.

"Of course," Jerove said, "it is completely within your right to refuse his request. You are not of his order, after all."

"I thank you for your concern," Merssa replied. "But I feel Cafior's will must have played a part in his decision, and I must obey."

"Indeed." Jerove's outrage was replaced by disgust. "Then I guess that will be all."

Exiting the Grand Cathedral, Merssa headed back at a brisk pace to where her companions were quartered. She realized her actions would most likely harm her chances of ever gaining title of High Paladin, but the words Borse said the previous night made her realize that duty to Cafior was more important than duty to city, and she would better serve Him in questing for the orbs.

Breakfast was quick, and Merssa barely uttered a word other than to inform her company she would be joining them to hunt down the orbs. Her news was met with sighs of relief and many smiles. Merssa wished she had had more time to spend with her companions, and with Borse, but there was too much to do and too little time in which to do it. With that in mind, she reported to Nilborg's quarters immediately following the meal, forgoing the agreed upon "after lunch" engagement. Nilborg did not seem surprised, and he was ready for Merssa when she arrived.

Of the other Palidurians invited to join the expedition, Nilborg informed Merssa that all had respectfully declined with the exception of Rholmar; the Paladin of Arronaus wished to learn more and arrived to the meeting after lunch. Rholmar listened carefully to Merssa's words, holding no ill will toward her for the confrontation they recently shared. He admitted he was hard pressed to march into Neja, as duty commanded, but he was swayed by Merssa's report and decided hunting down the orbs would better serve in defeating the evil.

Soren also wished to join Merssa and Nilborg—the High Paladin of Soleran had originally voted to march into Neja, but a couple days of thought had changed his mind. Unfortunately, Soren could not do so. The law demanded at least one member of the High Order from each sector remain within the city at all times, so all Soren could do was give his support and wish them well.

The next couple days saw the streets bustling with messengers running from sector to sector while the city prepared to mobilize a force over five thousand strong. Though it paled in comparison to Palidur's full strength, it was the largest assemblage of paladins, priests, and warriors to march from the Holy City in more than a hundred years. Armories were opened and their well-maintained contents distributed among the soldiers, and holy warriors were filled with excitement while the Paladin Knights maintained faces of stone.

Merssa received little sleep over the next three days while she continued to meet with Nilborg and Rholmar, and only Borse saw her on a regular basis, often joining her for lunch and dinner. She tasked Borse with keeping the company informed of all progress, to which he always replied, "Of course." On the third evening, Merssa treated her guests to dinner at Pleasant Vale. That night, it seemed not even the Ironside brothers could remove her smile.

CHAPTER 21

DIMARR

Upon the morning of the fourth day since the planning began,
the day Merssa's companies were to depart, two mages,
Melac and Wezlok, arrived to Palidur to join the quests for
the orbs. They bore scrolls from the Council of Wizards detailing the
most recent scouting reports, maps, contact names, and the like, and
were immediately ushered to Merssa and Nilborg. Merssa recalled
Melac's name from the Council as a trusted friend, but she was a bit
leery of Wezlok, for he was a Lorian; an elf of Maple Lore Forest.
Lorians were known to carry an air of superiority, and the arrogant,
disgusted look upon Wezlok's face did nothing to dispel that belief.
Merssa had never met a Lorian before, since they bore no desire to
interact with the "lesser beings" of the world and rarely ventured
from their forest. Wezlok was taller than the Salenti folk, but not so
tall as Vermallon elves; probably more akin to Dakreal elves,
standing a few inches higher than Merssa. Unlike the typical brown
or black hair of the Dakreal clan, however, Wezlok's hair was white.
To Merssa's knowledge, even elves of other forests held contempt for
Lorians, and Lorians only tolerated other elves in return. Merssa
decided Wezlok would join her mission to the north, so she could
keep an eye on him.

Just before lunch, the planning stage was completed at last and
Merssa took in a deep breath. It was time to begin. For that reason,
she did not hesitate to act when Eraim informed her there were no
horses available. Merssa had tasked the small elf with retrieving the

Salenti horses and Ironside steeds, as well as procuring eight additional mounts, but Eraim reported, with more than a bit of sarcasm, "Due to the city's mobilization, every horse is being prepped for the march to Neja." Merssa immediately made her way to the stables, and the stable keeper's story changed before her commanding gaze. She was issued just enough animals to fulfill her request.

Merssa said her goodbyes to Nilborg, Selanna, Eraim, and Arkor as the four departed with Rholmar for Tenvale, and also to Vikur, who headed to Ironside Keep with Melac. Seeing no point in informing Jerove or Arduer of her own departure, for it would only delay her longer, Merssa led Borse, Pallit, and Wezlok through the north gate. A great weight seemed to disappear when she was on the road at last, shortly replaced by a strong feeling of resolve unlike any she could recall.

They crossed Palidur Bridge and rode deep into Sendorum, passing through several villages and a few cities that lined the way. Many Sendor eyes followed Merssa's contingent: Pallit in his chain shirt with a sword at his side and a bow and quiver fastened to his saddle; Borse dressed in light leather armor with a large hammer strapped to his steed; and Wezlok—though the elf bore no visible weapons, his eyes pierced like daggers at any gazing his way too long. But the Sendors held no fear and city guards offered no hindrance while they passed, for Merssa rode at the lead, donning her silver armor and golden mace, and folks smiled and waved, hailing the Palidurian Knight.

The journey to Tribenor lasted two days, and most conversation during that time was between Merssa and Borse. Wezlok said little as he lagged behind, and when the elf did speak it was usually in his native tongue, of which Merssa knew little. Wezlok would then become annoyed as he repeated himself, translating it slowly into the common speech, but Merssa let it go without comment. She did not wish to burden herself with pointless confrontations so early in the mission.

They immediately reported to the King's Bounty Tavern, where they were to meet the Council's scout. Upon entering, Merssa spotted two elves quite out of their element, sitting as far from other patrons as possible. They had dark hair and were dressed in road-worn black cloaks over green leather, and leaning against the wall next to them were exquisite bows of dark wood with intricate etchings—obvious weapons of Vermallon warriors. One spotted Merssa and rose, standing as tall as Pallit. The elf gave a nod, confirming he and his companions were the ones Merssa sought.

"I am Eimell," the elf greeted them as they arrived to the table, and he offered the open chairs with a wave of his hand. "Please tend to your hunger and thirst at once."

"We're fine." Merssa's response was apparently to Wezlok's disliking, as the Lorian's eyes rolled ever so slightly.

Her company took their seats.

Eimell scanned the surrounding patrons with visible distrust. He then nodded with satisfaction before speaking just loud enough for Merssa to hear.

"We caught word of the blue orb as described by the Council of Wizards. Apparently, an escort of ghouls possessed it and were heading west after the Wind had ceased, but they were discovered by Death Hunters in Virch and destroyed. The leader of the hunters informed us he discovered the sphere and kept it. He described it as cold to the touch, with an impenetrable swirling mist trapped inside."

Merssa nodded, thinking back on the orb in the Silent Marsh and the effect it had had on Poluran's hand when the dwarf touched it. Evidently the orbs were not all the same.

"Unfortunately, a thief lifted it a couple days later," Eimell continued, "and it took a bit of tracking after that.

"It passed into Harbnum, where the thief attempted to rob an Andrian. The barbarian put him to the sword, and witnesses say the thief rose again, as a zombie, and was slain a second time. The Andrian claimed the thief's possessions as retribution for the crime. His name is Dimarr, and he is a tribal leader in southern Andria among the foothills of what you call the Coranthiar Mountains."

"Where exactly among the foothills does he dwell?" posed Merssa. "There is greater than three hundred miles along the northern border."

"Alas, our part ends here," Eimell said. "But we have arranged for you to meet someone familiar with the area. Her name is Arrikan, and she will be expecting you in nine days' time at a tavern called Griffon's Roost in Bouldertown."

Wezlok rattled off several words in the elfish language, but all Merssa gathered was "Do we know…" and "…the workings of…"

Eimell shot the Lorian wizard a cold glare before speaking to Merssa in the common speech. "If the thief's rising was *not* due to the orb, it is anyone's guess as to what evil was at work."

Wezlok released a sigh. "I would like to examine the body," he said in common.

"It was burned." Eimell's response was lacking in patience. "And the ashes have long been scattered about the countryside." He turned to Merssa and his tone became businesslike once again. "We wish you luck on your road." The elf and his companion rose. "And may Galenfial carry you on winged feet." Eimell nodded, and he and his companion grabbed their bows and strode out the door.

"Galenfial would not lower himself," mumbled Wezlok of the elfish deity. Though he said it quietly, Merssa was sure it was meant for her ears, for he used the common speech.

"Perhaps we should fill our bellies and take advantage of a good night's rest," Borse suggested, as if reading Merssa's growing annoyance.

"Well," Merssa gazed out the window at the darkening sky, "if it's to be nine days, then we are in no hurry and a night here should bring no harm."

Pallit choked, drawing Merssa's glare. Yes, she would normally have insisted on an immediate departure, but that was before… She was not quite sure what it was that was different. Merssa hoped she was not growing soft.

"I still do not understand something." Wezlok gained her attention. "How did the undead march about your lands unnoticed while they carried these orbs in the first place?"

"There is much you do not understand." Merssa glared at the elf, though she was still disgusted by the thought of Poluran allowing a group of ghouls to pass by him on horseback. "For now, all you need realize is unless we retrieve them, your forest will suffer the same fate as *our* lands."

"Excuse me." Borse caught the attention of a passing barmaid. "We are in need of food and refreshment."

"I shall turn in for the evening." Wezlok stood. "My need for sustenance is not as strong as yours. I will be ready at dawn's first light."

"I don't know why we need a mage," Merssa said after the wizard had gone.

"I believe Selanna's aid was most beneficial to you in your earlier travels." Borse raised a brow. "Is that not true?"

"Most definitely," answered Pallit emphatically.

"But why one of Maple Lore?" Merssa posed. "I don't see why the Council entrusted one such as this elf with a task so important."

Borse gave a half smile. "As you said yourself, his homeland stands to suffer as much as ours. Though he is very different from us, I sincerely doubt he will pose a threat to the mission."

"I hope you're right." Merssa could not shake her doubt, but Borse was probably correct, as usual.

They had dinner and enjoyed a couple drinks, and Merssa's mood lightened as the night wore on. Before the hour grew late, they retired to their rooms.

Merssa arrived to the tavern an hour before sunrise with Borse and Pallit, and she was surprised to find Wezlok there already. The only other patrons were a few farmers, gathering energy for a long day's work.

"I apologize for last night," the elf said, and Merssa's surprise became shock when she saw breakfast ready and waiting. Still, arrogance remained in the mage's tone when he added, "Let us begin again."

After eating they took to the road, and it did not take long before Wezlok fell several paces behind, causing Merssa to question the elf's desire for a fresh start. But she had more important things to think about and focused on the journey ahead.

The skies were favorable as the cool morning yielded to a warm, late-summer day, and to the east a dark line spanned the horizon and the road veered toward it. Soon the tall maples, oaks, birches, and cedars of Vermallon Forest became clearer and the road turned back to the north, but also a wide path led beneath the canopy of leaves—Vermallon Road.

Merssa turned north and entered Harbnum, following the road along the forest's edge. They continued so for several days and the air became cooler, especially with the evenings, but many villages lined the way and provided lodgings at night. This offered more than just protection from the cold, for Vermallon Forest was quite untamed, housing not only elves, but also hobgoblins in the middle region and goblins to the north among the hills. It was also rumored there existed ogres, spiders of abnormally large sizes, and wolves with glowing eyes that spit fire, but Merssa had never heard these reports from any reliable sources. She did know, however, that bandits hid within and preyed upon travelers when opportunity presented itself.

On the fifth day since entering Harbnum, the road veered west around Diral Hills before turning northwest, and soon the Coranthiar Mountains came into view: a jagged line often disappearing into distant, unmoving clouds. The mounds were not so breath taking as the Stone Eagles or lush as the Varlimor chain, but the peaks were never without white caps and were perpetually circled by large birds.

The next day crawled by as rolling hills shifted their course left and right and the road rose and fell. On the following day, at the advice of a villager, they rode hard until dusk, and as the last traces of light faded, Merssa spied Bouldertown less than a mile away.

The city was set atop a wide hill, and surrounding it was a wall of stone running from immense boulder to immense boulder. The gates opened before the company, revealing buildings of stone upon wide cobblestone streets, and several more boulders decorated various intersections like unrealized statues. The early night was alive with recreation.

While Pallit and Wezlok stabled the horses, Merssa and Borse reported to the Griffon's Roost to secure a table for dinner. Upon entering, Merssa's attention was drawn to a tall man at the bar. He was dressed all in black, as was usual, but strapped to his back was not one but two swords.

"Vecnor!" Merssa said, after which the entire room raised their drinks and shouted.

"Vecnor!"

"What took you so long?" The large man grinned. "I heard in Vermallon you aimed for this place, but I would have thought you'd have been here yesterday."

Merssa rolled her eyes. "Even now is too soon. Our nine-day journey took only eight."

Vecnor chuckled as he lifted his beer from the bar and followed her to a table where Borse was now seated. Borse stood briefly and greeted the large warrior. Pallit entered, but Wezlok was not with him. The ranger offered Vecnor a nod and took a seat.

"The elf said he had something to take care of," Pallit explained under Merssa's raised brow.

"Well, we'll not wait for him," she said. "Let's eat."

While they ate, Merssa informed Vecnor of all he had missed, including the meeting with the Council of Wizards. Near the end of her report, their meal was just about finished and Wezlok joined them with four keys in hand.

"I have procured rooms for the evening," the Lorian informed

Merssa, placing the keys onto the table.

She really did not know what to think of the elf. "This is Wezlok of Maple Lore." Merssa introduced him with a wave of her hand.

Vecnor gazed at Wezlok, then thrust his hand forward with a grin. "I am Vecnor. It's good to have you with us!"

Wezlok hesitated, seemingly not too eager to participate in the human formality of arm clasping, but he extended his at last and it disappeared within Vecnor's grasp.

"I've heard of you." The elf displayed a forced, unconvincing smile.

"Great!" Vecnor slapped Wezlok on the back in Vikur-like fashion, almost flopping the mage onto the table.

The remainder of the night was spent in small talk, in which Wezlok offered no words. The elf chose to skip supper, but he did drink wine from a goblet very slowly, showing distaste for the vintage with a small cringe every time he took a sip. Merssa eventually asked Vecnor of his whereabouts after parting company in Neja, to which he replied that he had other matters to attend to and he quickly changed the subject. As the tavern room dwindled to less than half capacity, Wezlok excused himself and headed to his room, and shortly afterward Pallit did the same. Borse went to the bar to procure one last round for those that remained, and while he was occupied, Vecnor shot Merssa an impish grin.

"I see you and Borse have taken a shine to each other."

Merssa felt her cheeks flush and she opened her mouth to put Vecnor in his place, but then she saw Borse speaking to locals at the bar. The priest held their undivided attention while most likely sharing words of Cafior. He turned Merssa's way, as if hearing Vecnor's comment, and gave a wink that brought a broad smile to her lips.

"He is very wise."

"That he is." Vecnor nodded. "But this is a good thing. I've never seen you smile as much as this night."

"That is not so!" Merssa scowled as best she could, under the circumstances.

"Yes, my lady." Vecnor bowed. "I stand corrected."

The next day seemed like it would never end. Vecnor and Pallit passed much of the time wandering about the city while Wezlok remained within the confines of his room, emerging only for lunch. Merssa never strayed far from the tavern, becoming impatient for Arrikan's arrival, and Borse remained with her, always brightening her mood before it could turn too dark. During lunch, Vecnor entertained them by explaining life in Harbnum and Andria, to which only Pallit seemed to show interest—the ranger appeared genuinely impressed with the scope of Vecnor's knowledge beyond swords and combat.

Nearing suppertime, Merssa was having tea with Borse when the tavern door opened. Merssa looked up, as she did every time someone entered, and a tall woman stood in the doorway, covered from head to toe in dirt and carrying a spear. The stranger's long hair was unkempt and its color undeterminable, and when the woman threw back her cloak, lifting a cloud of dust, Merssa noticed a sword strapped to her side. Everyone in the tavern shouted.

"Arrikan!"

Merssa rolled her eyes. She had grown tired of the patrons' enthusiasm, but at least she knew the woman to be the scout she was waiting for.

Arrikan scanned the room until her gaze fell upon Merssa. Without a hint of emotion, the woman approached. "Merssa Goldmace?" she inquired in a surprisingly feminine voice.

"I am." Merssa gave a single nod. "And this is Borse."

Arrikan gazed about the room. "Is it safe to speak?" she asked in a hushed voice as she took a seat.

"Why wouldn't it be?" Merssa lowered her voice, scanning the tavern. The room was half full and two patrons sat nearby.

"As I have found," Arrikan replied, "there are prying ears and eyes in unlikely faces."

Merssa turned to Borse, who nodded.

Borse closed his eyes and took in a deep breath, and while he slowly exhaled, he opened his eyes and scanned the occupants. "I sense no evil here," he said.

"All the same…" Arrikan nodded toward the two men at the next table.

"Very well." Annoyance crept up Merssa's throat. If Borse said all was fine, that should be enough. But Arrikan, of course, did not know that. Merssa stood.

Arrikan balked, staring at Merssa with visible surprise. Merssa had seen it before—others expecting her to stand much taller than she did. So what if she stood more than a foot shy of the scout? One did not need height to destroy evil; only the will to do so. Merssa led the way to a table away from the others and they sat.

"I apologize for my lack of trust," Arrikan said, looking back at the patrons. "But I have seen strange things as of late."

"Such as?" Merssa raised a brow.

"I believe there are others who would claim the object you seek," Arrikan explained. "I have overheard questions of a blue orb, and inquiries as to the whereabouts of Dimarr. I, myself, have been approached by such inquisitors, but Eimell was very insistent I speak to no one but you of such matters."

"Who else could possibly…" Merssa trailed off. "Trannum," she whispered to Borse.

"Or, perhaps there are others that share our quest," he offered optimistically.

Merssa gave a wry smile. "That would be comforting. But we cannot risk it. Other than those who have seen what I have seen… Nobody could possibly know. We must leave immediately."

"I'll gather the others." Borse stood and swiftly exited.

Merssa stared at Arrikan, troubled by the woman's words. "*Do you know where to find Dimarr?*"

Arrikan nodded. "I know where his village lies."

"Are there others who know? Anyone else that might be able to guide other interested parties?"

"I can't say with certainty," Arrikan admitted. "There are none in *these* parts that I know of. Most folks around here would never brave the wild lands of the north. But, I suppose, if one were to ride into Andria and knew the speech, it would only be a matter of time before they found someone willing to assist them for a price."

"Are you weary?" Merssa asked. "Can you ride tonight?"

"You needn't worry of me." The woman radiated confidence. "I spend more time in the mountains than elsewhere. I'm always ready."

Merssa was impressed. She might like this scout.

"Replenish your supplies. Meet us out front as soon as you can."

Arrikan nodded and exited.

Merssa sat a moment longer in thought. The fear that it was too late began to haunt her.

They gathered outside the tavern, and Arrikan's face lit up when Vecnor approached.

"How've you been, Vecnor?" The scout's smile passed from ear to ear. "It's been a couple years."

"Too long," Vecnor commented as Arrikan gave him a hug.

Merssa was surprised Vecnor had not revealed he knew the guide personally the previous day, but she could not recall if she had mentioned the name. She quickly introduced the others, and she could not help noticing the lack of interest between Arrikan and Wezlok, but it was not surprising.

"Let's ride," Merssa said once all were ready.

They exited Bouldertown beneath the dying light, and Arrikan led them along a chilly, northwesterly road a few miles before veering down a hunting trail due north. They kept a hurried pace by the light of the growing moon a couple miles farther before stopping to camp, and Arrikan hung a small kettle once a fire was started. After everyone was settled, they were served hot tea. Wezlok declined the beverage, preferring the contents of his flask.

"Tell us about Dimarr," Merssa said to Arrikan. The road had done nothing to inspire conversation, and now that they were stopped, Merssa needed something to distract her from the increasing cold.

"He is a tribal leader." Arrikan gazed into the flames. She seemed unbothered by the chill. "He has a small hunting village of about sixty people. It's always been a quiet place. They keep to themselves."

"How far is it?" Merssa inquired.

"Ten days at least to the hunting grounds." Arrikan raised her eyes to meet Merssa's. "But we can do nine if we press."

"Nine it shall be." Merssa needed to reach the orb before anyone else claimed it. "We haven't time to spare."

"There is another way," Arrikan mentioned. "It's quicker than trekking around the mountains, but I don't know how skilled you are at mountain travel. If time wasn't an issue, I wouldn't even bring it up."

"You need not worry of us," Pallit said. "With my assistance, it shouldn't be too difficult."

"Have you any experience in the Coranthiar Mountains?" Arrikan's demeanor was suddenly cold.

"I know mountains," Pallit replied. "And with the exception of our elfish friend here," the ranger waved a hand toward Wezlok, "we passed through the Stone Eagles not too long ago."

"The mountain way it shall be," said Merssa.

"Very well." Arrikan's tone held a touch of doubt.

"This is all very nice," Wezlok uttered the first words he had spoken all day. "But if we are to scale those large hills tomorrow, I think some rest is called for." He headed to where he had placed his bedroll, several yards away from the others.

"Do not stray too far," Arrikan warned. "The fire will keep away most beasts, but some will not mind creeping about the edges of the light."

Wezlok rolled his eyes and continued to his blankets.

"I'll guard tonight," Arrikan told Merssa. "The rest of you should get some sleep."

"Take first watch," said Pallit. "Wake me halfway till dawn. We should *all* get some sleep."

Arrikan stared at the ranger as he crawled beneath his blanket.

Merssa shifted her attention to Borse. The dark circles beneath his eyes had been growing darker with every passing day. "You look tired. Why don't you get some rest?"

Borse smiled and nodded before taking a place next to Pallit.

Merssa finished her tea and then turned in herself.

Merssa could not sleep. The night wore on and a cold breeze found its way across the camp, causing her to shiver and reminding her briefly of the Wind of the Dead. But Arrikan hardly took notice and this eased Merssa's mind.

"It's the mountains," the guide said without a glance. "The days will grow colder still where we're going. And the nights..." Arrikan shook her head.

Merssa nodded, sitting up and pulling her blanket over her shoulders.

Arrikan scanned the others of the company, all of them having found sleep easily enough. She then frowned. "If you don't mind me asking, do you think Borse is worthy of the road ahead? It's not an easy one."

"He is a very special man," Merssa said, half smiling as she gazed upon the resting priest. "Though he appears a bit frail on the outside, the strength of Cafior is in him." Staring at Arrikan, Merssa added, "You needn't concern yourself."

"What of the elf? He is silent and his eyes seem mysterious, if not mischievous."

"He is of Maple Lore, as I'm sure you have guessed," Merssa replied, and Arrikan nodded. "I shall have to trust in the Council's decision to send him, and I believe him to be silent only because he has nothing to say."

"And Pallit?" Arrikan looked at the ranger. "I admit I've never seen the likes of the Stone Eagles, but does his skill match his tongue?"

"He was once one of the King's Rangers in Neja," Merssa said. "I think you'll find him most helpful." After a bit of thought, she asked Arrikan a question. "How do you know Vecnor?"

"I met him some time ago, when I was young. He doesn't look much different than he did then. Must be in his late forties by now, but he looks strong as ever."

Merssa was a bit confused by the calculation and began to wonder if she knew Vecnor at all. She had met him eight years prior, and now that she thought about it, he had not really changed much in that time.

"He's never around long," Arrikan added, "and usually a couple years pass before he comes around again."

"That's Vecnor," Merssa murmured. Gazing at the near full moon as it peeked from beyond the clouds, she yawned. "I recommend you wake Pallit before too long. I'm going to try and get some sleep."

Merssa awoke to Pallit's voice just before sunrise—Arrikan had evidently decided to accept his offer to guard. After a cold breakfast, the company moved on.

The sky brightened and the area became clearer, and Merssa realized they no longer followed any discernable path. Not far to the north, dark clouds were pierced by the mountains, now close enough to make everything around her seem small, and rain appeared imminent.

"We'll be in the mountains by nightfall," Arrikan said after they stopped to care for the horses and have lunch.

The guide kept the break short, impressing Merssa, and they remounted and moved on. Before long the way became rough and the company was forced to dismount, and they led the horses for the remainder of the day. Though the terrain did not compare to that of the Stone Eagles, Wezlok's lack of mountain skills were obvious and he experienced a few complications. The elf often expressed frustration in his own language, to which Vecnor would snicker and add to Wezlok's annoyance, but Pallit walked behind the wizard, leading both of their horses and assisting when necessary. All things considered, Merssa thought the trek not too difficult and they reached their destination well before dusk.

They entered a small campsite, mostly level and clear of debris, and in the center was a stack of firewood—Arrikan had obviously prepped it several days ago, leading Merssa to wonder if all rangers kept areas ready in such a manner. Pallit set the wood alight, and while he did so Arrikan produced furs from a niche within some boulders and passed them out. Had the guide known they would come by this route? Or was she simply prepared for every contingency?

As dusk brought back the cool breeze, they enjoyed a hot supper prepared by Pallit. The air grew colder than the previous night and clouds continued to threaten, but the rain held off until morning.

What began as a light drizzle became a downpour by noon. The winds picked up as well, blowing cold from the mountaintops, and at times Merssa found herself willing to trade the chill for the rougher travel of the Stone Eagles. The furs proved most useful then, but also they became heavy as they were quickly saturated.

The rain persisted over the next few days, and Pallit and Arrikan continued to keep watch through the nights. Beginning on the third evening the two guarded together, and while Merssa laid beneath her blanket waiting for sleep to claim her, she heard them trading stories. Arrikan spoke of griffons roaming the mountaintops, and how barbarians hunted them and they hunted the barbarians in return, making quite a sport of it. Pallit shared battles against goblins and ogres from when he was a King's Ranger, but never did he mention his experiences near the rorbak, at least not while Merssa was awake.

On the fourth day the rain changed into snow, and soon a layer of the white stuff covered the ground. The air was bitterly cold and the wind cut through Merssa's layers, and they huddled close that night for a bit of added warmth—even Wezlok lowered his standards to sit very near to the fire. The cold grew more intense with every hour, making sleep almost impossible, and by morning the furs were iced over and crunched when anyone moved. Merssa felt her patience with the journey beginning to wane, but then Arrikan made an announcement that eased Merssa's mind.

"That should be the worst of it. Our descent begins today."

Merssa's sigh of relief was not the only one she heard at that moment.

The pace picked up—whether due to the thought of warmer temperatures or the downhill trek, Merssa was not sure. When the snow fell far behind and gave way to rain, Merssa considered it a welcome change, and in the end they exited the mountains by lunchtime of the third day since that snowy night. Overall, Merssa found the journey far less treacherous than Arrikan had led her to believe.

"We are a day ahead of schedule," Arrikan informed Merssa, glancing Pallit's way. "He is as you said. I have never seen anyone take to these peaks so quickly. We should reach Dimarr's hunting grounds before nightfall."

They moved into the foothills north of the mountains and headed northeast. The air warmed and the rain ended, as the dark clouds remained over the mountains, and Arrikan stashed the soaked furs near a large boulder and produced dry cloaks for all. Merssa definitely liked this guide.

They mounted for the first time in days and traveled east. Firs and cedars blanketed the foothills, interrupted often by deep valleys overgrown with fields of tall grass and wild flowers, and colorful birds and insects fluttered everywhere. About the peaks to the south, Merssa spied large birds circling.

"The griffons hunt today," Arrikan commented. "Let's be thankful the weather kept them away while we were up there."

The scenery continued to grow more pleasant throughout the day as the hills became tame. Wildlife seemed uninterested in the large company and presented no hindrance, but after a few hours Arrikan shook her head and frowned.

"Is something amiss?" Pallit asked, riding beside the scout.

"We should have seen somebody by now." Arrikan glanced about and drank from her skin. "Or at least a sign of hunters. The grass is undamaged. No one has been through here for at least a week."

"Let's press on," said Merssa. She appreciated the concern for things out of the ordinary, but life, at the moment, was not ordinary. Time was pressing and they needed to find the village.

They continued without obvious trails or markers, but Arrikan seemed confident with their route. After another hour, Wezlok brought them to a halt.

"Hold!" The elf cocked his head to one side.

Merssa detected nothing, save for the songs of birds and buzzing of small wings.

Wezlok listened intently before dismounting. The elf carefully picked his way through the brush, and after twenty paces he stopped and called back. "Here!"

Merssa and the others dismounted and rushed to find Wezlok's discovery. A dark-haired man in a wolfskin tunic lay among the bushes, his hand clutched over a chest wound that had obviously been bleeding for some time. The man panted heavily as he gazed at the figures now huddled above him, his eyes half closed.

"*Arburk momard!*" the man said, coughing. "*Arburk momard!*"

"He is of Dimarr's tribe," Arrikan said. "He says, 'Blue ice.'"

"The orb," Merssa murmured. It had to be.

"*Burk*," Arrikan said to the man. "*Arla buk.*"

"Arrikan!" the Andrian said with a weak smile, and after Arrikan repeated her words, he spoke again and she translated.

"'Blue ice. Dimarr's treasure…evil. Hunting no good. All is changed.'" Arrikan paused when the man broke into a fit of coughing, but then he calmed and continued. "'Dimarr seeks blue power now. Death is new beginning. I…do not want…his curse.'"

"Can you help him, Borse?" Pallit asked as the barbarian's eyes began to flutter.

"I can try." Borse knelt beside the man.

"*Naugh!*" the Andrian shouted, his eyes opening wide. He rattled off another sentence and Arrikan translated.

"'No! I must reach Bashnu. You must help.'" Looking at the others, Arrikan explained. "Bashnu is the god of hunting and battle."

"Why wouldn't he reach Bashnu?" asked Merssa.

Arrikan repeated the question, and the barbarian answered.

"He says we must make sure he dies." As Arrikan finished her translation, the barbarian's eyes glazed over and he ceased to move.

"Poor soul." Borse reached to close the dead man's eyes.

"Watch out!" shouted Merssa, pulling her mace.

As she voiced her warning, the dead man grabbed Borse by the wrist and hissed with hatred. The corpse had become a zombie. Vecnor's boot quickly stomped onto the barbarian's skull, and his sword flashed into his hand and he cleaved the zombie's head while Borse scrambled away.

"Just as the thief in Harbnum." Wezlok spoke more out of interest or curiosity than shock.

"He transformed so quickly," Borse said in horror.

"The curse infects all who touch the orb," Merssa thought aloud, turning all attention on her. She looked to her companions and slid her mace through the loop on her belt. "We best not touch it, then."

Merssa made her way back to the horses and the others followed, Wezlok moving slowly as he stared a moment longer at the body with great interest.

"From what the Andrian said," the elf mentioned after they had ridden a bit farther, "it does not seem likely that Dimarr will part with the orb willingly. Not if it is his treasure."

Merssa refused to look at the wizard. "That has always been a possibility."

"I only wish to be sure we are *all* prepared to do what is necessary."

Merssa glanced back to see the elf eyeing Arrikan, and the guide noticed this as well.

"You seem to know these people pretty well." Wezlok had evidently listened to some of Arrikan's conversations with Pallit over the past few nights. "I want to be sure you are not a hindrance if it comes to—"

"That man back there did not seem a willful participant!" Arrikan snapped. "And I'm sure there will be others of the tribe that feel the same!"

"Enough!" Merssa put up her hand. "We will do what it takes for the sake of Vaeldor." Glaring back at Wezlok, she added, "But no *more* than is necessary."

Wezlok gave a sly grin, one Merssa would have loved to have slapped from his face. But now was not the time…and the elf was not completely in the wrong.

Arrikan was then silent while they rode. The trees became patchy in several places, giving way to open fields, and after a couple hours the scout came to a halt.

"There." Arrikan pointed to the right.

Within the shadow of a mountain, a hill was nestled against a towering cliff, nearly devoid of trees. The descending sun revealed a small waterfall atop the mound, as well as a few wooden buildings, but most the village remained hidden from view.

Arrikan stayed within the trees and led the way almost to the cliff wall, where a brook raced from the hilltop, and there they dismounted. Vecnor gave his usual command to Umbarc to guard and they left the animals behind, venturing as far as the cover allowed. The trees ended at the base of the hill, however, and the village remained concealed by the rising slope.

"It's too quiet," Arrikan whispered. "By this time the day's hunt should be over and the bounty roasting on large spits. There should be music and dancing to celebrate."

"I can hear a few people walking about," Wezlok said. "Women, by the sound of them."

"Maybe Dimarr is not here," suggested Merssa.

"Only if the hunt has run long," Arrikan said. "Or if they've traveled beyond their borders."

"Perhaps they hunt prey of a different sort these days." Wezlok raised his brow, receiving sharp glares from both Arrikan and Pallit.

"I liked it better when you did not speak." Arrikan's tone was laced with venom.

"Hush!" ordered Merssa. "If Dimarr is gone, I only hope he left the orb behind. I do not wish to be around come nightfall." With a sigh, she added, "There's only one way to find out."

Merssa left the cover of the trees and marched up the hill, her mace hanging at her side, and the others followed. The rest of the village came into view and Merssa noticed a dozen or so wooden structures, a large, untended garden, and three cold fire pits with large spits lying nearby. From the waterfall a stream collected into a small pond that shed a soft blue glow, and within bathed a few women. The rest of the villagers, consisting of a dozen women, children, and elderly, ceased all activities upon noticing Merssa and her company, and some lifted clubs and spears and delivered menacing glares. Upon spotting Arrikan they seemed to relax a bit, but one woman stepped forward with a large axe. The barbarian had long dark hair and was wrought in muscle.

"*Durk!*" Arrikan called, stepping forward with a hand in the air.

The woman repeated the word, but her suspicion did not fade.

The bathers exited the pond quickly, gathering their skins and dressing while more women issued from the buildings. Arrikan began a conversation with the large woman, and while the scout did so, Merssa glanced Vecnor's way and nodded toward the pond. Vecnor gave an understanding nod and began slowly moving that direction, and at that moment the lead woman began yelling angrily.

"What is it?" asked Merssa with alarm.

"She is Dimarr's chief-wife," Arrikan explained. "I asked about the blue ice and she ordered us to leave. She calls us bandits."

Merssa considered the villagers. Greater than a score of women were present and armed, some appearing more nervous than angry, and the elderly and children had disappeared into the buildings.

"We need to look in that pond," she said to Arrikan. "Can you keep them occupied?"

"She'll hear no more words." Arrikan was desperate. "It's leave now or stay and fight."

Merssa took in a deep breath. "I'm sorry." She pulled her mace. "We cannot leave without the orb."

The chief-wife gave a cry that was echoed by some of the women, and half of them charged forward. The chief-wife bore down on Arrikan with the axe, but Arrikan twirled her spear and expertly deflected the attack aside. The scout countered with the shaft of her weapon across the barbarian's head, but there was no visible effect. The chief-wife brought the axe back again, and Arrikan ducked before thrusting her weapon and driving it completely through the woman's chest. The barbarian gasped and staggered, collapsing with wide eyes, and with visible sadness Arrikan drew her blade and prepared for the next attacker.

The exchange took place in just seconds, and Merssa moved a few paces toward the pond before being cut off by two women. The barbarians towered above her, but skill prevailed and Merssa easily fended one to the side and brought the second to the ground with a crunching blow to the knee. She dodged another attack from the first one before catching the barbarian in the ribcage. The woman cried out and collapsed into a heap.

Vecnor was then next to Merssa, wielding one of his swords in his right hand and a dagger in his left. He emitted a roar and charged toward the bulk of the villagers, causing several to flee, but three held their ground and hissed with wild hatred. They attacked savagely, but after a display of parries and dodges, Vecnor brought the pommel of his sword onto one's head, punched the second in the face, and headbutted the third, leaving all three dazed upon the ground.

The path to the pond was unimpeded, but Merssa hesitated as she checked on Borse. The priest was faced with two women and appeared awkward with the oversized hammer, but he caught the barbarians off guard when he raised the weapon overhead with ease. Borse fended off their advances before spearing one in the stomach with the haft, and he surely broke the leg of the other with the hammerhead. Pallit was nearby, and two women were motionless at the ranger's feet.

To Merssa's surprise, the fight was over as quickly as it began. The company had slain only four villagers, a much better result than she had thought possible, and all women still on their feet retreated into buildings. Merssa turned back to the pool.

"Merssa!" Arrikan shouted.

Merssa looked to see the four corpses rising; blood seeped from open wounds, but snarling faces showed they felt no pain. The undead chief-wife lunged for Arrikan and the scout danced back, bringing her blade about and severing the zombie's head. Vecnor struck down another zombie and Pallit moved to defend Borse, defeating the third, but the final zombie wrenched the ranger's ankle and he fell to the ground. Before the creature made another attack, Borse's hammer crushed its skull.

The zombie battle was over quickly as well, and several villagers reemerged to help the wounded and unconscious to safety. Merssa was glad to see this, and she turned back to the pond to find Wezlok standing at the water's edge.

"I hope you're not planning on messing with that thing," Merssa warned as she stepped beside the elf.

Wezlok gazed into the center of the pool, where a point of blue light illuminated the water. "I must admit, I am fascinated…" the elf mumbled, almost to himself—although he spoke the common tongue. "Of course, my intentions mirror your own," he added, turning to Merssa.

Merssa nodded, glad to see the elf did not succumb to the orb the way Poluran had in the Silent Marsh. "Now I just have to figure a way to get it out without touching it."

"I drank from the stream that flows from this hill," said Pallit with concern as he limped to the water's edge with Borse's help.

"If the orb can turn one into the undead," Wezlok posed, "what powers does it bestow upon the water?"

"The stream looks normal enough," said Borse. "The blue light seems contained within the pond. It does not travel with the brook."

"Is it safe to touch the water?" Merssa thought aloud.

"I'm not sure," Borse admitted.

"How do we get it, then?" Arrikan gazed back at the village, her eyes darting from building to building.

"I'll get it." Vecnor waded into the water.

"No!" shouted Merssa, but he did not stop.

The pool never rose above Vecnor's waist as he neared the middle, and the blue glow was immediately drawn back into the orb when he pulled it from the water with his gauntlet. Turning to face the others with a triumphant grin, Vecnor's smile quickly vanished. Merssa looked over her shoulder to spy more than two dozen horsemen entering the village, all riding horses as large as Umbarc.

"The hunters!" Arrikan gasped.

A large barbarian rode at the lead—undoubtedly Dimarr. He raised his sword, shouting a battle cry that echoed into the valley below, and the horsemen charged.

Merssa advanced with mace in hand, but did not make it far before Vecnor raced past her with both swords drawn—he would not be taking it easy this time. He flashed his blades in a flurry, unhorsing five riders by the time Merssa arrived. The hunters spilled onto the ground and Merssa and Vecnor dispatched them before they could regain their wits. But then there were the horses to contend with.

Like Umbarc, the animals were trained in combat, and one grazed Vecnor's shoulder with its hoof, causing him to wince while he slashed its massive forelegs and took it down. Vecnor and Merssa dropped three more of the beasts before the fifth one knocked Merssa to the ground and nearly trampled her—she quickly rolled aside as Vecnor struck it with a mighty blow.

Rising to her feet, Merssa surveyed the hill. Wezlok brought his hands together in a clap that sounded into the distance, and half a dozen barbarians and horses slammed together, as if invisible walls had crushed them. A few hunters lay motionless upon the ground, pierced by arrows from Pallit's bow, and now Pallit drew his sword to join Arrikan against the unmanned horses. From across the field, Dimarr yelled something in his barbaric tongue and pointed his sword toward Borse, who stood over the orb near the pond with hammer ready.

"No!" Merssa gasped.

She moved to block Dimarr's path, but four riders closed on her. Anxiety swelled in Merssa's chest at the thought of Borse alone with the chieftain and it was suddenly hard to breathe, but then Vecnor came roaring, gaining the attention of the horsemen and clearing her way.

Merssa intercepted Dimarr, but she was not prepared when the chieftain leapt from the saddle and pinned her beneath his great size. Dimarr withdrew a dagger and slipped it into her side before regaining his feet, and he pointed at her while barking an order to his horse. The mount charged with an angry snort.

Merssa struggled to her feet, the pain in her side only a minor distraction as her mind went to Borse. And now a stupid horse stood between them! She danced to the side of the mount's charge, catching a glimpse of Dimarr slashing Borse's right arm and then his leg. The scene caused her to gasp and the horse struck her chest and sent her tumbling. Merssa rolled to her feet, feeling deep pain beneath the dent left in her breastplate, and her focus shifted to the horse. She needed to dispatch it, and fast; and almost as if in answer to a prayer, two arrows pierced the animal's skull. One arrow she recognized as Pallit's and the other she assumed was from Arrikan. The beast did not go down right away, but staggered about, and Merssa left it behind to die as she hurried to Borse.

Borse was on one knee, his hammer now several feet away. Horror was on his face as Dimarr's sword rose for the final blow, but Merssa's legs carried her faster than she thought possible and her mace crashed into the back of the barbarian's head. She felt the skull shatter beneath her blow, and Dimarr's sword fell free as the mighty hunter collapsed onto Borse.

Dropping her mace, Merssa used all her strength to roll the chieftain's body aside. Borse was alive. He looked upon her with relief, but his expression moved to concern when gazing at her wounds. His eyes then snapped above her and grew wide, but the zombie-Dimarr towered over her for only a moment before Vecnor's sword cleaved its head from its shoulders.

Merssa scanned the hilltop. Pallit and Arrikan were dispatching one zombie-barbarian while Wezlok launched bolts of fire that reduced the remaining undead to crumpled, flaming corpses. All but the elf seemed to have taken injuries.

Villagers stepped from the buildings and lifted weapons, moving slowly as they measured the strength of the wounded invaders. They seemed hesitant to continue the battle, but Merssa was not sure how long that indecision would last.

Merssa turned back to Borse. The wounds to his arm and leg were gruesome and he bled from the scalp. She then noticed the orb, not far away; the cause of all this bloodshed. The Council's orders were to bring it to Tikken City, but Merssa could not risk losing it if the barbarians decided to attack.

She kicked the sphere several feet away and knelt before it, using her body to shield Borse. The golden glow encompassed her mace as she closed her eyes and whispered a prayer to Cafior, and she brought the weapon down with all the strength she could muster…

Merssa opened one eye. The orb was shattered. But unlike the larger one in the Silent Marsh, it had not exploded. With a sigh, pain nearly overwhelmed Merssa and she felt she might pass out, but she bared her teeth and forced herself to her feet. She noticed Wezlok's state of shock to witness the destruction of the evil sphere, but the elf's emotionless expression quickly returned.

"What of the remaining villagers?" Pallit regarded the barbarians as he and Arrikan joined Merssa. He was still limping and Arrikan bled from a wound on the left arm. "They have probably all been in contact with that hellish thing."

"We must cleanse this place," Wezlok said coldly.

Merssa watched the barbarians. They were dragging their dead from the area, and though some were aglow with hatred, most bore looks of relief. Arrikan had been correct. They seemed thankful to be rid of the blue ice.

"We will not decide their fate," Merssa said at last. "For good or evil, they will be spared. We have done what we came to do. Now let us leave this place while we still live."

The disgust on Wezlok's face as he walked away was unmistakable. It was not a decision Merssa felt she would have made a year ago, not even a couple months ago, and she was not sure it was the right decision even now. But in her heart, she felt it was the only decision that could be made.

Vecnor lifted Borse and headed down the hill with Wezlok while Arrikan assisted Pallit and followed. Merssa walked with heavy steps to the rear with mace in hand, just in case, but the villagers made no attempts to hinder them. Once within the safety of the trees, they stopped.

While Merssa fished out her healing herbs, Vecnor set Borse upon the ground. Merssa heard Borse recite a prayer, calling upon the power of Cafior, and a warmness encompassed the area. Looking up, Merssa saw a soft brown light surrounding Borse's hand, and he massaged his arm and leg until the wounds vanished, leaving nothing but the blood that had escaped.

Merssa stared in awe. Priests that could heal without the aid of herbs, by merely asking their deity for the blessing and channeling it through their body… It was rare. Nilborg could do it. Jerove could do it. But those were the only two Merssa had ever seen accomplish such a feat. While she contemplated this, she felt warmth engulf her as Borse placed his hands upon her wounds. Moments later, they were gone.

"Thank you," was all Merssa managed, and Borse smiled briefly before moving to tend to the others.

Wezlok waited impatiently upon his horse while the healing was administered, and once all were ready, they mounted and left the hill behind.

"We'll return to Palidur at once," Merssa said. "I pray the other quests have found success as well."

Chapter 22

Serpent's Range

Ironside Keep was the most magnificent structure ever built by dwarves for humans. At least, in Vikur's opinion it was. Centuries old, it had been constructed upon Varlimor Pass; a sentinel against raiders attempting to invade Sardina by means of the only safe passage through the mountains.

The keep was carved into the mountainside itself, and cleverly positioned upon the inside of a long, outward-curving road. The stretch of the pass before the stronghold provided little room for soldiers' ranks or instruments of war, and tower guards could spy an army rounding the bend and fire bows and catapults while receiving minimal resistance. The advancing force was then left with two choices: retreat or an all-out charge. The latter had only happened once in history, to Vikur's knowledge, and ended badly for the opposing army. Few enemy soldiers had been able to make their way up the snaking road rising to the front gate, and even then, they never came close to breaching the keep. Of the remaining ranks, most were felled by arrows or worse, having fallen or been knocked into the greater than one-thousand-foot drop on the northern side of the pass. It was said on that day that two hundred keep soldiers defeated an army of ten thousand.

Long had Vikur's line reigned over the pass, and even after peace between Marcove and Sardina had been won, his family continued to call it home. The garrison was reduced to fifty, the minimum number of soldiers necessary to run the keep's defenses, and unnecessary barracks and storage rooms were converted into guest rooms and a tavern—the latter added by Vikur himself, so he could enjoy fine ale and tell his tales without interruption.

As much as Vikur detested being tied to the stronghold, he could not imagine life without it. And because times remained peaceful, he was free to come and go as he pleased, instead of sitting around, getting fat and losing his edge in battle like his fathers before him. The soldiers did not mind his absences much, as long as they received their monthly wage, and Vikur paid them well.

Vikur arrived to the keep with a conjurer called Melac, whom the Council of Wizards had recommended for the task of claiming Trannum's orbs, according to Merssa. The conjurer had performed many important tasks for the Council of Wizards in the past and was quite skilled in his arts, but with this information coming from Melac, Vikur was not sure how much weight to allow it. Melac stood nearly as tall as Vikur and kept a clean-shaven head. He appeared young, as mages go, but talked with the wisdom of the Council at times. A staff of oak was strapped to Melac's horse and he wore red robes, and in Vikur's opinion he was a bit muscular for a mage, bringing forth thoughts that the man had, perhaps, chosen the wrong profession in life.

The visit to Ironside was short, so Vikur spent most his time within the tavern, sitting in his large chair and regaling the patrons—two Marcs, three Kalmirans, two Sards, and Melac—with tales of past adventures. Before lunch the following day, Vikur and Melac set out, bearing east on the pass toward Marcove, and the soldiers bade them safe journey as they rode from the gate.

The trip to Denvale took more than half the day, but the pass was quiet and they entered the walled village near dusk. Once an outpost to deny hostile forces entry into Marcove, years of peace converted Denvale into a place of commerce and its gates were only closed after dark. All but two of its many towers were now storage buildings, the barracks had become inns and taverns, and houses were squeezed wherever they could fit, making it a bit cramped. More annoying for

Vikur were the cows, chickens, and sheep roaming the streets, often getting in the way and leaving messes that usually went ignored for hours. Most times it was more than he could bear. But livestock was Marcove's chief source of trade, for much of the land east of the mountains was incapable of growing decent crops, and bringing harm to the animals was a crime severely punished.

Vikur and Melac stayed at the Bandit Inn. It was a fitting name within Marcove, Vikur always thought, for the kingdom was loosely held together and bandits and hobgoblins often roamed unchecked. Vikur had never thought very highly of the Marcs for this reason, and he was glad he would not have to stomach their dominion for long. Soon, he and Melac would enter Kalmaar.

Kalmaar… A vast realm from the Border Hills to the Batorn Gulf, boasting the strongest military in all of Vaeldor. Many great swordsmen trained within the kingdom dedicated to Brondor, and it was rumored Vecnor had been born there, though the large man never confirmed it. The realm had been plagued by civil wars throughout its history and the throne changed hands many times, but King Karrak's family brought an end to the strife and provided peace spanning nearly two centuries now.

Karrak was the eighth of his bloodline and had ruled longer than any before him. While in his prime, Karrak was the greatest swordsman in the land, and as he aged his skills waned, but his love for battle remained and led to the creation of the Brondor Tournaments. These annual contests of skill and strength, including one-on-one combat, mass battles, war games, and such, sometimes led to the death of its participants, but only when one failed to yield to a superior opponent. Warriors traveled from near and far for the privilege of competing in the tournaments and a chance to claim the treasured rings: golden bands set with an emerald and bearing Karrak's coat of arms. Vikur wore three such rings. By the end of the tournaments, the king hosted a great feast for the survivors, some of which sported more bandages than clothing. Vikur did so love Kalmaar!

Vikur and Melac ate an almost satisfying dinner at the Bandit Inn while Melac spoke about magical feats, but Vikur did not pay much attention. He could not help wondering if the mage could hold his own in an arm-wrestling match, and for the duration of the meal, it was all Vikur could think about. Afterward, they turned in for the night, and with the rising of the sun they left the village behind.

The journey across Marcove passed quickly enough and without mishap. Vikur knew how Marc bandits operated, cowards that would not risk their lives against a well-armed warrior such as himself in the open, so he stuck mainly to the plains. They skirted the Mentrial Woods and veered north toward the rising land, ignoring most roads, and camped for one night under the stars. Had they followed the easier path on the road through the forest, things might have been different. In that woodland, bandits grew bold.

Melac was a stranger to lands east of the Varlimor Mountains and proved very inquisitive during the journey, but Vikur felt no compulsion to play tour guide, only shrugging and nodding to most questions. Once they arrived to the winding path through the Border Hills, however, Vikur's anticipation rose and he decided to share his knowledge at last.

"These hills once crawled with goblins," Vikur said, "but King Karrak placed outposts every few miles to keep the road safe. You can see the first tower from here." He pointed to a turret a few hundred yards away, rising high to survey the surrounding area. "And though Kalmaar holds no claim over the hills, Marcove has never objected to the Kalmiran soldiers manning the towers."

"Fascinating," commented Melac. "Will we meet this King Karrak?"

"Alas, no." Vikur could not help the slight dejection in his tone. He loved the king. "The king resides in the north of Kalmaar. We are to meet our contact at Tarm—excuse me, *Duke* Tarm's castle in the south."

"Do you know this duke personally?" the mage asked.

"I assisted him in clearing out bandits north of the Border Hills several years ago." Vikur briefly remembered the fun he had had that week. "That was before Tarm was duke. Before he was *married*. He was a general then, of King Karrak's largest army. His success granted him the title duke, and now he governs all of southern Kalmaar."

"I noticed a slight alteration in your speech when mentioning he is married."

Melac never seemed to miss a thing. Vikur sighed.

"Lady Mayry is a true lady and noblewoman. Do not forget that." Vikur knew he could not. Mayry never seemed happy to see Vikur, and she especially hated listening to the stories he and her husband shared. Vikur was most uncomfortable in her presence.

Travel through the hills was uneventful, and archers watched from the towers while the two passed, some recognizing Vikur and hailing him. After a few hours they emerged into Kalmaar, and to the north stood the walled city of Barraday. It was immense, challenging even the size of Tikken City, and overlooking it upon a hill was the castle of Duke Tarm, where Vikur was to report and find what the Council of Wizard's scouts had learned of the orb's location.

Vikur was recognized immediately upon reaching the gates, and he and Melac were escorted through the busy streets and to the duke's stronghold. Melac seemed to be looking everywhere at once, trying to take the scenery in without much luck, and they did not slow until they reached the inner bailey of the castle. From there they were ushered to the audience chamber, where Tarm sat upon a throne before a gathering of citizens, listening to a petty squabble between two noblemen. Next to the duke was the Lady Mayry. Both were dressed in royal robes of blue, and though the duke wore no crown, a golden tiara adorned with rubies was atop Mayry's head. Appearing quite bored, Tarm stroked his neatly trimmed mustache while listening to the two men bicker back and forth.

"You shall pay five pieces of silver for the use of his horse," Tarm said, silencing the two. "And I'll hear no more of horse theft among cousins!"

A grin split the duke's face upon spying Vikur across the room.

"Enough!" Tarm waved his hand. "That will be all today. Clear the chamber!"

The gathering grumbled as they were ushered from the room, their complaints unheard for at least another day, and the doors shut with a hollow boom. Only a couple soldiers remained.

"A sight for sore eyes!" said Tarm as he walked to greet Vikur. The duke stood a head shorter, but a sense of cunning was in his eyes.

"Tar—" Vikur spied Mayry's raised brow. He really needed to get used to speaking properly before her. "Duke Tarm." Vikur bowed low. "My lady." He added another bow.

"Nonsense!" Tarm slapped Vikur on the back and led him toward the thrones. "There are no titles among warriors."

Though Vikur knew the duke to be sincere, he sensed the contradiction within Lady Mayry's gaze.

"This is Melac," Vikur waved a hand toward the mage, "sent by the Council of Wizards."

Melac appeared nervous and unsure of what to do. The conjurer bowed awkwardly, his eyes darting to and away from Lady Mayry. Vikur frowned, unsure of what had come over the wizard, and returned his attention to Tarm.

"Is my contact here?"

"He is." Tarm took his seat. "He will be here shortly." The duke gave his wife a sideways glance and turned back to Vikur with an impish grin. "I'm going with you."

"What?" Vikur was caught off guard. "But—"

"I am the sworn protector of all southern regions of Kalmaar." Tarm sat tall. "It's my duty to rid the kingdom of this evil." His grin reappeared. "Tarm and Vikur together again!"

"Very good." Vikur forced a smile, recognizing the disapproval on Mayry's face.

The doors opened and two guards stepped inside.

"Xorlunder, Elloria, and Boler," one of the guards announced, and three figures entered. The guards exited, pulling the doors shut.

At the lead of the approaching three was an elf dressed in gray leather with a fancy bow over his shoulder and a sword strapped to his side. Though Vikur had never met a gray elf of Orlenfel, this elf surely hailed from that clan. His skin was almost as gray as his armor and silver hair hung below his shoulders. He was taller than the warrior elves of Vermallon, standing as high as Vikur, and although his frame appeared thin and fragile, his strides were confident. The feature Vikur found most striking was the white irises upon black eyes.

To the left of the elf was a woman bearing an unmistakable symbol of Brondor about her neck, a silver medallion of crossed swords, as well as a golden amulet depicting the snarling head of a stallion, a typical emblem for Kalmiran soldiers. She was dressed in black and white robes, her chain armor beneath rattling with every step, and two swords hung from her belt, one to either side. To the right of the elf was a grim looking warrior, short in height but wrought in muscle. The man's light-brown hair was set into braids, as were his long sideburns, and Vikur recognized him to be a barbarian of Nomedd. On the barbarian's back was a large, two-headed axe.

"Your Excellence." The elf bowed low. "I am Xorlunder of Orlenfel. With me are Elloria, Kalmiran priestess of Brondor, and Boler of Nomedd."

The two bowed at their introductions.

"Permission to address you, my lord," Elloria said, her sharp voice laden with strength.

Vikur had seen many battle priests, as they were called, more skilled at killing than healing, but he had never enjoyed the company of one. This could be interesting.

Tarm nodded, granting Elloria's request.

"I was a Death Hunter in the north." She beamed with pride. "But over the past several weeks, I noticed our path always returning to the Serpent's Range. It seemed too much a coincidence to me that undead, with no sense of organization, kept choosing a southward route near the mountains. I brought it to the attention of my commander, but he failed to see it the same. So when I met Xorlunder and heard what he had to say, I knew right away I needed to join with him. This evil must be snuffed out at its root."

"The Weend of the Deed was not felt by my people," Boler said in a deep voice without proper decorum, bringing about one of Mayry's frowns usually meant for Vikur. Tarm appeared unconcerned. "But we have sheered een your battle, for many undeed wandered eento our reelm. I have been seent to put an eend to eet."

Xorlunder spoke next, revealing himself to be the scout Vikur sought. The elf kept his story brief, telling only that he followed all traces of the orb to the southern end of the Serpent's Range, commonly referred to as the Serpent's Mouth due to the numerous razor-like stalagmites that plagued the area—the Serpent's fangs.

"We'll depart for the Serpent's Mouth as soon as possible," announced Vikur at the end of the report. Merssa would have been proud!

"I'll ready a small contingent," said Tarm.

"I should add, uh, if I may." Melac gained everyone's attention. "The Council of Wizards believes there are others that seek the orb as well." The mage's eyes darted in and out of contact with Tarm's. "I only mention this, uh, my lord, because too much of a delay may, um, work against us in our, uh, efforts."

Vikur could not help but gawk. Melac had spoken almost nonstop since departing from Palidur. Now, words seemed to be difficult for the mage.

Tarm studied Melac. "I understand. But I know what it's like along the Serpent's Range, and it's not a friendly place. I'll keep it to a score, then. We'll depart from the courtyard in an hour's time."

"As you wish." Melac bowed.

Vikur felt his shoulders slump slightly. It seemed Tarm was taking charge of the mission. But what could Vikur do? Merssa would not allow it, of that he was sure, but there was something about Merssa that allowed her to do what she did. Outside the walls of

Ironside, Vikur just could not find the words that came so easily to her. But he knew Tarm, and the duke needed to be in charge.

Xorlunder, Elloria, and Boler bowed and departed.

Tarm grinned, turning to Vikur and rubbing his hands like a greedy tax collector. "This is going to be fun!"

An hour later, twenty soldiers stood within the courtyard, and Tarm seemed to know them all by name. Also present were fresh horses for all. The beasts were exquisite in appearance, and Vikur knew immediately they were from the Batorn region. In Batorn, horses of exceptional speed and stamina were bred. Vikur had never ridden one before and he was looking forward to it.

"Amazing animals," commented Melac to Vikur, sounding freer and more confident than he had in the audience chamber. "I have read about these creatures, but never before have I beheld them."

Vikur raised a brow. "You seem to have found your voice again."

"Oh." Melac's cheeks flushed. "My apologies. I have, in the past, uttered words not taken quite rightly by royals, and, well, sometimes it is better to say nothing at all than to be misunderstood. And, well, that Lady Mayry—"

"What about my Lady Mayry?" Tarm was suddenly behind Melac. The duke's armor reflected the bright sunlight, and strapped to his side was a blade made for kings.

"Only that she…is a pretty pony—" Melac stammered, receiving a quizzical look from Tarm. "Uh, that is, as pretty as one of these beasts. Well, they *are* beautiful horses and…I mean I wish she were *my* bride. No, no, no! I am overwhelmed by how she—"

"Please stop speaking!" Tarm barely held back his laughter. "If she were to hear a word of what you have just dropped upon my courtyard, I fear you would never leave the dungeon!"

Vikur almost laughed himself, but he spied the arrival of Lady Mayry, unpleased as always, and found his composure.

"Ah," Tarm said. "My pretty pony has arrived!"

Vikur thought he saw flames shoot from Mayry's ears. He glanced back at Melac.

"I told you I cannot speak before royals," Melac said quietly.

"And now I know it to be true." Vikur grinned, and he and Melac climbed onto their saddles.

Tarm placed a kiss upon Mayry's cheek before mounting, and Vikur detected sarcasm in her farewell and thought it odd she did not remain to see them off. Instead, Mayry turned on her heels and strode back into the castle. Hopefully Tarm had not mentioned any more of Melac's comments to her.

They exited the courtyard, Tarm leading the way with Vikur and Xorlunder to his flanks. Melac, Elloria, and Boler followed with the soldiers bringing up the rear. The city streets were traversed with ease all the way to the north gates, as they had been kept clear ahead of the contingent, and soon the company was galloping off along the northern road.

The day passed and the pace was quick. Vikur thought it the best ride he had ever experienced—no rumors could ever capture the reality of the horses' skills—and he felt as if he could have slept in the saddle the entire time without worry of falling. Come night, the soldiers took care of all labors in a most disciplined fashion, setting up camp and taking care of the animals, and before long a fire was roaring and dinner was served while the soldiers watched the perimeter.

The meal was a good hearty stew, and while they ate, Vikur and Tarm took turns telling stories to entertain the company. Tarm spun a yarn almost as well as Vikur, and they continued until all had been served an after-dinner wine. It was at that point that Tarm insisted Vikur speak of his journey into Trannum's lair. Vikur obliged, but his tone was grim as he relived the ordeal. He shared everything he believed pertinent, but omitted a few details, such as the battle with the Ragab, the dunarchins, and the cloud that had been placed over his mind by the undead wizard. Vikur found those parts too disturbing and did not wish to bring nightmares to his new companions, nor himself for that matter.

Come morning, the soldiers packed up and they moved on. Now

and again horsemen were seen, most likely bandits, but the duke's company was more than a bit dissuading and the brigands kept their distance. By midday of the third day, the Serpent's Range came into view, its peaks rising like black spikes into the sky, and as dusk approached, they neared the Serpent's Mouth. The area was almost bare of vegetation, giving it an ominous appearance, and already Vikur spied some of the Serpent's fangs: small pointed rock formations with razor-sharp edges, appearing black and uninviting.

"Horses have been here recently." Xorlunder had dismounted to scan the ground ahead. "They passed into the north."

"How many?" Vikur inquired.

"Hard to say." Xorlunder shifted his eyes from the ground to the distant north. "They rode in a single line, walking slowly. A score, maybe."

"What do you think?" Tarm looked at Vikur. "What if these are the 'others' your wizard mentioned?"

Vikur was caught off guard. He had not expected Tarm to inquire as to his thoughts. "Let's follow them. If they're after the orb as well, it could save us some searching. Or at the very least let us know who they are."

Xorlunder went on foot while the others rode twenty yards behind, and they followed the trail at a slower pace so as not to lose it in the fading light. After a couple miles the tall elf stopped and motioned for Vikur to approach.

Vikur and Tarm dismounted and joined the gray elf, who was gazing into the distance. Vikur peered forward, spotting a gathering of dark shapes, but they were too far off to discern exactly what they might be.

"They are the horses we follow," Xorlunder said. "But no riders. They stand perfectly still. There is something unnatural about them."

"Let's have a closer look." Vikur unsheathed his sword.

Leaving a few soldiers behind, the company proceeded on foot. As they drew nearer, Xorlunder brought them to a stop.

"They have open wounds." The elf was a bit startled. "But they bleed not." He sniffed the air. "They are undead."

"This is not good," said Vikur. "They have beaten us to the orb."

Tarm frowned. "Maybe. Maybe not. Even if they have, they'll return to their horses eventually."

"Perhaps we should wait in ambush," suggested Elloria. "The terrain is very accepting of such a plan."

Vikur was uncomfortable with the idea. "No. They may not have found it yet. And we don't know for certain they will, or that they'll return this way. For all we know, they will take the item and continue through to the other side." He shook his head, staring at the dark spires. He bore no desire to enter into the Serpent's Mouth, but he could not take that chance. Merssa would not take that chance. He turned to Xorlunder. "Can you track through these mountains?"

The elf nodded.

"Then we follow the riders," Vikur said to Tarm. "I know it's not a desirable path, but I do not wish to waste time sitting here for who knows how long. Who, or whatever is ahead of us could perish in the mountains and we'd never know it. But we'll leave some of your men behind, in case they return."

"What about these feelthy beests?" Boler stared in disgust at the undead horses.

Vikur grinned. "Let's return them to the grave!"

They hewed the undead mounts without mercy. Only a few offered any resistance, but they were no match for the force against them and all eighteen were destroyed. Tarm gave orders to half his men to drag the corpses a hundred yards to the north, and they used ropes and horses to assist them in the feat.

"It's getting late," Elloria said as the last rays of the orange sun reflected high upon the dark spires. "Perhaps we should start fresh in the morning."

Vikur shook his head. "We'll move as far as we can. There's no time to spare."

Too bad Merssa had not heard him say that!

Tarm selected ten soldiers to accompany them into the

mountains, and while the company readied their gear, Xorlunder searched along the rough terrain until locating the trail he sought.

"I have seen tracks as these before," the elf said. "There is no warmth to them. Never was. They must be made by the undead, but they are unlike any ghoul or zombie tracks I have seen. Those abominations slide, waddle, and drag their feet, but these…these are steady strides. No one is different from another."

Vikur's mind went back to the dunarchins. He thought again of mentioning the special soldiers of Trannum, but his tongue would not move, as if bringing them up would ensure it *was* dunarchins that had made the trail. From the recesses of Vikur's mind shone two fine points of blue light and he shook his head clear.

"Let's go."

The beginning of the trek was not so bad; the Serpent's fangs were scattered and spaced far enough apart so as not to present too much of a threat. It was not long, however, before the growing shadows crept onto the trail, making things a bit more difficult, and Xorlunder's pace slowed and they lit several torches. The small stalagmites became more numerous then, ranging from a few inches to a few feet in height, and several held shreds of wool, obviously torn from heavy cloaks—it seemed the creatures were unconcerned with being followed. The company marched single file, as no one wished to take a tumble and get cut—or worse impaled—upon the fangs. Once a few miles were behind them, Xorlunder located an area large enough to accommodate the entire party and they made camp.

"We should have a fire," Melac suggested.

"Ees that wise?" Boler posed.

"Undead dislike fire," Elloria pointed out.

"And fighting in the dark would be an advantage only *they* would enjoy," Melac added.

Vikur needed no more information. "Stoke the fire! By all means!"

The night was warm and pleasant, but sleep came hard for Vikur, as his dreams were filled with undead creatures sneaking up in the dark. With the return of the sun, he breathed a sigh of relief and they packed up and moved on.

The way grew difficult as the fangs continued to crowd them, but the travelers they trailed were evidently unconcerned, and signs of their passing grew so numerous that even Vikur could track them like an expert hunter. Xorlunder slowed the pace and they picked their way carefully, but caution was not enough—not all could escape getting their own cloaks snagged and torn. At one point a soldier lost his footing and gashed his arm on a small spire.

"Curse these fangs!" the man said through clenched teeth while Elloria wrapped his arm.

The ground rose higher and the number of fangs began to decline, most of them having become too tall for anyone to fall upon. This made the trail much easier and Xorlunder moved more swiftly, but often the elf slowed again, for groupings of more threatening fangs came and went.

"They know exactly where they are going," said Xorlunder during a short break for lunch. "There is no doubt in their steps. They never double back."

"What if they already retrieved it and have taken an alternate route?" Melac posed. "They may have already exited the mountains."

"I do not believe so." Xorlunder furrowed his brow. "Though they are greatly faded, there are signs this way has been used before, both as an entrance and an exit. I am sure they are to return by this route."

Most the day had passed when they happened upon a cliff overlooking a lush valley. The floor stretched a couple hundred yards to another cliff wall, where a waterfall cascaded into a pool, and from there a river flowed into a large lake surrounded by trees and thick brush—a scene worthy of a romantic portrait, and highly unexpected by Vikur. Xorlunder did not appear so impressed, and the elf's eyes narrowed upon the trees.

"They are down there," Xorlunder said.

Try as he may, Vikur saw only trees. "What do you see?"

"Eighteen figures walking within the shadows of the trees." Xorlunder paused, squinting again. "All are armed except for one that carries a pack."

"They found it!" Vikur pounded his steel fist onto a nearby stalagmite, chipping the stone and receiving a small cut. Hoping nobody noticed, he added, "We must go after them."

"Remember," Xorlunder said, "they'll be returning this way."

"Excellent!" Tarm grinned. "Let's prepare an ambush."

"Eet won't do any good," warned Boler. "Een Nomeedd we atteempteed seeveral ambushees… All eendeed badly."

"If they are ghouls," Melac said, "they will smell us well before they reach us."

"Now that I have seen them," Xorlunder never took his eyes from the valley, "I am positive they are neither zombies nor ghouls. They move as fluent as any human."

"Dunarchins," mumbled Vikur, gaining everyone's attention. He should have said something earlier. "They are undead unlike any I have ever seen. And from what Selanna has told me, they are capable of thought. They do not simply act on hunger or hatred of all things living. They plan, and they fight without worry of pain or fatigue. They do not suffer from the light of the sun. Trannum's elite warriors."

The faces before him were mixed with concern and disbelief.

"I don't like the sound of this," said Tarm. "How is it even possible?"

Vikur shook his head.

"When will they reach us?" Melac looked into the valley, but Vikur doubted the mage could see the undead warriors.

Xorlunder scanned the sky. "After dark."

"Perhaps we should back off." Elloria gazed back the way they had come. "It would be better to fight tomorrow when the light returns."

"They will march through the night," Xorlunder said. "We could not move far enough to avoid a confrontation before morning. And besides, this is the only spot where they *must* come through us. If we relocate, they could sneak around us in the dark. If what Vikur says is true, that just might be what they would do."

"He's right." Vikur nodded. "We'll face them here."

Time crawled while they made ready their preparations. Xorlunder started a small fire while Elloria handed out cold torches, and Tarm placed his soldiers strategically about the area, an eager look upon the duke's face.

As the sun dipped beyond the mountains and shadows engulfed them, all was quiet. Vikur's heart pounded in his ears and he gripped his sword, looking back and forth from the cliff's edge to Xorlunder. The breeze played with the fire and the dancing shadows added an element of foreboding to the gray elf—his tall, thin frame appeared almost as a deadly statue with sword in hand, head bowed, and eyes closed. Xorlunder's eyes snapped opened as sets of pale lights rose from the darkness below.

"Now!" the elf commanded.

Tarm and five soldiers immediately set torches alight, after which Melac raised the campfire to over ten feet to reveal four dunarchins. The creatures were just as Vikur remembered, with yellow skin wrapped tightly about their bones and hollow, bottomless eye sockets hosting points of light that burned pale blue. The undead firstborns were not surprised by Vikur's company and they advanced with weapons ready.

Vikur attacked the lead figure, but the dunarchin fended him off and countered with surprising speed. Vikur was briefly caught off guard, but he was not a three-time champion swordsman of the Brondor Tournaments without reason, and he skillfully fended off the attack before taking out the creature's leg with a savage slash. He then severed its head and its eyes faded.

Tarm arrived to Vikur's side, attacking the second dunarchin with sword and torch. The fire seared the undead warrior's dried flesh while the duke's sword cut into it with every slash and it was quickly dispatched. Together, Vikur and Tarm struck down the other two, but the remaining dunarchins stormed the area and drove them back several paces.

Vikur and the duke slew another dunarchin each, but as Vikur turned aside an attacking blade it grazed his head. His right eye blurred—he was not sure if it had been struck or if blood from his scalp had blinded it—and when he retreated to clear his vision, he saw a dunarchin force Tarm against the point of a spire. Vikur charged, ramming his shoulder into the creature and knocking it to the ground, and Tarm split open its skull.

"Find the pack," Tarm said, and the duke moved to engage a nearby dunarchin to give Vikur time.

Vikur scanned the undead warriors, searching for the pack the elf had mentioned. The light of the fire remained bright and he saw Xorlunder dancing about the jagged rocks while two dunarchins pressed. The gray elf leaped skillfully onto a stalagmite, feet firmly upon its blunted sides, and brought his sword in an arc that seemed to leave a trail of white-hot light in its wake, severing the head of one dunarchin. The sight momentarily distracted Vikur—had Xorlunder used magic? The other dunarchin inflicted a wound to Xorlunder's free hand, but the elf gracefully spun about, hopping into the air and landing back into his original position, and with precision, he sliced the undead warrior's weapon arm off at the elbow—the light trailed the sword again and left a smoldering wound. Xorlunder brought his sword back across the chest and neck with great speed and the creature collapsed.

Vikur shook his head clear and scanned the corpses. Neither had the pack.

With a sword in each hand, Elloria put forth a combination of attacks and efficiently struck down an undead firstborn in seconds. The priestess seemed unaware of the small cut on her arm as she pressed another dunarchin, and she lost one of her weapons when the creature sent it flying into the darkness. The fiend was destroyed with the assistance of one of Tarm's men, but the soldier lost his life in the process and Elloria received a wound to her leg that impaired her movement. Neither dunarchin bore the pack.

Nearby, Boler split a dunarchin's head wide open with his axe, then flailed the weapon in a battle rage to take down a second one shortly after. The barbarian's wild movements brought injuries onto himself by the many fangs around him and he was left with cuts to his legs and arms. Still no pack in sight.

Vikur spotted one of Tarm's soldiers motionless upon a spire with chest split wide, and a second soldier thrust his sword into the killer's stomach. Vikur was surprised to see a brief showing of pain on the dunarchin's face, but the look was quickly replaced by rage and it lowered its shoulder and rammed the guardsman toward a fang. The warrior nearly avoided the pinnacle, suffering a gash on his arm and falling to the ground, and another guardsman thrust a torch into the dunarchin's face, causing it to retreat. As it did so, it slipped on a loose stone and fell, its leg nearly severed along a sharpened spire, and the soldier skewered its head upon his sword. No pack.

Melac held a torch, standing above two of the duke's men—both were unmoving and bled from nasty gashes. The mage blew onto the fire, issuing a blast of flame upon a dunarchin, and the creature ignited instantly. It screeched as it staggered onto a couple spires, where it ceased to move.

Vikur saw no package on Melac's victim before the flames had claimed it, but then he spotted a late arrival to the battle: a dunarchin bearing no weapons. There was a crackling of energy upon its fingertips and it issued forked bolts of lightning upon three soldiers. The men convulsed and screamed, and if the lightning did not kill them, their bodies tumbling onto the fangs of the dark mountainside had surely finished the job.

"Undead wizard!" shouted Elloria.

The priestess moved with a severe limp, but even so, she was a competent warrior and crippled another dunarchin before Boler cleaved its head. Boler then fell to his knees when lightning encompassed his body. Elloria attempted to rush the undead mage, but another dunarchin slashed her arm and her sword clattered to the ground, leaving her weaponless. Vikur charged, screaming his battle cry, and dropped the creature before it issued another blow.

Vikur turned to face the dunarchin mage and spied it at last: the leather bag strapped to its side with a bulge to suggest a box inside. It had to be the orb. The dunarchin hissed, and before Vikur could act, it fled from the trail and into the night.

"No!"

Vikur felt panic rising. He could not allow the orb to get away and he gave chase, running as fast as he could so as not to lose sight of the fleeing shadow. It was immediately obvious the dunarchin was not hampered by the darkness or the razor-like rocks surely slicing its body, and Vikur ignored them as best he could, but the wounds were rapidly growing in number. Another fang gashed Vikur's foot and he knew he would soon lose his quarry, so he leapt onto the dunarchin's back and rode it onto a spire that pierced its body. Unfortunately, Vikur felt the point enter his stomach as well.

With teeth clenched, Vikur heaved himself from the stalagmite and onto his back. He thought it odd, but there was no pain. He was sure his body had gone numb—it was the only explanation—and while he lay panting, he felt evil eyes upon him. Turning, Vikur saw the foul creature staring from atop the spire.

"Foolish being!" it hissed in a dry, hoarse voice. "I feel the blood of the firstborn in you. *You* will join our ranks!" With its final word, sparks crackled within its eye sockets.

"No!"

Vikur mustered what strength remained and swung his armored fist onto the creature's skull. Its eyes flickered, but they continued to burn into him. He pounded again and again, until the lights faded at last, and then collapsed onto his back.

Several minutes passed while Vikur viewed the stars, and in the distance came muffled voices, though he could not understand them. He felt consciousness slipping away and his body began to float, and the stars diminished as a peaceful darkness covered him like a blanket.

"Here!" Vikur attempted to shout, but he emitted little more than a hoarse whisper. Then, like a rush, he fell to the ground and his body was wracked with pain. He coughed up blood and the stars returned, and suddenly a shadowy figure stood above him. It was Xorlunder.

Torchlight surrounded Vikur as the rest of the company arrived. He marveled at how he had caught the dunarchin without first impaling himself—the Serpent's fangs were more numerous than any region of the mountains he had seen.

"Are you all right?" Xorlunder scanned Vikur's body.

"I can't move." Vikur winced. "Make sure it has the orb."

Xorlunder retrieved the pack and removed from it a box. It was cube-shaped, and although bound in leather, Vikur was sure its craftsmanship was exquisite. The elf pulled a key from a chain about the dunarchin's neck before unlocking the box, and slowly lifted the lid to reveal a blue, luminescent orb. Vikur gazed at it, feeling a sudden desire to stare deeply into the swirling mist within, and quickly turned away. It was just as Merssa had described.

"Close it," Vikur said, not knowing what evil it might unleash. "That's it."

Xorlunder snapped the lid shut and locked it.

Tarm squatted next to Vikur, the duke's arm held tightly against his gashed side. "What now?"

"We take it to Tikken City." Vikur winced again, as speaking brought more pain.

Vikur was lifted to his feet by Xorlunder, the elf exhibiting surprising strength for such a thin frame. The motion brought Vikur additional agony, but allowed him a better view of what was left of the company. Other than the elf and Tarm, Melac was assisting Elloria and only two of the duke's men were present, one leaning heavily upon the other. Boler was not among them.

Vikur kept one arm around Xorlunder's shoulders while the elf led them a short distance to an area less plagued by sharpened rocks, and there Elloria bandaged wounds and provided splints and slings. The priestess first tended to her own leg, then moved to Vikur, using small amounts of some medicine on his many cuts and gashes and shaking her head often.

"It is amazing you survived that chase," Elloria muttered, surely using up a good portion of her supplies.

"I am Vikur," he managed to say, hoping he was putting forth a grin, as even his mouth hurt.

Elloria let slip a faint smile. "Thank you for your assistance back there." And without awaiting a response, she moved on to her next patient.

The company settled in for the night, and Vikur was sure none would find sleep, judging by the faces around the fire. In truth he doubted he would be able to close his own eyes, but with his blurred sight, spinning head, and the warmth of the blanket someone placed upon him, Vikur could not help but sleep.

With the coming of light, Vikur awoke to see the others readying to continue. He was able to gain his feet without assistance, and though he still ached, he felt able to move on. Elloria's medicines had surely done their job.

They began the journey back without even a thought of breakfast, as everyone appeared eager to exit the mountains, but it took time to relocate the path—Vikur's jaunt had taken them some distance to the north. The pain of Vikur's wounds grew worse as they pressed on and he noticed he was not the only one suffering, but Elloria provided strange herbs to chew on and the aches eased enough to keep their legs moving. After two days, they emerged at last, and the soldiers that had remained behind greeted them.

It was only lunchtime, but they could travel no farther and chose to rest until the next morning. Elloria produced more medicines from the packs on her horse and continued treating their wounds throughout the remainder of the day.

"You need to rest," Elloria told Vikur. "Your foolish run through the fangs has left more gashes than I can stitch. But they should close up fine with the medicines, given the chance."

"Foolish run?" Vikur winked. "Or brave pursuit?"

"Foolish." Elloria left no room for humor. "But, I suppose, you achieved your objective."

"Not to mention I saved your life," he said. "Let us not forget that."

"But it was you that decided we should enter the mountains," she pointed out. "Had we awaited them in ambush when they returned to their horses, as I suggested, none of this may have been necessary."

"But…" Vikur was at a loss. Boler had claimed the undead could not be ambushed. Xorlunder said the creatures would avoid confrontation and sneak around them in the darkness. Did she not remember any of that? "It's what Merssa would have done," Vikur mumbled.

"Who?" Elloria frowned.

"Never mind."

"You need to try and avoid activities for at least a week," the priestess said once she was finished, and she left Vikur to his thoughts.

Vikur awoke with a start. Glowing blue eyes plagued his dreams. Not wishing to return to them, he exited his tent to get some fresh air.

Stars dotted the sky and the waning moon provided little light, but there were plenty of torches planted about the area. Vikur reached high to stretch, but stopped short upon aggravating his injuries. Though he continued to improve, the stomach wound was deep and hurt more than even Ragab's horn had. Elloria claimed Vikur would need a week without activity. How little she knew him. He was Vikur!

Blinking the sleep from his eyes, Vikur spotted a blue glow, barely visible beyond some boulders, and his heart raced. He grabbed his sword from the tent and moved to the rocks as fast as he could, but stopped when he found Tarm kneeling on the ground, gazing silently at the orb nestled within the open box. With a heavy sigh, Vikur winced in pain.

"Vikur?" Tarm was a bit startled.

"What are you doing?" Vikur searched the surrounding darkness for glowing eyes.

"Oh." Tarm closed the lid. "Nothing. Just curious, I guess." The duke cleared his throat. "How can something so small contain so much power?"

"It is but one of five," Vikur said. "And it's evil."

"Yes, of course." Tarm locked the box and placed the key around his neck. "We best get some sleep." He yawned. "Long ride tomorrow."

Vikur nodded and they headed back to the campsite. The duke returned the box to its tent, where three guards stood alert.

"Carry on," Tarm ordered the men, who nodded. After a glance toward Vikur, the duke stepped into his own tent.

Vikur stood in thought. Shaking his head, he decided to walk the perimeter.

The camp was secure and all guards alert at their posts. The soldiers welcomed Vikur's intrusion into yet another boring night and gave greetings, but their words fell on deaf ears. Vikur did not think Tarm guilty of any evil, for he had known the duke for years and bore much respect for the man. No. If evil was afoot, the orb was to blame. And the more Vikur thought about it, the more he realized he must do something.

Quietly, Vikur went to where the horses were corralled and saddled his steed; the pain in his stomach made it difficult, but he forced his body to finish the task. Making sure no one was around, he led the animal outside the perimeter to the south, beyond the range of the guards, and commanded it to stay. Doubling back unseen, he approached the tent with the orb.

"I need to see the orb." Vikur attempted to walk past the guards, but they did not move.

"Sorry, sir," one guard said. "Only the duke has the key."

"Just let me see the box, then," Vikur said. "To make sure it's all right."

"Sorry, sir," the guard repeated. "No one handles the item. Those are our orders."

Vikur thought about the guard's words. They allowed Tarm to take it completely from their sight, but would not let him even look at the box? He opened his mouth to mention this, but decided it was pointless.

"Very well."

Vikur turned to walk away, but came back with a sucker punch, striking the soldier square on the jaw and knocking him out. Vikur landed another punch, stunning the second guard, and as the third soldier attempted to pull a sword, Vikur grabbed hold of the man's hand and forced the blade to the ground. He then broke the guard's nose with a headbutt and dropped the man to his knees. The second guard recovered and ran, calling out an alarm.

Vikur entered the tent. It was empty, with the exception of the box resting upon a boulder. He snatched the box, and after hastily cutting an exit to the rear of the tent with his sword, he exited. His stomach bandages were showing signs of blood as he ran to the south, but Vikur did not stop until encountering a couple guards near the perimeter.

"What's happening, Lord Vikur?" questioned one.

"We're under attack!" Vikur yelled, holding the box behind his back. "All hands to the duke!"

The men hurried toward the tents.

Reaching his horse, Vikur climbed onto the saddle. His armor and all of his possessions were back in his tent, but he had his sword, and that was all he needed. He spurred his horse into the darkness without looking back.

Chapter 23

Tenvale

"Mind you stay within your means," Selanna said to Vikur before parting company in Sardina. "Do not try to be what you are not."

Vikur chuckled with confidence. "I'll see you in Tikken City!"

The Lord of the Keep nodded for Melac to follow, and the two rode east toward Ironside Keep to begin the hunt for the orb in Kalmaar.

That had transpired a couple days ago, and now Selanna sat in a small tavern just outside the border of Tenvale, awaiting her contact. She was pleased for the most part with the company she traveled with. Eraim was with her, of course—where else would Eraim be? Then there was Nilborg, the High Priest of Soleran, who was a pleasant, elderly man to say the least, and Rholmar, a paladin that seemed to carry himself well. Rounding out the company was Arkor, making for a very capable group in Selanna's mind. She did not care too much for the tension between the Paladin of Arronaus and Arkor, however—the altercation in the streets of Palidur had not been forgotten, and they often made negative comments toward one another under their breaths. The squabbling evidently wore upon Nilborg as well, and the priest attempted to keep the peace with little success. Selanna had questioned Merssa about the wisdom of placing the two together, but Merssa gave Selanna one of those stern looks and said, "There are more important things at hand. If they get out of line, don't give them any dinner."

It was just past lunch when a woman entered the establishment, stirring Selanna from her thoughts. Standing nearly six feet by Selanna's estimation, the newcomer appeared exactly as one would expect a human scout to look. The woman's dark hair was pulled tightly into a long brown ponytail and she wore loose clothing beneath her light leather jacket—ideal for lengthy travel. After a brief word with the barkeep, who nodded toward Selanna's company, the woman approached.

"Selanna?" the woman asked, to which Selanna nodded. "I am Ladonia, sent by the Council."

Selanna detected a slight accent, placing Ladonia's origin in Philen. It was obvious Ladonia worked to conceal it for some reason.

"Please," Selanna said, "have a seat."

Ladonia nodded and sat with a slight show of elegance, as one with a noble upbringing that was either trying to hide it or had not practiced it for some time. "The item you seek has fallen into the hands of a wizard by the name of Solett," Ladonia said.

Merssa would have been impressed with this scout. No small talk. No tales of how she tracked it over days and days.

"He is a high standing mage," Ladonia continued, "and from what I have learned, he discovered it while investigating the Wind along the Ladal Mountains. Supposedly he intended to take it to Witchdoor, to the Temple of Vou for observation and testing, but the priests there say he never arrived. It would seem he took it home instead, and he has not been seen since."

"Typical mage," Arkor mumbled.

There was a thump beneath the table and the one-armed warrior glared at Eraim, who refused to make eye contact but wore a smirk with pride.

"In fact," Ladonia added, "*none* of his many servants have been seen lately, and those that live near him report a blue light at night, shining through shuttered windows."

"This is unfortunate," said Nilborg. "What if we have to take it by force? Will we be able to perform such a feat?"

"Let us not forget that Tenvale is ruled by wizards," cautioned Selanna. "They live by a code you would not understand and the laws will seem strange to you. Punishment for breaking them can be severe."

"I suppose you wish to simply knock on his door and ask for it?" Arkor raised a brow.

"So we're to assume he's evil?" Rholmar's disdain was obvious in his tone. "He's a wizard and he found a toy. He's probably playing with it before turning it in."

Selanna thought of commenting on the paladin's choice of words, and pointing out that wizards did not *play* with magical *toys*. But it seemed Arkor had enough remarks for all.

"All I'm saying is that informing him of our intentions will not be met well. Wizards do *not* take kindly to being told what to do."

Rholmar's jaw clenched. "Just because you lack the mannerisms to converse with intelligent beings —"

"Please!" Nilborg intervened. "We have a few days yet to discuss this matter…and hopefully in a bit more amiable tone. For now, it is the laws of Tenvale that concern me. We shall have to rely on you, Selanna, to guide us through."

Selanna nodded. It would be difficult, but she could handle it.

"Hasn't the strange behavior of Solett turned any heads?" asked Rholmar of Ladonia. "What if we appeal to the king wizard, or whatever they call their leader?"

"All behavior in Tenvale will seem strange by your standards," Selanna tried to explain. "Mages conduct experiments all the time, disappearing for months in some cases. It is not uncommon. No laws are broken, so long as damage is limited to their own property. Even a servant's death is acceptable, and the servants know this."

"So there's nothing we can do?" Arkor spread his hand and hook out in frustration. "We just allow him to keep the damned thing?"

Selanna spoke quickly as Rholmar's mouth opened.

"I am only saying that we must be discrete. We will surely be outside the laws of the land, and to be caught would bring harsh punishment. If a wizard inquires as to our business, you are all my servants." Seeing the disapproval from Arkor and Rholmar, Selanna could not help but smile. The thought of how much more fun it would have been had Merssa been with her floated briefly across Selanna's mind — or even Vecnor. "Just for our time in Tenvale," she added. "It is the best way to avoid scrutiny. They do not look kindly upon outsiders of the craft."

"Sounds like a city I know." Arkor directed his comment toward Rholmar, who returned a sharp glare.

They entered the Wizard Kingdom, and while they passed through settlements, there was ample evidence to support Selanna's claims. Of course, none of it came to Selanna as any surprise. Spell casters walked about as nobles while all others were treated as peasants, regardless of any wealth. The more powerful the mage, the higher their rank in society, and the ranges between the powers were vast, from Trickster to Master Wizard. Low-ranking mages usually served as city guards and kept suspicious eyes on all foreigners, often pushing them to be on their way. For this reason, Selanna kept her companions close, as fewer questions were asked while she was present. Selanna also adjusted her personality to one of superiority, speaking down to officials in a most brutish manner at times, for beauty afforded her no favor — this was reinforced by the fact that Eraim was extended absolutely no courtesies. Had Selanna been a citizen, she would surely be ranked above most mages, and playing her part with confidence and arrogance kept most city guards at a distance. Such were the ways in Tenvale.

And so, they made their way across the realm. Rholmar and Arkor bore sour looks the entire time while posing as Selanna's bodyguards, and more than once Selanna needed to scare away an official that questioned their loyalty toward her. Nilborg was convincing as Selanna's sage, and Eraim always enjoyed playing a handmaiden, usually speaking in made-up accents and groveling before Selanna for coins. Ladonia surprised Selanna, as the woman assumed the role as cook and never strayed from it, often insisting on actually making the meals while on the road, which Selanna was not entirely satisfied with. Ladonia only knew how to make sausages, which Selanna did not partake of, and some kind of tart, of which Selanna was sure was supposed to have some amount of sugar in it. She was positive Ladonia had seen someone cook once, but doubted the scout had ever actually attempted the task before. This went on for a bit more than four days, until they reached the western edge of the dominion, and it was only just after noon when they arrived to Rrimmburd, a large city off the Queen Arman Lake.

They settled within a tavern and enjoyed a quiet meal as best they could until the sun touched the water. The company was grim, and Selanna knew it had nothing to do with having been her servants over the past several days. No one wanted to battle a wizard, not even Selanna. Solett was a high-ranking member of Tenvale, and that meant he had power. Real power.

"His house is a couple miles to the south," Ladonia interrupted Selanna's thoughts, "built on a small rise along the beach and extending to the water below. It is three stories in all, with the main door on the second floor upon the cliff, but also there's a small iron door on the beach below."

"I suppose we'll just knock on the main door," Arkor muttered.

Selanna did not want to listen to yet another disagreement between the one-armed warrior and paladin, so she spoke quickly.

"We shall see if the iron door is accessible." She received the anticipated stare of disapproval from Rholmar and continued. "It is the best way. I fear the worst, and the orb is too important."

"And what if, in the end, we are simply thieves breaking into a wizard's house?" posed Rholmar. "I do not wish to be on the wrong side of the laws, as strange as some of them may be."

"You need not worry of that," Selanna assured him. "Remember, you are my servants. *I* will be the one to answer for it."

Of course, that was not wholly true, Selanna knew. In Tenvale, if a wizard was sentenced to imprisonment, the wizard's servants would be sentenced as well. But Rholmar did not need to know that.

Nor would he be pleased to learn what imprisonment in Tenvale meant. Selanna shuddered at the thought.

"We should go now," Ladonia said.

Selanna nodded and they exited the tavern.

They left their horses within the city stables, so the mounts would not draw attention while standing outside the wizard's house, and headed south on foot along the lakeshore as the sun dipped low across the water. The city fell behind and they encountered nothing, save the occasional home along the water's edge. The houses were large and each one unique, as their owners would have had a hand in their construction, and every wizard possessed a structure to reflect their needs. Each had plenty of space between them, at least a quarter mile, like a farmhouse leaving plenty of room for crops and livestock, but there were no crops and no livestock. The space was simply to protect neighbors from any mishaps within each home's laboratory. As Selanna glanced upon each house, she wondered how she would shape her own. She pursed her lips as she realized she had no idea. But one thing was certain: there would be many more trees about.

Only a trace of sunlight remained when Ladonia stopped and pointed to the next house. It was large, set partially upon a small cliff and extending down and over the water, where four stone pillars supported it. Just as the scout mentioned, the front door was on the second level upon the cliff facing the road, and below, the lower level was set above a narrow strip of sand. No lights were visible through the few shuttered windows that existed upon any of the structure's three levels.

"There is the trail down to the beach." Ladonia pointed to a dirt path falling down a slope. "It leads to the iron door."

The descent appeared steeper than it felt as they made their way to the beach. From there, Selanna saw more clearly the portion of the house set above the water. The beach narrowed to a three-foot strip beneath the structure, and between two of the pillars was an iron door set into the cliff wall, barely discernable within the shadows.

Selanna led the way to the door. She closed her eyes, exhaling slowly while summoning her sight, and opened them again. Everything touched by magic was revealed to her and she spotted a faint residue. The door obviously possessed magical wards, but they were aged and weakened—Solett had evidently lost interest in maintaining the magic's potency. With a wave of her hand, Selanna released some energy and the residue faded to nothing. She looked at Eraim and nodded.

Eraim stepped forward with tools in hand. After a few seconds she stepped back, disappointment clouding her face. "That was not even a challenge. I could have done it with my eyes closed."

"Stand aside." Arkor stepped forward with sword in hand.

"We're not here to murder this man," Rholmar said. "And I still object to entering in such a manner; as thieves in the night!"

"We've been over this." Nilborg placed a hand upon the paladin's metal shoulder. "I'm afraid, in this matter, we must assume the worst. The orb must be procured before the necromancer learns of its whereabouts."

Rholmar appeared unconvinced. "Then I'm going first." He stepped past Arkor, his weapon remaining in its scabbard.

Arkor said nothing, but the hint of a smirk crossed the one-armed warrior's lips.

The rusted hinges screeched when Rholmar opened the door, and Selanna produced her ball of light to reveal a rough-hewn corridor carved into the cliff and coated with moisture. After ten feet it was reinforced with thick wooden beams that formed an arch, and after another ten feet it turned right.

Just before the wooden beams was another iron door, which Rholmar found to be unlocked. The door squealed louder than the previous one, opening into a chamber containing a small boat, fishing nets, and the like. With barely a glance at the room's contents, Rholmar continued along the hall and around the bend.

The tunnel stretched another ten feet, ending with a spiral staircase leading a short distance to a trap door. Rholmar ascended, motioning for silence as he reached the top, and listened carefully.

There was no sound. He pushed the door. It rattled, but did not open.

"Locked," the paladin whispered loudly.

Eraim climbed the narrow steps and viewed the door. "I'll need a boost."

Rholmar allowed Eraim to climb up his back, and she knelt on his shoulders with perfect balance. She fit a dagger into the crack, sliding it a short way until it caught something, and then pulled a piece of metal from her belt and worked it into the seam. After a few seconds, Eraim placed the tool back into her belt, dropped to her feet, and nodded.

Rholmar pushed the door open, its hinges screaming just as the others, and above was darkness.

Arkor shook his head. "The wizard has surely heard us by now. Probably preparing his defenses."

Rholmar pulled himself up and Selanna willed her light to follow. Eraim went next and then Selanna.

They stood at the end of a corridor stretching thirty feet before branching left and right, and all down its length were doors to either side. It was obviously the portion of the house sitting above the water. The others filed into the corridor and Arkor and Eraim began opening doors. Selanna stood between the two to get a view of either side, and Ladonia joined Rholmar at the far end of the hall, where the paladin stood guard. The first door Eraim opened revealed another spiral staircase leading up, and the remaining doors led to rooms containing barrels, crates, linens, and other storage.

Selanna moved to the intersection. The left hallway contained a single door a short distance away, while to the right the numerous doors continued, all on the right side, and at the corridor's termination was a large door bearing strange markings. Rholmar looked at Selanna, and she nodded toward the door with the runes.

The paladin led the way, but stopped five feet from the large door, seemingly hesitant to move any closer. Selanna stepped past him. Intricate runes were etched into the wood, but fresh carvings had been added, overlapping the older markings.

"What do you make of it?" Rholmar asked.

"The original runes would be Solett's. A sort of wizard's mark." Selanna looked closer. "But it is quite unusual to alter them."

"I doubt he's feeling himself," Arkor commented as he and Eraim arrived.

"But the new ones..." Selanna felt the blood drain from her cheeks as the carving became clear: a triangle, within which an oval extended beyond two of its borders. She had seen it before, upon the floor of Trannum's lair and on several books from the necromancer's library. "This does not bode well."

"Is it trapped?" Rholmar asked.

Selanna studied the door. She detected nothing, as expected. Wizards did not usually trap things within their own homes. She shook her head.

Rholmar stepped forward and tried the latch. The door swung open without a sound. Beyond, a laboratory was dimly lit by the waning moon through an open window facing the lake. All was quiet and still, until a movement to the right within the shadows caught their attention.

"I am Rholmar, Palidurian Knight and Paladin of Arronaus." His hand moved to the hilt of his sword. "Who—"

Two figures stepped into the moonlight. They staggered, appearing intoxicated, but the smell of death proceeded them and Selanna knew them to be zombies. She sent forth her light and revealed it to be so.

Rholmar pulled his sword and charged, decapitating one of the walking corpses in a flash. The second zombie made a feeble attack, but its clawed fingers could not penetrate the paladin's breastplate and he dispatched it as well.

"Was that my first lesson in manners?" Arkor said from the doorway, receiving a cold glare from Rholmar.

The others entered and Selanna willed her light to illuminate the entire chamber. A few tables existed, all of them bare, and several jars and containers were cracked or broken and strewn about.

"The zombies are dressed as servants," Ladonia pointed out.

"This is most disturbing." Nilborg gazed at the bodies. "We best ready ourselves for anything." He pulled the morningstar from his belt.

"This is not the main laboratory," said Selanna. "It is too small. The other will be upstairs."

"The stairs are among the storerooms," Eraim said. "The rest of the doors lead to servants' quarters, but they appear quite unused."

"Let's return to the stairs without delay," Nilborg said to Rholmar.

Everyone held their weapons ready while Eraim led the way to the spiral staircase. Rholmar then ascended first and the company followed.

The stairs emptied into the back corner of a lounge containing a large hearth and two doors, one across the room and one to the left—the main entrance, judging by the cloaks hanging next to it. What caught Selanna's immediate attention, however, was the state of the room. The furniture appeared as though a wild animal had chewed it up and claw marks marred the plaster walls.

"There's a body." Arkor pointed his sword at a pair of boots sticking out from behind the sofa.

Selanna followed the one-armed warrior with her light as he moved cautiously to get a better look. It was the corpse of a human mage. The throat was ripped out and the clothes shredded, and Selanna recognized the uniform to be the same as Rrimmburd's city guard. The man possessed many other savage wounds as well, and all appeared fresh.

"Perhaps they did send someone to check on Solett," Arkor said. "Unfortunately, they have not received his report yet."

A growl came from the cold, dark fireplace, where a set of pale blue eyes hovered within. Selanna sent her light forth to reveal a dog covered in soot, and though open sores plagued its body, no blood issued. It growled again, bearing bloodstained teeth, and its eyes flared as it lunged for Arkor.

Arkor slashed his blade, adding to the dog's many wounds, but the animal rolled to its feet and lunged again. Arkor raised his left arm, and its teeth sank into the wooden shaft as the animal pushed the one-armed warrior over a tattered chair and to the floor. The dog released the arm and went for Arkor's throat, but Rholmar's sword came in an uppercut, nearly decapitating it. The animal tumbled to the side, its head dangling, but still it moved. In an attempt to emit another growl, a strange gurgling came from its wide-open throat and sickly black liquid bubbled out, but Mithkahr severed the remainder of its head and the body flopped to the floor.

Arkor ripped a piece of cloth from the chair and wiped the black ichor from his armor. The fluid reeked a sour smell and his eyes watered. "What in the Abyss was that thing?" he spat. "I did not know dogs could be turned into ghouls."

"I am not so sure it was a ghoul," Selanna murmured to herself. She received a concerned look from Eraim, who had just wiped the dark blood from Mithkahr.

"I sensed great evil from that animal," said Nilborg. "And the feeling I get from the rest of the house is suddenly very powerful."

"I was hoping zombies was all he had learned." Selanna shook her head. "But it appears Solett has discovered much more than that from the orb. That beast's eyes shared the same light as the dunarchins."

The company paled with these words, with the exception of Ladonia. Perhaps the scout was not aware of the undead firstborns.

"I doubt *anything* is alive here." Ladonia glanced about the room.

Rholmar headed for the door opposite the hearth. "We best get back to it, then."

The paladin led them into a hallway bearing more doors, all to the left side. They checked each in turn, finding a dining chamber, kitchen, and a couple guestrooms, and all contained fine furnishings but were devoid of occupants. At the far end of the hall, Rholmar turned left and into a short corridor bearing a single shuttered window, and around another bend the hallway ended at a large door.

The door bore runes identical to the ones downstairs, complete with the additional markings.

Rholmar flung the door open to reveal another laboratory, twice the size as the first and showing signs of recent use. Tables were covered with books, bottles, and jars, as almost every inch of space was in use, and wisps of smoke drifted to the floor from a brazier hanging in the center. Four pairs of blue eyes appeared within the shadows of the room, two sets to the immediate right and the other two across the chamber.

"Dunarchins!" shouted Arkor as he stepped next to the paladin.

Selanna sent her light to the near corner to reveal Arkor's guess to be correct. One dunarchin was dressed as a servant and the other had the dark skin of a Dale from Holindale, and both held swords.

Arkor and Rholmar met the two. The Dale-dunarchin fought with the prowess of a hardened veteran while the servant's skills were lacking, but the absence of fear made both of them vicious. Arkor and Rholmar proved superior, however, and the undead firstborns were quickly defeated.

The other dunarchins split up as they moved around the tables, and Eraim made her way up the middle of the room toward one with Mithkahr in hand, her blade emitting its red glow. With a feint, she drew the undead warrior's attack and slapped its blade aside. She then spun, severing the dunarchin's leg and bringing it to her level, and in a flash, she split open its skull.

Ladonia's skills paled in comparison to the others of the company and the final dunarchin backed her against the wall. Nilborg arrived to Ladonia's aid, holding his symbol of Soleran high and yelling in the tongue of his deity—a language coming only to worthy priests in times of need. The dunarchin threw its arm over its eyes, as if the symbol shed the very light of the sun, and Ladonia plunged her sword into the fiend's chest where its heart once beat, dropping the dunarchin to its knees. The same black liquid that seeped from the dog coated Ladonia's blade, and when Nilborg's morningstar crashed into the dunarchin's skull the creature collapsed.

All was quiet.

Selanna lowered her hands. She had stood ready, in case any of her companions needed assistance, but now she gazed intently about the room. The presence of magic was everywhere, as well as the feeling of extreme power. "The orb is here," she said. "Find it quickly, but be careful of items you do not recognize."

While the company began their search, Selanna's attention was drawn to an open book. She held her breath as she skimmed the current page, reading Solett's most recent entries, and she turned back a few pages. The wizard had written complete instructions for the creation of dunarchins.

Selanna's attention shifted to the nearby brazier. The smoke issuing was not smoke at all, for it drifted wistfully to the floor. She reached up and touched the brass bowl. It was ice cold.

"Who dares to trespass?" came a hoarse whisper from the open door. Standing there was an older man in brown robes. He was tall, completely bald, and his clothes appeared to have been worn for days. "Who dares to trespass?" he repeated in a more forceful tone while staring blankly ahead.

"I am Selanna of Salenti." She stepped forward. "I have come to help you."

"To help…me?" The man spoke barely above a whisper and his lips twisted into a grin.

"The orb," Selanna said. "It is affecting your mind. You must resist its power."

The wizard chuckled. "Foolish elf! The orb and I are one!" The last couple words came out in a hiss, and his eyes began to shed the same eerie blue light as the dunarchins. "And you shall all join us!"

Arkor charged as the man began an incantation, but the one-armed warrior bounced off an invisible barrier and crashed to the floor. Blue wisps of smoke issued like snakes from the wizard's fingertips, slithering to the ceiling and gathering into clouds, and from them flew small humanoids on bat-like wings. The creatures showed many pointed teeth as they began to giggle, but with a command from the wizard, they snarled and descended onto Selanna's companions.

Nilborg raised his holy symbol against one of the fiends, but the imp spit smoking saliva onto the priest's hand and laughed when the symbol fell to the floor. It then sank its claws and teeth into Nilborg's shoulder, and Nilborg winced in pain as he ripped the creature loose and slammed it onto a nearby table. The small monster stopped laughing and shook its head in an attempt to regain its senses, but Nilborg's morningstar crushed it and it disappeared in a puff of blue smoke with a fading cry.

Rholmar swung his sword at an imp and it flew quickly around the blade, sticking its long tongue out at the paladin. It did not see the dagger in Rholmar's other hand until the weapon was planted firmly into its stomach, and it vanished in a puff of blue smoke.

Arkor used his false arm as bait, allowing an imp to sink its teeth into the wood. The creature released its bite, shaking its head in confusion, and Arkor brought the pommel of his sword onto its skull. *Poof!*

A second imp attacked Arkor from behind, biting into the one-armed warrior's neck, and he fought desperately to get at it, but the pest danced out of reach with every swipe and returned for another taste. Selanna was about to send aid, but Rholmar snatched the creature and squeezed the life from it. Another imp came to within inches of the paladin's head and Arkor returned the favor, cutting it in half. *Poof! Poof!*

Eraim rolled beneath a table and out the other side as two imps descended upon her. One pursued, raking Eraim's cheek with its claw, and she swung Mithkahr in retaliation, but the creature flew quickly from the weapon's path and taunted her with a maniacal laugh. The second imp landed on her back, but lost its hold when Eraim quickly rolled over it. She came back with her blade and the little monster vanished in a blue cloud with a shriek. The first imp took to throwing vials of strange liquids from a shelf, hovering beyond Eraim's reach.

Again, Selanna was about to send aid, but her attention was stolen by Ladonia's shriek of pain. Several small wounds were upon the scout's arms and cheeks as she did all she could to keep one of the blue fiends at bay. It laughed mockingly as it darted in and out of reach, and every time Ladonia made a feeble attack, it scored another hit and quickly retreated to the ceiling.

Selanna cast two small globes of green light, and one flew to Ladonia's aid while the other raced to Eraim's. The imps attempted to dodge the missiles, but the spheres proved too fast and agile, chasing them under and over tables, around bottles and vials, and destroying them both.

"Solett!" Selanna turned back to the door. "You *will* hand over the orb!" In her words was woven a spell, but it had no effect. The wizard's will was too strong.

"I am Solett no longer!"

The wizard's glowing eyes bore into Selanna, and from his hand issued three small, fiery spheres. Selanna brought her hands up and the globes bounced aside. One struck the ceiling above Nilborg, raining small stones and dust onto the priest's head. The second one exploded on a table next to Eraim while she evaded another flying creature, showering her with glass and setting fluids alight. The final globe flew straight for Rholmar, and the paladin was unaware while he battled an imp. Arkor shoved Rholmar free of its path and it exploded on the wall, causing little damage — proper laboratories were built to take such abuses.

Selanna launched a table at the wizard, but a word from Solett's lips shattered it into harmless splinters. She then released two green spheres and he waved them aside, where they harmlessly darkened the walls. Solett dropped a portion of the ceiling and Selanna raised her hands to counter, but a couple chunks of stone hit her on the shoulder and scalp, the latter causing a trickle of blood to run down her cheek. Several more spells were issued back and forth, and more tables, bottles, and books were destroyed.

The melee with the imps was over and Selanna could see Ladonia hiding beside a large cupboard for shelter from the magic battle. Eraim joined the scout while Nilborg cautiously circled to the right of the wizard, but Selanna knew the priest would be of no assistance. Arkor and Rholmar rushed from the left and Solett waved a hand, as if they were nothing more than pesky insects, and cast them into the far wall.

The orb's hold over the wizard was too strong. Selanna had held her full power in check, trying to subdue Solett, but she had to end the battle before one of her companions was hurt too badly. Turning to the brazier, she fired a green ball of light, and Solett shrieked as the brass bowl flew into the air and its contents spilled onto the floor. Time seemed to slow while frozen pieces of coal shattered upon the flagstones and the orb was revealed to all. It bounced with a loud *clang* several times and rolled across the room until reaching the back wall.

"No!" cried Solett, ignoring all else as he sped toward his coveted treasure.

With great sorrow, Selanna released one last spell and a beam of green light emitted from her palm. Solett revealed pain at last as the glow engulfed his body and he dropped to his knees, and the light of his eyes faded and he collapsed and ceased to move. Selanna closed her hand, shaking her head, and the spell ended.

"Is this it?"

Eraim's voice snapped Selanna from the pity she felt for Solett. She moved across the room to where Eraim squatted above the blue sphere. The orb was smaller than the one in Sistama, but it held the same swirling mist and Selanna could feel the power contained within.

"It is," Selanna said. "And we must destroy it. I can now see that its power is too great for anyone to possess."

Eraim gave Selanna a quizzical look—her friend knew all too well she never desired the destruction of magical objects. Selanna's attention returned to the corpse of Solett briefly, and then moved to the books that had survived the magic battle.

"It possessed Solett," Selanna explained, "and that could not have been an easy feat. And these books…" She lifted one from the floor. "They have been written before. I have seen the likes of them in the library in Sistama. We must destroy the orb before it does to others what it did to him."

"I'll do it." Arkor walked to where Eraim watched over the sphere.

"Wait," Selanna warned after a moment of thought, remembering how the orb within the swamp had exploded, but she was too late.

Eraim scrambled from the area as Arkor's blade fell. The weapon did not have the same effect as Clanghorr, however, and *it* shattered while the orb remained whole—not a scratch was left upon the sphere's smooth surface. Arkor fell to his knees, cringing in pain.

Nilborg rushed to the one-armed warrior, holding a small root. "Place this under your lip. It will ease the pain." Nilborg stared at the orb with both awe and fear. "*Can* we destroy it?"

"I believe so." Selanna looked at Eraim. "Ready Mithkahr."

Rholmar and Ladonia helped Arkor from the area while Eraim hesitantly raised the blade. Selanna began to chant, and the blue vapor of the orb pulsed while she did so. She continued, her chant growing louder, and the orb's light grew brighter. Her voice became almost deafening in her ears as the sphere continued to match its will against hers, but in the end, Selanna proved stronger and its glow dimmed slightly.

"Now!" Selanna shouted, and Eraim brought down Mithkahr.

There was a great hissing noise, followed by a high-pitched wail that seemed to pass into the distance, and then silence. The orb lay shattered in a thousand small fragments.

Chapter 24

Garthglen

Poluran sat on Melballa, squinting at the fields before him. Streams cut through tall reeds feeding stagnant, green-freckled ponds, and birch, maple, oak, and willow trees were loosely scattered about. It was not the Silent Marsh by any means, but Garthglen was a swamp nonetheless, and Poluran did not look forward to entering it.

Next to Poluran was Massima, scout to the Council of Wizards and one of the dark-skins of Holindale. Poluran put little faith in barbarians, though he had never met a Dale before, and this particular one did not even possess a decent weapon—strapped to the scout's horse was nothing but a stick the man called a quarterstaff! But the Council spoke highly of Massima, so Poluran decided to give him the benefit of the doubt…for now.

Also present for the hunt of the orb was Brem, priest of the forest goddess Frayorna. Poluran had met the marteese several times in the past when passing through Neja and trusted him. Then there was Malgabi of Marcove, who was on a journey through Virch and heard the call for warriors; Rybeal of Philen, a wizard Seac the Seer personally recommended; and finally, of all search parties formed, Poluran's was chosen to host not one but two krukari!

First there was Gruzim, who had had no desire to cross the King Arman in pursuit of the other orbs and even less to enter Palidur—a feeling reciprocated by Merssa. Then there was Norik. Norik was almost as hideous as Gruzim to look at and just as tight lipped, but he was smaller in stature and carried a battleaxe. And if having two krukari was not bad enough, they had no love for one another. Poluran thought the abominations would get along for lack of friends, but they proved his theory quite out of place. They had to be separated in the riding order, for they often bickered, and through those times Poluran was grateful for Malgabi. The Marc seemed to have a knack for keeping peace between the two, and this caught Poluran by surprise. He had only known Marcs to be greedy and self-serving. He never would have guessed a citizen of that realm could prove so diplomatic.

It was quite a collection of characters, Poluran thought when they departed from Tikken City, but over the two-day journey to the swamp, no one questioned his authority and that was a good start.

"Tell me about this place again." Poluran interrupted the choir of locusts and frogs.

Massima scanned the direction of Poluran's gaze, as if trying to see what held his attention. Sunlight glinted off the scout's dark, clean-shaven head, and upon either shoulder a tattoo of fire revealed devotion to the deity Silcor. The man's dark eyes held Poluran for a moment, and the barbarian smiled, ready to recite the story a fourth time.

"Long ago," Massima said in a heavy accent, enunciating each word carefully, "settlers lived in this swamp, for it was renowned for hunting and fishing. But the land became infested with terrible creatures and they abandoned their homes."

"Unnaturally large reptiles…" Poluran sighed.

"And trolls," Massima added.

"Trolls," Poluran muttered. "That's all we need." He turned back to the scout. "What of the orb?"

"At night," the barbarian replied, "people claimed to have seen a pale blue light shining from deep within — "

"Like a pillar of light," Poluran finished.

"Thank goodness Trannum's minions have not retrieved it yet." Rybeal joined the two. The mage spoke in a manner reflective of high social standing.

"Perhaps they were eaten by trolls," Poluran suggested.

"That is unlikely." Rybeal frowned. "Trolls feed on living flesh, as do the reptiles. They would have no interest in undead and probably ignore them, if not avoid them."

"Then why haven't zombies reclaimed it?" Poluran posed.

"I cannot say for sure," the wizard mused. "Perhaps it is the watchful eyes of the surrounding lands. The undead may not be able to find a safe road."

Poluran gazed at the sky. It was just past midday and large clouds floated lazily overhead. "How far is it to the village?"

"A day, perhaps," Massima replied, "according to the maps from Tikken City. There is an old road that should take us there, but we do not know for sure the village is where the orb lies."

Poluran shrugged. "Seems a good enough place to start. Let's ride."

Marking the beginning of the road was a long pole protruding from the ground—Massima claimed to have placed it a couple weeks prior. Once a wide trail of packed dirt, the road was barely discernable through tall grass, wild flowers, and reeds, but it held firm beneath them. Poluran was grateful for this, for it would allow them to avoid hidden pools of quicksand, and the occasional streams interrupting the path proved shallow and were easily crossed by the horses. Poluran also appreciated other features Garthglen held from the Silent Marsh, such as a view of the sun, and though the air was thick and insects swarmed heavily, it was an easy tradeoff for ghouls and impenetrable fog.

As the company pressed farther, willow trees draped over the path as the swamp worked harder to cover up the road, forcing Massima to dismount often and make sure they still followed it. The infestation of bugs also worsened and it seemed the critters were all of the biting varieties, but at least there had been no sign of enormous reptiles…or trolls.

The day passed and a thin fog settled with the sinking of the sun, and when the road veered west, large shapes loomed to either side ahead. They drew nearer and it was evident several buildings once existed, but now only three structures of stone stood, tattered but intact, and the rotted remains of wooden constructions were barely visible amongst the overgrowth.

"This isn't the village, is it?" Though Brem appeared elfish, his voice lacked the melodic tone of that heritage, proving he was only half elf.

"No," Rybeal replied. "It was most likely an outpost, or quarters for hunters."

"Whatever it was," Poluran said, "it'll serve us well for the night."

They gathered into the northernmost building. Most of the roof was missing and its doors and shutters had fallen long ago from their hinges, but unlike the other two structures, all of its exterior walls stood. Littering the floor throughout were the remains of wooden rafters, shingles, and stones of various sizes, and of its five rooms, three were useable without much clearing.

Once all was made suitable, Norik led the horses to the room farthest back while the others settled into the large, central chamber and a fire was lit. They had a bit of supper, save for Gruzim, who moved to the front room to keep watch on the growing shadows, and while they ate, Poluran's attention was drawn to the barbarian. The Dale held colorful objects, some dark and shriveled and others orange or yellow, and there were white and red colored chips.

"What have you there?" Poluran inquired while laboring on smoked meat.

"These are fruits from my land." Massima held up a dark, shriveled piece for Poluran to see.

Poluran ceased chewing and stared. He had eaten many apples and seen grapes before, but he did not recognize anything in the barbarian's hand.

"They are normally much larger and filled with sweet nectar," Massima explained with a smile, "but the juices have been removed to survive the journey."

"Is that so?" Poluran considered the shriveled pieces. Nope. He still did not see it. They could not be fruit.

Massima slowly chewed a single orange piece and then a red chip. The Dale's chewing stopped and he looked again at Poluran, who was still unsure if the pieces were actually food.

"Would you like some?" the scout asked.

"If you insist." Poluran accepted a handful and tossed most the pieces into his mouth. They felt waxy on his tongue, but when he bit down his taste buds were overwhelmed with flavor and he closed his eyes and exhaled with delight. "Mighty fine, my good man!" Poluran accidentally shared bits of chewed fruit with the scout. Tossing the remaining pieces into his mouth, he chewed more enthusiastically and nodded several times in satisfaction.

Soon the swamp grew cool and dark and the company huddled closer to the fire. Poluran noticed Malgabi was absent, but the Marc returned from the front room, where he most likely made another attempt to make Gruzim feel like part of the company. Poluran did not understand why the man wasted time on such matters — Gruzim was a true loner. Taking a seat next to Norik, Malgabi opened a jar and began rubbing a light-brown salve onto his arms.

"What have you there?" Poluran lifted his brow.

"A special ointment from a rare plant in my land," the Marc replied. "This place causes my skin to rash."

"Will it keep bugs away?" Poluran lowered one brow.

"Sorry, friend." Malgabi smiled. "It treats only rashes." He capped the bottle and returned it to his pack.

"Hmph!" Poluran snorted, searching his arms. Red welts dotted his skin, but no rashes.

Crickets, bullfrogs, and the like filled the air while the night progressed, but also there came mysterious noises Poluran could not place. A strange clicking was emitted to the distant north followed by an answer to the east, and from the south came what sounded like wolves growling, followed by a long hiss. Gruzim, however, reported seeing nothing when Poluran inquired.

The hour grew late and the strange sounds faded, but sleep seemed difficult for all and they remained awake, passing the time in various ways. Malgabi held quiet conversation with Norik while Brem and Rybeal wandered to a window with blankets draped over their shoulders. Massima explained to Poluran the process of drying fruits, to which Poluran nodded but held no comprehension. It seemed like a lot of work to eat a piece of fruit, but he could not argue with the results.

"There it is!" Rybeal gained everyone's attention, pointing through the window opening.

Interrupting the night was a spire of blue light to the southeast, visible through the missing roof, but everyone hurried to the windows. Poluran climbed atop a pile of rubble to gain a better view and Massima joined him, the barbarian standing only a head taller. The distant, pale light pierced the sky, and Poluran recognized it to be the same color as the orb in the Silent Marsh. A chill traveled the length of his body.

"It's miles away." Brem now crowded the rubble pile. "A day perhaps, if the road remains tame."

"Now it is certain," Poluran said under his breath. "It's here." Turning from the window, he stepped down. "Let's get some rest."

Poluran and Massima stood within the front room, sharing the second watch. The bog was unchanging and the spire continued to shine through the night as they listened to the never-ending song of the insect army. Poluran gazed at the barbarian, noticing the Dale would have been undetectable in the shadows were it not for his light-colored clothing—nothing more than a loincloth and vest made from the fur of some large, spotted animal.

"Have you any more of those fruits?" Poluran scanned the scout's pouches. There were five in all.

Massima smiled and extracted a handful. "Here." He handed them over. "I only packed enough for myself," the Dale added as

Poluran gobbled them without hesitation, "but enjoy." Massima provided another handful.

The next couple hours passed slowly, and Massima spoke of life in Holindale, revealing himself to be a hunter of large game within the desert territory. The barbarian went into great detail about tracking through the sand and the difference between several animal paw prints, but Poluran shut out most of the information, so as not to forget things more important in life. Poluran took his turn once the barbarian seemed finished with the tale, describing the great halls of Rornibur. He must have fallen silent at some point, having drifted into memories of the Undermountain he had not seen in over three years now, for Massima stirred him with a question laced in alarm.

"Did you hear that?"

Poluran put an ear to the swamp. The bugs' chatter continued, but now from a distant location. He grabbed his axe and peered through a window, and not far away he spotted a shadowy figure approaching. It was lanky, standing just shy of ten feet in height, and though it walked upright, its hands nearly dragged along the ground.

"Stoke the fire and wake the others," Poluran instructed Massima. "We have a troll, and it's not likely alone."

While the Dale carried out his bidding, Poluran kept watch on the figure. It crept along slowly, now hunched over, and occasionally stopped to sniff the air like a dog on the hunt. As it neared to within twenty yards, it darted to the side and disappeared from sight, and at that moment Poluran spotted its friends—at least two others had been walking single file behind it and moved in the opposite direction.

Massima returned with his staff in one hand and a torch in the other, just as a troll stuck its large head through the doorway. The monster's jutting brow concealed its eyes within deep pits of shadow and the nostrils of its hooked nose flared as it sniffed. It opened its maw wide enough to swallow a child whole and hissed, exhibiting many long teeth. Poluran raised his weapon to strike, but Massima lunged with the torch, and for a moment the monster's eyes were revealed—two small, blood-shot orbs dominated by large red pupils.

The creature reared as the fire struck it in the face, and before the orange sparks hit the floor, it disappeared.

Poluran ran to pursue, but stopped at the doorway, thinking better than to leave the protection of the stone walls. He scanned the swamp for the beast, but his attention was drawn back to the room when Massima cried out.

The torch fluttered on the floor and blood flowed from three long scratches on the barbarian's arm, and perched atop the wall was the troll, glaring down at them. It pounced, pinning Massima to the floor, and opened its mouth to taste the Dale's flesh, but Clanghorr scored a lethal hit, severing its head in a single swing and spraying the nearby wall with a shower of green blood. The body thrashed briefly and collapsed, rendering Massima helpless beneath its weight.

Grabbing hold of the monster's arm, Poluran attempted to lift the corpse, but the slime of the marsh made it hard to get a solid grip. Then came the sound of battle from the other room.

"Forgive me." Poluran dashed off.

Within the central chamber were two more trolls. Rybeal stood before one, and the creature writhed on the floor as flames issued from the wizard's open palm. The other troll was nearby, its head and one of its powerful claws protruding through a large window, and Norik's axe lay several feet away as the fiend held the krukari against the wall and several inches above the floor. Brem avoided the troll's gnashing teeth while swinging a small blade in an attempt to free Norik.

Poluran's attention was stolen when he heard the horses whinny, and another troll entered from the backroom. Malgabi was first to contest it, but the creature smacked the Marc aside and squared off with Gruzim, the krukari expertly twirling the long spear.

Poluran charged the window, screaming as he waved Clanghorr overhead, and cleaved the arm that held Norik. The troll roared and snapped at Poluran, its teeth smacking with enough force to sunder a small tree, but only a single tooth grazed Poluran's scalp as he ducked. Brem inflicted a long cut beside the troll's snout, but the monster ignored the marteese, looking to even the score for its lost appendage. Poluran sliced off a portion of its jaw and the creature emitted a sickly roar as its greenish blood sprayed. It retreated into the bog, its wail echoing for miles.

Only one troll remained, and already Gruzim had placed many cuts and punctures onto its hide. Malgabi struck the creature as well, but the Marc seemed only a nuisance and was knocked aside again by a slap of the beast's claw. Gruzim put forth a combination of attacks with his mighty spear, slashing with the sharpened edges and following with the haft, and the troll collapsed when one of its legs was cut nearly from its body. It lashed frantically with both claws, but Gruzim severed its arms next. The krukari's lip curled into a wicked grin and the troll's eyes pled for death from beneath its deep brow, but Gruzim prolonged its agony, turning the point of the spear downward and slowly piercing its chest. The swamp creature emitted a horrible cry.

Poluran stepped forward, bringing down Clanghorr and slicing through the troll's neck. The wailing ceased. He never thought he could feel pity for such a terrible monster, but Gruzim's display was more than Poluran could bear, and the krukari appeared to be enjoying it a bit too much.

Brem was removing Norik's breastplate to inspect the warrior's wounds, so Poluran headed for the front room to help Massima, ignoring the glare issuing from Gruzim. Massima stepped through the doorway, clutching a blood-stained rag over his arm.

"I'm sorry I left you," Poluran said.

Massima nodded with a painful smile. "It was necessary. Think not of it again."

After tending to Norik's injuries, Brem treated the Dale's arm with a sap-like liquid from a jar. The priest then inspected Poluran's scalp—Poluran had already forgotten about the gash.

"It's not serious." Brem rubbed some sap on the cut.

The substance felt sticky and had a surprisingly pleasant aroma. Poluran touched it with his finger to get a better whiff, if not a taste.

"It's not for eating," Brem said quickly.

Poluran reluctantly wiped it upon his pant leg, still wondering how it might taste upon a good slice of fresh-baked bread.

"Your cut should be better by tomorrow," the priest added before walking away.

After seeing that Rybeal was unscathed, Brem attempted to check on Gruzim and Malgabi, but the two were dragging the corpses from the building and insisted they were unharmed.

Poluran shook his head, gazing at the long streaks of green blood left on the floor. Norik was then next to him.

"Two horses are dead," the krukari reported, and Poluran's mind went immediately to Melballa. "Brem's and Massima's," Norik added, easing Poluran's mind.

"Leave them," Poluran said, "and bring the rest in here with us." He gazed at the sky. "Morning isn't far off. We'll be leaving soon enough."

While the swamp brightened, they ate a light breakfast. Poluran assisted Massima in finishing the remainder of the fruits and offered salted meat in return, but was surprised to learn the barbarian did not eat meat. Wasn't the man a hunter? He wore an animal's skin! Poluran did not understand.

Upon exiting the stone building, Brem doubled up with Rybeal and Massima remained on foot, the barbarian insisting he was more comfortable that way. They set out into a light haze at a brisk pace, and before the sun's light touched them, nearly a mile was placed between them and the outpost.

The haze lifted and the path became a bit clearer as morning wore on, and with the arrival of the noon hour, the rivers and streams grew more numerous and willows sagged depressingly into moss covered ponds. Now and again a loud *hiss* caused alarm, as alligators and crocodiles protested the company's intrusion, but most the reptiles kept their distance. A few strayed too close and met quick ends upon the edges of Clanghorr and Norik's axe. Two others were impaled by Gruzim's spear, and Poluran was thoroughly impressed when Massima dispatched an aggressive croc without assistance—he was sure the staff would snap, but was dazzled by the way the barbarian twirled the stick and finished off the twelve-foot lizard.

A few hours later, all signs of the road disappeared and the ground softened. Massima exhibited signs of frustration, picking through tall weeds and over and around fallen trees, and luck smiled their way when the Dale spied a bridge to the south. Closer inspection revealed an aged construction of stone, chipped and cracked and missing portions in several locations, and stagnant green water was overgrown with weeds and dotted by lilies of yellow and white below.

Poluran dropped from Melballa and gazed up and down the bridge's span. He slid the edge of Clanghorr along the stone, cutting a shard as easily as slicing bread, and scrutinized the rock. He sniffed it, stared some more, and licked it. It tasted solid enough. Dropping the shard, he nodded.

"It'll hold," Poluran informed the others. Feeling their unbelieving gazes, he sighed. "I'll go first."

The ailing construction proved solid, and not a creak or groan was heard while Poluran led Melballa onto it. He did not make it far before Massima joined him, but the others remained behind and watched. Just over halfway across, Poluran's gaze was drawn to the water, for several lilies were suddenly pulled together and floated toward the bridge. Massima halted to see what had grabbed Poluran's attention, and as the lilies neared, they saw a reptile over forty feet in length. The creature's color matched the water so perfectly that Poluran had not noticed it while it rested, but now he saw it plainly. It resembled a crocodile, but possessed six legs and a longer snout, and it remained submerged as it made its way in serpent-like fashion. Poluran's hands clutched the haft of Clanghorr as he prepared for the monster to leap, but it passed beneath the bridge and continued along the river's path until disappearing into the swamp. Poluran released a deep sigh.

"Such beautiful creatures," said Massima, gazing in the direction the lizard had departed. "That is," the barbarian added before Poluran's raised brow, "when they're not trying to eat you."

Poluran snorted.

They continued safely to the other side. The bridge was no Korban, but its strength could not be denied and Poluran gave it a quiet thank you. The others followed…one at a time.

Massima discovered the old road again, and after a hasty meal the company resumed their trek. A few miles later, the air cooled rapidly, and farther on, frost covered the ground and a thin fog obscured sight beyond a couple hundred feet. Their breath grew thick and the swamp was suddenly devoid of sound, save for the crunching of vegetation beneath them, and shadowy forms of trees became distorted, appearing as lurking trolls ready to strike. Other than the ice, Garthglen was beginning to remind Poluran of the Silent Marsh.

"Guess I should've brought a fur," he mumbled to Massima.

As soon as the words escaped Poluran's lips, he realized he had complained to the wrong person. The barbarian shivered beneath the small catskin and raised a brow in response.

The horses began slipping on patches of ice, forcing the company to lead the animals on foot. They draped blankets over their shoulders as the cold became more intense, but Poluran felt little relief—though there existed no breeze, the stale cold found its way into his layers and chilled his soul.

"Why is it so cold?" Massima was unable to seize the chattering of his teeth. "It is as if the Wind of the Dead has settled here."

The comment alarmed Poluran and he scanned the area for ghouls, but nothing moved.

After another quarter mile, large silhouettes loomed suddenly before them. A closer look revealed several structures spread over a wide area.

"This is it." Rybeal gazed about. "The village."

Nothing stirred. Nothing made a sound. There were no ill odors. There were no odors at all. The many buildings were in various states of decay, much like the ones encountered the previous day, only some of the structures of wood were still standing, dilapidated as they were.

"Let's have a look around," Poluran said. "Stay in pairs and ready your weapons."

They began methodically searching the village, and Poluran hoped his company took care not to unsettle any of the buildings—some of the leaning structures appeared ready to collapse at any moment. Massima worked with Poluran, Brem with Rybeal, and Malgabi and Norik seemed to be following Gruzim. By the time dusk arrived, they had covered half the village with no sign of the orb.

Rybeal located an old blacksmith's shop that seemed sturdy and the company gathered there. It possessed three windows, much too small for a troll's head, and Brem led the horses to a few stalls littered with ancient horseshoes. Massima and Norik gathered anything that would burn, and with Rybeal's magical assistance, a fire was started within a central hearth. The flames kindled old coals and the company circled around to thaw their weary bones.

"Well," said Malgabi with hope as he gazed through a window, "it'll show itself sooner or later."

"The sooner the better," grumbled Norik, not sharing the Marc's enthusiasm.

The shadows of night moved in, and Malgabi stood near the door while the others had some supper around the fire. Poluran munched cold, stale bread, glancing Massima's direction every now and again to make sure the scout was not hiding fruit. But the barbarian possessed only rations others were willing to share.

After the less-than-satisfactory meal, Poluran stepped from the hearth to check on Malgabi, and as soon as Poluran was a few feet away from the fire the chill stung his teeth and froze his lungs. He did not know how the Marc could bear it.

"No sign of the light yet," Malgabi reported.

"You should warm yourself." Poluran looked out the door at the thin fog that seemed to glow within the darkening village. "You'll catch your death in this chill."

"I'm all right," the Marc said. "I'll keep watch a bit longer."

Poluran shrugged and eagerly returned to the warmth of the fire. A short while later, Malgabi stood.

"There it is!" The Marc grew excited.

Poluran took in a deep breath to warm his insides before grabbing Clanghorr and pulling his blanket tighter about his shoulders. "Let's go."

They lit a few torches and followed the pillar of light to an area Rybeal and Brem had searched earlier. The blue spire penetrated the fog within an alley between a couple two-story structures, issuing through a fissure in the ground five-feet long and four inches at its widest point. Poluran dropped to his knees to have a look, and his heart raced when he spied the orb within a small chamber below.

"There's a cellar." Poluran rose to his feet. "The entrance must be in one of these buildings."

To the right was a solid construction of stone, and to the left a partially collapsed mixture of stone and wood. Poluran gazed at the leaning structure and shook his head.

"Don't let it be that one."

They searched the stone building thoroughly, but found no underground entrances. Returning to the alley, they gazed at the half-crumbled building.

"How are we to enter that?" Brem frowned.

"Perhaps we should wait until morning, now that we know where it is," suggested Rybeal. "It would be dangerous to enter this place in the dark, and I will be better able to assist when the light returns."

"I don't wish to stay in this place a moment longer!" Malgabi spat. "We'll catch our deaths in this cold!"

Poluran was taken by surprise. Until that moment, he would have thought the Marc quite comfortable with the surroundings. "We'll return to the fire," he said. "Let us warm our minds first."

Back in the smithy, Massima added the remainder of the wood and flammable debris to the glowing coals and they ignited instantly. The company warmed their bodies before anyone spoke.

"If we enter that building," Brem said, "it will likely collapse on top of us."

"And as I have said," added Rybeal, "I may be able to help, but I hesitate to use my powers in the dark. I could make matters worse."

"Perhaps we could dig our way to the orb," suggested Massima.

Poluran shook his head. "The crack passes through ten feet of frozen land. We haven't the proper tools."

"That won't be necessary." Malgabi said.

The Marc entered, followed by Norik, and Poluran thought himself foolish he had not noticed the two were missing.

"We had a look about," Malgabi said. "There seems no safe entry into the ground level, but we found an accessible window on the second story. Beyond that, a staircase looks very much intact."

Poluran raised a brow with doubt.

"Unless, of course, you would like to spend the night here," the Marc added.

Poluran thought hard, his focus resting on the fire. He had no desire to stay one night in the frozen region of the marshland. Still, working in the dark with humans and half breeds was pointless. But their wood supply was exhausted and the blue lips of his company unmistakable. It would be a long, cold night.

"Let's have a look."

They returned to the alley, where Malgabi's knotted rope dangled from an open window on the second level of the wreckage. Poluran eyed the rope with doubt and sighed.

"I'll go first," volunteered Malgabi, and the Marc was scaling before Poluran could respond.

The building was tilted away slightly and the ascent appeared easy enough. Soon the Marc disappeared through the window, sticking his head out again to see if anyone followed.

Poluran was uneasy. He had a bad feeling, but what else could he do? "The rest of you stay here," he grumbled.

He began to climb, nodding for Massima to follow. The barbarian complied, skillfully working his way up with one hand on the rope and a torch in the other, and they arrived to the window without mishap.

Malgabi waited at the top within a small chamber. The floor was missing, but two planks spanned the opening to an archway on the opposite side.

"Norik and I checked it out," the Marc said. "The boards are sturdy."

Malgabi led the way across the bridge, the planks groaning with every step, and they passed safely through the arch. Beyond, only a portion of the floor remained about the edges of a larger chamber and a dark pile of rubble lay ten feet below, while across the room was the staircase Malgabi spoke of.

Poluran placed a hand on Malgabi, halting the Marc, and stepped past him. Fearing a hasty descent, Poluran then placed his back against the wall and shuffled as lightly as he could around the hole. The partial floor proved solid and they reached the staircase without mishap.

Gazing down the steps, Poluran's vision pierced the darkness and he saw a mass of debris—he wondered if they would have to dig their way into the cellar. The steps appeared sound, just as Malgabi had mentioned, but Poluran did not wish to press his luck.

"One at a time."

Malgabi shrugged, and Poluran led the way.

The room below was almost completely buried beneath the remnants of the upper level. An old bar was barely visible, as well as the smashed remains of clay mugs, bottles, kegs, and tables and chairs, and not far away, a dark archway led deeper into the dwelling. Through the wreckage existed a path to the arch. Whether natural or otherwise, Poluran could not tell.

"This must have been a tavern," he said. "Be alert. And don't touch *anything*."

Poluran moved down the path and through the archway. A large cooking pit dominated an old kitchen, and upon the floor were dilapidated cupboards and bits of pottery. To the rear, next to a sturdy table that survived the war of time, was a square hole in the floor. All that remained of the trapdoor that once covered it was a pair of rusted hinges, and the torchlight revealed a steep stairwell leading into the cellar.

"The first sign of luck." Malgabi grinned. "The entrance is not buried."

"I would not call it luck," said Massima. "This route has been made by hands and not by chance, of that I am sure. The orb was placed here by the exact path we walk."

"What does it matter?" Malgabi gave way to annoyance. "It's getting colder and we must retrieve it, however we can. Let's just get it and get out of here."

Poluran hesitated, taken slightly by Malgabi's hasty tone. It was Poluran's own eagerness that had summoned Hezeb in the cellar of the stone cabin. "Let's get the others."

He turned back, ignoring the Marc's sigh, and they returned to the window to find the remainder of the company huddled in the alley. Poluran had them climb the rope, and they all carefully made their way to the kitchen. Poluran then grabbed Massima's torch and descended into the cellar.

The stairs were relatively free of debris and emptied into a storage room laden with smashed crates. Broken barrels and bottles left pools of ice here and there and the fleeting thought of a belt of ale floated through Poluran's mind, but he doubted there was any to be had. A thin shadow was present on the wall to the right, from floor to ceiling, and after following a narrow path, Poluran discovered it to mark a door obviously meant to have been secret—a small stone wedged into its frame betrayed it.

Handing the torch to Massima, Poluran set Clanghorr against the wall and dug his thick fingers into the seam. He pulled the door open with a jerk, and from the shadowy corridor beyond came high-pitched screeches. Dark, ghostly figures flew through the opening, and their glowing blue eyes scanned the company while unseen mouths wailed the eerie shrieks again.

"Wraiths!" shouted Brem.

One wraith descended onto Massima, and the barbarian swung his staff in defense, but the weapon passed harmlessly through its ghostly presence. The Dale stumbled backward, losing his footing on a patch of ice, and fell to the floor as the creature locked onto his throat with its dark fingers.

Poluran grabbed his axe and rushed to Massima's aid, stopping short when a wraith blocked the path. Clanghorr sang as Poluran swung the mighty blade, and the weapon reduced the spirit to black vapor floating harmlessly into the shadows overhead. A second wraith attacked and Poluran dodged to the side, his shoulder sundering a crate attempting to hamper his movement. He swung Clanghorr again, destroying the undead fiend.

The wraiths continued to wail, drowning out most other sound, but Brem's voice rose above them. The priest held high his holy symbol, a silver tree with golden leaves, and his body took on a green aura, causing the undead to cower as he pressed them into a corner.

"Death returns to thee!" Brem called out. "Taste the sting of Almighty Frayorna!"

The marteese struck three wraiths with his blade, extinguishing their eyes forever, and the surviving few raced back through the open doorway.

The room was quiet.

Poluran went to Massima. The barbarian was pale and panted heavily. His eyes stared toward the ceiling, wide with horror, and black marks were visible where the evil fingers had clutched his neck.

"Help him," Poluran urged Brem.

The priest hurried over, appearing nothing more than a small marteese again, and checked on the barbarian. He bowed and shook his head. "There is nothing I can do."

"What about that sappy stuff you used yesterday?" Poluran was desperate.

"It will not help him." The priest looked at Poluran. "The wounds left by the wraiths are different. They are beyond my skill."

Poluran knelt beside Massima, suddenly wishing to question why Brem had joined the quest. Instead, Poluran took the Dale's hand. "I am sorry, my friend."

"Don't…" Massima clutched Poluran's arm. "Don't let… I can feel it… Don't want to be…" The scout's body stiffened, and he stared at nothing as he released his final breath.

Poluran stood, tightening and loosening his grip on Clanghorr. Anger chased the cold from his veins while he waited for the transformation he knew would come. Massima's head snapped toward Poluran, snarling with hatred, and Clanghorr quickly returned the barbarian to the Realm of the Dead. Glancing at the others, Poluran saw three dark scratches on Norik's cheek and a handprint on Rybeal's forehead. Stern faces showed the two to be ready to continue.

"Three got away," Rybeal said. "Back the way they had come."

Without a word, Poluran walked through the opening, and behind him Malgabi held the torch to illuminate the way.

A short corridor ended at another chamber—most likely a storeroom for the better vintages of the tavern, but empty wine racks lined the walls. A blue light spilled through an archway on the opposite side and Poluran approached, searching for the wraiths. Nothing stirred while he crossed the floor.

The next room looked to have once been a treasury. A couple empty chests lay open on the floor, their contents taken long ago, and in the middle was the orb, resting neatly upon a pillow like a royal jewel. A single ray of blue light issued from it and through the long, narrow crack in the ceiling. Though it was not evident from above, Poluran could now see the fissure had been carefully carved to let the light shine out, but allow nothing to enter from above — nothing, that is, except for wraiths.

Still there was no sign of the dark ghosts. Poluran figured they exited through the hole, not wishing to face the priest a second time, and he turned his attention to the orb. It was a much smaller version of the one he shattered beneath the stone cabin, and the desire to destroy this one washed over him.

"Did the Council not want us to bring it to them?" inquired Malgabi, obviously reading Poluran's emotions as he tightened his grip on Clanghorr.

Poluran glared at the Marc, remembering the case Seac had provided. It was a box of lead in which to transport the orb to Tikken City unharmed—a point the Seer emphasized. The Council hoped to use it; to learn from it a way to combat Trannum. But now the thought of taking the evil frigid power of death to civilized lands did not seem wise.

"Let's return it to the Council," said Rybeal with a cough, the touch of the wraith obviously wearing upon the wizard. "It is for the greater good."

Poluran relaxed his grip at last. The urge to shed a tear for the fallen scout nearly overwhelmed him, but nothing was forthcoming—either rage held it in check or it was too cold to weep. Pulling the pack from his shoulder, Poluran produced the box and carefully nudged the sphere into it with his axe. He shut the lid and locked it with a key he wore around his neck.

"Let's go."

As they reentered the storage room, Poluran felt a chill emanating from the case, worse even than the shards that had pelted him in the Silent Marsh. The box did nothing to shield the cold, and while he ascended into the kitchen, his joints stiffened. Determined to continue, he made his way through the tavern and up the steps to the second story, but his body went numb and he stumbled near the top.

"Are you all right?" asked Malgabi with concern.

"The orb," Poluran said through chattering teeth. "It's freezing my bones!"

"Perhaps we should carry it in shifts," suggested Rybeal.

Poluran glanced at the others. He trusted Brem, and the Council obviously felt the same about Rybeal, but he would never put faith in a krukari and Malgabi had been acting queer as of late—perhaps the cold was affecting the Marc's mind. Poluran handed the pack to the wizard, pulling the tall man down to his size.

"Brem and us only."

Rybeal nodded, accepting the package.

The wraiths emerged from the shadows below and immediately swarmed the wizard. One raked a claw across Rybeal's hand and the pack dropped to the floor, and the other two dragged the mage several feet away.

Poluran gasped. "The orb!"

Fighting his frozen joints, Poluran swung Clanghorr and reduced the creature hovering above the pack to vapor. He then scrambled for the box, but one of the spirits abandoned its assault upon Rybeal and descended onto Poluran's back. Dark claws passed through Poluran's armor without effort and he felt the icy fingers penetrate his flesh. His head began to swim as Norik lifted the pack, but the krukari hesitated.

"Get it outta here!" Poluran shouted, and Norik ran from sight.

Poluran rolled to face his attacker, but saw only smoke as Brem stood above him, again surrounded by the green glow. The only other person present was Rybeal, coughing up blood. The wraiths were gone.

Suppressing the sickening feeling now invading his stomach, Poluran pushed himself to give chase. He rounded the collapsed chamber and passed through the archway to find Norik skewered upon Gruzim's spear—the mighty weapon was completely through Norik's back.

"Gruzim!" Poluran charged onto the planks with Clanghorr ready.

Gruzim yanked the spear free, allowing Norik's body to fall through the window, and spun, taking a defensive position. "He betrayed us!" Gruzim shouted, causing Poluran to halt. The krukari eyed Clanghorr's deadly edge while maintaining his usual sneer. "He and Malgabi! Malgabi's got the orb."

Poluran moved around Gruzim, keeping a watchful eye, and peered through the window. Below stood Malgabi with the pack.

"Well done!" the Marc gave a wave. "Master sends his many thanks!" And he ran off into the darkness.

Chapter 25

Of Secrets and Plots

It had taken two days to ride from Tikken City to Garthglen, and Gruzim sat on his horse, watching Massima and Poluran discuss the swampland while they prepared to begin the search for the orb. Gruzim decided to join the quest for the orbs after the encounter with Trannum; he could think of little else since that day within the crypt beneath the rorbak. To his dismay, he was forced to follow the scrawny dwarf. The only other option had been to sail to Palidur—like Gruzim would ever set foot in such a place! And so he went with the dwarf, treating the weakling as the leader of the expedition. It was the only way to learn more.

Gruzim took no real delight with any in the new company, and he especially disliked Norik. Even though Gruzim's "krukari brother" did not say much to the others, the oaf was far too willing to serve, and this made Norik weak. Then there was Malgabi. The Marc spoke to Gruzim as an equal, and Gruzim detested this, for there existed no such being. He was Gruzim! Unmatched in strength or skill. He could feel Malgabi probing with odd questions and comments now and again, and though the Marc did well to make it seem innocent conversation, Gruzim was no fool. Gruzim noted similar conversations between Malgabi and Norik as well, so he decided to keep an eye on this human.

Gruzim gazed at Poluran, still holding council with the Dale, and now the wizard joined them, as if enough time was not wasted with talk already. The wizards of Tikken City must have been desperate to make the dwarf the leader of the company.

"Let's ride," Poluran said.

It was about time.

The first night in the bog was not without its fun. Gruzim had never encountered trolls before and looked forward to testing their skill, and sure enough, the creatures found them at the hunter's outpost. One dropped into their midst through the missing ceiling, but the wizard immediately set it alight with magical fire. A second one stuck its monstrous head through a window, pinning Norik to the wall with a powerful claw as the fool attempted to race to the front room to get the dwarf. Malgabi intercepted a third one, but the creature seemed uninterested with the Marc and slapped the warrior aside. The monster then turned Gruzim's way. Battle at last!

Gruzim squared off with the beast, testing its strength, and found it swift and aggressive, but no match for his talents. He toyed with it, inflicting several wounds deep enough to hurt, but not enough to kill too quickly. Gruzim was greatly annoyed when Malgabi joined the fray, and he stepped back to allow the troll free reign to attack, but the monster only slapped the Marc aside again.

Returning to his prey, Gruzim put on a show with his spear that caused the troll to fall back. He took great pleasure in severing its limbs and watching it squirm, but then it begged for death. How disappointing. And he could not believe his eyes when the dwarf stole his kill. Gruzim *lived* for the kill!

The trolls were defeated and everyone survived—a surprising outcome. The priest tended to the others in turn and offered to check Gruzim's wounds—like he had been touched! Even if he had, he would not accept the aid of a priest. Only the weak were in need of such things, and sometimes death was the only cure. Gruzim also noticed Malgabi was in no need of care. But why would the man be? The troll had shown no interest in the Marc.

The next day, though cold and dim, brought more light onto the situation. When they entered the frozen area of the swamp, not only did Malgabi seem unhampered by the cold, but something else was amiss. The human's breath was not visible. Gruzim wondered if the Marc breathed at all, and it baffled him that no one else had noticed. Their minds were so bent upon finding the orb that Trannum himself could have accompanied them and none would have been the wiser.

They reached the village at last, and the feeble dwarf insisted everyone pair up to search. Gruzim shook his head and walked off on his own. He needed no assistance. But upon noticing Malgabi and Norik following him, he decided it time to confront the Marc.

"What part of Marcove you from?" Gruzim posed after Norik went to check on a small building.

"The south." Malgabi eyed Gruzim with suspicion.

"And you wish to…make sure the orb is taken care of?" Gruzim remembered the weakling mentioning this in a conversation from a few days ago.

"That is correct," the Marc said slowly.

"And just *how* would you take care of it?" Gruzim raised a brow.

"How do you think?"

"You needn't worry of me," Gruzim assured the man. "Your business is your own. As is mine."

"Is that so?" Malgabi's eyes darted about, seeking out the locations of the others of the company.

"The time will come when you must do your bidding and I must do mine." Gruzim turned from the warrior. "You best pray there's no conflict." He walked away, leaving the Marc to ponder his words.

Later that night, they followed the orb's light into an alley and climbed up and down the ruins of an old tavern. Within the cellar the dwarf freed half a dozen wraiths—a foe worthy of far more respect than trolls. Gruzim had learned long ago about the life-sucking touch of the dark ghosts, and it was a memory he did not wish to relive. He immediately stepped closer to Malgabi, and just as Gruzim anticipated, the creatures never looked their way. The Marc stood poised with a defensive posture, but it was just for show, of that Gruzim was certain. Gruzim saw the wraith attacking the barbarian and could have possibly saved the Dale's life, but instead he marveled at the scene. The priest took on a green glow and killed a few of the spirits while a couple met their ends upon Clanghorr, and the surviving wraiths fled.

At last they found the blue sphere, and Gruzim could feel its power. He heard talk in Tikken City of the orb in the Silent Marsh, but to behold one… He wondered what great powers it possessed, and what he might accomplish with it. But that would have to remain a mystery as he watched the dwarf scoop the orb into a box.

They made their way from the tavern and the wraiths returned to claim their treasure, or perhaps to assist one they were familiar with. In the commotion, Norik ended up with the package, and Gruzim followed the worm through the arch to find Malgabi waiting at the window. Norik never saw the Marc's dagger coming, and the blade sank deep into Norik's stomach. But Malgabi was foolish to think such a wound would be enough.

"Move no farther!" commanded Norik as Malgabi put a leg outside the window with the box in hand. Blood seeped from Norik's stomach, but he stepped forward with his axe. "You're not taking that!"

"My friend." Malgabi maintained his arrogant tone. "Great treasures await you from the master. Just turn around and the wealth of Vaeldor is yours."

Norik swung the axe, slicing through the Marc's right shoulder and into the chest cavity. It was a mortal wound for any man, but the attack served only to disarm Malgabi and cause the man to wince.

Now Gruzim's assumptions had proven true. He did not know exactly what Malgabi was, but Gruzim knew his own future depended on the next few seconds. With a mighty thrust, he shoved his spear into Norik's back, and Norik screamed as Gruzim jammed the weapon until it emerged through the breastplate.

Malgabi smiled, pouring his skin salve onto the gaping cut, and Gruzim watched the Marc's wound close.

"My business is my own," Gruzim scowled. "I do this not for you, but for me. Tell your master that."

Malgabi nodded and allowed himself to tumble into the alley, evidently having no need for the rope.

Gruzim noticed the silence behind him. The wraiths had been defeated. The dwarf shouted Gruzim's name and he jerked his spear free, barely able to bring it into a defensive position—one lucky hit from the axe would be the end of him.

"He betrayed us!" It was all Gruzim could think to say. "He and Malgabi! Malgabi's got the orb!"

The dwarf eased up. The fool was buying it. Poluran peered out the window, and Gruzim kept a wary eye on the axe while doing the same.

Malgabi waved. The idiot hung around to say goodbye. Gruzim had half a mind to throw his spear.

"Well done! Master sends his many thanks!" After the fool's attempt at humor had failed, Malgabi ran off into the dark swamp.

Everyone stood in shock for several seconds, realizing their failure. Gruzim saw they all had suffered much from the wraiths, and he probably could have killed them if he took the dwarf out first, but he thought better of it. No telling how many more trolls and large crocs were in the swamp, and he might need to feed one of them to the beasts before it was over. No, he would let them live…for now.

Gruzim might have killed them after exiting the marsh, but the incompetent Malgabi had dropped the healing salve, and it did not take long for the mage to deduce its properties. Before leaving the frozen village, the company had quite recovered from their ailments, and though Gruzim's skills in combat were unmatched, he was not foolish enough to take on a healthy wizard and a dwarf bearing a weapon as lethal as Clanghorr at the same time.

The pathetic bunch tried to track Malgabi, but without the barbarian it was hopeless. Two days later, they found their way beyond the borders of Garthglen, and that night, while Gruzim and Brem were on watch, Gruzim slipped away into the darkness. It was time to return home.

Chapter 26

Bitter Reunion

A somber mood hung over the audience chamber like a dark cloud. Seac, the only Council member present, gazed at the orb seekers before him from his throne, his mind deeply troubled. Nearly two months had passed since the edge of Clanghorr destroyed the orb in the Silent Marsh, and the hunts for the remaining orbs were unfolding.

Vikur was first to return to Tikken City. The Lord of the Keep had ridden for two weeks with almost no rest before sailing from Palidur, possessing wounds that should have killed him. He was ushered to a bed immediately, where he received care for a few days.

Shortly after Vikur was on the mend, Merssa arrived with Borse and Pallit. Wezlok was not with them, having decided to return to Maple Lore, and though Merssa claimed Vecnor to have been a part of the quest, the large man apparently parted company before they arrived to Sendorum. Later that same day, Selanna and Eraim rode in from the south with Arkor, Rholmar, and Nilborg. Merssa called for an immediate council with the Palidurians in the library and Borse joined them, but Seac was not privy to their conversation, and the elves remained within their quarters—at least, the servants believed them to have been confined to their guestroom.

Finally, on the following day, word of Poluran's arrival reached the Council, and Seac called all companies to the audience chamber, where they presently awaited the dwarf. Seac had grown concerned with Poluran's absence; he thought the Garthglen company would return before all others. The Council had spent almost a week now with the orb Vikur brought, the only orb to survive thus far, and Seac hoped Poluran had found success as well. But with the opening of the large doors, the grim faces of Poluran, Rybeal, and Brem did little to reinforce this hope. Seac also noticed the pack he had issued for the orb's transportation was not with them.

"Before we get to discussing the orbs," Seac began the meeting, "let us first hear what news Poluran brings."

Poluran appeared reluctant to speak, but eventually found the words. "We lost it. We had it…but we lost it."

A deafening silence followed until Poluran spoke further. The dwarf described briefly the icy marsh and village, and his face paled when telling of the wraiths and traitors, Malgabi and Norik.

"I'm still unsure as to Gruzim's involvement," Poluran added. "The wretch disappeared into the night as soon as we exited the bog."

"Why would living souls assist one such as Trannum?" Nilborg exhibited shock and disappointment. "I can understand Solett falling beneath the power of an evil orb, but to willingly serve—"

"Though I believe krukari to be capable of anything," Rybeal interjected, "Malgabi was not among the living, I think. In his hasty departure, he dropped a salve he had been applying to his skin. Upon closer examination I discovered it to be a powerful healing agent. I believe he was using it to keep his skin from decaying, so he would appear to be alive."

"It is a healing salve unlike any I have encountered," added Brem. "I know not of its origin."

"Perhaps Malgabi is the necromancer's attempt to create undead capable of blending with the living," suggested Rybeal.

"Impossible!" Merssa, as usual, disagreed with what she did not understand. "Undead are incapable of intelligent thought. Even ghouls are led by hunger and not intellect."

"Do not fool yourself," said Selanna, "lest you forget that ghouls transported the orbs to their original locations, as Poluran witnessed in Sendorum before this all began. And the dunarchins that stood by

Trannum's side in the halls beneath the rorbak are capable of independent thought, according to Trannum's journals. The undead firstborns retain the wisdom and skills possessed while living, though the process twists their minds and bends their wills toward hatred. What fills my heart with dread is that Solett created these creatures himself, and wrote a tome matching Trannum's word for word." Selanna held forth a large book. "I procured this from Solett's laboratory. Though a powerful wizard, he was not strong enough to resist the orb, and somehow became an extension of the necromancer."

"Dunarchins are fearsome opponents indeed," Vikur said, "and I witnessed one that used magic."

The Lord of the Keep had spoken of the battle versus Trannum's elite warriors when he first arrived to Tikken City, so only Seac knew the tale, but now Vikur shared the horrid memory with the others. He shuddered when speaking of the undead mage upon the stalagmite and his voice became a bit hesitant, and just as with his earlier report, Seac believed Vikur withheld some details. Vikur's explanation that he rode off with the orb because he feared for the safety of his companions did not sit well with Seac, and from the look on Selanna's face, she surely felt the same.

The room fell silent, and Seac used that moment to collect his thoughts before addressing them all.

"Though we have not had much time with it, we have worked day and night studying the orb from the Serpent's Range. From it we have ascertained that although each orb possesses the ability to create undead, each also contains powers unique unto itself. The one within our keeping has the ability to organize the undead, even those with no intelligence whatsoever." Seac glanced at Merssa, knowing she would be the most resistant to accept such a statement. "And it would seem the one formerly within Garthglen possesses the cold energy the Wind of the Dead carried across the lands. Of the other two," he eyed Merssa and Selanna, still in disagreement with their reasons for destroying the items, "alas, we know not their true functions, and perhaps never will. The orb within the Silent Marsh combined them all, allowing them to share their powers over great distances. Upon its destruction the communication was severed, and the less intelligent undead began wandering aimlessly while others attempted to retrieve or protect their master's most valuable treasures."

"What does it mean with the loss of the orb in Garthglen?" Nilborg inquired.

"The orbs are very powerful," Seac replied, "each containing a portion of Trannum's strength —"

"We've heard this before." Merssa's arms were folded across her chest. "With the destruction of the orbs, Trannum is weakened. Yet when we tracked him into his crypt, he didn't even seem to notice the loss."

"That, my dear, is because the orb was but a fragment of his power." Seac controlled his mood as best he could. He had grown quite accustomed to interruptions from the paladin, but he was extremely drained and tired. "At the time we did not realize the existence of the other four, nor thought them possible. Though I do not expect all here to understand, nor will I go to any great lengths to explain it, with their destruction, Trannum does indeed lose the energy they contained forever. And to answer the question posed by Nilborg, with their return, he can draw the power back into himself if he so desires."

"Then why allow any orbs to survive at all?" demanded Merssa. "Why were we not given instructions to smash them and be done with it? By your own admission, as long as they exist the necromancer can draw from them. Had Poluran destroyed the orb within Garthglen, it would not have been taken."

"It is wise to know your enemy, is it not?" Seac posed. "The orbs contain power beyond any we believed possible, and already we have learned much from the one we possess. It is our hope to discover the purposes and weaknesses of our enemy, so that a proper plan of action can be made. After that, the item will certainly be destroyed."

The room gazed at Seac, not wholly convinced. He had expected this, even from Selanna, but Rybeal's doubtful gaze caught Seac by surprise. Rybeal, Seac knew, aspired to join the Council one day. Once a chair was available.

"You needn't fully understand all of this," Seac said. "But you must trust us."

"Palidur searches for Trannum in the Stone Eagles," Nilborg said, "but Merssa tells me the crypt is deserted. Is there any way to discover the necromancer's whereabouts through the orb you possess?"

"Though the orbs and Trannum share a bond," Seac explained, "they cannot communicate with one another. The destruction of the orb in the Silent Marsh, as I mentioned, severed the link, including that between orbs and their master. We cannot use the orb we possess to find him, just as he could not know of its presence here. So, for now we can only wait and keep our eyes and ears open."

The shifting of Merssa's feet meant she desperately wished to say something, and it would not be pleasant. So Seac decided to bring the meeting to an end.

"I know there are more questions, but I must return to the orb. This meeting is adjourned for now."

He rose and proceeded to the smaller door, unhesitating even when Merssa voiced his name.

Merssa was not pleased. The arrogance of the Council disgusted her. Their quest for knowledge cost her an orb, and she feared what consequences it might bring. If only she had met up with Vikur before he reached Tikken City...

"Have my ship ready," Merssa snapped at Mordan, and then she turned to Nilborg. "We must return to Palidur immediately."

Nilborg nodded, and he exited the chamber with Borse and Pallit.

"You two," Merssa said to Vikur and Arkor. "Return home and see if there's anything to learn."

She looked at Selanna and Eraim and opened her mouth, but then shut it. Giving those two instructions was pointless. They might obey; they might not. In the end, they would probably learn more than anyone else. Merssa nodded, and they returned knowing smiles.

"What about me?" Poluran stood, defeated.

Merssa considered the dwarf. She did not know what she wanted to say, if anything. She knew, rather felt he had done everything possible to retrieve the orb, and she honestly held no ill will toward him—her anger lay with the wizards. Had a proper plan been in place to destroy the orbs, Poluran would have succeeded. But still…

"Come with us," offered Vikur. "We could use the company."

Merssa nodded her acceptance of the idea, and Poluran gave a wry smile of appreciation.

Selanna was in no hurry to depart from Tikken City. She knew not why, but she felt there was something more to be learned before returning to Salenti, and while the others prepared for departure, she and Eraim wandered about the gardens. They were not there long when Elgarroth arrived.

"Master?" Selanna was surprised and delighted, but deep down she had trouble truly feeling either emotion. "It is great to see you."

"Hello, my dear." Elgarroth smiled warmly, but then he frowned. "You look troubled."

"It is the orbs," she said. "We lost one. And for once I agree with Merssa. At first I sided with the Council's desire to study them, but after seeing what they can do… They should have been destroyed immediately."

Elgarroth sighed. "It is the way of wizards. You know this. The destruction of magic is never our desire."

"And there is something the Council is not telling us," Selanna added. "Of that I am certain."

"Only of their fear of Trannum," Elgarroth said. "The power they have discovered within the orb is greater than any one of them, and the necromancer possessed the ability to create five such items."

"*My* fear is that there may be six."

Eraim's voice came from behind Selanna. Selanna had forgotten her friend was there.

"What do you mean?" Selanna posed.

"Nothing." Eraim was suddenly shy. "It is just the prophecy. *Power of five, united by one.* What if the "one" is not part of the "five," and another is out there somewhere?"

Selanna shared a look of concern with her mentor.

"I know," Eraim said. "It is silly. If another one existed, then the Wind of the Dead would have had another origin and we would have heard—"

"If he has reclaimed two such orbs…" Selanna shook her head. "How strong will he be? Strong enough to take the one the Council holds, if he so chooses."

Elgarroth stared blankly at Selanna, as if in deep thought. "Perhaps. I shall speak with the Council and be sure they have considered such a possibility." He turned. "Until next time."

"Evil days lie ahead," Selanna said somberly after Elgarroth had gone.

"Perhaps I am mistaken." Eraim shrugged. "The wise minds of the Council and even yourself had not thought it to be so. Who am I, after all?"

"Let us hope you are right."

Selanna received a slightly offended look from her friend. She could not help but smirk in response.

Chapter 27

Passage of Time

Years passed after the quest for the orbs concluded. There were no more reports of rising dead, no clues as to Trannum's whereabouts, and Palidur's quest into the Stone Eagles had borne no fruit. Every few months, several of the orb seekers gathered in Tikken City to discuss the sleeping evil, and most kingdoms from Kalmaar to Philen kept watch over their dominions for signs of the necromancer. It was not long, however, before the wandering undead diminished, making their rising little more than a nightmare for most. The following years saw many kings abandon all quests to find the creator of the orbs, not wishing to waste any more resources chasing a ghost. Had it not been for the new custom of constructing walls around graveyards, just in case the dead rose again, one would have thought the existence of the skeletal wizard to be nothing more than a story to frighten children.

Life marched on…

The years saw a great gathering in Palidur to witness Merssa and Borse exchange vows. The couple later repeated the ceremony outside the city, for many friends wished to celebrate the unity but were prohibited by Palidur law.

The following year, Merssa was named High Paladin of Cafior. She eagerly accepted the position when Arduer retired due to health complications at the age of sixty-one, and the High Order had little choice in the matter, for Merssa was the favorite among the people of the Cafior Sector. There was then tension within the Grand Cathedral, as Merssa fought to change some of the traditions she had grown up with, and Nilborg and Soren backed her cause to make drastic changes to the city's treatment of outlanders. The process was slow and tiring, but Merssa kept to her convictions, even when pressured to step down by others—now that she was a member, only she had the authority to dismiss herself. Merssa also saw to it no member of the Order forgot about the necromancer, and Trannum's name was brought up at every meeting.

Though Borse was not wholly comfortable within the white walls, feeling the great churches should be open to all, he moved into the Holy City to be with his wife. And while Merssa performed her duties, he often wandered into the surrounding lands and mingled among the commoners. Farmers grew to know and love Borse and followed his teachings, and crops flourished better than any believed possible. Borse turned aside all praises, insisting it was Cafior's blessings and not his presence that brought good fortune, and he urged them to show thanks by paying homage to the deity.

Merssa and Borse desperately wanted children, but it seemed it was not meant to be. And so they remained content with their love for each other, as well as their devotion to Cafior.

A spark had ignited between Rholmar and Ladonia after their time together in Tenvale, and in the year following the wedding of Merssa and Borse, they decided to wed as well. It was then that Rholmar discovered his bride to be a renegade princess of Philen and eldest of three daughters—Ladonia had run away from her duties of royalty to pursue the adventurous life of a scout.

At Rholmar's urging, Ladonia returned to make amends with her father and was eagerly accepted back into the king's good graces. Rholmar was then faced with a difficult choice, for Ladonia came to realize how much she missed her home, and with a heavy heart he said goodbye to his beloved Holy City.

The two were joined in matrimony before the king's court and an entourage from the Arronaus Sector of Palidur, and with the king's permission, the chief priest of the castle stepped aside to allow Garren, High Priest of Arronaus, to preside over the event. At Rholmar's side, to the surprise of many, was Arkor. The two became great friends after the quest for the orbs, and those who knew Arkor agreed the one-armed warrior's dark moods had almost vanished after the friendship began. And just as Ladonia, Arkor found faith in Arronaus through Rholmar, as well as a new outlook on life.

The king of Philen was pleased with Rholmar's skills in combat and tactical sense, and after a few years called him son, not having been blessed with one of his own. Rholmar was named Duke of the Eastern Border and given a castle outside Crynora, but he immediately began renovations, making the city reminiscent of the one he loved. With the king's blessing, Crynora was renamed West Palidur.

Pallit and Arrikan were also united, enjoying a small wedding within the Griffon's Roost of Bouldertown where they had first met. Borse performed the ceremony, and he and Merssa were guests of honor.

Pallit never returned to Neja, making a new home in Harbnum, and he and Arrikan spent most of their time in the mountains, where they built a large house and gave birth to their son, Magneer.

Vikur married a commoner from the city of Charndova, and his choice of brides did not shock most, for he often preferred the company of simpler folk. Poluran was present for the wedding, as well as the birth of Vikur's son, Ballrik, ten months later. Vikur was most grateful for the dwarf's company, especially when his wife's health failed during delivery of the child, and Poluran was given a permanent room within the keep.

Poluran split his time between Ironside Keep and Rornibur over the next few years, but felt out of place within the halls of the Undermountain, for his warnings of Trannum's return fell on deaf ears—the dwarves were more concerned with mining rorbak, now that the evil spirits had passed. So Poluran packed up Melballa and said goodbye, returning to Ironside for good. There, he happily played the part of uncle to Ballrik, since Arkor had left to live in Philen.

Trannum was forever on Selanna's mind, and she and Eraim remained alert for signs of the necromancer's return. They journeyed often to Tikken City for updates on the Council's research into the orb and to see if there were any discoveries as to Trannum's whereabouts, but always the news was little to none.

Selanna poured over the books from Sistama, and she was able to use the tome from Solett's laboratory to better translate the Ancient Moclen script. She grew well versed in the language then and thought of venturing back into Sistama to seek more of the writings, but Eraim convinced her otherwise. Selanna learned much about dunarchins, wraiths, and ghouls, and became something of an expert on undead, but she did not delve too deeply into their methods of creation, for it was far too disturbing.

One of the Sistama tomes especially intrigued Selanna, for its final pages touched upon another form of undead, but the text was incomplete; perhaps continued in another volume. Though the information was vague, it filled Selanna with dread and her desire to return to the dark swamp grew. But she knew it was a feat she could not perform alone, and Eraim would never agree to accompany her.

Elgarroth spent much of his time in Tikken City and Selanna held audience with him often, but he offered no help in the matter of the tomes, for his time was filled with concerns of his own. After six years, Elgarroth proved difficult to track down, even within his

Vermallon home.

As for the rest of Vaeldor, most returned to their ordinary lives. For some, their part tells another story.

Chapter 28

Tarm

Duke Tarm sat at the dinner table. Though many years had passed, he could still feel the cool, smooth surface of the blue sphere upon his fingertips. The orb had changed his life forever when it touched his mind, helping him to realize his true path in life. He was not meant to be a mere duke. He was meant to be king! That was his destiny.

The orb revealed this and more. Tarm was foretold of an impending doom, after which only the chosen would remain masters. And he would be king of those masters! The fool, Vikur, ran off with the orb, thinking there existed a defense against the rising power. This angered Tarm at first, but would not serve to alter his new path.

A couple months after the orb opened Tarm's eyes, the power behind the sphere sent a messenger. Malgabi was a pompous warrior claiming to be a Marc, but Tarm knew this to be untrue, for the man lacked the characteristics of those dwelling within the kingdom to the south.

"You are to raise an army. One larger than you currently boast." Malgabi presented many valuable jewels. "Master's gifts should help, and more will come."

"King Karrak will be curious as to why I'm increasing my forces," Tarm said.

"That is why you must do it in secrecy."

There was obvious disrespect in Malgabi's tone. Normally Tarm would not tolerate such insolence, but life as he knew it was over. He accepted the jewels.

Tarm went to work immediately, devising plans without help from advisors or close friends—not even his wife was aware of his actions. He hired diggers from Marcove to enlarge his dungeon and miners from villages near the mountains to increase his stock of iron. The Marcs passed through the servants' entrances beneath the cover of night with picks and shovels and hauled wagons of loose dirt to distant wild country—servants were left to clean all messes, too fearful to inquire as to the sources. The miners were not allowed near the castle; Tarm personally collected all iron deliveries a few miles outside of Barraday, not wanting any witnesses to these transactions, and transported them to his secret cache while the castle slept.

It took more than five years to complete the secret chambers, including forges to expand the armory and war rooms where Tarm spent late hours planning. Once every few months, Malgabi returned with more jewels and to check on Tarm's progress, but the messenger never seemed satisfied. Tarm desired greatly to run the man through with his sword, but he knew he could not. He would just have to bite his tongue until the deed was done.

The next step was to find the soldiers Tarm needed to strengthen his forces, but he could not simply travel in search of mercenaries. He felt a wall moving quickly against his back and realized he could no longer do it alone. So he called for a meeting with his most trusted generals.

Standing before the three warriors he had known practically all his life, Tarm revealed his intentions to claim the throne. He added that under his rule, those loyal would receive power and wealth beyond their greatest dreams, and upon completion of his speech, the men sat with faces of stone. At that time, Tarm produced some of the trinkets provided by the so-called Marc and the generals' eyes lit up. They eagerly agreed to do whatever it took, and they set out to gather supplies and find mercenaries within Marcove and Sardina—soldiers with no fealty to the Kalmaar king.

The next burden was to explain all to Mayry, and when Tarm

finally found the courage, he was surprised with her enthusiastic acceptance. Shortly after, he found Mayry speaking with Malgabi, as if the two were old friends, and realized she had probably known all along. The idea of being queen made Mayry absolutely giddy and she spoke of bearing a child, a task she had previously claimed to be impossible. Tarm grew suspicious and might have inquired further, but the thought of having children was overwhelming and he decided to let it be.

Fourteen years had passed since Malgabi's first visit. The armory was stocked and the Border Hills teeming with mercenaries—Tarm had to end the watch of the northernmost towers within the rolling terrain to keep the soldiers hidden. Sturdy tents and a few structures were then erected to house the men and protect them from goblins and ill weather, and over the years, the encampment grew almost into a village and families were started. But the mercenaries trained daily and awaited the opportunity to live as wealthy nobles under Tarm's rule.

Thus far, Tarm had avoided suspicion from the north, but he was not sure how much longer his luck would endure. King Karrak had trusted Tarm for more than thirty years, and as time passed, guilt gnawed at his insides. But there was no turning back.

These thoughts floated through Tarm's head while he sat before his favorite meal, lamb in wine sauce with dumplings, but his stomach was unsettled. Across the table, Mayry's appetite seemed well enough for them both.

"Duke Tarm." A guard interrupted the meal. "The messenger, Malgabi, requests audience, my lord. He claims it is of great importance."

Tarm's heart raced as he stood. Could it be time at last?

He left the dining hall with Mayry clutching his arm in excitement. Within the audience chamber, seated upon Tarm's throne was Malgabi, appearing no older than the day they first met. A guard was pleading with the Marc to step down, but Malgabi only smiled.

"Forgive me, my lord," the guard begged. "I told him not—"

"It's fine."

Tarm could feel the disdain in his own voice. While he dismissed the soldiers, Mayry proceeded to the thrones. Tarm followed once the doors were shut.

"That is my seat." Tarm felt his hands trembling as he fought to conceal the mounting rage.

Malgabi looked upon the thick wooden chair and shrugged. "So it is." The worm flashed an arrogant smile as he rose and offered a sarcastic bow.

Tarm took his seat next to Mayry. His wife's smile never faltered.

"I bring grand news!" Malgabi beamed. "It is time."

Tarm felt the blood rush to his head. He was filled with both fear and excitement, just as the day he first saw the orb, and all guilt retreated to the shadowy corners of his mind.

"Gather your forces," Malgabi instructed. "I'll return in three months. And then we march."

"I am in no need of your assistance in this matter," Tarm said. "I have had more time than necessary to plan the assault."

"I *will* assist you." Malgabi took on a rare, serious tone. "That is the way it is going to be. The way the master wishes."

Tarm released a heavy sigh of frustration.

"There are elements of the war you are not aware of," Malgabi explained. "For instance, you have allies in the north."

"Nira? Selt?" Tarm was a bit confused. No kingdom would dare stand against King Karrak.

Malgabi shook his head and smiled. "They are called the Zurkan."

"Benasti?" Tarm could not believe his ears. He would never have recruited the aid of hobgoblins and krukari, and especially not the Zurkan. They were an elite krukari force, their name meaning "Soldiers of Blood" in hobgoblin, and were certainly not creatures worthy of trust. Only a fool would consort with such scum.

"That is correct." Malgabi's grin took on a mischievous aura.

"They are ready and eager."

Tarm lightly tapped his fist upon his chin. The idea of fighting beside Zurkan made him ill. He would rather hunt them down than call them comrade. But, he supposed, they could serve a purpose; perhaps limit his own casualties. "Very well."

"Three months." Malgabi spun on his heels and boldly exited without proper etiquette.

Mayry's face was aglow. She seemed to want it as much as Tarm, if not more.

The first order of business was perhaps the hardest, for Tarm had to dismantle parts of his existing army. Over the years the generals took note of those they felt would join the cause, but there were many they were sure would not. The latter soldiers were placed into small groups and sent on petty missions, but little did they realize they would never return, for mercenaries awaited in ambush. Of the soldiers that were spared, little convincing was necessary to gain their loyalty, for they realized there to be no choice in the matter.

Next, weapons and armor were distributed and soldiers and mercenaries placed into squadrons; and generals, captains, and lieutenants took their commands and issued orders. All was ready with a few days to spare.

Malgabi arrived a week late. Tarm had half a mind to ride without the man, but thought better of it, and if their existed a reason for the tardiness, Malgabi did not share it.

"You are in complete control for now." Malgabi laughed at Tarm's scowl. "Consider it a test. If all goes well, you have nothing to lose and everything to gain."

Tarm was not impressed.

The next morning Mayry gave Tarm a kiss, deep and passionate, and she radiated excitement and pride unlike any he had ever seen. The march began, and women, children, and elderly gathered to see the seemingly endless parade of knights and soldiers marching through the streets. Feelings were mixed within the large city, for many did not agree with the mission, but all wished for the safe return of their loved ones.

The army was greater than forty thousand strong, larger than the king's personal guard and equal to half of Kalmaar's total forces combined. Tarm led the main host on a direct route while the generals broke east and west, and they battled northward, easily neutralizing the smaller baronies. Tarm hated to admit it, but Malgabi fought well by his side, showing no fear in combat, but it was Tarm that paved the way on the battlefields, unmatched in skill. Anyone taken prisoner was given the choice to join or die, and most chose the former. There would be no aid coming to the king from the south!

A fortnight after the campaign began, they neared the region of Burmagaard. The way had been easy thus far, as Tarm's plans proved well laid out, and while they closed on the capital city the battles grew fewer. This came as no surprise. Tarm had anticipated it. According to his calculations, Karrak would have pulled all local forces to him and put forth a call to arms, but no one would answer in time. Next, messengers would arrive to parley in an attempt to delay Tarm's plans.

With the rising of the sun the following morning, two such messengers arrived on horseback. Tarm met with them on neutral ground, and at the lead of the contingent that followed him was Malgabi.

"King Karrak is confused as to why you have brought this attack, Duke Tarm," one messenger stated. "He is sure there has been a misunderstanding, and wishes to reach a peaceful resolve before any more of our kindred's blood is shed."

"Return to your king!" Tarm spat. "And inform him the only peaceful resolve will be the unconditional surrender of the crown!"

The messengers stared coldly before turning to ride back, but they moved no more than a few paces when an arrow streaked by Tarm's head and struck the lead rider in the back. Whipping around, Tarm saw Malgabi nock a second arrow.

"Cease!" Tarm commanded.

Malgabi let loose the bowstring, piercing the back of the second messenger. The Marc held a pompous grin while the horses rode away, one with an empty saddle and the other dragging its rider by a single foot.

"It's better this way," Malgabi said, maintaining the smile. "The king's men will know we're taking no prisoners."

"It's barbaric!" Tarm started his horse toward the encampment, again fighting the urge to strike Malgabi down.

Later that day, the battle for Castle Darmhorng began less than a mile south of Burmagaard. The armies were evenly matched, but upon the dawn of the following day, the remainder of Tarm's forces arrived. His generals flanked those loyal to the king and Karrak's troops fell back within the city walls. Tarm's soldiers cheered and gave chase, but the generals halted the advance and issued orders to lay siege.

While all was made ready, Tarm noticed the approach of Malgabi. It was the first he had seen of the man in several hours—he had hoped Malgabi met his end somewhere on the field, but the worm appeared unharmed.

"All is going well!" Malgabi boasted. "It is better than you planned!"

"It would seem." Tarm was not completely confident. The king's army had not lost even half their numbers before their hasty retreat, and Karrak had never joined the battle. It did not make sense. "Light the fires," he ordered a general. "Let no one escape in the dark."

The night was quiet and there came nothing from Darmhorng or Burmagaard—no attacks by catapults or bows and no more requests for parley. While the soldiers relished in the apparent victory, Tarm wracked his mind in an attempt to realize what the king was hiding. When twilight replaced the night sky, the answer was revealed.

From the west came the blaring horns of Morimont, and hundreds of drums vibrated the battlefield as a legion of dwarves approached. Karrak had always been in good standing with the stocky folk, but Tarm never dreamed they could be convinced to meddle in the affairs of humans. Nowhere in his plans had he accounted for such a variable.

The dwarves marched in perfect sync with faces of stone. Tarm ordered his archers to release a volley of arrows, but the Morimont soldiers raised shields to form an almost impenetrable barrier and very few missiles found their mark. With a roar the dwarves charged, waving axes, hammers, and picks, and Burmagaard's horns sounded as the gates opened and the king's forces poured through, led by Karrak himself. Even in his advancing years, the king showed much vigor and personally defeated one of Tarm's generals without a scratch to show, and in Karrak's wake his troops followed with strength and confidence unseen the previous day.

Tarm could not believe his eyes. His plans had been laid out perfectly, but the tide was turning against him. It was all wrong. He witnessed some of his soldiers surrender before the king and shift their allegiance, and any of his men caught in the path of the raging dwarves were left trampled underfoot with gashes and mangled appendages.

"Curse Karrak!" Tarm cleaved one of the king's soldiers. "Curse him and his love of the mountain folk!"

"All is not lost," Malgabi called. "I told you of our reinforcements. And here they come!"

Horns filled the air again, this time from the northeast, and Tarm saw the plain red banners of Benasti. Never before had such a force marched from the evil forest, and a chill raced down Tarm's spine.

The advancing army looked at least fifteen thousand strong, three times the size of the dwarfish force, and the front ranks were filled with hobgoblins and krukari. These foot soldiers lacked order and discipline, but made up for it with savagery and hatred, and behind them the Zurkan marched in perfect ranks or rode upon large wolves. The elite Benasti warriors wore spiked armor as dark as night with blood-red cloaks draped over their shoulders, and concealing their faces were skull-like helmets. The Zurkan raised swords, axes, and spears into the air several times as they grunted, and a hush almost captured the battlefield while all witnessed their approach.

The Benasti foot soldiers screamed as they charged, and though the dwarves dropped four for every one of theirs to fall, they were greatly outnumbered and quickly overwhelmed when the Zurkan joined the fray. The Benasti elite killed all in their path in a most brutal fashion, even striking down their own foot soldiers if they moved too slowly. One warrior in particular stood out from them all. This krukari was larger than the others and lacked the red cloak and skull helmet. He fought ferociously with a wicked spear, thrusting and slashing its blade, and around him his subjects chanted, "Gruzim! Gruzim!"

Soon Karrak's soldiers were pinned between the warriors of Benasti and Tarm's army with no path of retreat, and Karrak called for his men to cease. Tarm issued a similar order, but had it not been for Malgabi shouting in hobgoblin, Tarm was sure the Zurkan would gladly have continued until all humans were dead.

The battle was over and more than thirty thousand corpses littered the ground. It was an hour before dusk when King Karrak met Tarm on the battlefield, and with visible reluctance the crown was surrendered. Tarm watched Gruzim step behind the defeated king and saw bloodlust in the krukari's eyes.

"He's to live," Tarm said loudly enough for all to hear.

Gruzim released a low growl and his lip curled into a scowl.

"He is to live," Malgabi repeated, and only then did the krukari stand down.

Tarm turned to his one surviving general. "Secure the castle!"

The general smiled and the men cheered.

CHAPTER 29

THE HIGH ORDER

ews of the fall of King Karrak traveled swiftly to Palidur. The High Order sent scouts to investigate, but by the time they reached Vermallon Forest, Tarm's forces had already pushed their way to the Great East River. The many elfish clans of Vermallon worked together to disallow westward advancement, and Nira held strong at the only two bridges spanning the mighty river to prevent northward movement as well. Word then reached the Holy City from Ironside Keep that Kalmirans had conquered Marcove. The weaker kingdom stood no chance against the organized attack and crumbled quickly, but Vikur vowed that no forces would breach the mountain pass.

How Duke Tarm managed to pull off such a feat, the High Order could not fathom, and the strange alliance between Tarm and Gruzim, the new king of Benasti Forest, plagued them even more. The Order gathered within the Grand Cathedral every day since the incident became known to discuss the matter, and at the tenth such meeting, some of the members were shocked to find a pair of elves within the High Temple. Merssa had granted Selanna and Eraim access into the most sacred hall, and those that opposed the elves' presence were powerless to argue the point, for Merssa had the backing of both Nilborg and Soren—the High Priest and High Paladin of Soleran felt the matter important enough to break tradition.

Merssa began the meeting by recapping all that had transpired beyond the Varlimor Mountains, to which Jerove and Garren nodded impatiently.

"We know all of this," said Trakinir. The Arronaus paladin was just as outraged as the two priests and made no attempt to conceal it.

"But what we have not considered is the possibility that Trannum is behind it," Merssa pointed out.

Trakinir's scoff was echoed by Garren and Jerove. The three seemed eager to abandon all thoughts of the necromancer over the past several years, but no meeting ever concluded without Merssa sharing her encounter with the undead wizard or the images he imparted upon her. Lately, they had grown more outspoken with their displeasure for the topic, and Merssa knew they believed her "obsession" to be out of control.

"Some feel we have seen the last of the necromancer." Selanna's voice outraged the same three members. "It is easy to believe that we foiled his schemes and that his creations were not enough to combat the forces of elves, humans, and dwarves. But very few have faced his dunarchins, and we have not seen all he has to offer, I assure you.

"I have read from tomes that Trannum has written." Selanna was undaunted by the glares. "Though incomplete, they contain enough information to reveal that he has yet to show his greatest creations. Let us not forget the remainder of the prophecy, as told by the Council of Wizards."

"*Alas! the One that Evil brings,*" Eraim recited. "*Takes the land, takes the kings.*"

Garren clenched his fists, the Arronaus priest's ire obvious on his face. "We do not know the conflict across the mountains to be anything more than the conquest of a duke! True, Tarm has formed a strange allegiance with the Benasti scum and their lord, of whom I believe some of you are familiar with." Garren gave a sideways glance toward Merssa with the latter part of his statement. "But Kalmaar's history is riddled with such internal wars. The king's crown has moved from bloodline to bloodline. Who's to say where true royalty lies there?"

"They've lived peacefully for well over a century under Karrak's line," Merssa said. "He was beloved by all, and at one time believed unconquerable, even by this Order."

"Still," Soren maintained a calm demeanor, "we must be careful in this matter. We need more information before we can choose a proper course of action."

The comments of the Soleran paladin dismayed Merssa. She counted on his support, as well as Nilborg's, but she knew Soren to be thorough and patient, so she was not surprised.

"For now," Soren added, eyeing Merssa with obvious understanding of her apprehension, "Tarm's advance has been stalled in Nira. And as for Ironside Keep, let's not forget the fortress was built for the very task it now performs. So they are stalled there as well."

"I remember when you were hasty to march into Neja," commented Selanna, receiving many ill looks. "But you are not so brave when it comes to Kalmaar."

Garren and Jerove were rendered speechless, fury burning within their eyes as their lips quivered but issued no sound. Even Merssa was held in shock.

Trakinir rose to his feet. "You will *not* speak in such a manner! You should not even be here!" The Arronaus paladin turned toward Merssa. "And let this serve as sufficient reason why!"

"It is not fear of Kalmaar, Selanna." Soren still did not give into the outrage. "It is the needless killing of innocents. If it is indeed an internal war Kalmaar has been faced with, it is not our part to intervene. We cannot assume it is the workings of Trannum."

"Nor should it be wholly excluded," added Nilborg. "We must not allow Trannum to build in power. Not if we can prevent it."

Though Merssa had grown used to the Soleran priest's constant support, she always appreciated when Nilborg's words echoed her own thoughts.

"I suggest we reinforce Ironside Keep," said Jerove from the seat next to Merssa. "We can do the same for Nira, at least until we've learned more of the true nature of the union between Tarm and Gruzim, and then we can make an *informed* decision."

"That is the *least* we can do," said Merssa. But she knew it was the best she could hope for…for now.

"You always have the right to proceed with a mission of your own." Jerove's sarcasm was felt as he looked from Merssa to Nilborg. The Cafior priest still took exception with the expeditions to recover the orbs all those years ago. "But now it is time for the *Order* to decide what the *city* shall do."

Selanna and Eraim were escorted to a private chamber within the Cafior portion of the cathedral. While Eraim gazed at portraits of priests and paladins long departed, Selanna paced the floor, feeling the meeting had not gone well. But she hoped at least that eyes had been opened.

"What will they do?" Eraim asked after a few minutes.

Selanna sighed regretfully. "I think we both know."

Merssa entered, a scowl planted on the paladin's face. "We will *'look into things.'*" Her sarcasm was more than obvious. "The fools!"

"What do you mean?" Selanna inquired.

"We shall assist Nira and Ironside Keep, as Jerove suggested," Merssa replied. "We will also send a small force back into Neja to search Trannum's lair again, and there could *possibly* be an expedition into the Silent Marsh if the venture into the Stone Eagles proves fruitless. Furthermore, we will work with Vermallon spies to see what we can find of the Kalmaar-Benasti pact." Merssa did a poor job of pretending to agree with the words, unlike Merssa of the past. It was Borse's influence, Selanna was sure.

Eraim gasped, her eyes wide. "Tell me you are not returning to Sistama!"

Merssa shook her head. "I do not believe the Order will ever come to that decision. They have placed enough on the plate to keep them busy for a while."

"My mind often wanders to Vikur's tale of the Serpent's Range," Selanna mentioned. "His running off with the orb seemed strange. I have wanted to speak with him further on the matter, but the tomes have taken up much of my time. Even now, I have not fully translated them."

"Tarm was with Vikur when he hunted the orb," Eraim reminded Merssa.

"You believe Tarm may have been affected?" Merssa furrowed her brow. "Like Solett?"

"There are many strange factors," Selanna replied. "Tarm's role in slaying goblins and hobgoblins to settle southern Kalmaar is legendary, yet he aligned with Benasti. All of this must have taken years of preparation, but how was it accomplished without King Karrak's knowledge? How did the duke amass such an army?"

"The king had total trust in Tarm, and he was no fool." Merssa bit her lip in thought. "Yet Tarm turned on him like a rabid dog."

"I will go to Kalmaar," Selanna said after a pause. "That is what Soren was hinting at. You need more information. I will find what I can and return as quickly as possible."

"Be careful." Merssa's concern was genuine, but her eyes were grateful.

Chapter 30

Darmhorng Dungeon

Selanna and Eraim left Palidur immediately. While riding through Sendorum, Selanna could not help but enjoy watching life endure, seemingly unaffected by the dangers beyond Vermallon Forest—life as it was meant to be. Sendors tended to fields, fed livestock, haggled over prices of mundane items, and frequented their favorite taverns. Selanna wondered if the citizens were simply unaware, or if they believed the evil would never reach their realm. If she had her way, it would be the latter.

Nearer the Vermallon Forest, things changed. Villages had doubled their guard and hunters spent less time trekking through the trees, for wolves had grown to terrible numbers and bandits were running rampant. Vermallon elves, though unseen most of the time, normally kept the dangers of the forest in check, but since the elves' departure to the eastern edge, things were very different. A few hunters even reported seeing an ogre and a one-eyed giant.

Selanna and Eraim entered the forest, leading Lilli and Dandi through the trees and avoiding Vermallon Road—surely bandits were watching it day and night. That evening, Selanna had to ward off a couple packs of wolves with magical bursts of flame, but they encountered little else until the next day, when they met up with a forest patrol.

Tall Vermallon elves presented themselves, dressed in brown and green leather with well-crafted swords strapped to their sides. The warriors held bows as long as Selanna was tall, but their arrows remained in their quivers.

"These are not the days to be wandering Vermallon," the lead figure said in the elfish tongue. "War is at hand. Perhaps you best return to Salenti."

Selanna sensed the shifting of Eraim's feet. Most Vermallon elves lacked respect for the combative skills of their Salenti cousins, and the speaker was evidently among that majority. Eraim took exception, standing as tall as she could and puffing out her chest, but no one seemed to notice.

"We aim for the House of Elgarroth," Selanna informed the soldier.

The patrol shared small chuckles. The leader then spoke again.

"The enemy is only leagues to the east. And though we watch the border night and day, I cannot promise you a safe journey. Nor can I promise you success in your quest to find the wizard's home. I have lived in the southern domain all my life and have never seen it."

Selanna gave a knowing smile and the tall elf frowned. It was a response that never ceased to amuse her, when one came to understand she was no stranger to the mysterious wizard.

"Very well." He turned to his contingent. "We will leave them to their own affairs." He gazed back at Selanna, exhibiting a dubious look she had become quite accustomed to. "You are on your own from here."

"I thank you." She bowed.

Selanna ignored the remarks that ensued as the warriors disappeared beyond the trees, not caring to listen to the words of those too ignorant to understand the great Elgarroth Sandanari. Glancing at Eraim, Selanna noted a disturbed look. Evidently Eraim had chosen to hear the comments.

Selanna took the lead and they headed east. She could not help but smirk while recalling the remarks of the Vermallon elf, about never having seen the House of Elgarroth. It was a place even the most competent trackers failed to find. The soil left no evidence of anyone having passed through and trees shifted to steer away trespassers, but this posed no problem for Selanna, for she had become quite accustomed to the magic over the years. After a few more miles, she and Eraim entered the clearing where the small house stood, and Selanna sighed in relief to find the wizard at home.

Elgarroth sat upon a log, puffing on a long thin pipe, and did not seem surprised at their approach. He motioned for them to sit on a log across from him and an elf servant silently led Lilli and Dandi to a water trough.

It had been some time since Selanna last spoke with Elgarroth and there was much to discuss, but she had no idea where to start. Elgarroth seemed to sense this and went first, speaking of the past six years, but mainly he stated common knowledge while revealing little of his own actions during that span. None of it was news to Selanna. When Elgarroth inquired as to her discoveries, Selanna informed him of all she had learned, including recent events in Palidur. Elgarroth stared in his usual, emotionless way.

"At what point did Gruzim become Lord of Benasti?" asked Eraim after a moment of silence.

"It would seem he was born there," Elgarroth answered. "A prince, as it was." He puffed on his pipe before continuing. "A custom exists there, you see, where the sons of the Benasti king are sent into the world to live among the 'hated enemies' for a time. Those that return may then compete for their father's title in a battle to the death, if they so choose."

Eraim gasped. "How barbaric!" Her expression twisted to one of confusion. "But why would a king send his sons to live among those who might…" She shook her head in disbelief.

"To learn about their enemy," Elgarroth replied. "Only the strong can survive such a test. And when they return, it is with the wisdom of those that would oppose them."

"Did you know?" inquired Selanna. "That he was a Benasti prince, I mean?"

"No one could have known," Elgarroth explained, "lest they were of Benasti themselves. Only a dozen or so of the many krukari roaming Vaeldor are of Benasti royalty, and it is nearly impossible to tell which, for Benasti rulers carry no noble mannerisms."

"What of the union between Tarm and Gruzim?" Selanna posed. "Is it all a coincidence, as Palidur hopes? The prophecy states that Trannum will take the lands, does it not?"

"Trannum is sly and crafty." Elgarroth's eyes narrowed on nothing in particular. "He has had much time to prepare, and he is in no hurry. If this is his doing, he has revealed nothing to say so. There has not been seen any undead in the duke's conquest."

"I am sure it is his doing, nonetheless," Selanna said. "I can feel it. This charade he has created, using Tarm and Gruzim, will certainly grow to a greater evil. Sardina, Sendorum, and Harbnum may think the mountains and forest protect them, but I feel these barriers only serve to keep things hidden."

There was a long pause as Elgarroth drew from his pipe.

"Your convictions are strong," he said at last. "But have you the courage to act upon them? Palidur needs proof of the necromancer's involvement before they will act. Humans remain in their homes, hoping bad dreams will pass with the night. And while Vermallon elves guard only their own interests, Nirans battle for their very lives. Even Merssa, with all her influence, cannot give cause to rise up and fight an unseen foe."

"Where do I begin?" An overwhelming feeling enveloped Selanna, like she was too small to make a difference.

Another period of silence followed. Not even the insects seemed willing to answer Selanna's question. As her heart sank, Elgarroth spoke.

"Perhaps you might start with King Karrak."

"He is alive?" Selanna was shocked.

"Certainly." Elgarroth blew smoke into the air. "Tarm placed him within the dungeons of his own castle, in Darmhorng. I know not why the duke allows him to live, but there he is."

"How do we get into the dungeon?" Eraim asked, a bit despairingly.

"Between the two of you," Elgarroth regarded Eraim, "I believe it is within your means."

Eraim's shoulders slumped. "Perhaps," she mumbled to herself.

Silence followed for several more minutes. Selanna would have loved nothing more than to stay and chat with her mentor longer, but time was pressing. Elgarroth nodded, as if reading her thoughts, and she and Eraim took their leave without another word.

The next task was to cross the Great East River; the widest waterway in all of Vaeldor, boasting a swift current over its entire length. Only two bridges existed east of Vermallon for safe passage, but opposing armies were known to be encamped on either side. Eraim, however, informed Selanna there was another way.

"Remember when Selt occupied Nira?" Eraim looked over her shoulder while she spoke, as if afraid Dandi and Lilli might fall behind.

"That was over a century ago," Selanna said, almost as a question. Actually, Selt had oppressed Nira many times throughout history, but the last time Selanna recalled any occupation, she had been much younger. That had to be the occasion Eraim was referring to, but Selanna thought it to be odd. Eraim was only twelve years Selanna's elder. For what purpose had Eraim been roaming Vaeldor so far to the east?

Eraim nodded and continued. "Well, during that time I had need to pass into Kalmaar, and I did not wish to go through Varlimor Pass—such a horrid way to travel!" Her eyes cautiously scanned the surroundings. "I used a hidden ford, built by scouts for safe passage in times of danger. My hope is that it still exists."

Again, Selanna thought it odd. Why would her friend have a need to pass into Kalmaar at such a young age? She considered asking, but decided to leave it be and they moved on in silence.

They traveled slowly for some time, avoiding Vermallon patrols in hopes of keeping the remainder of their journey secret—the less that knew of their passage, the better. The task was not too difficult, for the watch over the far southern region seemed lacking, most likely due to the fact the forest became denser and prevented any sizeable force from marching by that route.

Soon rushing water reached their ears and Eraim picked up the pace. Moments later, the river came into view, cutting through the forest in great haste, and the roar of a waterfall was unmistakable. Eraim led the way upstream a short distance and the roar grew as Candermane Falls came into view.

The magnificent waterfall was just south of the rapids, falling several hundred feet from a stream within the Varlimor Mountains, and it strengthened the river as they joined forces and sped off to the Batorn Gulf. The water was a bit tamer west of the alliance, though still a dangerous place for a swim, and it was there that Eraim began searching the foliage.

"It is here!" Eraim exhibited a touch of excitement. "And it looks to have been well maintained."

Stowed away in a large collection of thickets near the water's edge was a raft big enough for four travelers and their horses, more than enough room for Selanna, Eraim, and their animal companions. A rope traveled beneath the water from one side to the other, barely detectable as it exited the river and passed through the thickets, and it was anchored to a large tree on either side, where great care had been taken to conceal it with vines and dirt. Selanna had to admire the artistic prowess, for she could barely discern the rope's presence, even when staring directly at it.

Eraim pulled some of the rope from the water and locked it into a harness upon the raft. Selanna eyed the area suspiciously while Eraim slid the craft partway onto the river, but there were only trees, bushes, and water. Once all were aboard, Eraim applied all her might and began pulling them across, exhibiting the hidden strength Selanna was well aware of. The current dragged them downstream until the rope was taut, but it held and they reached the other side without mishap. Eraim disconnected the rope and allowed the river to conceal it again before hiding the raft within nearby bushes.

"What if the raft had been on this side?" Selanna asked.

Eraim smiled. "I cannot reveal all our secrets."

They traveled uphill, following a narrow path along the western edge of the mountain stream to the falls. The way then grew steeper and icy water sprayed them while they scaled wide stone steps next to Candermane. A small ledge provided some relief a bit more than halfway up the waterfall, and upon the ridge, hidden among a few pine trees, Eraim revealed a dark tunnel that bore into the mountain. Selanna produced her small light and they entered.

The tunnel was dank and the walls saturated with moisture as they passed beneath the falls, but after a little more than a quarter mile, the roar of Candermane faded and the passage became dry. They followed the snaking tunnel for a day and a half and emerged into the wild country of Nira, well south of the warfront. Selanna breathed in the fresh air, feeling as though her lungs had been deprived for weeks.

Eraim continued to lead the way east over the next few days, avoiding scattered villages as they entered civilized lands. A couple patrols of humans donning blood-red tabards were seen—typical garb of Benasti soldiers—but escaping detection was not difficult, for superior eyes and ears gave Selanna and Eraim plenty of warning while they were still far off.

"How strange it is that Benasti has humans in their ranks." Selanna spread her blankets upon the ground as they settled in for another fireless night.

"They were not Kalmirans," Eraim said. "Their hair was lighter and their faces rounder."

"Seltans?" Selanna furrowed her brow.

"I am sure Gruzim does not wish to insult his own soldiers with the menial task of border patrol," Eraim remarked. "And what other race of humans east of Vermallon would work with Benasti? I can think of none other than the Seltans."

Selanna shook her head with disgust. Selt was infamous for seizing any opportunity to gain power.

They pressed farther east the next day and veered a bit to the north, passing through more settled lands of the region to remain beyond sight of Benasti Forest and the evil lurking therein. Seltan patrols came more frequently then, so they took to traveling at night. While the sun shone, they hid among trees or within tall crops of farmlands, and Dandi and Lilli never betrayed their position. They spied on villagers while in hiding, finding oppressed and frightened people. Nobles were treated as peasants, and peasants, if they survived, were worse off than animals. Life beneath the rule of Tarm and Gruzim was grim indeed, and Selanna felt sickened that she was powerless to do anything about it.

They reached the Batorn River and the full moon shone off its seemingly still water; a reflection worthy of a portrait. The image was distorted, however, when they crossed the shallow waterway on horseback and entered Kalmaar at last. The night grew late by the time they reached the first of three bridges over Orlenfel River, about an hour before the rising of the sun. The water was much deeper and wider than the Batorn River and the bridge was teeming with soldiers, so they continued east. Over the next evening, they found the other bridges just as guarded.

"They possess the land north and south of the river," Eraim said. "Why do they guard the bridges so heavily?"

"Perhaps the pact between Kalmaar and Benasti is not such a friendly one." It had not escaped Selanna's notice that the soldiers to the south were Kalmiran, while those north of the bridges were hobgoblins.

"How are we to cross?" Eraim asked.

"We will have to continue to Orlenfel," Selanna thought aloud.

"That is two days from here," Eraim complained. "Can you not just use your magic?"

"I dare not." Selanna frowned. "I fear it would bring unwanted attention."

"And what if the gray elves do not welcome us?" Eraim posed.

To Selanna's knowledge, neither of them had ever been to Orlenfel, nor had they ever met a gray elf. The Orlenfel elves were known to be almost as territorial as those of Maple Lore—at least that was how they were portrayed in Salenti. But Selanna often wondered about the accuracy of that belief.

"Vikur spoke highly of Xorlunder," Selanna said. "*He* is of Orlenfel."

Eraim sighed and nodded.

They moved on, arriving to Orlenfel two evenings later without mishap, but found the forest besieged by thousands of Benasti warriors. Unlike humans, hobgoblins and krukari could see well into the shadows of night, and passing unnoticed would be difficult.

Selanna gazed at the many bonfires. "I think a bit of magic is in order now."

With a wave of her hands, several of the fires rose to more than twenty feet and released sparks that created small explosions. Many shouts ensued and soldiers ran about, and Selanna and Eraim met no resistance while they bolted their horses into the safety of the trees. Less than a hundred feet into the woodland, however, they were quickly surrounded.

From the trees dropped fifty elves, taller than even those of Vermallon, with bows loaded or swords ready. They wore gray leather and their weapons were exquisite in make, and the white irises of their eyes almost glowed against their grayish skin in the shadows. Most had hair the color of silver, but there were a few that possessed white.

"That was pretty risky," one elf said in the elfish tongue. "We might have killed you before we noticed you were not hobgoblins."

Selanna raised a brow. "Had you made that mistake, I would have doubted you to be elves."

"Very good." The gray elf held his cold stare. "But you are neither of Orlenfel nor Vermallon. What brings you here?"

"We are of Salenti Forest," Selanna replied, "and our business is our own. But I assure you it bears no ill toward your folk."

"Is that so?" posed the elf. "Our commander will make that determination."

Selanna and Eraim offered no resistance and were led deeper into the woodland. They arrived to a battle encampment large enough to support a few hundred soldiers, though only fifty were present, and were escorted into a large tent where a gray elf was busy writing on a piece of parchment. Behind the seated elf stood a female, tall and slender with long silver hair and sharp, beautiful features; an obvious family resemblance existed between the two. The seated elf ceased writing and looked up.

"Who have we here?"

"Intruders from Salenti Forest, Commander," the guard said. "Or so they claim."

The elf nodded and the warriors left.

"I am Selanna," Selanna said. "And this is Eraim."

"And what brings you here in such dark days?" the commander posed.

Selanna hesitated. "We are not able to discuss our business with you, I am afraid. Only that we are on an important journey and must not be delayed."

"These are strange times." The elf motioned to the female, and she poured three goblets of wine. "It is hard to tell your allies from your enemies. The only ones we find we can trust are ourselves."

The female placed a goblet before the elf and handed one to Selanna and one to Eraim.

"May I inquire as to whom it is that addresses us?" Selanna asked.

"Please, forgive my manners." He bowed his head. "I am Xorlunder, commander of this outpost. And this is my daughter, Lorylla."

"Xorlunder?" Eraim brightened. "The one that guided Vikur through the Serpent's Range?"

"You know of that?" He raised a brow.

"We were on a similar mission in Tenvale," Selanna explained. "And now that I know who you are, I am a bit more at ease."

Xorlunder sipped his wine, but then raised his head in alarm.

"Does your mission have something to do with the orbs?"

Selanna nodded. "It would seem they affect the minds of some. Even possess them."

"Poor Vikur." Xorlunder shook his head. "He was a good man."

"It is not Vikur I speak of," Selanna said. "He is still a good man. He returned the orb to the Council of Wizards without hesitation, though I am not sure that was best."

"Duke Tarm." Xorlunder sighed. "Now it begins to make sense. Vikur put much trust in that man. When he ran off with the orb I was going to ride after him, but the duke assured me it was not necessary; that he had men in position. He said Vikur had gone mad and I believed him." He pounded his fist onto the table. "Now the Benasti knaves sit outside our forest! They dare not invade, and I do not believe they intend to. They are only to make sure we stay put. We could slay them, but then what? Are we to take on all of Kalmaar and Benasti?" The fire in Xorlunder's eyes dwindled. "So we sit and wait. Wait for a sign." He considered Selanna. "Perhaps that sign is you."

Lorylla refilled their glasses and Xorlunder drained his immediately. Turning back to Selanna, he gazed into her eyes, as if attempting to read her thoughts.

"Tell me what part the orbs play in this war?" he asked at last.

"Not the orbs, but their creator," Selanna said. "And as for the part *he* plays, I have only my beliefs for now. I hope to learn more from King Karrak. It is Darmhorng we aim for."

"My dear," Xorlunder's face showed great sorrow, "I am afraid you are too late. I doubt very much the king is alive."

"Word has reached my ears that the king of Kalmaar lives," Selanna said. "A prisoner within his own dungeon. A reliable source has told me so. And now it is vitally important we reach him. I would appreciate any help you can offer in this matter."

Xorlunder sat silently in thought. Again, Selanna felt as though he was trying to probe her mind.

"Very well," he said at last. "There is a path unknown to most Kalmirans. It passes very near to the Serpent's Range, through untamed lands and beyond sight of civilization. It has always served me well, but you best travel at night." Xorlunder stood and opened the tent flap, revealing the brightening forest. "As you can see, morning is not far off. If you like, you can stay and get a fresh start at dusk."

"We *could* use some rest." Selanna had been feeling a bit fatigued for several days, but she had not given it a thought, as her mind was bent on getting to Darmhorng. But now sleep did not seem like such a bad idea.

"Then you shall have it." Xorlunder whistled and a guard appeared. "Rest well under our watch. Let your dreams be troubled not."

Selanna opened her eyes and gazed at the gathering dark, feeling well rested for the first time in weeks. The tent flap opened, awakening Eraim as well, and Lorylla entered.

"It is time." Lorylla's voice was deeper than Selanna would have thought, but it suited the tall elf.

Outside, no fires burned and there were fewer guards than before. Those present moved swiftly about, taking down tents and loading packs onto exceptional horses—surely mounts of the Batorn variety. Selanna and Eraim found their own supplies were replenished and their animals ready for travel. Xorlunder stood next to Dandi and Lilli, admiration plain upon the commander's face.

"Your horses are exquisite," Xorlunder commented, reaching down to brush Dandi's mane, like one petting a dog. Dandi did not seem to mind. "They are built very much like Batorn horses, but intelligence shines in their eyes, greater even than the Andrian breed. I have never met Salenti horses before. Quite exquisite."

"Is everything all right?" Selanna was given to concern. Though Xorlunder showered praise upon their wonderful animal companions, there was no joy in his voice.

"All is as well as can be expected." He looked at Selanna and

Eraim. "We should be going."

With his daughter and ten warriors in company, Xorlunder led them to Orlenfel River, where two rafts bore them across. He then gave Selanna and Eraim directions for the best route to Burmagaard while they walked swiftly toward the woodland's southern edge.

"Once you arrive," Xorlunder added, "I know not how you will access the castle, nor find the king."

"You need not worry of that," Eraim said quietly, as if speaking to herself.

Xorlunder looked as though he wished to say more, but the smell of Benasti was suddenly heavy in the air—the forest was coming to an end. He gave Lorylla a nod, and she immediately led the contingent of gray elves silently to the west and disappeared.

"There is greater than a hundred out there," said Eraim, peering through the trees.

"Yes." Xorlunder's eyes were angry. "Are you ready?"

Selanna nodded. "Thank you. I wish you well."

Xorlunder turned his attention to the dark shapes meandering outside the trees. Cupping his hands about his mouth, he whistled a rising note.

A volley of arrows exited the forest, each missile finding its mark, and eleven shadows fell. The Benasti soldiers scrambled about and another volley dropped eleven more. The gray elves then charged, leaving the cover of the trees and drawing swords, and Benasti horns sounded in answer—a low tone that vibrated the forest.

What Selanna witnessed next, only for a moment, were tall, proud warriors skilled with both blade and magic. Swords became alight with searing heat; fingers released flashes to blind opponents; and warriors leapt to unnatural heights, performing impossible stunts. The stories she had heard of the skill of gray elves as a youth mentioned splendor and grace, but now Selanna saw it for the lethal beauty it truly was.

"Go!" Xorlunder commanded.

Selanna and Eraim rode hard from the forest and over the hills to the south. There was no time to see if any spied their departure, and they continued until all sounds of battle were long faded. Not far ahead was the unmistakable Serpent's tail—slender mountains rising sharply into the dark sky—and the west and north revealed no signs of pursuit. It seemed the distraction had worked.

Travel was easy after that, just as Xorlunder promised. There existed no villages along the Serpent's spine and they encountered no hunters while skirting the foothills. On the fourth night they turned west, leaving the mountains behind.

The next night they crossed a large road running north and south, and smaller roads were scattered as farmhouses and villages began cropping up. The following evening, they encountered the main road into Burmagaard and kept to the south of it, and early the next night, still a few miles east of the capital city, troops were camped on and off the road, forcing Selanna and Eraim to tread more carefully. When Burmagaard came into view at last, so did thousands of tents and bonfires.

"They have an entire army outside the city." Selanna felt defeated. "This will not make entry an easy task."

"We are entering by another route," Eraim said. "Follow me."

They skirted the encampments while soldiers enjoyed drinks and laughter, circling the mighty walls of the city until reaching the western side. To the north, the castle butted against Lake Garaard and a twenty-foot wall allowed no access by way of the water, but Eraim continued west without hesitation and Selanna followed. They rode another few hundred yards before they came upon a copse of elms and maples, and there they dismounted and led their horses into the cover of the trees.

"Remember when we last visited Darmhorng?" Eraim asked.

"That must have been over forty years ago," Selanna said, her brow furrowed in thought.

Eraim nodded. "You wished to visit with King Karrak. I do not recall exactly why. I did not really care. I just wanted some excitement." She began poking around a collection of large boulders.

"But there was no excitement for me, because you spent most your time talking with the castle wizard."

"I remember." Selanna smirked. "I thought maybe I could learn something from him. I did not realize I would be the one doing the teaching."

"Like I said," Eraim gave Selanna a boring-eyed look, "*no* excitement. So I wandered about the castle in search of anything interesting, and I 'accidentally' discovered King Karrak's secret escape tunnel." Eraim stomped her boot upon the ground, and Selanna heard the hollow sound of a hidden door. "I just hope it has remained the same."

Eraim dropped to her knees and removed a thin layer of soil, revealing a small wooden door. She then worked the dirt about the door's edges before slumping her shoulders with a heavy sigh. "The mechanism is missing. I do not possess a tool for this." Eraim looked up at Selanna. "This one is for you."

Selanna nodded and stepped before the door. She closed her eyes and concentrated, and her mind floated free and hovered above. She could see her body standing motionless among the trees while Eraim kept watch on the surroundings, and upon the ground the trapdoor became transparent, revealing a dark passage below.

Selanna floated through the wood and into the tunnel. Turning back, her vision pierced the darkness and viewed three bolts holding the door firmly in place, one on each of three sides while the fourth possessed large hinges. All fittings were rusted. Selanna focused on the bolts, reaching with her mind, but they would not budge. She concentrated on just one, and it moved slowly back from the door. She then did the same with the second bolt. The third one was a bit more defiant, but it could not resist her will for long, and after completing the task she rushed back into her body and her eyes fluttered open. She released her breath, feeling the drain of the complicated spell, but she had plenty of strength remaining.

Eraim squatted above the open door, staring at rusted iron rungs leading down some twenty feet. "Yuck!" She scrunched her nose.

The tunnel walls were saturated with moisture and the floor appeared muddy. "This is worse than Candermane Tunnel."

Selanna sighed. "Time to soil our boots."

While Eraim shared a quiet word with their animal companions, Selanna descended into the hole and brought her small light into being. The floor was indeed muddy and the passage long and dank. Eraim joined Selanna after fastening a single bolt to hold the door shut and they proceeded.

Puddles of muddy water were gathered in many places, some as deep as a foot. The ceiling was inconsistent, sometimes seven feet high and other times only six, but there were no twists or turns and they followed the tunnel some distance before it ended abruptly.

"Have they closed it off?" Selanna felt a twinge of panic rising.

Eraim shook her head. "The wall opens up," she whispered. "Into the dungeon."

"Might King Karrak be nearby?" Selanna lowered her voice.

"There are two areas of cells, if memory serves. We will enter very near to one and the other is beyond a guardroom."

Selanna nodded and Eraim began feeling along the wall. Upon pushing against a stone, a grinding noise was emitted as a hidden door began to slide open. Selanna quickly used her powers to void all sound until the movement ceased, her heart racing, and a narrow opening allowed access into the back corner of a storage room. Crates filled the dark chamber, leaving a small path to a wooden door on the far side, and Selanna sent forth her light to lead the way, dimming it to the strength of a candle.

Eraim moved to the door, and after finding it locked, she produced tools from her pouch. In seconds the lock was picked, and she opened the door slowly before peering into a dimly lit corridor beyond. Pulling Mithkahr, Eraim proceeded into the hallway and Selanna followed.

The corridor stretched twenty feet before turning left and right. In the distance Selanna detected laughter, and she knew Eraim heard it as well, for Eraim began creeping without a sound to the intersection. Selanna did the same. To the left the hallway traveled a short distance to a door reinforced with steel bands and possessing a barred window, and to the right was the first set of cells Eraim had mentioned: a dead end with five heavy wooden doors to either side, each with a window of bars. A single torch cast weak lighting upon the doors and no guards were present.

Sliding around the corner, Eraim moved along the wall toward the cell doors. As she reached the first one, it was obvious she was too short to see through the window.

Selanna allowed her light to fade and followed. Though not as skilled as Eraim, Selanna moved almost as silently until she stood before the first door. She rose onto her toes, peering through the window and detecting the shadows of four occupants within. Allowing her vision to adjust, Selanna saw they were soldiers. Each was dressed in tattered tunics bearing King Karrak's coat of arms over ill-treated wounds, and not one raised an eye to meet hers. Moving across the hall, Selanna found the opposite cell contained six more, and the rest of the cells proved no different. There were at least fifty soldiers in all, and King Karrak was not among them. Some of the faces were grim and some showed defeat, while others were either sleeping or dead; Selanna could not tell which.

"I believe these are King Karrak's personal guards," she whispered to Eraim.

"Do we rescue them?" Eraim whispered back.

Selanna shook her head. "Let us find the other cells."

Eraim moved back through the intersection to the single door, where the sounds of laughter and chatter were strong. This time Eraim leaped, grabbed hold of the barred window, and pulled herself up to have a peek. After a couple seconds she dropped quietly to the floor.

"There are four jailers having a game of cards," Eraim whispered. "Quite distracted. The far door is the one we want. It is open." She regarded Selanna. "It will not be a problem for me…"

"You need not worry about me," Selanna said. "I will meet you on the other side."

Eraim shrugged and went to work on the lock.

Selanna whispered an incantation and her body became transparent. A couple seconds later, she vanished altogether. The spell would be draining, Selanna knew, but not so much as the one she used to open the trapdoor—both were advanced, needing more concentration than mere attack or defensive spells. A couple decades ago they might have been enough to exhaust Selanna's strength, but she had grown significantly under Elgarroth's guidance, and she would still have plenty afterward.

Selanna looked around and found she was alone. Eraim was gone and the door was ajar. Peering into the chamber, Selanna saw the distracted jailers. There was no sign of Eraim, but Selanna was sure her companion had fared well, for the guards merrily continued with their game. After quietly squeezing beyond the door, Selanna closed it to a crack. She then walked slowly across the room—not normally a difficult task when one is invisible, but the guards were pigs, and bones, scraps, and empty tankards forced her to place her steps carefully. Upon reaching the far side, Selanna found the opposite door open a couple of inches. She pushed it softly, but the hinges squeaked and she stopped. Glancing back, the guards remained unaware, so she whispered her spell of silence and quickly slid through before pushing the door almost shut. She had no idea how Eraim had managed without magic.

The corridor beyond was long and possessed eight cell doors, each twenty feet apart. Unlike the previous doors, they were made of thick iron bars from floor to ceiling with a crossbar at their midpoint. A couple torches upon the walls dimly illuminated the passage, but the first cell on the left shed a light of its own.

Selanna moved slightly down the corridor before becoming visible and releasing her spell of silence. She jumped with alarm when the shadows stirred beside her. It was Eraim.

"You startled me," Eraim whispered from the darkness.

"I startled *you*?" Selanna caught her breath. She returned her attention to the corridor.

The cells were larger than the ones containing the soldiers, and within the illuminated cell sat King Karrak. He possessed luxuries not normally afforded prisoners, including decorative blankets, plush pillows, a wine decanter, silver goblet, fine clothing, and a large bowl of grapes. The decanter, however, was full and the goblet appeared dry, and there was not an empty stem on the grape vine. The king sat on the cold stone floor, dressed in rags while the goods were piled in the center of the cell. The only prop he used was the small lantern providing the light.

Selanna stepped before the door and Karrak immediately rose. She put a finger to her lips and a small smile brightened the king's aged face as he sighed.

"I am deeply sorry, sire." Selanna bowed.

"The other cells are empty," Eraim said. "This will not take long." She gazed at the lock while fishing through her pouch.

"No!" Selanna and King Karrak whispered sharply in unison.

Eraim appeared more than a bit confused, but neither Selanna nor the king offered an explanation.

"How did this come to pass?" Selanna asked.

"I'm not entirely sure." King Karrak held a puzzled but stern look. "The duke raised an army both foreign and domestic. How he could afford such a muster, I'll never know, but he must have planned it for some time. I never saw it coming. I allowed him to rule over all of southern Kalmaar as if it were his own." The king shook his head. "Apparently that wasn't enough.

"Word reached me of his rebellion about a week before he arrived to Burmagaard. I was enjoying a feast with my dwarf friends at the time and they offered aid in the matter." Karrak grimaced. "But I never expected him to consort with the likes of Benasti!" He spit the foul taste of the words onto the pile of gear.

"We were overwhelmed. The dwarves were slaughtered. I had to surrender or all my subjects would have suffered the same fate." Karrak was visibly pained, and his sorrow brought a tear to Selanna.

But his face grew stern again. "So he puts me here!" He glared at the luxuries. "And mocks me with gifts! I wish *he* were here, that I may spit on *him*!"

Karrak's outburst was louder than Selanna was comfortable with, and it was not long before she heard footsteps outside the door. Eraim quickly opened the cell across the hall and they stepped inside, just before the wooden door squeaked open and the sound of a single pair of boots approached. Selanna and Eraim shrank into the shadows of a corner as a guard stepped before the king.

"Are you in need of anything?" The soldier's demeanor was surprisingly polite.

"I need your master's head on a spear!" King Karrak growled.

"I'm sorry, sire." The guard maintained the respectful tone. "That is not within my power." His eyes began to wander about the area.

"You look at me when you're speaking!" Karrak grabbed the jailer by the uniform and jerked him with surprising strength, slamming the man's face into the bars and surely breaking his nose. "I am a prisoner, you oaf! And you will treat me as such! Now go back to your games with your cowardly friends!" The king released the man with a shove.

"Sorry, sire." The jailer staggered a bit as blood trickled from his nose and across his lips. He seemed both embarrassed and ashamed, and after a quick bow, he headed back down the corridor.

Selanna and Eraim waited until the door shut, and Eraim sighed when they heard the lock engage as well. After a moment of silence, they returned to King Karrak's cell, finding him with head bowed.

"Sorry about my outburst," he said quietly

"Was it wise to treat the guard so?" Eraim asked.

"He won't do anything to me!" The king was annoyed again. "None of the fools will. The duke wants me alive and well. At first I believed it to be out of respect and the friendship we once shared, but then I overheard him talking to someone. They were in the guardroom, but my ears are as good as ever. The man he spoke to informed him I must be kept alive, sounding more like an order than a request. Apparently, I have loyal subjects that pledged fealty to the duke to ensure my safety, and they dare not mass an assault upon the castle while I live. I am a hostage."

"Do you know the man that Tarm spoke with?" inquired Selanna.

The king scowled at the mention of the duke's name. "I heard his name once or twice. Sometimes the guards speak of him, though not very fondly." Karrak thought for a moment. "Malgabi. That's it. They refer to him as the Marc, but his accent betrays his origin farther south. It's almost gone, and he's done well to hide it, but it's there all the same. He's Nomish. I have no doubt."

"Malgabi!" Selanna said to herself in alarm. It was the connection she was searching for. She turned back to the king. "I am sorry, sire, but we must go."

"Right." Eraim pulled out her tools and eyed the cell door.

Selanna placed a hand on her companion's arm. "We cannot."

Eraim was thoroughly confused.

"It's all right," the king assured them. "I appreciate the loyalty, but I am no thief in the night. I am a prisoner of war, and shall remain so. Escape in such a way would shame me in the eyes of Brondor, and I would certainly fall from His graces if I allow it to happen."

Eraim's shoulders slumped and she put the tools away, staring sadly upon the king.

"Go now," Karrak urged them, and even in rags he appeared regal. "You've stayed longer than you should, and I'm happy to have seen another friendly face. But I will not have you imprisoned or killed on my account."

"Until we meet again." Selanna's eyes welled up.

The king nodded with an encouraging smile.

They slipped back down the corridor. Selanna's heart was filled with sorrow, so much so that she nearly walked into Eraim as they reached the door. Eraim had stopped abruptly and her head was cocked to one side.

"They are not so loud anymore," she pointed out.

Selanna realized the laughter of the jailers had ceased. Peeking through the barred window, she saw only three of the guards present and the card game had ended.

"Apparently the king's outburst has sobered them. But there is something I can do." Selanna waved her hands and whispered a chant. After a few seconds, she ceased and turned to her companion. "It should be safe now."

Eraim picked the lock and opened the squeaky door to reveal the guards fast asleep. Taking in a deep breath and holding it, Eraim walked quickly across the room and through the opposite door. Selanna followed, breathing normally and matching Eraim's pace.

No one stood in their way while they made it back through the storage room and into the filthy corridor. After sliding the secret door back into place, they moved swiftly down the long tunnel and up the ladder. They exited into the trees and Eraim held the trapdoor in place while Selanna used her powers to fasten one of the bolts.

It was still a couple hours before dawn, and Eraim turned to Selanna with troubled eyes.

"I do not understand," Eraim said. "If his loyal subjects stay their hands only because he is a prisoner, as he claims, his escape could put things to right."

"He would have to turn his back on Brondor," Selanna tried to explain. "That is something he would never do, just as neither you nor I would turn our backs on Galenfial."

"Or Vou?" Eraim raised her brow.

Though Eraim would never wholly understand the workings of Vou, Selanna knew her companion had as good an understanding of the Source of Magic as any non-mage. "Perhaps." Selanna offered half a smile.

"Has it anything to do with your strange Code?" Eraim referred to the cryptic Code of Wizards; a way of life most users of the arts followed to remain in Vou's good graces. "Something about 'not altering the fate of an individual' or such?"

"Something like that," Selanna muttered. She looked squarely at

Eraim. Her friend would never wholly understand. "Try to find solace in that he does not wish to be rescued."

"Would you rescue me if I were in need?" Eraim posed as they saddled up.

"Who could ever capture you?" Selanna chuckled. "And even so, *you* would not need *my* help. It would be the other way around."

"You begin to sound more like Elgarroth every day," Eraim said. "You do your best to not answer my questions."

"Why, thank you." Selanna accepted the compliment.

Chapter 31

Repentance

Selanna greatly desired to return to Vermallon to inform Elgarroth of her encounter with King Karrak, but she suspected her mentor already knew more than he had revealed. It did not escape Selanna's attention when King Karrak commented how nice it was to see *another* friendly face. So she and Eraim headed south, for Selanna also wished to speak with Vikur.

Kalmiran soldiers were stationed mainly within cities and several patrols marched upon the roads, so Selanna and Eraim stuck to traveling at night and remained within the wilderness. Selanna was surprised to find the path through Border Hills lightly manned and the journey across Marcove was almost effortless, but passing through Denvale proved tricky, for the city was swarming with soldiers, both Kalmirans and Marcs. Eraim procured a couple uniforms and they disguised themselves as guards, and though the outfits were baggy, it was a detail not easily distinguishable within the dark alleyways. When the hour was late, Selanna provided a small show of fireworks above the city to distract the tower guards, and she and Eraim slipped quietly onto the mountain pass.

The mountain road was barren, and to either side cliff walls rose steeply to heights of at least three hundred feet—a subterranean tunnel without a roof. Come morning, the wall to the right gave way to a sheer drop, and after another mile the pass followed a long curve to the north. The wind whipped, dancing with their clothing and coating them with mountain dust, and as the morning sun brightened the sky, they discarded the uniforms into the chasm. Shortly after, the road curled back to the west before turning south and the keep came into view—a magnificent structure carved into the face of the cliff at the apex of the curve.

Though Selanna had not been born at the time of its creation, she knew how, centuries ago, hundreds of men lost their lives when the king of Sardina decided to open trade with eastern lands and ordered the road to be built. The king was not aware of the large hobgoblin population within Mentrial Wood, nor the barbarian raiders of Nomedd, and the pass became an entry point for invaders. And so Grellmor, seven generations before Vikur's reign, commissioned the construction of Ironside Keep and spared no expense. This brought an end to the raids, as hobgoblins, bandits, and barbarians viewed the mountains as impassable once again, and over time the pass became a road for merchants and travelers, and the keep more of an inn than a fortress—the way Selanna had always known the stronghold to be. But now it was returned to its militant status, and a loud horn sounded as guards hurried about the tall towers and arrows were aimed at the road from the battlements. One of the guards evidently recognized Selanna and Eraim, and they could hear his shouts.

"Do not fire! Hold your fire! They are friends!"

At the top of the snaking path that led to the keep, the large portcullis began to lift. A guard then wound his way down to meet Selanna and Eraim, and Selanna released the magical energy she held ready, just in case any arrows had come.

"Morsum," Eraim whispered.

Selanna smiled. Her companion never seemed to miss the smallest of details, or forget even an unremarkable guard's name.

"Hello, Morsum." Selanna hailed the guard.

"His Lordship will be most happy to see *you* two!"

Morsum motioned back toward the gate, and a stable boy came running. After an angry snort and stomp of Lilli's hoof, Eraim decided to assist the lad.

Selanna followed Morsum into the keep, and right away she noticed additional changes since she had last visited. The most obvious was the Palidurian soldiers everywhere.

"Lord Vikur is in the training room with young Ballrik," the guard informed her. "But I'm sure he won't mind the interruption."

"I see you have company," Selanna said.

Morsum sighed. "Yeah. Reinforcements, they're called, from the Holy City. They outnumber us three to one. They even have their own commander, a paladin by the name of Krelnamir." He stopped and glanced about before speaking in a hushed voice. "He and Lord Vikur are often at odds with the organization of the keep."

They continued down the corridor.

"All has been especially stressful as of late," the soldier added. "Lord Arkor does not come around anymore, not since moving to Philen, and Poluran is visiting Rornibur. He's been gone a couple months now and I don't know when he'll return. I think the Palidurians make him uncomfortable. Lord Vikur spends most his time training Ballrik. It's probably the only thing that keeps him sane."

They reached their destination and Morsum opened a pair of doors. Beyond was a room Selanna recalled to have been used to host parties in the recent past, but now it was set up with dummies, targets, and the like, and Vikur was present, instructing his son on technique with a wooden sword. Ballrik had grown since Selanna last saw him, standing as high as his father's chin. He was a dozen years in age now and looked nothing like Vikur. Some claimed Ballrik took after Arkor in appearance, but Selanna realized the lad to possess the image of his late mother. Vikur halted the lesson and a large smile crossed his face.

"Selanna!"

He strode over and embraced her, and Selanna was a bit startled when her breath was squeezed from her body and her feet lifted from the floor. She might not have minded so much, had Vikur not been drenched in sweat.

"Hello, Vikur," she said after he released her, wiping the moisture from her arms and cheek. "And how are you, Ballrik?"

"Fair." The boy seemed grateful for the interruption.

"Let us leave this room," Vikur suggested. "The lounge will be much more comfortable…if it's not being used at the moment." The last comment was mumbled beneath his breath, but it did not escape Selanna's ears.

Vikur and Ballrik led Selanna down the hall without cleaning up or toweling off. Selanna wrinkled her nose in disgust. They entered the lounge, normally filled with patrons in the not-so-distant past, but now only a servant and Eraim occupied the large room. Eraim sat, drinking from a steaming cup Selanna was sure held tea, and Selanna was pleased to see Vikur treat her friend to the same welcome she had endured—she was further amused to hear the squeak and spat of outrage that ensued.

Vikur was immediately handed a tankard and he drank deeply. The servant seemed to assume Selanna wished for some hot tea and he placed a mug before her. She accepted it with a smile. Vikur drank deeply from his second mug before speaking of his situation.

"A few weeks ago, a paladin by the name of Trakinir shows up and offers assistance in watching over the pass." Vikur glanced about, almost as if making sure no one else was listening. "Though I did not desire any help, I could think of no justification to deny the request. But little did I know—"

The door opened and a warrior dressed in shining armor and a brown cape similar to the one Merssa normally donned entered. There was an air of arrogance about him as he approached, and with nothing more than a glance toward Selanna and Eraim, he whispered into Vikur's ear. The man's attempt to conceal the message failed, of course, and Selanna heard every word. Apparently her and Eraim's approach had stirred up the Palidurians, and the warrior was not pleased. As the man exited, Selanna was sure a smile formed briefly on Vikur's lips.

"That's Krelnamir," Vikur said with obvious sarcasm. "He's a subordinate to Merssa and was sent to make sure all is 'operating smoothly.'" He grinned. "You two gave them a little scare. So I guess that makes your visit even better!"

A breakfast consisting of eggs and bread was served, and the rest of the morning went uninterrupted while Vikur spoke of heroic deeds of his past. Some tales involved journeys Selanna and Eraim had been on as well, and though Selanna found many flaws with his facts, she said nothing. Once the meal was ended, Ballrik excused himself and eagerly left the room.

"We have been to see Xorlunder," Selanna said after the boy had gone.

Vikur took another deep drink, his mug shaking just a bit. "How is he?" he asked with a poor attempt to appear apathetic.

Selanna stared intently. "He informed us of additional facts involving the Serpent's Range and the orb."

Vikur sighed, gazing at the table and shaking his head. Then he slowly revealed his story in full, sparing Selanna his normal embellishments. She listened closely to every word.

"I did not think Tarm would come to this," Vikur admitted at the story's conclusion. "I didn't want to believe... I thought if I took the orb..."

Selanna placed a hand upon his arm. "You could not have known."

Selanna informed Vikur of King Karrak's imprisonment, and though Vikur was pleased the king still lived, he was deeply saddened. Selanna also warned Vikur not to get any ideas about entering Kalmaar, knowing him to be capable of action before thought, and once all was said, Vikur seemed relieved to have finally unburdened himself. They then enjoyed a glass of spiced wine.

The remainder of the day was spent wandering the keep, and Selanna found the inn rooms converted to barracks and storage — no evidence suggested the stronghold had ever served any other purpose. Vikur's soldiers seemed just as stressed as their lord, so Selanna and Eraim took a small amount of pleasure in teasing the

Palidurians. They received a few threats of banishment by Krelnamir, but Vikur informed the paladin they were guests of honor and to be treated as such. The following day they bade Vikur farewell, and though Vikur was disappointed, he understood and wished them well.

The path to Palidur was easy enough after that, and upon arrival Merssa called for a meeting of the High Order. Selanna informed the Order of their journey into Kalmaar, as well as Malgabi's involvement and Tarm's fascination with the orb, but Trakinir, Garren, and Jerove still failed to see a solid connection to Trannum.

"Malgabi may be nothing more than a link between Tarm and Gruzim," said Jerove. "I know the Council across the lake believes him to be a minion of the necromancer, but we do not know this for fact. We only know that the carelessness of the Council and a dwarf allowed the man to steal the orb. Perhaps he, himself, is using it to spread evil, as did Solett of Tenvale."

"Even if that were true," interjected Merssa, "we must find him and destroy the orb, lest we allow Trannum to claim it."

"I agree," said Soren. "But we know not where he resides, be him Marc or Nomish, and we cannot go walking into the eastern realms with an army to investigate. A small force must be assembled, one under a flag of peace and intent upon the orb and Malgabi only. As much as I am saddened by King Karrak's fate, we cannot be the justice for every land."

"And if we discover the matter goes beyond the orb," added Garren, "only then will further measures be considered."

"I would like to offer my services on this quest," said Selanna, receiving a glare from Garren, Trakinir, and Jerove.

"Nonsense!" Trakinir waved her off. "*I* will lead the force. One made of Palidurians."

After the meeting concluded, Merssa had Selanna and Eraim join her at her new living quarters. Members of the High Order were provided large, two-story homes, with the exception of the Soleran Sector of course, and it possessed more rooms than Merssa and Borse could ever find use for. But Merssa seemed pleased with it. After pleasant greetings with Borse, the priest poured them all a glass of wine and started a fire within an exquisite hearth adorned with angels bearing swords.

"Of course, it should be *me* leading the investigation into Malgabi," Merssa said, getting to business. "But I feel the more exposure they get to this evil, the more they'll understand. Regardless of their stubbornness, they are as much against the spread of evil as am I."

The last statement was rather optimistic for Merssa, Selanna thought, but as she watched Borse pat Merssa's hand, Selanna was sure it was he that counseled his wife to this thought pattern. Selanna found it rather agreeable. In the end, they would need the full support of Palidur, and Selanna knew Merssa could not muster that alone.

"I am not giving up on this matter," Selanna said while the others sipped from their goblets. "I will continue to find out what I can."

"I'm counting on that." Merssa's look was stern. Not *all* of the paladin's ways had vanished.

Over the next several months, Selanna made many trips into Kalmaar. Most were done without Eraim's assistance, as Eraim was busy with fact-finding missions elsewhere. Selanna reported to Merssa all movements of Tarm and his Benasti allies, and she also kept an eye and ear out for Malgabi, but it seemed the mysterious messenger had disappeared.

While traveling alone, Selanna employed a spell taught to her by Elgarroth, disguising herself as a human soldier. Under this guise, moving about the territory was generally an easy feat. She returned to Darmhorng once a month to see King Karrak, regardless of whether she had any news to share. On her seventh such visit, the year was late and early winter had already dropped enough snow to fill an entire season, and though the king could not see this, the prison walls emanated the chill of the outside air. Karrak appeared much older since the last time Selanna had seen him, but it was his eyes that concerned her. They were no longer sad, but worn.

"You need to end my misery," Karrak told Selanna.

"I cannot do that, my lord!" She spoke almost too loudly.

"I am never to see the light of day again," he said somberly. "And I will never die in battle, as I hoped. I gave away that chance to save those loyal to me. It is a coward's way, I know, but lately I've had this fear that they plan something dire for me. Something other than what they've revealed. I do not wish to become anything other than what I am."

Selanna could not hold back her tears as the king sat before her, a defeated warrior surrendering all that remained of his dismal life. She did not wish to relinquish hope that he would one day rule again, but she knew it would never come to be. She could not take his life, but a thought occurred to her.

"Perhaps I *can* help," she murmured softly. "I will be back."

With a deep breath, Selanna made her way to the guardroom. Two jailers were playing cards, one was asleep, and two others were sharpening swords. Leaning against the wall, not far from the door, Selanna spied a battleaxe next to the cot of the sleeping guard, and an incantation formed upon her lips. The weapon lifted just above the floor and slowly floated toward her. At one point a guard glanced around and Selanna halted its motion, but the other jailer ordered him to play a card and he returned to his game. Selanna continued her spell until the weapon was within reach, and she opened the door just enough to grab it before returning swiftly to the king's cell.

"Take this." She handed Karrak the axe. She then concentrated upon the cell door and the lock opened with an easy incantation. "You shall have your battle!"

King Karrak smiled and stepped from the cell. He placed a fatherly hand on Selanna's shoulder and brushed a tear from her cheek, and then headed for the guardroom, leaving his smile behind.

Selanna watched from the doorway as Karrak strode proudly into the room and brought looks of shock to the guards. The unarmored king, well into his seventies, wielded the axe like a champion and a great battle ensued. He slew two jailers before the sleeping soldier woke and joined the fray, and then a sword sliced Karrak's left arm, rendering it useless. The king continued with the weapon in his right hand and killed a third guard, and Selanna gasped when a blade pierced deep into his stomach, feeling the cold steel as if it were she that had been struck. King Karrak took down the final two soldiers with one mighty swing before collapsing to the floor.

Selanna rushed into the chamber. Karrak was covered in blood, both his and that of the jailers', and he gazed at her and coughed. Then his lips formed a smile.

"Thank you…" was all Karrak managed before passing from the Realm of the Living.

"May Brondor accept you into His halls with open arms, my lord." Selanna closed his eyes.

"He was a great warrior," came a voice from the iron door that led into the castle. It was Tarm.

Selanna rose, feeling great ire stir within. She took in a deep breath to gain control of her emotions.

Tarm entered, eyeing the dead guards before turning his gaze to Karrak. "I had the utmost respect for him."

"Yes, I can see that!" Selanna snapped. "You shall pay dearly for your deeds before it is over."

"Yes," Tarm said, barely above a whisper. "I most certainly will."

Selanna eyed him suspiciously. Tarm's sword was sheathed and his hand never drifted near the pommel, but she found herself wishing he would draw it and give her a reason to destroy him.

"I have no intention of attacking you." Tarm smiled, as if seeing Selanna's thoughts. "I've known many wizards, and from what I have learned of your Code, you cannot harm me unless I threaten you. Is that not right?"

Selanna glared at the pompous man. He was more or less correct, though he did not completely understand. The Code of Vou forbade her to strike down a mortal who posed no threat to her, but there were ways around that particular law. In this case, however, Selanna would not insult the Keeper of Magic with technicalities.

"I *will* pay, indeed." Tarm's smile failed. "I have done a great evil...and there is no way to make it right."

"Who is your master?" Selanna demanded. "Where is the orb?"

Tarm looked away. "I was tricked. That damned orb! It filled my head with evil thoughts... Desires that were not my own. It distorted everything!" He shook his head, suddenly angry. "And that blasted Malgabi! I am nothing but a puppet!"

Selanna began to wonder if Tarm remembered she was in the room

"And now," he turned her way, "they're digging up the dead!"

"The dead?"

"Ancient crypts." A glint of insanity was in Tarm's eyes. "The Royal Crypts of Kalmaar. Malgabi brought orders to recover the bodies of two kings of old: Cadorn and Radaam. The blasted Marc also sent Gruzim's soldiers into Benasti to find the grave of one called Anduiff...Some krukari king from centuries ago. I'm surprised those corpses didn't rise with the rest of them when the Wind of the Dead plagued the land."

"Whom does Malgabi speak for?" Selanna asked. "Who is his master?"

Tarm stared blankly before answering. "We both know that answer. But I fear to utter the name."

Selanna furrowed her brow. "What use has he for dead kings?"

Tarm shrugged. "No good, I promise that." He stared with his mouth open, as if he wished to say more, and for a moment he appeared the noble Duke of Kalmaar and not a power-driven rebel. Then he found his voice. "Will you grant me a great favor?"

Selanna wanted desperately to spit on him, but she was caught off guard when tears welled in his eyes.

"What would you ask of me?" She said the words slowly, her eyes darting back and forth from Tarm to the stairwell leading into the castle. Was he stalling?

"I know you have been visiting him." Tarm looked again at the king's corpse. "It took me a while to figure out how, but I discovered the tunnel."

Selanna was alarmed. "How long have you known?"

"A few months." He shook his head. "I guess part of me was hoping you would rescue him…but…"

"What is it you wish of me?"

"Meet me at the tunnel's end," Tarm said. "I will be there shortly."

Selanna looked at Tarm, and every fiber of her being begged her not to trust him. But curiosity got the better of her and she nodded.

Exiting the dungeon, Selanna followed the tunnel until emerging through the trapdoor. She half expected to find soldiers waiting in ambush, but only Dandi was present within the trees. Nearly half an hour passed, and Selanna was about to leave when a noise came from below. Tarm climbed out of the tunnel bearing a small bundle of blankets, and Selanna heard a baby fussing within.

"Mayry has blessed me with a child at last." Tarm beamed. "A boy, after all these years. I never thought I would see the day."

Selanna gazed at the man, unsure, and his smile faded.

"Take him." Tarm held forth the bundle. "I do not wish for him to be raised here…amongst all this." He gazed at the many bonfires in the distance, visible through the trees to the east. "Never tell him of his parents. Never tell him…"

"What am I to do with a human child?" Selanna stared in disbelief.

"You shall think of something." He choked down a lump in his throat. "You must do this not for me, but for him. He is innocent. Please, give him a chance."

Selanna accepted the child.

"Goodbye, my son." A tear rolled down Tarm's cheek as he kissed the infant one last time.

"What is his name?" Selanna inquired, suddenly moved to sorrow for a person she desperately wanted to hate.

"I wish him nothing from his mother or myself." Tarm shook his head. "Any name we have given him must be lost."

Selanna nodded and climbed onto her horse, cradling the baby in one arm. She looked hard at Tarm, noticing the same worn look she had seen in King Karrak's eyes. "I hope you find peace."

Her feelings were trapped between shock and confusion, and she realized several moments had passed without another word. Selanna cleared her throat and rode off into the night.

CHAPTER 32

TAKES THE KINGS...

Merssa sat in her church alone. The turmoil beyond the mountains was ever on her mind, and the most recent news Selanna brought, the pillaging of dead kings, certainly played a part in the Prophecy of Trannum. *"Takes the land, takes the kings,"* Eraim had recited before the High Order, but they would not hear it, save for Nilborg. Soren was still not wholly convinced and genuinely feared the killing of innocents, so Merssa could not fault the Soleran paladin, but the others maintained the opinion that it was the mere conquest of a duke to become king and all else was supposition. Merssa sometimes wondered if the Order did not fear Trannum enough, or if they feared him too much.

Not even the disappearance of Trakinir persuaded the Order to take stronger actions. The High Paladin of Arronaus set out with a company of ten last summer on a quest to find Malgabi, but there had been no word from them. In Trakinir's absence, a temporary replacement was elected to the High Order, an event unheard of in the city's long history. Hubrid had been one of Garren's loyal followers for as long as Merssa could remember, and she shared many confrontations with the young paladin before rising to her current rank. She suspected this fact served as motivation for choosing him. But Hubrid could not be fully promoted to High Paladin, for he had yet to fulfill his obligations to the city, and therefore he was not allowed to vote on Palidur affairs. If only Rholmar had not moved to Philen, he would certainly occupy the chair where Hubrid now sat. Then Merssa would have a fair chance to argue her beliefs. And maybe then she could gather the votes necessary to execute a proper plan.

Though the continuing strife plagued her mind, Merssa also had cause to celebrate. Selanna had brought to Merssa an infant boy to raise as her own. Borse was excited as well, but not so much as Merssa, for she had given up hope that the day would come when a baby would need her love. Selanna would not reveal from where the child had come, nor any information of his past, but Merssa chose not to press the mage and rejoiced in her good fortune. She named him Cavalor, after her grandfather, and left his side only when duty called.

And so, Merssa sat in her church, praying to Cafior for guidance. On one hand there was what she believed to be the greatest evil since the Uustaag gathering in the northwest, and on the other hand there were the immediate needs of her son. In the end, she knew duty would prevail. The High Order could prevent Merssa from sending a Palidurian force to investigate matters further, but they could not stop her from gathering a contingent of Cafior warriors. She knew Jerove would frown upon such actions, but she could stay put no longer. The sentinels placed within Nira and Ironside Keep would not be enough to thwart Trannum once the necromancer chose to renew his attack.

Later that evening, Merssa and Borse discussed the matter at length. Borse was supportive of her convictions, and he admitted to feeling a disturbing presence he had not felt since his days in Neja, distant as it was. By dawn, it was decided Borse would care for their son while Merssa led an expedition to uncover the truth once and for all.

"Who better to begin Cavalor's teachings than you, after all?" Merssa teased, to which Borse gave a sympathetic smile.

Merssa put off her departure until spring's thaw, and was deeply saddened when the day arrived to bid Cavalor and Borse farewell. She led a group of twenty warriors to Ironside Keep to speak with

Krelnamir, the paladin commander she had placed there, and upon arrival Vikur gave her a strange look. It took Merssa only a moment to realize the cause of his distress.

"I am not adding to your numbers," she assured him of the soldiers in her company. "They are with me, and will depart when I do."

"That's good news." Vikur appeared as though the world had been lifted from his shoulders.

Krelnamir had little to report, much to Merssa's dismay, for life on the pass was uneventful.

"Other than the elves, Selanna and Eraim," Krelnamir appeared to have tasted something sour while he uttered the names, "nothing has approached from the east since I've been here. The only challenge has been keeping the men focused."

Merssa remained at the keep for a couple days to question others, but there was nothing more to learn. So she returned to Sardina and headed north.

It rained on and off while she led her contingent through Sendorum, but Merssa cared not, for it mirrored her mood, and Vermallon Road was abandoned and nothing hindered her passing — bandits would not dare attack a squadron of Palidurians and there were no Vermallon elves, at least none that were seen. Upon entering Nira, Merssa was surprised to find winter had not ended there. Snow was scattered in patches and became more constant nearer the bridges, and beyond the river were settled large armies with Kalmiran flags flying high and Benasti banners just beneath them. The Palidurians stationed north of the bridge reported no attempts by the enemy to advance.

"We have them contained, my lady," reported the commander of the area. "But truth be known, it seems they're content. Perhaps the war is over. Maybe they're satisfied with what they have."

"Perhaps," Merssa responded, not believing the assumption for a moment. The enemy was not stalled, merely waiting. What Trannum was waiting for, Merssa did not know, and she desperately wished to gain a firsthand look at things Selanna reported. Perhaps Merssa might discover something the mage had missed. But she lacked the skills of Selanna and Eraim, and she would have to rely on their eyes.

Feeling her mission had been a waste of time, the desire to return to Borse and Cavalor grew strong. But Merssa was determined to learn something of use and headed to Tikken City.

Heavy rains continued to pound Sendorum, drenching her and her men and coating them with a layer of mud, but the sun burned through the clouds over Virch and provided early summer warmth. Merssa was grateful for this and appreciated the chance to clean from the rode and bathe the horses. Upon crossing Korban Bridge, the clouds vanished and it seemed summer was in full swing over Moclen.

Merssa arrived to Tikken City and was granted immediate audience with the Council of Wizards, but upon reaching the audience chamber, she found Seac alone.

"I was hoping to speak with the entire Council," she said. "I have come to learn more of the names Cadorn, Radaam, and Anduiff."

"Indeed, I anticipated this." The Seer's shoulders slumped slightly. "And I have the information you seek."

Merssa nodded. "Please proceed."

"Cadorn was a great and evil king of Kalmaar over a thousand years ago, before even the Ancient Enemy of the North was known," Seac said. "He ruled through fear and was most known for his unmatched skill in combat. He bullied his subjects, killing them when it pleased him, and ruled for many years until his demise at a feast, when he drank poisoned wine. No one knew who performed the deed, but many were grateful.

"Radaam also ruled over Kalmaar, nearly three hundred years later. He worshipped the dark deity, Thard'Dun, and was skilled in both battle and the magical arts. His reputation for torture was renown in his day, and made him one of the most feared rulers in the kingdom's history. It was rumored he killed his own sons so that no one thought of taking his throne, and he claimed he found a spell to grant him immortality. In the end, he died at his own hands when the spell went awry.

"Anduiff was the original Lord of Benasti, about the same time as Radaam's reign. The evil lord pillaged lands from Selt to Virch, showing mercy to no one, and of all krukari throughout history, it was said his treachery was the darkest since the Ancient Enemy. His life was claimed by old age within his evil woodland."

Merssa pondered the Seer's words as a chill crept up her spine and into her scalp. What could Trannum possibly want with these corpses? She was not sure she wanted to find out.

"But there's more," Seac said. "Our scouts have reported other dead kings being taken as well. There is Jurack of Beit, Dunuthar of Selt, and Gulthar of Marcove. Each was evil and terrible in their time, and it is rumored the body of Velgaad was discovered."

"The dwarf king that brought about the fall of Lornibur?" Merssa asked. It was taught in Palidur that Lornibur was the birthplace to all dwarves. But during the reign of King Velgaad, the underground city fell into darkness, forcing the dwarves to wander Vaeldor in search of new homes and forming the clans that existed today. From what Merssa had learned, the body of the king was dismantled by his subjects as punishment for his acts, and the pieces were dispersed about Lornibur before the city was intentionally collapsed.

Seac nodded. "Histories are sketchy, but all agree that he fell into evil ways out of greed. It is believed he existed in the days of Cadorn, and that the two schemed together at times."

Merssa shook her head. "What are Trannum's plans with these corpses?"

"We do not know, alas," the Seer said somberly. "We attempted to find an answer from the orb, but have been without success."

A sudden horror overcame Merssa. "What about—"

Seac held up a hand, as if anticipating the question.

"The body of the Ancient Enemy of the North was never seen again after the Battle of Balgorn, when the wizard, Welmirth, felled the mighty warlord in his own citadel and cast him into Balgorn River. That was a long, long time ago, and I doubt even Trannum would know where to begin looking for it."

"That does not mean—"

"Selanna feared as you do, and she rode to the north to speak with the Guardians of Lothen Forest, only to find from the elves that there has been no activity in the desolate realm of Helmland. It remains an uninhabitable wasteland."

"Where is Selanna now?" Merssa had not seen the elf in nearly six months, and she was growing concerned.

"I believe she left for Vermallon Forest," Seac replied. "Perhaps to speak with Elgarroth. That was over a month ago, and from there, I know not her destination."

"I would request you send word to me in Palidur immediately upon her return," Merssa said, to which Seac nodded.

She bade him farewell and returned to her men.

Three months had passed since Merssa's journey began, and there was little to show for it. Her work was far from done, for she barely knew more than before she left the Holy City, but her desire to see Cavalor and Borse was too strong to bear. Merssa returned home.

Several years went by, and Merssa spent her time carrying out her duties, raising her son, and loving her husband. The enemy in the east remained in the east and there was still no sign of Selanna—even Eraim was alarmed with the mage's long absence. News of events across the Varlimor Mountains was then scarce and proof of Trannum's involvement never surfaced. The Wind of the Dead drifted into myth and legend, and though Merssa always seemed happy with her family life, the future for Cavalor held her in fear.

With the High Order, Merssa's relationship was forever tainted, save with that of Nilborg and Soren, and she was especially disappointed in Jerove. She had hoped for more support from the

High Priest of her order. The disappearance of Trakinir was never resolved and another company was sent to look for him, but no sign of the paladin could be found, nor the company he led. There were many attempts to convince Merssa to step down from the High Order, but she would not do so. She could not, for they needed constant reminding of the sleeping evil beyond the mountains. Merssa's only hope was that it would not be too late before action was taken.

Chapter 33

Ironside Keep

Vikur sat in the lounge of Ironside Keep, sipping from a glass of wine and feeling more at home than he had in a long time. Over six years had passed since the High Order of Palidur sent soldiers to aid in the watch over the mountain road, and in all that time there had not been so much as a spy attempting to sneak by in the night.

Vikur marveled to find the warriors of the Holy City still immersed in their duties. Though their arrival had been viewed as a major inconvenience at first, the relationship between Vikur and his "guests" had greatly eased. Even the strife between him and Krelnamir had subsided. Vikur remembered when he and the paladin spent much of their waking hours in verbal confrontations, disagreeing on the best ways to deploy soldiers and protect the pass. Vikur was Lord of the Keep and had trained his entire life for that very task, but Krelnamir had other views. Over the past few years, however, they grew close, sharing meals, telling stories, and conferring on most military decisions. Now, they were like old friends.

After the first year of the watch had passed, Palidur began rotating soldiers. Half of the guards would be granted leave as new recruits took their place, and six months later the second half would journey home when the next contingent arrived. Only Krelnamir's position remained unchanged, for the Holy Knight of Cafior swore to keep his post until the matter was resolved.

"Lady Merssa is correct in this matter," Krelnamir told Vikur at one point over a glass of wine after dinner. "There is more to the uprising in Kalmaar than just mere conquest. Of all of Palidur, only the High Paladin Merssa has faced Trannum, and she alone knows of the great evil the undead wizard poses. It matters not that she has found no proof to convince the remainder of the High Order. I know in my heart she is correct, and I will not waver."

Vikur had faced the necromancer as well, and he fully agreed. But not all Palidurians felt as Krelnamir, and Vikur overheard a few of the most recent arrivals grumbling about "Lady Merssa keeping the orders alive," and how Nilborg was "still following the beliefs of the Cafior paladin." But they did not dare mention such things within earshot of Krelnamir.

During the winter of the third year of Palidur's support, Vikur began looking forward to the arrival of new soldiers. Krelnamir finally trusted Vikur to train the recruits, offering little interference, and since the winters had grown long, the final traces of snow lasting until early summer, training was all that existed to keep Vikur busy — that is, when he was not honing his son's skills. Over the past couple years, however, Ballrik had grown restless and a bit rebellious, so Vikur accepted Krelnamir's assistance in the matter. Ballrik's interests were renewed at learning some of the Palidurian ways, and Vikur found the lessons fascinating as well, though a bit conservative for his liking.

It was now mid-autumn. The mountain pass had already accumulated enough snow to fill an entire winter, the cold season having begun earlier than even last year's, and it was wearing upon Vikur's bones. The wine in his glass did little to warm him, but he preferred to save the ale for when Poluran returned from Rornibur. Then they would drain a few kegs to get through the frigid months! Though Poluran called Ironside home, the dwarf always spent the last month of autumn within the Stone Eagle Mountains.

"I best keep my affairs there in order," Poluran would reason. "No telling what trouble they'll get into if I stay away too long."

With the early snowfall, Vikur hoped the road to the keep could still be traversed.

His thoughts were interrupted when Ballrik entered. Now eighteen years in age, Ballrik had grown into a fine warrior. The resemblance between them ended there, however, as Vikur saw more of Arkor in the lad than himself. Though Vikur had not seen his brother in almost a decade, it was as if the one-armed warrior still roamed the stone halls, for Ballrik exhibited the same attitude toward the keep Arkor had: always wishing for a more eventful life someplace else.

"The stores are full." Ballrik gave his report with obvious disinterest. "We should have enough supplies for six months. Maybe the sun will shine by then." The last part he mumbled to himself, though it did not escape Vikur's ears.

"The winters are long, I know." Vikur felt his patience waning. "But let's not be bitter already. It has only just begun."

"Yes, sir." Ballrik did not even fake respect.

Vikur bit his tongue. He knew his son wished for warmer surroundings and freedom to travel. The lad had hinted on more than one occasion that he wanted to live with Uncle Arkor in Philen.

"I don't understand why you're so loyal to this place," Ballrik muttered, acting more ambitious than usual. "It's just an elaborate cave, after all."

"For generations, our family has vowed to protect the pass. And our word holds as strong now as ever." How long had it been since Vikur's father said the same words to him? When he exhibited the same indifferent attitude? The thought made Vikur feel slightly ill, but he continued with the lecture. "One day the responsibility will fall onto you."

"I don't want to be tied to this place!" Ballrik glanced at the walls, as if they were moving in. "You speak of countless travels and battles. *I* want to travel. *I* want adventure."

Vikur remembered saying those words himself. Now *he* was the enemy. "Why don't you see to your other duties."

Ballrik left the room, mumbling many more choice words beneath his breath.

Vikur awoke with a start. A low drone filled his ears—a horn was sounding. The fire still burned high within the hearth, so he had not been sleeping long, and he became annoyed with Krelnamir for running a drill at such an hour. As Vikur's head cleared, he realized it was no drill, for he detected distant calls and shouts.

Grabbing his sword, Vikur hurried to the window and pulled open the shutter. His room was located in the central and tallest tower, granting him a full view of the rest of the keep as well as the road below, but a frigid breeze greeted him and he could hardly make out the other towers through a thick curtain of snow. The horn continued to blare from the east tower, a warning that something approached from the direction of Marcove, but the night revealed nothing as far as Vikur could see.

He poked his head through the window for a better look, and within the east tower Vikur saw silhouettes of three guards. One guard was at the horn while the other two fired crossbows into the snowy night. Vikur peered onto the pass again, following the direction of their fire, and strained to penetrate the veil. A mass of dark shapes was slowly approaching!

The figures bore no torches, and the front ranks seemed to be using shields to push snow into the chasm to the north. Several of the plowmen tumbled into the gorge as well, disappearing into the depths, but the dark horde continued its pace. Vikur stared in disbelief, wondering how an army could march under such conditions. Beyond that, they should have perished from the cold, if not the treachery the snow brought to the road. Then Vikur held his breath. Within the mass he spied many sets of cold blue dots glowing faintly in the night. It was a familiar sight, burned into memory from years ago.

"Dunarchins!"

It was not an army of Kalmirans or Marcs that approached, but a legion of undead!

Horns sounded from the north tower, above the gate and below Vikur's room—a high-pitched tone signaling the keep was under attack. Vikur thought it odd, for the undead were still several minutes away, and he quickly donned his chain shirt and raced from the bedchamber with his sword in hand.

"Ballrik!" he called as he sped down the tower steps and neared his son's room.

The young warrior stepped through the door with sword in hand, sleep evident in his eyes. "What's happening?"

"Stay close," Vikur ordered and continued downward.

They entered the center of the Great Hall, a long chamber connecting to all towers. Palidurian soldiers were scattered and rushing to their posts, some half suited in armor, and they proved quickly their value, as none were panicked and all remembered their training of the stronghold's defenses.

Vikur headed immediately for the east tower, for the screaming of its horn had ceased. Before he arrived, Krelnamir came rushing from its stairwell with a look of horror.

"What is it?" Vikur shouted above the din.

Krelnamir was pale and stared blankly, as if Vikur was not there. But then the paladin blinked and was suddenly aware.

"Wraiths!" He shuddered. "Wraiths flew into the tower. We never saw them coming. They have been destroyed, but I am the only survivor."

"The other towers!" Vikur looked over his shoulder and then back to Krelnamir. "We'll take the north. You check the west."

Krelnamir nodded and sped off.

"You three!" Vikur hailed soldiers rushing through the hall, halting them in their tracks. "Man the east tower. See why the catapult is not firing. And set fire to your arrows. It's the undead we face!"

"Yes, sir!" They moved quickly up the steps.

Vikur ran to the north tower with Ballrik on his heels. As they reached the door, an inhuman screech greeted them and two wraiths passed through the cracks of the portal. Their eyes were bright with hatred upon their shadowy bodies and they immediately attacked.

Vikur jumped back, knocking Ballrik to the floor—his son had been following a bit closer than he realized. The first wraith streaked past, but the second struck Vikur, its icy hand passing effortlessly through his chain shirt and flesh. He felt the chill of death as the phantom grasped at his heart, but he would not be taken so easily. Bringing down his sword, a blade handed down through generations, Vikur caught the creature by surprise. Though most weapons passed harmlessly through their ghostly forms, it tasted the steel edge of his blade and its link to the living world was severed. It dispersed into a hissing black mist that quickly dissipated.

The other wraith held Ballrik pinned to the floor, one of its dark claws clutching the lad's throat and the other reaching into his chest. Ballrik writhed in pain as he struggled to breathe, and the sight was more than Vikur could bear. He brought his blade in a vicious arc as he roared with rage, and by the time he refocused, Ballrik was gasping at his feet while blackish smoke momentarily filled the air.

"Let's get out of here!" Ballrik coughed, slowly climbing to his feet. His eyes were wide with horror.

"Pick up your sword!" commanded Vikur, spying the blade on the floor. "They will *not* take the keep!"

At that moment, Vikur heard a distant crash. The gate was under attack.

"To the gate!"

Vikur ran down the hall to the open iron door accessing the lower levels. Ballrik followed with sword in hand, but the lad's pace was hampered, as the life-draining effect of the wraith's touch had evidently left him in a weakened state. Vikur could not afford to wait, and he descended the long stairwell to the entry chamber.

Upon arrival he found the large entry doors smashed and the portcullis twisted in a way no mortal hands could have accomplished.

A score of zombies and skeletons littered the floor, as the Palidurians stood tall in defense of the keep, but more undead poured through the breach and dunarchins were close behind.

With a battle cry, Vikur jumped into the fray. He hewed heads and limbs from all that opposed him, rarely needing more than a single swing…until he reached the dunarchins. Faced with the more challenging foe, Vikur changed his mode of attack, taking care to pay a bit more attention to defense, and slew four of the creatures. The morale of the guards rose high and they were filled with renewed strength, and Ballrik arrived at last, taking out a pair of undead in Vikur's wake.

Three dunarchin mages entered, and energy crackled between their bony fingers. They launched lightning, dropping three soldiers to torturous deaths, but Palidurian archers arrived through a nearby door and fired upon them. It took twice the arrows than it would have for living foes, but the bowmen were swift, exhibiting speed to almost rival that of elves, and the mages were destroyed before their lightning brought too much damage.

At last, the chamber was cleared and all was quiet. More than two score of undead littered the floor, along with the bodies of eight guards, and the soldiers glanced about uneasily while awaiting the next wave. When nothing was seen or heard, they cheered in victory.

Vikur bled from a few wounds, but felt no pain as he gazed at the twisted gate. The pass had been plagued with undead and surely they were not defeated, but nothing else entered through the battered doors except for loose snow upon a chilled wind. The cold then grew more intense, and Vikur's breath obscured his vision as fear crept into his body. The room fell silent and he turned to find the keep's defenders pale with fright—four of them dropped their weapons and ran screaming up the stairs. Ballrik was among those brave enough to hold their ground, and they all viewed Vikur with wide, questioning eyes.

From outside came a hollow roar that ended in a long hiss. In all his days, Vikur had never heard such a sound and he shuddered. The snow began to swirl as large, flapping wings drew near, and the hair on the back of Vikur's neck stood when a dark thought entered his mind: Trannum has come! The fallen defenders of the keep began to moan and stir—their corpses had transformed into zombies, as if the Wind of the Dead had returned!

The fear rolling in the pit of Vikur's stomach grabbed a firm hold. "Fall back! We're sealing off the level!"

The soldiers eagerly complied and ran up the narrow steps. Vikur and Ballrik followed, stopping to force the first iron door closed and dropping its bar into place. At that moment, Vikur realized allies might still be present within the lower levels of the keep, but there was no turning back. Halfway up the stairs, the second door squealed in protest, but Ballrik joined Vikur and it shut with an echoing *boom*. They continued upward, returning to the Great Hall, and closed and barred the third and final door.

The sound of battle still raged within the west tower, and from the east approached five guards with weapons ready. They were pale and sighed in relief at the sight of Vikur.

"We dispatched wraiths in the north tower," one of the men reported. "But it was costly. We lost better than a dozen men."

"What about the catapults?" Vikur asked.

"They are snowed in and the wind is strong." The guard shook his head in despair. "Even if we try to dig them out, wraiths circle them like hawks."

Vikur turned to his son. "Ballrik. Take those three." He waved a hand at three of the Palidurian archers. "Give aid to Krelnamir in the west tower."

Ballrik nodded and did as instructed, though reluctance was obvious in his eyes.

That left Vikur with one archer and nine guards, three of which were of little use as they leaned heavily upon one another to remain standing. Vikur turned to watch Ballrik speed away, touched by the fear he might never see his son again in this lifetime.

Dread suddenly captured the Great Hall as the air became frigid and frost crept along the seams of the iron door leading to the lower levels. Vikur backed away with his blade held ready.

"Stand your ground!"

He issued the order, but did not look to be sure the soldiers complied. He waited, expecting a battering ram to come next, or that of an iron door being blasted from its hinges, but that was not the case. There was a distant *clang*, followed by the creaking of the first door slowly swinging open. Moments later, another *clang* sounded and the second door swung open.

Vikur detected the nervous rattling of armor. "Hold your ground!" Looking over his shoulder, he noted the fear in the soldiers' eyes. "They will not take the keep!"

All was quiet. Even the battle within the west tower had ceased — either Ballrik and the reinforcements had helped, or… Vikur could not finish the thought. His attention was drawn to the distinct sound of a single pair of metal boots walking casually up the stone steps. The aura of terror increased as the sound stopped just beyond the iron door, and several guards retreated a few paces. Five wraiths then issued through the cracks of the door, ignoring the hall's occupants and immediately lifting the iron bar. While the wraiths went about their task, the dozen or so corpses within the hall began to rise.

"No!" shouted Vikur, rushing the door.

Two of the dark spirits abandoned the iron bar to meet him. Vikur quickly slew the first, then twisted from the reaching claws of the second before returning it to the Realm of the Dead.

The heavy bar hit the floor.

The remaining wraiths attacked Vikur as the door swung open, and a rush of frigid air swept over the hall while the guards fought the newly risen zombies. Vikur slew two more wraiths, but the final one leaped onto his back and knocked him to the floor, its claws sinking deep into his weary body. He could no longer find the strength to lift his arms in defense, and through blurred vision he saw a dark, heavily armored figure step through the open iron door. From its helmet shone a set of pale blue eyes, similar to that of a dunarchin's, but Vikur could tell this was something much worse. His eyes closed and he saw nothing more.

CHAPTER 34

ONE WINTRY DAY

It was the harshest winter Nilborg could recall. Though only halfway through, the sky had dumped enough snow upon Palidur to fill two such seasons, and every day brought more chilled winds from the southeast, riding dark clouds that rarely revealed the sun's light. Winter months normally presented little hindrance in northern Sardina, and passing in and out of Palidur was seldomly a difficult task. Even through the coldest stretches, the King Arman hardly accumulated enough ice to make a difference and transport by ship was always a viable route. But this winter was different. Though the city was well maintained—horses, plows, shovels, and wagons were used to keep the roads clear and cart snow outside the walls—the surrounding lands did not fare so well and travel outside Palidur was non-existent. A thick layer of ice covered the shoreline and extended beyond sight, imprisoning all ships within the harbor as well.

Nilborg sat at his desk, gazing out the window at the falling snow. He sighed. The next meeting of the High Order was to be held in a week, and he worried that Soren and Merssa would not be able to return in time. Being his only allies in all decisions concerning Trannum, Nilborg feared what might happen in their absence. Almost three months prior, weeks before the first snowflakes touched the tall white buildings of the city, the two paladins left on a holiday for Philen. They were dear friends to Rholmar, Duke of West Palidur, and wished to be present for the birth of the duke's first child. Nilborg desired to be there himself, but Palidur law demanded at least one member of the High Order from each sector remain within the city at all times. So he feigned fatigue when Soren offered to stay—at Nilborg's age, it was an easy thing to do.

Three soldiers donning dark-blue cloaks came rushing in. They panted heavily, and upon their faces was alarm.

"Your Excellence!" one said as they bowed.

Nilborg felt his heart pick up speed. "Yes?"

"There appear to be fires to the south and east. Many fires. It looks as if Courtin and Dellabville are alight."

Nilborg rose. The villages were not far away and had always been in good standing with the city, especially with that of the Soleran Sector. The winter had been so harsh that there had been no contact with any of their citizens in a month.

"Are you sure they are not bonfires?" Nilborg asked. "Perhaps lit for warmth?"

"They are not, Your Excellence," the soldier replied. "The smoke is black and very thick."

Nilborg sat again, staring blankly at his desk. In his mind Merssa's voice rang out: *Trannum is behind this*. "Alert the other sectors," he said. "And put together a couple squadrons to investigate."

"But the snow—"

"We must find a way!"

Nilborg's harsh tone caused the soldier to flinch. But the man nodded, exhibiting both uneasiness and embarrassment, and the three departed as swiftly as they had arrived.

Alone again, Nilborg sighed heavily. Could it be Trannum's doing? Or was Tarm marching on Palidur? For the latter to be true, either Ironside Keep had been defeated, a task not easily performed, or the line of defense about Vermallon Forest, including thousands of elves, the Niran army, and Palidurian troops, had failed. Or what if neither had occurred? What if the fires were simply coincidence? No. Two villages do not go up in flames, not at the same time. Nilborg saw no choice but to call for an emergency meeting.

The Order met less than an hour later. Besides Nilborg, present were Jerove of Cafior and Garren and Hubrid of Arronaus, Hubrid having been fully promoted to High Paladin only last year. Nilborg relayed the news, but realized the others were already aware.

"And what do you expect us to make of this?" Garren raised a brow.

"That something evil is afoot," Nilborg replied. "We must take action immediately."

"And whom do you expect we'll find behind it all?" Jerove asked, but did not wait for an answer. "Trannum?"

"That is irrelevant!" Nilborg grew hot. "Whether Trannum, Tarm, or some other evil, it demands our immediate attention."

"Did you not already send scouts to investigate?" posed Garren.

"I did."

"Then I suggest we await their findings before we rise up in arms," Garren said. "Perhaps too many fires were lit for warmth. It is, after all, a difficult season upon us. There's no sense placing our city in a state of emergency for sheer carelessness, is there?"

"Let us vote on the matter," Jerove suggested with a wave, and Garren nodded.

After a show of hands, the result was three to one, with the High Order deciding to take no further action until the scout parties returned.

Nilborg shook his head. Without another word, he exited.

Two days later, the scouts returned and were immediately escorted to the Grand Cathedral, where the High Order was assembled and waiting.

"What news do you bring?" asked Jerove once the meeting was called to order.

"It is grave, Your Excellencies," the lead figure said. "The villages are indeed burning, but it is more dire than that. They are infested with zombies."

Nilborg stared at the soldier in horror. "The undead!"

"What of the villagers?" Hubrid leaned forward in his chair. Though he had sided against Nilborg, the Arronaus paladin spent much of the past couple days pacing the city walls in anticipation of the scouts' return.

"We saw no survivors," the man replied somberly.

"And what of the zombies?" asked Nilborg. "Could they be remnants of the corpses that rose years ago with the Wind of the Dead?"

"I don't believe so," the soldier answered. "They were fresh. There was little or no decomposition. And many were dressed as Marcs and Kalmirans, but also there were some bearing the crests of Ironside Keep and the Sard army."

"Then Ironside *has* fallen." Shock gripped Nilborg, making it hard to breathe.

"That's not all," the soldier added. "We spotted a few of our own as well. Soldiers that had been allocated to Ironside Keep to guard the pass."

The room was silent. Jerove and Garren shared a concerned look, one touched with horror. Hubrid dismissed the scouts.

"We must mobilize immediately," said Jerove after the doors had shut, avoiding Nilborg's gaze.

"Perhaps we should maintain our forces here," suggested Garren, The High Priest's face as pale as the snow. "If the undead march against us next, we shall be in need of our full strength."

"Garren," said Nilborg. "We cannot forsake the people of Sardina. What if these abominations turn south? We must destroy them immediately."

"Sardina has their king and their army," Garren retorted. "Besides, what if all of Sardina has fallen already and their corpses march upon us?"

"Palidur has never shown fear in the presence of evil!" Nilborg stood. "And with or without the assistance of the High Order, the warriors of Soleran will march!"

Nilborg almost regretted the words as he said them. It was an outburst they would have expected from Merssa, but never before had he shown anger within the Grand Cathedral. The ways of Soleran, however, were clear. Nilborg could not count the times he recited the sacred text, *Defenders of the Defenseless*, within the walls of his church. To turn his back on Sardina now would be turning his back on Soleran.

"It would seem the dead are rising again." Nilborg calmed his voice as he sat. "Perhaps the Wind of the Dead blows, but we fail to notice under the cover of winter. If we wait too long, the spring may see us besieged by a number of undead even our Holy City cannot withstand."

The Order passed the vote to march, three to one. Only Garren opposed.

The great horns of Palidur blared—the citywide call to arms, unheard for several centuries—and in less than an hour, nearly twenty thousand Palidurians were ready to march while thousands more gathered their gear. Within the Grand Cathedral, hundreds of priests pooled their powers of prayer and the Heavens opened a portal within the clouds to allow the sun to shine through. The city cheered. An hour later, the north and south gates opened and two forces marched, one bound for Courtin and the other for Dellabville.

Hubrid led the way east while Jerove headed the force to the south. High Priests did not normally partake in military assignments, but in Merssa's absence, Jerove took it upon himself to fill in, breaking the rule of maintaining at least one member of the High Order from each sector within the city at all times.

"I must do what I can to make this right," Jerove had said to Nilborg. "I have been wrong for too long... I only wish Merssa was here."

"Take care, old friend," Nilborg said to him. "Be safe."

The snow was deep, but the Palidurians marched with

unwavering determination beneath the light of the sun. Horses trampled a path before the soldiers, and the soldiers used shovels to get through the deeper drifts. No one was above digging and progress never slowed as the day wore on.

Nilborg stood upon the wall, watching Jerove's force become small in the distance. What began as a mass of shining silver beneath cloaks of brown and blue diminished into a dark wisp upon a sea of white. Only three thousand soldiers remained within the city, and most walked the battlements, sharing Nilborg's view. A shaky breath exited Nilborg's body and he closed his eyes to pray.

CHAPTER 35

HALLOWED LAND...

Merssa and Soren arrived to the Council of Wizards, answering the summons of Seac the Seer. They had spent a week within Tikken City already, along with Borse and Cavalor, passing the time until it was safe to go home. Reports claimed the King Arman to be frozen solid on its eastern edge, making passage by ship impossible, and the harshest winter known to Sardina and Sendorum had evidently covered those realms with several feet of snow. It seemed odd, since winter in Moclen was mild at best, and a shadow of doubt crossed Merssa's mind. But there was little she could do under the circumstances, and she and Soren decided to stay put until the weather softened.

The Seer was alone when they arrived, and he apologized, offering a brief explanation that the Council was "dealing with important matters." Seac's face was long and troubled, and heavy circles beneath his eyes revealed lack of sleep. Though he had seemed old since Merssa first met him nearly two decades prior, this was the first occasion she recalled him to appear absolutely worn.

"Why have you called us here?" Merssa asked, unable to conceal her growing concern.

"I wish it were to bring good tidings," Seac said somberly, "or to ask of Rholmar's newborn son...but it is grave news I bear. Palidur has fallen."

Merssa was stricken mute with disbelief. Time seemed to stand still and an awful lump worked its way from her stomach and into her heart.

"How?" Soren managed.

"Legions of undead."

Merssa's shock gave way to rage. "Trannum!"

"It would seem," said Seac. "From what little information we have received, an army assaulted the city, led by a new breed: dark warriors upon flying skeletal beasts."

"They were Death Lords." Selanna's voice came from the chamber doors. "Corpses of great and evil kings of old. And with them they carry the skills of their former lives, as well as powers bestowed upon them by Trannum."

"Selanna!" Merssa felt both relief that the mage was alive, and anger with the elf's long absence. But while Selanna moved heavily across the chamber, Merssa was reminded of their journey through the Silent Marsh, when the mage's power was completely drained, and she was moved to concern. "Where have you been?"

"Dark roads," Selanna replied with great weariness. "After last I saw you in Palidur, I returned to Kalmaar. From there I traveled south into Marcove, and then into Nomedd, following the path of evil before me. That is where I found *him*." The elf's face paled even more.

"Trannum," Merssa said, barely above a whisper.

Selanna sat heavily upon a Council seat near Seac, as if her legs had lost all strength to support her. The Seer did not object. She gave Merssa an exhausted nod.

"I shall summon the Council immediately." Seac rose to his feet, moving more swiftly than Merssa would have thought possible, and disappeared through the single door to the wizards' chambers.

Merssa turned back to Selanna. "What have you seen?"

"I shall tell you in good time," the mage replied in a soft voice, as one drifting into slumber. Then she focused on Merssa. "For now, take comfort that Nilborg lives."

Soren's attention was captured with these words. "Where is he?"

"He rests in a temple in Larkorn, with what is left of your city's people." Selanna shook her head. "He is beside himself. You should go to him, both of you, before he loses all hope. Much of what has happened he can tell you, for I was not there."

Merssa stared at the elf a moment before turning to Soren. She desperately wished to hear what news the mage bore, but it was obvious the Soleran paladin's mind was already made up to leave, and her desire to see Nilborg was strong as well.

Biting her lip, Merssa nodded. "Very well. But when will I see you again?"

"I will meet you there," Selanna replied. "I promise. Now go. He needs you."

"Do *not* delay too long," Merssa warned, and she and Soren exited the chamber.

They found Borse and Cavalor within the Council library. Borse was reading aloud from a book on Tikken City history, most likely discussing the creation of the Council of Wizards, and though only seven years old, Cavalor listened with the understanding of one twice his age. Borse stopped short upon seeing Merssa and Soren enter, and the expression on Merssa's face must have been grave, for her husband was immediately moved to concern.

"Palidur is no more." Merssa felt numb as she uttered the words. It was as if someone else had said them from far away.

After relating all she and Soren had heard, they gathered their gear and set out for Larkorn without delay.

Selanna woke when the shutting of the wizards' door resounded throughout the chamber. The Council approached in single file and onto the dais, and one member stepped before her, his face filled with great annoyance. Selanna rose from the chair and allowed him to sit.

"I have informed the Council of your news thus far," Seac said once all members were seated. "Please. Tell us what you know."

With a deep breath, Selanna spoke. "After searching Kalmaar and Marcove for Malgabi with no luck, I remembered King Karrak's comment that the Marc's accent seemed Nomish, so I journeyed to

Nomedd. What I found there was a land of walking dead. Thousands of zombies and skeletons, as well as dunarchins, ghouls, and wraiths roam unchecked. It was quite draining on me, but I was able to conceal myself and walked many days until discovering their spawning ground."

Selanna paused, feeling the blood drain from her face as memory took her back. "At the base of the hills, south of the Varlimor Mountains, is an old castle containing many laboratories, just as Trannum's tomb in the Stone Eagles. Within them, ghouls are being bred from stockpiles of corpses and prisoners wish for death as they are transformed into dunarchins... The elite warriors can only be made from living flesh, you see." She shook her head. "Trannum has been creating these creatures, unhindered for several years now, and his army is at least eighty thousand strong.

"Dunarchins operated the laboratories while Trannum remained hidden, but his markings were unmistakable and I could feel his presence. Fearing he might feel mine as well, I decided to leave and inform you of what I had learned." Selanna paused as a shiver of horror nearly overwhelmed her. "That was when the kings arrived."

"The corpses?" asked Seac.

She nodded. "They took the kings into a dungeon laboratory I had not seen. I knew I needed to learn of his plans for these bodies, so I stayed a bit longer...and that is where I finally found *him*. He must have been down there, preparing for their arrival." Selanna took in another labored breath. "There were vats of dark fluids and a cauldron of some sickly yellow substance, and the bodies were placed upon stone slabs surrounding a pedestal that held the orb from Garthglen." She gazed off in the distance as her face twisted in disgust. "I witnessed the entire procedure, though I will not speak further of it, and once the embalming was complete, Trannum chanted for several hours until the light of the orb faded. At that moment the eyes of the kings were kindled. The Death Lords were born.

"They radiate the same cold air as the Wind of the Dead, and raise all corpses around them. They also carry with them terrible weapons, and the necromancer imbued them with other powers, of that I am sure. But I dared not remain long enough to learn more."

The Council began their silent speaking to each other, but Selanna sensed their apprehension.

"The tale does not end there." She regained their attention. "Even while some of Trannum's minions sought the bodies of the kings, others collected and pieced together enormous skeletons, constructing great beasts to carry these new generals. Undead dragons."

Selanna fell silent again as the wizards began to murmur, this time foregoing their little silent trick. Seac raised a hand and the whispers ceased.

"Please, my dear," the Seer said, as a father listening to a child's report. "Continue."

"I am not sure where he procured the remains of such creatures," Selanna admitted, "but I believe he scoured the mountains of Borlean and Ladal, seeking ancient battle grounds."

"That is where the final days of the Dragon Wars took place," Seac said, as if voicing his thoughts aloud.

"The creatures were reconstructed as whole as possible, some as long as fifty feet or more," Selanna said. "Though their wings are but skeletal remains of better days, they are able to fly nonetheless, and their roar travels many leagues, striking fear into all that hear it. But the darkest power they possess is their breath. The fire is long extinguished from living days, but has been replaced by a cloud of death."

"Tell us of this cloud," said a wizard to Seac's far right with wide eyes.

"I had the displeasure of witnessing a test upon Nomish prisoners." Selanna shook her head with revulsion. "Sickly yellow vapors surrounded them, and for a moment they screamed. When the cloud dissipated, all that was left were withered bodies. It was as if the years had run through them until all life was spent."

"The orb never hinted at any of this," one wizard whispered to another.

"He knows you have it," Selanna said. "And he plans to take it."

"Is that so?" Seac raised a brow. "You know this for certain?"

"I heard him speak of it to the Death Lord, Cadorn," Selanna replied.

The wizards stared at her for several moments, until Seac spoke again.

"We knew this day would come. We knew that one day we must destroy it."

"Must we?" posed a wizard to the Seer's right. "Surely, in the hands of mere mortals, it would be in danger of returning to its creator. But it is *not* in the hands of mortals."

"Might I remind you of the arrogance of Palidur?" Selanna spread her hands. "Is Tikken City the next great city to fall?"

The wizards glared, some anxious and others outraged.

"Perhaps we should discuss this matter in chambers." Seac attempted to break the tension, or perhaps end the conversation. It did not work.

"Tell us, Selanna," another wizard said in a suspicious tone. "How is it you were able to gain so much knowledge without discovery? Ghouls could surely have smelled you at fifty yards, even if you were able to *hide* as you claim. Perhaps Trannum knew of your presence, and you have become but a messenger without realizing it."

"True, escaping detection would seem impossible," Selanna admitted. "That is why I had to become one of them."

The wizards glared, unimpressed or confused. Selanna felt almost as Elgarroth, and it brought a smile to her lips. She did indeed escape detection, using the same spell she had employed to mimic a Kalmiran soldier when passing in and out of Darmhorng Castle. She became a ghoul, and the power provided her with the stench as well. Getting used to the smell might have been difficult at one time, as well as learning to walk like one of the foul creatures, but Sistama had done well to prepare Selanna for that. Unfortunately, the ghouls turned out to be underlings to the dunarchins and she was kicked around often when found in areas off limits. After a year of studying the dunarchins, she decided to promote herself and took on their form. It was only then that she gained access into the castle's lower levels, where she learned of the information she had shared and more. But for now, she would say no more on the matter. Selanna's intentions at the moment were to keep the Council busy and conceal other activities—a task she felt she had accomplished.

"I must go." She saw relief in the eyes of some, and concern for unanswered questions within others.

"We thank you for your insight, Selanna," Seac said, "and will consider your words carefully."

Selanna bowed and exited the chamber.

It was dusk when Selanna made her way from the city and north along the road bound for Korban Bridge. After a mile, she dismounted and looked about, and within the gathering shadows along the King Arman, she detected a dark figure.

"Any problems?" she inquired.

The figure stepped from the tall reeds and held aloft a leather sack. Its rounded bottom revealed success. The bag was opened and a blue glow spilled out, revealing Eraim's smiling face.

Selanna nodded in satisfaction. "Very good. Now let us do what must be done."

Taking care not to touch the orb, Eraim rolled the sphere from the bag and onto a flat stone. She raised Mithkahr as Selanna began to chant, just as in Solett's laboratory, and once the spell was complete, the blade fell and the orb was shattered.

"Trannum will know it has been destroyed," Selanna said. "Tikken City will be safe."

"The Council will not realize the service we have provided," Eraim remarked. "But perhaps one day they will be grateful."

Selanna could not help but release a small chuckle. "You always think that."

Eraim shrugged.

They carefully swept the pieces of shattered glass into the leather sack and climbed onto the backs of Dandi and Lilli. It would be a few days to Larkorn and Selanna desperately wanted sleep, but sleep would have to wait. Eraim led the way slowly, to Selanna's relief, and they headed north.

Chapter 36

Larkorn

Nilborg sat in the small chamber alone. The head priest of the Soleran temple within Larkorn had graciously converted the storage room to accommodate Nilborg, and there he spent most his time. He emerged into the Hall of Worship when no one else was present, to pray and pose his many questions, but he received no answers. Several bandages adorned his body, and though he possessed the means to heal his wounds, a great burden of guilt rested upon his shoulders—he did not feel worthy of Soleran's Touch until his doubts could be resolved. That time, however, seemed far off, and all hope was slipping away.

Then Soren and Merssa arrived.

The paladins gazed upon Nilborg as if he were an elderly man for the first time he could recall. He invited them to have a seat within the confines of his small room, and there they shared some wine and conversation. Merssa spoke of Borse and Cavalor, having decided to leave them at an inn for the time being, and Soren bragged of Rholmar's newborn son, Montac, and how large the infant was. The conversation continued this way for some time, but then Merssa steered the subject to the topic Nilborg most wanted to forget.

"How did it happen? I must know."

Nilborg's smile vanished and he became silent with thoughts of the recent past. When at last he found the words, he told the tale with a trembling voice. Merssa shook her head somberly when he mentioned Jerove's change of mind in Trannum's involvement, but

Nilborg spared them Garren's views toward the end, not wanting them to think less of the Arronaus High Priest. The paladins nodded in agreement when Nilborg mentioned the Order's decision to march, as if casting their votes to the declaration made weeks ago.

"It seemed the right decision at the time, and I gave full support," Nilborg said. "And from what Hubrid explained, we marched with the wrath of the gods behind us and destroyed zombies by the thousands. Ghouls and wraiths fled for cover or perished at the sun's touch, and though the dunarchins were a force to be reckoned with, we greatly outnumbered them. All seemed well in hand..." He trailed off until rediscovering his voice. "Then the clouds returned, darker than before.

"I knew them to be unnatural, and our hearts grew uneasy within the walls of Palidur." Nilborg shuddered at the memory. "Younger soldiers abandoned their posts, searching for places to hide from the unseen evil... I can only imagine how the warriors within the villages felt." He paused, hesitant to finish the tale, and he felt his eyes widen. "Then came a terrible sound...a strange roar that pierced my soul and echoed forever. The air grew colder and the dread became stronger. Garren and I gathered all priests we could find so we might combine our prayers, and we knew our efforts to be working, for our men returned to their posts. We took heart that our words of faith reached the battlefields as well..." Nilborg's voice failed and he closed his eyes to gain control. "We were not prepared for what happened next.

"Upon the fifth night after our soldiers marched, they returned at last. I was not atop the wall when this occurred, or I might have realized something was amiss. They bore no fires and marched without order or rank. The tower guards, perhaps overjoyed with their return, sounded the horns and opened the gates without thought. It was too late when we noticed the open wounds and rigid movements. They were zombies."

Nilborg took a long drink from his goblet. With a deep breath, he continued.

"The zombies attacked, making a path for the dunarchins and ghouls, and wraiths flew into the towers and killed the sentries there. We had to pull back into the Cafior and Soleran sectors, sealing off that of Arronaus." Nilborg's lips trembled. "Then came three large creatures of bone from the clouds, and upon their backs were dark warriors of unspeakable terror. I had never sensed evil so strong in all my life." He glanced over his shoulder, as if one of the riders were watching through the window. "They descended onto Palidur and slew our warriors with horrible weapons and evil magic, and all around them our fallen rose up against us, adding to the enemy's numbers. And the bone steeds…" he trailed off as tears rolled down his cheeks. "The hideous breath…"

Nilborg began to weep. He fought to compose himself, and when Soren placed a friendly hand upon his shoulder, Nilborg found the strength to speak again.

"Hubrid was then by my side." Nilborg was torn between pride and sorrow. "He returned from Dellabville in the wake of the undead and battled through the city until he reached me. Many wounds plagued him, but he remained strong." Nilborg shook his head with great sadness. "He said there was no hope in defeating the riders, and he rushed me onto a ship with several other priests and as many Palidurians as he could. He insisted I find a way to combat these newest minions of Trannum. There were, of course, no paladins willing to abandon the city."

"Hubrid…" said Soren sadly. "In the end he proved worthy of his rank."

"Even in his efforts," Nilborg added, "all was nearly in vain. The ship was locked in the harbor by thick ice and would not budge. But he and the other paladins bought us the time we needed, and in answer to our prayers, the Heavens rained fire and broke the ship loose. As we sailed from the shore, I saw Hubrid fall at the hands of a dark warrior. Alas, the High Order is no more."

"Jerove and Garren did not board the ship?" Merssa asked.

"Jerove never returned from Courtin, not as far as I had seen,"

Nilborg replied. "As for Garren, he refused, as almost I had. But I realized Hubrid was right. Someone had to bring news. Someone who had seen what we're up against."

"I'm so sorry I wasn't there." Merssa bowed her head.

"I am not." Nilborg was stern and he looked her squarely in the eyes. "Had you been there, either of you…" He shook his head. "I am grateful Soleran and Cafior saw fit to lead you from Palidur at such a time. We were powerless against the assault." With his last statement, Nilborg hung his head in shame.

"It is not your fault." Merssa placed a hand upon his back. "There was no way any of us could have known."

"Had we listened to your words," Soren said regretfully to Merssa, "perhaps we might have been better prepared."

"That doesn't matter anymore." Merssa looked at them both. "Hubrid did right by seeing the ship safely from the harbor. Now we three will find a way to defeat Trannum, lest Palidur's downfall be in vain."

"Thank you." Nilborg gripped both paladins' hands tightly. "I shall be in need of both your strength."

Though Merssa's heart ached for the loss of her beloved city, there was no time to mourn. Trannum had resumed his war upon the living.

The next day, Selanna and Eraim arrived to Larkorn and Merssa called for an immediate council within the Soleran temple. Borse, Soren, and Nilborg were present, and Selanna spoke of her journey through Kalmaar, Marcove, and Nomedd. Merssa was both disgusted and angered. She had not thought it possible, but her resolve to confront the undead wizard grew with every bit of information the mage revealed.

"And, as you have already learned," Selanna added, "the size of Trannum's army grows with every living soul that falls before his Death Lords."

"Just as the prophecy forewarned," said Eraim. *"Living join through death."*

"What does the prophecy hold next?" asked Soren.

"Next, we fight!" Eraim pulled Mithkahr and held the blade high. Though the smallest of the company, the menacing look on the elf's face could have halted a troll.

"Do not forget: *Many a hero, born to die,*" came a voice from the door, which had been locked by Nilborg before the council began. Everyone turned to see Elgarroth.

"Master!" Selanna said with surprise.

Merssa's feelings were mixed. Sure, Elgarroth was a great wizard by reputation, and he seemed privy to knowledge no one else possessed. But why, then, was he incapable of stopping such evil before it happened? Merssa would never understand wizards, and she doubted she wanted to.

"We must mount a counterstrike immediately." She ignored Elgarroth's presence. "And after we take back Palidur, we —"

"Your first reaction will most likely play into Trannum's hands." Elgarroth brought Merssa more than a touch of annoyance. "You see, he is in no hurry. Every move has been carefully planned. Why do you think he has made no attempts to cross Palidur Bridge? Or destroy it so no one may cross against him? The ship bearing Nilborg did not escape by mere luck. There were flying beasts and Death Lords that could have prevented it. But they did not."

"What are you saying?" Merssa demanded.

"Now he waits," Elgarroth replied. "His trap is set. The survivors of Palidur will surely assemble all they can, Palidurians and outlanders alike, to take back that which they hold so dear. He has lined the walls with undead, and within the city is Cadorn, one of the mightiest Death Lords. The undead king is as cruel as he is evil, and with Trannum's magic he is even more terrible than days when he lived. All that fall before him will join him. There is no need to mount another assault upon the living, for they will surely come to him."

There was a long moment of silence while the wizard's words were absorbed. Merssa gazed at the table where she sat, as thoughts of fighting undead friends sent a chill down her spine.

"So we do not attack?" She turned to Elgarroth in disbelief. "We allow Trannum to rule over half of Vaeldor until he grows bored and decides to take more? That makes no sense."

"You most certainly take back the conquered lands of Vaeldor." Elgarroth added confusion to Merssa's annoyance. "But it is how, and when. Not now, and not through brute strength will you succeed. This is an effort for all of Vaeldor to resolve, not just the survivors of a once great city. There are many brave warriors that will come and offer what they can; many kingdoms that will lend aid. But hold no illusions; this is a campaign for the years. Your children, and your children's children will ultimately fight this war. But it begins with you."

"So when *do* we strike?" Merssa's patience was at its end. She wished to see Palidur again, before old age claimed her. She was a woman of action and did not understand the wizard's desire to stay her hand. But in the end, she would concede to Elgarroth's wisdom and she knew it. No matter Merssa's feelings for the elf, his knowledge exceeded all within the room.

"I know it is not the nature of humans to bide their time, for their days are short in this world." Elgarroth offered a soft smile. "But the day of truth will come. You will know when the time is right. For now, gather courage and strength, and look for those who would offer help. But never forget the treacheries of Tarm, Gruzim, and Malgabi; the enemy has many faces. Plan carefully the entire war, not merely a few battles of pride, and forget not who the enemy is, nor how long *he* has had to prepare. And always remember that your first reaction more than likely fits into his scheme."

Elgarroth bowed and turned toward the door.

"Master?" An anxious look was plastered over Selanna's worn face.

"I know, dear." He gave half a smile. "We shall meet again soon, and you will give me a full account."

Selanna seemed disappointed, but bowed and hindered

Elgarroth's departure no longer.

A moment of thought followed after the wizard had gone, until Merssa broke the silence.

"We must send word to Rholmar at once. And to every kingdom. Let them know all we have learned of the enemy. They will surely allocate soldiers to the cause, lest they be forever branded cowards." She sighed, gazing about the room. "Has anyone seen Vecnor?"

Heads turned to look at one another, but no one spoke.

Merssa shook her head. "I last saw him in Harbnum, but that was years ago. I wish he were here now."

They began the meeting anew, discussing Trannum well into the night, and Eraim recorded information onto scrolls to be distributed to kings across the land. All within the room gave accounts of what they knew of the necromancer's minions and the best ways to combat them, but Selanna provided most the information, drawing from secret travels and the ancient tomes of the Silent Marsh. Eraim produced a journal containing maps of the realms with markings to show where the forces of Trannum, Tarm, and Gruzim were last known, and the small elf traced the path the undead used to gain entrance into Sardina.

Merssa felt all blood drain from her face as a morbid thought crossed her mind. "Vikur!"

"He is alive," Selanna said. "I am sorry I did not mention it before, but I have seen much in the past few years. He is in Tenvale, but suffers from many wounds, the deepest being his failure in holding the pass."

Selanna relayed the events of Ironside Keep, as Vikur had explained them to her.

"Though his vision was blurred," Selanna added, "there is no doubt in my mind it was a Death Lord he saw before losing consciousness. And I believe it to have been Radaam, from other things I have been told."

"How is it Vikur survived?" Merssa inquired.

"It was Krelnamir," Selanna replied, "at least as Ballrik tells it.

Krelnamir stood between Radaam and Vikur, and while the two did battle, Ballrik took his father into the base of the central tower, where lies the family crypt. Within, he informed me, is a secret tunnel constructed when the keep was young. He carried his father deep into the mountainside, emerging east of Southwood and far from civilized lands. There, the snow was not so heavy and the undead were scarce, and he was able to evade them as he crossed into Tenvale."

Nilborg sighed. "Thank goodness they're all right."

"Vikur is not himself," Selanna said. "He sent his son to Philen, to live with Arkor, and is not well in spirit. I believe he would rather have perished in the keep, and this prevents his wounds from healing fully. I only hope Poluran will make a difference. I encountered him in Rivercross and he was quite eager to find Vikur when I told him the story."

"And you have not seen Vecnor in *all* your travels?" Merssa posed.

Selanna shook her head. "I have not."

"Where have you gotten off to, old friend?" Merssa gazed out of the window at drifting specks of snow. She desperately wished to have the large warrior's counsel…as well as his sword.

The council of Trannum lasted several days, and through the years that followed, most of the room's occupants returned to their homelands to bide their time and carry on with their lives.

Merssa moved closer to the line of evil. Placing several tents north of Palidur Bridge, she housed her family and what remained of Palidur's citizens, almost daring the enemy to cross the Great East River. There, Merssa would carry out her duties, raise her son, and love her husband. There, within Sendorum, she would be aware of any further advancement of the necromancer's forces. Never again would she rely on votes to determine the fate of the living. No matter what Trannum held in store for Vaeldor next, Merssa would never again be distracted. Her eyes were open, more than ever before, and she was ready.

This Concludes

ALAS!
THE ONE THAT
EVIL BRINGS

The story continues with

MIGHT

AND

STRENGTH

OF

EVIL BONE

Coming in 2022

Acknowledgements

I would like to thank my wife for her patience and encouragement, and my son for his contributions. I would also like to thank Mary Nichols and Peggy Kattelus. Their support, guidance, and writing skills made this series possible, and I owe them more than I could ever repay. Finally, I would like to thank all the family members and friends for the hours of reading they provided to help this story come to life.

ABOUT THE AUTHOR

Ronald G. Bellar was born in Ohio and raised in Michigan, one of the middle children in a family of ten. He has an associate's degree in electrical engineering and a bachelor's in automated manufacturing, but his love for numbers led him to a life in taxes and bookkeeping. He began writing when he was 15, but did not take it seriously until he was encouraged to do so much later in life. After coaching football for 31 years, he has finally retired his whistle, but his love for sports endures. He currently resides in Michigan with his wife and son.

Glossary of Names

Alabar (AL-uh-bar): Fast flowing river marking the western border of Neja.

Andria (an-DREE-uh): Barbarian realm, north of Harbnum.

Andrian (an-DREE-uhn): Barbarian native to Andria.

Anduiff (AN-doo-if): Death Lord. First Lord of Benasti Forest.

Arduer (AR-doo-er): High Paladin of Arronaus in the High Order of Palidur.

Arkor (AR-kor): Younger brother to Vikur. The one-armed warrior.

Arrikan (AIR-ik-in): Scout for the Council of Wizards. Mountain ranger in Harbnum.

Arronaus (AIR-uhn-us): Deity of the sky.

Balgorn (BAHL-gorn): River in Helmland. Called Blood River.

Ballrik (BAHL-rik): Son of Vikur.

Barraday (BAIR-uh-day): City ruled by Duke Tarm, located in southern Kalmaar.

Bashnu (BASH-noo): Barbarian deity of battle.

Batorn (buh-TORN): Gulf north of Kalmaar. Also, a breed of horse that lives in the region of the gulf, known for their beauty and great endurance.

Bayn (BAYN): A marteese. Battle mage from Neja.

Belsod (BEL-sahd): Bodyguard to Olinin.

Benasti (be-NAS-tee): Forest in northern Kalmaar. Largely inhabited by hobgoblins and krukari.

Bistrent (bis-TRENT): Dwarfish word for hurry; immediately.

Boler (BOH-ler): Barbarian warrior from Nomedd.

Borlean (BOR-lee-in): Mountains separating Desert of Fire from Tarn Arum Jungle.

Borse (BORS): Priest of Cafior from Cafdella.

Brakkeet (brah-KEET): Expletive in the dwarfish language.

Brem (BREM): A marteese. Priest of Frayorna from Neja

Bril (BRIL): A King's Ranger in Vol Maren, Neja.

Brondor (BRAHN-dor): Deity of battle.

Burmagaard (BER-muh-gard): Capital city of Kalmaar.

Cadorn (kuh-DORN): Death Lord. Ancient ruler of Kalmaar.

Cafdella (caf-DEL-uh): Village in Neja sporting rich soil.

Cafior (CAF-ee-or): Deity of the land.

Candermane Falls (CAN-der-mayn): Waterfall in northern Varlimor Mountains.

Cavalor (CAV-uh-lor): Adopted son of Merssa.

Charndova (sharn-DOH-vuh): City in Sardina, on the western edge of Varlimor Pass.

Clanghorr (KLANG-or): Ancient dwarfish battleaxe.

Coranthiar (kor-ANN-thee-er): Mountains across northeastern Vaeldor.

Corlan (KOR-luhn): Bodyguard to Olinin.

Courtin (KOR-tin): Small village outside of Palidur.

Craldek (KRAL-dek): Member of Council of Wizards.

Crynora (kry-NOR-uh): Large city in Philen.

Dakreal (DAYK-ree-uhl): Forest in Philen. Home to Dakreal elves.

Dandi (DAN-dee): Salenti horse belonging to Selanna.

Darmhorng (DARM-horng): Castle for the King of Kalmaar, located in Burmagaard.

Death Hunter (DETH HUHN-ter): Hunter of the undead.

Dellabville (DEL-uhb-vil): Small village outside of Palidur.

Dellen (DEL-lin): Captain of the Guard in Tikken City.

Denvale (DEN-vayl): City in Marcove, on the eastern edge of Varlimor Pass.

Dimarr (di-MAR): Barbarian chief in Andria. Possessed one of the orbs.

Diral (DYE-ruhl): Hills in northern Harbnum.

Dominelli (DAHM-in-EL-ee): Largest village of elves within Salenti Forest.

Dunarchin (DOON-er-kin): Undead created from a firstborn. Elite warrior, able to walk beneath the sun.

Dunuthar (DUHN-uh-thar): Death Lord. Former king of Selt.

Eastgate (EEST-gayt): Large city, located on the eastern border of Neja.

Eimell (EYE-mel): Vermallon elf. Scout for the Council of Wizards.

Ekland (EK-land): Barbarian territory north of Selt.

Elgarroth Sandanari (EL-guh-roth SAN-di-NAR-ee): Mysterious elfish wizard of Vermallon Forest. Mentor to Selanna.

Ellaville (EL-uh-vil): Village in northwestern Virch.

Elloria (el-LOR-ee-uh): Brondor priestess in Kalmaar. Former Death Hunter.

Eraim (ee-RAYM): Salenti elf. Master of many talents and friend to Selanna.

Fellna (FEL-nuh): Wife to Larman.

Frayorna (fray-OR-nuh): Deity of the forest. Mother of Nature.

Galenfial (guh-LEN-fee-uhl): Deity of the elves.

Garaard (guh-RARD): Lake in Kalmaar, north of Burmagaard.

Garren (GAIR-en): High Paladin of Arronaus in the High Order of Palidur.

Garthglen (GARTH-GLEN): Swampland in southern Moclen.

Guardians (GAR-dee-uhns): Vermallon elves living in Lothen Forest, tasked with watching Helmland for signs of evil.

Gothnelli (goth-NEL-ee): Original name of the Silent Marsh. Elfish for hunting ground.

Grellmor (GREL-mor): Ancestor of Vikur and Arkor. Commissioned the construction of Ironside Keep in the Varlimor Pass.

Gruzim (groo-ZEEM): Krukari warrior that travels with Bayn in Neja.

Gulthar (GOOL-thar): Death Lord. Former king of Marcove.

Harbnum (HARB-nuhm): Kingdom north of Sendorum and east of Beit.

Helmland (HELM-land): Wasteland north of the Stone Eagle Mountains, where the Ancient Enemy of the North once resided.

Hezeb (HEZ-ib): Demon.

High Riser (HI RYE-zer): Mountains in northern Philen. Home to the High Riser dwarves.

Holindale (HOE-lin-dayl): Barbarian territory south of Tenvale.

Hubrid (HUE-brid): Paladin of Arronaus from Palidur.

Ironside (EYE-ern-side): Keep on Varlimor Pass. Surname to Vikur and Arkor.

Jerove (jur-OVE): High Priest of Cafior in the High Order of Palidur.

Jurack (joo-RAK): Death Lord. Former king of Beit.

Kalmaar (KAL-mar): Kingdom boasting the largest military in Vaeldor.

Kalmiran (kal-MAIR-in): Citizen of Kalmaar.

Kamen (KAY-min): Farmer in Ellaville.

Karlsum (KARL-suhm): Baron of Neja. Lord over Eastgate.

Karrak (KAIR-ik): King of Kalmaar.

King Arman (AR-muhn): The largest lake in Vaeldor, north of Arman Forest.

Korban (KOR-bin): Bridge spanning the Squire River. Built by dwarves of Rornibur and named after their king of old. Made of rorbak.

Krelnamir (KREL-nuh-meer): Paladin of Cafior from Palidur. Placed within Ironside Keep to assist in the watch over Varlimor Pass.

Krukari (kroo-KAR-ee): One possessing both human and hobgoblin blood. Outcasts.

Ladal (lay-DAHL): Mountains separating Desert of Fire from Tenvale.

Ladonia (luh-DOHN-yah): Scout for the Council of Wizards.

Larkorn (LAR-korn): Large city on the eastern border of Virch.

Larman (LAR-min): Tavern owner in Ellaville.

Lilli (LIL-lee): Salenti horse belonging to Eraim.

Lothen (LOH-then): Forest in northwestern Beit, where the Guardians reside.

Lorian (LOR-ee-uhn): An elf from Maple Lore Forest.

Lornibur (LOR-ni-ber): Ancient home to the dwarves. Birthplace of all dwarfish ancestors.

Lorylla (LOR-i-luh): Gray elf of Orlenfel. Daughter of Xorlunder.

Magneer (MAG-neer): Son of Pallit.

Malgabi (MAL-guh-bee): Warrior out of Marcove.

Marcove (MAR-kohv): Kingdom south of Kalmaar.

Marc (MARK): Citizen of Marcove.

Marteese (mar-TEES): One possessing both human and elf blood.

Massima (MAS-i-muh): Barbarian from Desert of Fire. Scout for the Council of Wizards.

Mayry (MAY-ree): Duchess of Kalmaar. Wife to Tarm.

Mees (MEES): Elfish word for alarm.

Melac (MEL-ak): Wizard from Moclen.

Melballa (mel-BAHL-uh): Mule owned by Poluran.

Meldar (MEL-dar): Deity of the dwarves.

Mentrial (MEN-tree-ahl): Forest in Marcove. Houses many bandits.

Merssa Goldmace (MER-suh): Paladin of Cafior from Palidur.

Mithkahr (MITH-kar): Ancient elfish blade.

Moclen (MAHK-lin): Kingdom west of King Arman Lake. Home to Tikken City and the Council of Wizards.

Montac (MAHN-tak): Son of Rholmar.

Mordan (MOR-duhn): Steward to the Council of Wizards.

Morimont (MOR-i-mahnt): Home to the dwarfish king of Varlimor and largest city of dwarves within the Varlimor Mountains.

Morsum (MOR-suhm): Gatekeeper of Ironside Keep.

Neja (NAY-shjuh): Kingdom south of the Stone Eagle Mountains. The Bandit Kingdom.

Nejan (NAY-shjuhn): Citizen of Neja.

Nilborg (NIL-borg): High Priest of Soleran in the High Order of Palidur.

Nira (NYE-ruh): Kingdom north of Kalmaar and south of Selt.

Niran (NAIR-in): Citizen of Nira.

Nomedd (NOH-med): Barbarian territory south of Marcove.

Nomish (NOH-meesh): Citizen of Nomedd.

Norik (NOR-ik): Krukari warrior.

Olinin (OH-li-nin): Marteese wizard from Neja.

Orlenfel (OR-len-fel): Forest in northeastern Kalmaar. Home to the gray elves.

Palidur (PAL-i-der): The Holy City, located in Sardina. A Free city, it is governed by paladins and priests.

Palidurian (PAL-i-DOO-ree-uhn): Citizen of Palidur.

Pallit (PAL-lit): An ex-King's Ranger of Vol Maren. Protector of and friend to Borse.

Philen (FYE-len): Kingdom in southwestern Vaeldor.

Poluran (POH-ler-uhn): Stone Eagle dwarf from Rornibur.

Prack (PRAK): Servant at the Trapper's Inn in Sikilaville.

Presnin (PREZ-nin): Stableboy in Vol Maren.

Radaam (ruh-DAHM): Death Lord. Former king of Kalmaar.

Ragab (RAH-guhb): Demon.

Rholmar (ROHL-mar): Paladin of Arronaus from Palidur.

Rivercross (RIV-er-cross): Large city in Virch, near the Korban Bridge.

Rorbak (ROR-bak): Rare white stone native to the Stone Eagle Mountains.

Rornibur (ROR-ni-ber): The largest city of dwarves within the Stone Eagle Mountains.

Rrimmburd (RIM-berd): A large city within Tenvale.

Rybeal (RYE-beel): Wizard from Philen.

Salenti (suh-LEN-tee): Forest west of Moclen. Home to Salenti elves.

Sardina (sar-DEE-nuh): Kingdom east of King Arman Lake. Home to free city of Palidur.

Seac (SAY-ahk): The Seer. Member of the Council of Wizards of Tikken City.

Selanna (suh-LAHN-nuh): Salenti elf. Wizard and friend to Eraim.

Selt (SELT): Kingdom north of Nira, known for demon worshipping.

Seltan (SEL-tuhn): Citizen of Selt.

Sendor (SEN-dor): Citizen of Sendorum.

Sendorum (sen-DOR-uhm): Kingdom north of Sardina, east of Virch, and south of Harbnum.

Serpent's Range (SER-pents): Mountains in eastern Kalmaar. Infamous for sharp spires.

Sikilaville (si-KIL-uh-VIL): Village within Urell Coast, south of Tall Pines Forest.

Silcor (SIL-kor): Deity of fire.

Sistama (SIS-tuh-muh): Elfish name for the Silent Marsh.

Soleran (SOH-ler-uhn): Deity of mercy and light. Defender of the Defenseless.

Solett (soh-LET): Wizard from Tenvale. Possessed one of the orbs.

Soren (SOR-in): High Paladin of Soleran in the High Order of Palidur.

Stone Eagle (STOHN-EE-guhl): Mountains north of Neja. Home to Stone Eagle dwarves.

Tarm (TARM): Duke of Kalmaar. Rules over the southern border. Husband to Mayry.

Tenvale (TEN-vayl): Kingdom south of Arman Forest. Kingdom of Wizards.

Thard'Dun (THARD DOON): Deity of pure evil.

Tikken City (TEE-kin): Free city located in Moclen. Governed by the Council of Wizards.

Trakinir (TRAY-kin-air): High Paladin of Arronaus in the High Order of Palidur.

Trannum (TRAN-nuhm): Ancient necromancer tasked with researching Uustaag the Dark.

Tribenor (TRY-ben-or): Capital city of Sendorum.

Umbarc (UHM-bark): Andrian horse belonging to Vecnor.

Uustaag (OO-stahg): Warlord of Helmland of old. Ancient Enemy of the North.

Vaeldor (VAY-uhl-dor): The continent of all known kingdoms.

Varlimor (VAR-li-mor): Mountains separating Kalmaar from Sardina. Home to Ironside Keep and Varlimor dwarves.

Vecnor (VEK-ner): Large human warrior. Also known as Black Rogue and Black Death.

Velgaad (VEL-gahd): Dwarfish Death Lord. Former king of Lornibur.

Vermallon (VER-muh-lahn): Forest separating Harbnum from Nira. Largest forest of Vaeldor and home to Vermallon elves.

Vikur (VIE-koor): Lord of Ironside Keep. Brother to Arkor.

Vircan (VERK-uhn): Citizen of Virch.

Virch (VERCH): Kingdom north of King Arman Lake.

Vol Maren (vahl MAIR-uhn): Capital of Neja.

Welmirth (WEL-merth): Ancient wizard that defeated Uustaag at the Battle of Balgorn.

Wezlok (WEZ-lahk): Lorian elf wizard from Maple Lore Forest.

Wirth (WERTH): Proprietor of the Trapper's Inn in Sikilaville.

Witchdoor (WICH-dor): Capital City of Tenvale.

Xorlunder (ZOR-luhn-der): Gray elf of Orlenfel. Scout to Council of Wizards.

Zurkan (ZER-kin): Soldiers of Blood. Elite krukari warriors of Benasti Forest.

www.ingramcontent.com/pod-product-compliance
Lightning Source LLC
Chambersburg PA
CBHW061203190726
48288CB00001B/42